# I0727868

Cover design by: Aisling Elizabeth

Mistletoe MISTAKE

MELODY TYDEN

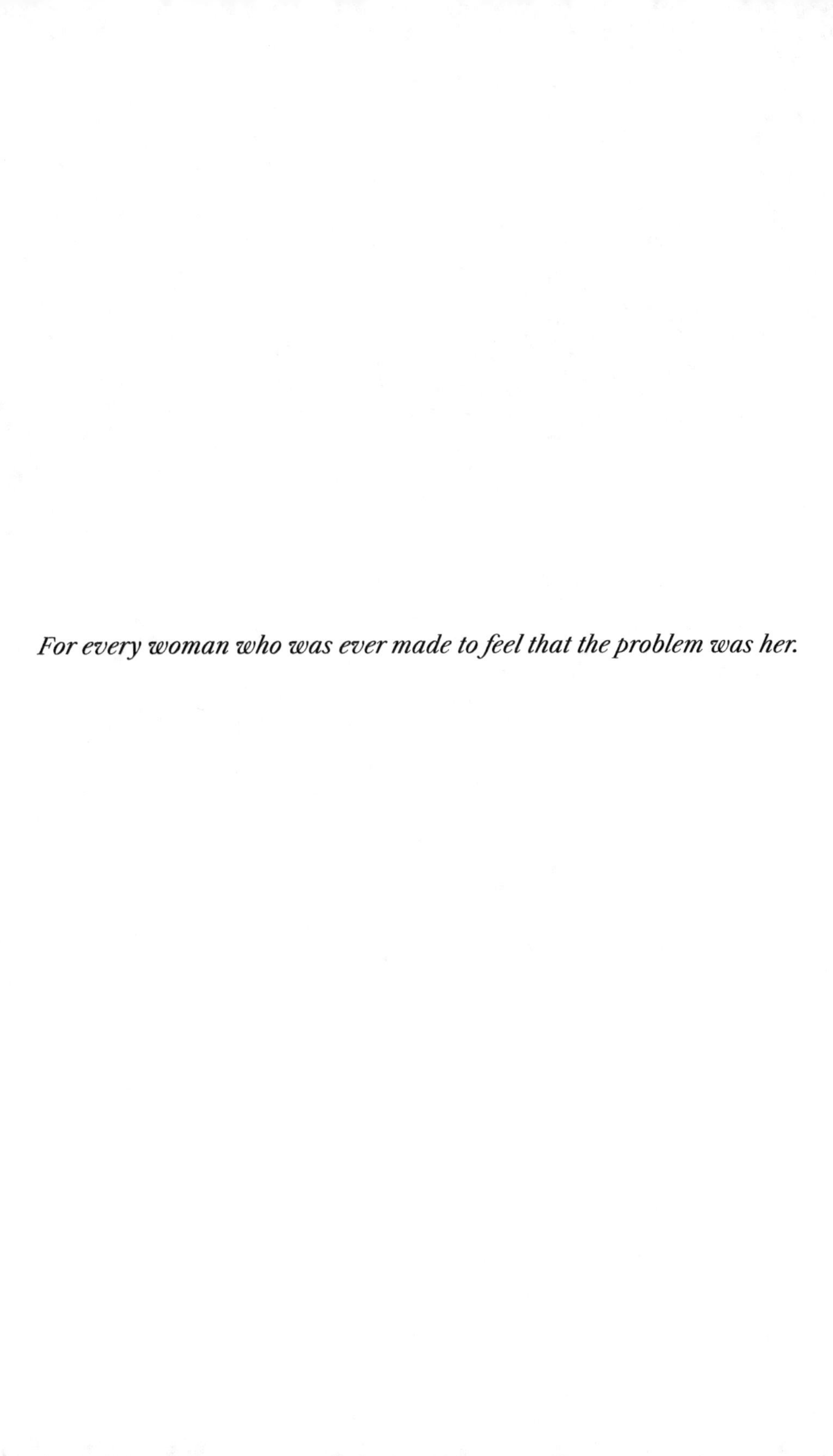

For every woman who was ever made to feel that the problem was her.

Chapter One

THE CHRISTMAS PARTY

~Gemma~

The insistent knocking at my office door pulled me out of my concentration so abruptly that I jumped in surprise. Time had slipped away while I'd been bent over my blueprints, and as I raised my head, I realized that the sky outside my London office had turned completely dark. Damn it. Just how late was it?

"Come in," I called out as I quickly rolled up the papers I'd been working on.

The door swung open to reveal the disapproving face of my colleague and best friend, Holly. Her blonde hair had already been swept up in an elegant up-do and her makeup looked flawless, as usual.

"I knew it!" she declared, her voice full of disapproval. "You haven't even started getting ready yet."

"I'm sorry, Hols. What time is it?"

"Time to go enjoy ourselves and forget about all of this." She spread her hands to include the whole of my office in 'this': the table I used for meetings with clients, the desk with my computer for paperwork, and the drafting table where I had been working now. "Open bar, Gemma. The clock is ticking."

With a laugh at her enthusiasm, I stretched my arms up over my head, rolled my neck to get the kinks out, and resisted the urge to remind her that I would be the one paying for the open bar in the end. As the owner of the company, I'd be footing the bill for the whole party.

"I am all in on the open bar tonight," I promised her instead. "I've got my dress and makeup in my bag, so let's go get changed."

That night, we were holding our annual Christmas party and traditionally, it had always been a night to remember. Or to *not* remember, depending on just how much we decided to drink, and after the year I'd had, no one would blame me if I overindulged just a little.

"So, about the dress..." Holly started, and my eyes narrowed suspiciously. The mischievous look on her face was a dead giveaway that she had something up her sleeve. "I thought we could try something different tonight."

"We?" I repeated, crossing my arms skeptically. "Or me?"

Holly had a history of trying to push me out of my comfort zone, especially when she thought I needed a pick-me-up.

"Both of us," she assured me. "It's just a little something to get us in the Christmas spirit. I've got everything we need in my bag, so let's go to the hotel and get ready there."

Since we were hosting the party at a nearby hotel, Holly and I had decided to get a room for the weekend. We had another event to attend tomorrow, and having the room would not only save us from having to go home in between, but also from having to walk from our office to the party in our high heels right now.

Knowing that arguing with her would be pointless until I saw what she had planned, I locked up the office behind us as we headed out into the early December night. Everyone else had already left since we'd given them the afternoon off before the party. Although my year had personally been a disaster, it couldn't have gone better for the company. We deserved to celebrate and that evening, I intended to do just that.

The walk from our small office in St James's over to the sleek hotel near Leicester Square didn't take very long, even with dodging all the other people out on the pavements. The Christmas lights twinkled above us, the air just chilly enough for scarves and mittens, and Christmas carols drifted out of the stores we walked past, already staying open late to welcome the holiday shoppers. I loved this time of year, or at least I always had, before this year. The thought of what should be happening this Christmas threatened to dampen my spirits, but I refused to give into the temptation. For one night, we were going to forget everything else and simply have some fun. 'Christmas fun', by the sounds of what Holly had said earlier, though she still hadn't told me exactly what she meant by that.

The hotel lobby buzzed with guests coming and going as we checked in, and as soon as we got to our room, Holly produced a bottle of champagne from the room's mini-fridge that she must have ordered to be waiting for us. With a satisfied grin, she held it up to me. "Shall we?"

"There's an open bar downstairs," I reminded her, though I couldn't help smiling at her infectious enthusiasm as I claimed one of the double beds for myself. The clean, modern style of the hotel room with its monochrome colours and abstract art on the walls felt rather bland despite the upscale furnishings, and I couldn't help comparing it in my head to our most recent project. No one would be using the word 'bland' to describe *that* hotel once they got a look at it.

"This is just a starter." Popping the cork like an expert, Holly poured out two glasses, offering one to me as she held hers up for a toast. "To Christmas and booze and finding a hot guy to snog on New Year's Eve!"

"I'll drink to that." The bubbles from the champagne tingled in the back of my throat as I took a large gulp, ready to get the alcohol into my system as soon as possible. At this rate, we'd both have a buzz going in no time. "Now, what's this about my dress?"

With a sparkle in her blue eyes, Holly threw open her small suitcase and pulled out two matching bright-red Santa dresses with short skirts and off-the-shoulder necklines, faux fur trim and a cinching black belt.

I burst out laughing in disbelief, nearly sending the champagne back out through my nose. "You can't seriously expect me to wear that?"

My laughter earned me a pout. "Oh, come on, Gem. This is our one party of the year that's just our staff. Every other party, we can wear proper dresses and be grown up and boring. Tonight, let's just be stupid and have some fun."

She did make a very good point. The upcoming Christmas season would be filled with dull client parties where we'd have to stand around in sparkly gowns all night, making small talk with rich business owners and our competitors. At our own party, on the other hand, we could do whatever the hell we wanted. There were some perks of working for ourselves.

Draining the last of my champagne, I gave in. "You know what? Let's do it. Sexy Santa, here we come!"

~Cole~

As soon as I entered the hotel lobby, my friend and right-hand-man, Jackson, leapt to his feet from a nearby sofa and headed over. He'd obviously been waiting for me.

"How did things go?" he asked as he fell into step beside me.

Not wanting to be overheard, I waited until we were in the elevator to answer him bluntly. "They're awful. Fucking terrible. We've waited three months for the designs and we can't even use them."

"It can't be that bad..." he started to say, but quickly clamped his mouth shut as he saw the scowl on my face. "I trust your judgement, of course, but maybe with a few adjustments..."

I shook my head emphatically. "There's no point. I've fired the company. We're going to have to start over."

He groaned as he ran his hand through his hair. He'd done that for as long as I'd known him; where I would release tension by swearing, he'd take his frustration out on his hair. "Okay, I'll start looking tomorrow. There's got to be somebody out there whose style you like."

"We should just bring in our usual team from New York." I'd been saying that for the last six months and he'd shot me down every time. He had an annoying way of getting me to do what he said, even though, as his boss, I made the final decisions. It probably had to do with him usually being right.

"You know we can't," he reminded me. "We want to use a local firm to show that we're invested in making this a part of the city, not just a big American company coming in and setting up another soulless hotel in the heart of London."

Since I'd heard it all before, I simply grunted. "Then find me someone whose work doesn't look like a soulless computer program spat it out."

"You're exaggerating, as usual, but I *will* find someone else. Tomorrow. For now, let's forget about it and get ready for this party."

I sighed at the reminder as the elevator doors opened to our floor. I had almost forgotten about the party. My company owned part of the hotel we were staying in and they were holding their staff Christmas party that evening. For some reason, Jackson had promised we would make an appearance.

He veered off to his room while I carried on to my suite at the end of the hall, my home for the next couple of weeks. Passing through the living room, I headed straight to the bedroom to check my appearance. Since I'd already worn a suit for my meetings that day, at least I wouldn't need to change. A quick shave and a splash of fresh cologne should do it, even though I hated going to these types of things alone. Having a woman on my arm usually helped to ward off any unwanted advances. However, I'd only arrived in London the night before, so I hadn't had a chance yet to reach out to any of my contacts here to help me find some suitable companionship. For the time being, I would have to rough it.

With my minimal amount of effort complete, I returned to the hall and knocked on Jackson's door. He appeared a moment later, having swapped out his tie for a new one decorated with Christmas lights in shades of red and green.

"Honestly?" I asked wearily. The Christmas season had just started and already, I was tired of it. I hated this time of year; too many bad memories, and it seemed to start earlier and earlier each year. It was only the first of December, for fuck's sake.

Jackson just grinned, not at all bothered by my disapproval. "We're not all Scrooges like you, Cole. Come on, let's go get a drink."

At least that was a suggestion I could get behind.

Making our way back to the elevator, we headed downstairs to the conference room floor. The elevator doors opened into a hallway with dark carpet, designed to cover any spilled drinks, and neutral beige walls, where people in suits and party dresses stood milling around. On either side of the hall stood a set of closed double doors in a dark wood that matched the floor, with muted music and talking drifting through them from the rooms beyond.

The doors on the left had a large sign reading 'Lytton Hotel Christmas Party', the party we were here to attend, so we started to head in that direction. Before we got there, however, the doors on the right opened and a woman walked out, immediately distracting us both.

Unlike everyone else around us in their formal attire, this woman wore a skimpy red Santa dress and hat, immediately drawing my eyes to her hourglass figure and the way the black belt cinched around her waist. Long, wavy red hair cascaded down from beneath her hat and over her bare shoulders. Her green eyes seemed to sparkle from within, and her plump lips were painted a shade of rusty red which matched her hair almost exactly.

We all reached the centre of the hallway at the same time, and we all stopped short simultaneously to avoid a collision. As my feet stopped moving, I couldn't help but stare at her. She was fucking gorgeous.

Her eyes met mine for a brief second and her mouth formed a warm smile before she turned the same look on Jackson. "Merry Christmas, gentlemen." Her British accent had a slight drawl to it that told me she'd already started drinking. One hand moved to her chest and my eyes followed it, taking in the swell of her breasts, just visible at the edge of her low-cut dress. A second later, I blinked in surprise as I realized several candy canes hung from the fur lining. She plucked two of them out and offered them to Jackson and me.

Jackson took his readily, giving her a wide smile in return. "Merry Christmas to you. Mrs Claus, I presume?"

When she saw his tie, her eyes lit up even further, which shouldn't have been possible. "Looks like someone is already in the Christmas spirit." She gave him a nod of approval before her eyes moved back to me. "Your friend, on the other hand, could use some work."

Since I hadn't taken the candy cane from her, she reached up and tucked it down my suit jacket, hooking the end around my lapel.

"A little better," she assessed, her eyes lingering on my chest for a moment before she looked back up at my face and gave me a wink.

I remained silent, trying to figure out what this might be. Did she work here? Part of the entertainment, perhaps? And if so, would there be a chance to pay extra for a little private entertainment later? The view I had down her dress was more than a little enticing.

"He's a lost cause, I'm afraid," Jackson was saying. "I'm Jackson and this is Cole."

"Cole?" she repeated, still looking up at me with her twinkling eyes. "Like the lump of coal you get in your stocking? That sounds appropriate."

Jackson laughed in genuine amusement. "You have no idea."

Her smile seemed to light up the whole room as her eyes remained fixed on mine. "Lovely to meet you both. I'm trying to find my friend, Holly, but I hope you enjoy your party."

"Holly?" Jackson asked. "Who does that make you? Jolly?"

With a laugh, she turned her charming smile on him. "Wouldn't you like to know?"

Winking at me one more time, she sauntered off down the hallway away from us. Jackson and I both turned to watch her go, taking a moment to appreciate her legs and ass in the short skirt of her dress and her high heels.

"Damn," Jackson muttered under his breath. "We're going to the wrong party."

Indeed. I looked over at the door she had come out of, where the sign read: 'Anchor Design Christmas Party'. That didn't give me any further clues as to why she would be dressed that way.

I shared my guess with Jackson anyway. "She must be working the party. Maybe there's more just like her inside our party too."

"In that case, let's get in there." Getting to the door first, he opened it for me and I headed inside, but not before taking one last glance down the hallway where the woman had gone. To my frustration, I couldn't see any sign of her.

~Gemma~

"Hols?" I called out when I got to the ladies toilet.

Her reply came from inside one of the stalls. "Yup, I'm here. I made it."

Sighing with relief, I leaned back against the sinks to wait for her. We may have overdone it with the champagne in our room earlier, and after she left the party to find the toilet, I suddenly got worried that she'd end up going into the wrong party on the way back. It seemed more than possible, so I figured I better go and check on her.

Not that it would be the worst thing in the world to end up at the other party, I couldn't help thinking as I remembered the two men I'd just bumped into in the hall. The one with the Christmas tie had been cute, with slightly curly blond-ish hair and blue eyes, but the other one... wow.

He towered over me, his height and build conveying power while his short, trimmed dark hair seemed to highlight his strong, angled jawline. An expensive-looking suit and tie completely covered him, but it couldn't entirely hide the toned body underneath. His eyes were dark and deep, and somehow, the fact that he hadn't smiled made him even more attractive. The intense look on his face had been sexy as hell, dark and smouldering.

My stomach fluttered as his eyes watched me, making me feel like a blushing schoolgirl more than I ever had while in school. Honestly, I couldn't remember the last time I'd felt such an instant attraction to someone, but it must just be the alcohol, I told myself. It had knocked my internal calibrations off course, making it impossible to accurately judge anything.

The men were American, or at least the one who'd spoken to me was. The other guy hadn't said a word, I realized. *Cole.* The memory of the firmness of his chest as I'd hooked the candy cane onto his suit, along with that unblinking stare, made me shiver.

He couldn't be more different from the last guy I'd been with, the one I thought I would be with forever, but that might be a good thing. My previous choices were obviously defective, so maybe I should be looking for something different.

When the stall door opened and Holly appeared, her Santa hat precariously close to falling off her head, I reached out and straightened it out before we made our way back to the party together.

A cheer went up from the crowd as we returned, which we acknowledged with a wave and a bow. We were blessed with an amazing team of employees, and I loved having a chance to kick back with them and their partners. Our party might not be big compared to the one across the hall, but we were all having a great time.

"Martini?" Holly suggested, and I nodded enthusiastically. Our event the next day didn't start until late afternoon and we had the hotel room upstairs for the night, so we might as well make the most of it.

After a couple more drinks and many dances, Holly and I managed to make it through our speech celebrating all our achievements for the year and we started to hand out presents to the staff. We'd got them all personalized ornaments, my own design of baubles containing miniature London landmarks, along with Marks & Spencer gift vouchers for their Christmas dinners.

"Thanks so much, Gemma!" My assistant Denise gave me a hug as I got to her with her bag of goodies. "You remember my partner, Neil, right?"

I gave the man next to her a warm smile, trying to focus my eyes on his face. "Of course. It's lovely to see you again."

He smiled back; or at least, one of him did. "Nice to see you too. Where's Edwin tonight? I hoped to get a chance to rub it in about his team's performance last night. He's still got shares in Tottenham, right?"

In spite of the many drinks I'd had, my mouth went dry as Denise stared at Neil in horror. It seemed obvious that she had already told him about me and Edwin, but he'd either forgotten or just hadn't been listening. I almost felt worse for her than for myself.

"I have no idea where he is. We broke up." I kept the smile pasted on my face as I stated the facts bluntly. It got a bit easier to say it every time I did, though the mention of the football club shares that I'd bought him as a gift added an extra sting.

Uneasiness quickly descended on Neil's face. "Oh, uh, well, I'm sure you're better off without him."

It looked like Denise wanted to murder him, so I figured I better help him out before things turned ugly. "I definitely am. Have a fun night, you two!" With a cheery smile, I moved on to the next person before he could stick his foot in his mouth any further.

When all the gifts had been distributed, I realized I hadn't used the toilet when I'd gone to find Holly, and I really needed to now. After letting her know my intentions, I headed back out the door. Music thumped from within the room across the hall and I tried to read the sign on the door as I walked by, which turned out to be easier said than done with my slightly blurred vision. By squinting at it for a while, I could make out that it seemed to be a party for the hotel we were staying in. Did the men I had seen earlier work here at the hotel? They seemed like management types, though I might be stereotyping them based on the way they were dressed. What would they think of me based on my dress, I had to wonder?

I took a step back, shaking my head at my inability to get the tall, handsome stranger out of my thoughts. After everything I'd been through this year, the last thing I needed would be to get hung up on a guy. Although, just fooling around with one for fun definitely didn't sound like a bad idea at all.

Briefly, I flirted with the idea of going into the party to see if I could find him, but I quickly realized I would stand out like a sore thumb and probably make a fool of myself in the process. He hadn't given me any indication that he would even be interested, and I hadn't drunk enough to completely lose my sense of shame.

No, the best course of action would be to use the toilet, go back to my own party, and put the whole thing behind me. By tomorrow, he would be nothing more than a fuzzy memory.

~Cole~

The hotel manager continued to drone on about holiday yields as I took another drink. We'd already been here a lot longer than I wanted to be, especially since, to my disappointment, no scantily-clad women in Santa dresses could be seen at our party. It must have been part of the entertainment for the other party, and the idea of going over there and seeing it for myself tempted me far more than it should have.

My self-control had won out, though, and now, I was simply bored and ready to return to my room. Tomorrow, I would get in touch with one of my contacts who could connect me with an agency here to provide women to meet any needs I may have. I preferred to handle things that way: keeping everything transactional to avoid any misunderstandings.

When my phone buzzed in my pocket, I gratefully took the excuse to leave the conversation, making my way out of the room and back to the hall where I took my phone out. The phone display showed my sister's name and normally, I would let it go to voicemail at a business function. However, at this precise moment, I answered it as the lesser of two evils compared to the dull party I wanted to escape.

As I expected, her call was simply to check up on me. Every year at this time, the same thing happened: she called me nearly every day, as if I might have some kind of breakdown every time I saw a Christmas tree. I reassured her that I would only be in London for a couple of weeks and would still be home in plenty of time for Christmas so she could keep an eye on me in person. My tone seemed to reassure her even if my words didn't, and after I'd hung up, I looked at the phone in my hand for a few seconds, wondering how upset Jackson would be if I just went back up to my room now and sent him a message to say I'd left.

Before I could decide, a flash of red caught my attention from the corner of my eye.

"I guess you have more Christmas spirit than I gave you credit for, Mr Lump of Coal."

When I looked up, the gorgeous redhead from earlier stood in front of me with a smile on her face, and my pulse rate increased as I took in the sight of her again. She looked even sexier the second time I saw her, and I couldn't help imagining what she would feel like, and taste like, for that matter. It had been a long time since a woman had this kind of effect on me. My interest had definitely been piqued, but I would only act on it if we were on the same page.

I also had no idea what she was talking about. What had she said? Christmas spirit?

"What?" I managed to ask.

With a laugh, she pointed up to the ceiling. Following her point, I looked up to see that I had inadvertently stopped to take my phone call directly beneath a fake sprig of mistletoe.

"You know the rules," she said as my gaze returned to her smiling face. "Anyone under the mistletoe gets kissed. Were you waiting here for me?"

Her tone was obviously teasing, but I never wasted time with flirting. I simply wanted to know if I had any chance of taking her upstairs with me. Could she be the kind of woman I was after?

"What would a kiss cost me?" I asked, trying to move the conversation onto more comfortable ground for me.

She laughed again, a light, musical sound that made my lips twitch against my will. "First one's free."

With those words, she took a step closer to me, close enough that I could smell her perfume: a feminine vanilla and spice scent so enticing that I had an irrational urge to bury my face in her neck and inhale it more fully. Then, to my surprise, one of her hands slid up the side of my face and pulled me towards her as she stood on her tiptoes to plant a quick peck on my cheek.

The feel of her hand and the smell of her, her body so close to mine and the sight of those twinkling eyes damn near made me lose control.

"You call that a kiss?" The words came out rougher than I intended, and before she could respond, my hand found her waist, pulling her closer to me as I pressed my lips against her plump red ones in an almost electric collision, sending a shot of pure desire through me.

She didn't resist me. In fact, her hands went to my arms and brought me even closer to her.

The door to the hotel's party opened, letting more people into the hall to join us, and the woman in my arms pulled back, giving an almost nervous laugh that made it clear to me that she wouldn't have stopped if not for the interruption.

Just having her close to me had already begun to make me hard, and I wanted to get even closer, but first, I needed to clarify the situation.

"Why are you here tonight?" My hand still rested on her waist, feeling natural there.

She gave a half-hearted shrug, her green eyes locked on mine. "For work."

So, she *was* working the party, as I thought, but in what capacity? "Dressed like this?" I asked, tracing the neckline of her dress with my free hand. The touch of my fingertips on her skin coaxed a sigh out of her, letting me know she felt this electricity between us just as much as I did.

"I just wanted to spread some Christmas cheer," she said, making an effort to keep her voice steady though I could still hear the tremble in it.

I leaned down so I could whisper in her ear. "What else would you be willing to spread?"

A shiver went through her body as my lips grazed her neck, and though she didn't answer me, her physical reaction told me what I needed to know: she wanted this too. Therefore, I moved on to more practical concerns.

"Are you finished for the night or do you need to go back?" Not sure how much longer I could wait, I internally prayed for the first option.

"I can leave. Are you making me a better offer?"

Her breath sounded shorter than before, and a satisfied smile began to spread across my face. That was exactly the answer I'd hoped for: she could be bought after all. I didn't imagine a girl like her would be cheap, but that had never been an issue for me. At this point, I would be willing to pay pretty much whatever she asked.

"What if I want the whole package?" I murmured, still keeping my lips next to her ear.

"Meaning?" Her hand pressed against my chest, sending the blood rushing south even more than before.

I pulled her even closer so she could feel just how hard she'd made me, and her body almost melted into mine. "Meaning you in my bed, all night, doing whatever I tell you to."

Her whimper had to be one of the sexiest fucking things I'd ever heard. I was used to the women I paid putting on a show for me, but if she was acting, she deserved some kind of award. It felt very real.

"You have a room here?" she whispered back, and my smile widened. "Yes."

Almost reluctantly, she pulled back from me so she could see my face. I didn't know exactly what she saw there, but I could only assume it matched the lust I could see in her eyes. It seemed to satisfy her, at any rate. Whatever she was looking for, she found it, based on her response.

"I just need to let them know I'm leaving."

She gestured to the doors for the party she'd been at, reminding me that I had completely forgotten about Jackson. I should fill him in too. "I'll meet you back out here in a couple of minutes."

With a nod, she quickly made her way into the other room, and I watched her go with an intense mix of satisfaction and anticipation. It had been a long time since I'd been this excited to get a woman in my bed, and I had a feeling this night would be worth every penny in the end.

As soon as that thought crossed my mind, I realized we hadn't actually agreed on a price yet. That went against my usual rules, but it didn't worry me too much. Whatever she asked, I could afford, and once we got up to my room, we could settle it then.

I really couldn't wait.

Chapter Two

THE MISTAKE

~Gemma~

My whole body trembled as I stepped back inside the party and caught Holly's eye from the door. In the middle of a conversation, she nodded at me to say she'd seen me, and I leaned back against the wall as I waited for her to finish, wrapping my arms around myself to try to stop my shaking.

I couldn't quite believe I intended to go upstairs with this man I had never met before and knew nothing about, and yet, I had no doubt that I wanted to do it. His words and his touch set me on fire in a way no one ever had before, but then, no one had ever spoken to me like that either. The only man I had ever slept with had always been very respectful, which I thought I wanted. Now, suddenly, I wasn't quite so sure. The thought of what might happen, of what Cole might say and do to me when we were alone in his room, had my heart racing.

"What's going on?" Holly asked as she walked over, giving me a curious look. "Are you okay?"

I nodded, trying to sound nonchalant. "Better than okay. I just wanted to let you know I'm going to leave now and you probably won't see me until tomorrow."

Her eyes widened in surprise before a wide grin spread across her face. "No way! Who's the guy?"

"He's attending the party across the hall," I explained, gesturing at the door behind me. "I don't know much about him, but he's just..."

I trailed off, unable to find an adjective to adequately explain what Cole did to me, and Holly's smile got even bigger as she watched me struggle.

"Lost for words, huh? This must be some man. Have fun, Gem! You deserve it. And be safe. You're just staying here in the hotel?"

I nodded again. "If it gets weird, I'll just leave. I've got my key and my phone." As proof, I grabbed my small clutch bag from the table where I'd left it earlier and held it up for her to see.

She wished me luck, her enthusiasm spurring me on as I returned to the hallway. The *empty* hallway, with no sign of Cole, and for a moment, I worried that he might have changed his mind. However, not more than thirty seconds later, the doors to the other party opened and he strode out, a smirk on his face and a dangerous gleam in his eye.

It felt like a magnet pulled me towards him as I walked forward. He didn't say anything, just put his arm around me as if it belonged there and led me over to the lift.

When the lift arrived, other people were already inside so we walked in and stood quietly, his arm still around my waist and his thumb tracing a circle on my hip. Nothing in the action was inherently dirty, but combined with the smell of his cologne and the firmness of his body next to me, it still sent heat through my body, leading straight to the steady pulse between my legs. I could hardly believe he'd turned me on this much by barely touching me.

As the lift doors opened on Cole's floor, he led me out and began walking down the hall towards his room, but as soon as the door closed behind us and we were alone again, Cole pushed me up against the wall of the hallway, pressing the length of his body into me. "What's your name?" he whispered, his hands running up my thighs and under my dress.

The idea that I would be doing this with someone who didn't even know my name would have been unbelievable to me just a few hours ago, but I sure as hell didn't want to stop.

"Gemma," I managed to gasp, though for a moment, I almost thought I had forgotten it. Focusing on anything that required brain power seemed impossible as he lowered his lips to my neck, sucking and licking at it while his hands rubbed my thighs, getting closer and closer to my already soaked knickers. My knees were ready to buckle. "Shouldn't we... go in your room?"

"What's the matter, Gemma?" I could hear the smirk in his voice even though I could no longer see his face. "Afraid someone will see you? That they'll see just how wet you are for me?"

With that, he pushed my panties aside and pressed a finger inside me while I grasped at his shoulders to keep myself upright. "Bloody hell," I panted as his thumb brushed my clit, making my thighs and stomach clench involuntarily.

A deep chuckle echoed in my ear. "Those aren't the words I would use, but I'm guessing that means you're ready for this."

Just as abruptly as he'd inserted it, he removed his finger and walked away, heading further down the hall and leaving me slumped against the wall. He didn't even look back to see if I would follow. He was so damn sure of himself, so in control, and for some reason, it only turned me on more.

Pushing myself away from the wall, I hurried after him, arriving just as he opened the door to his room. He went in first, holding it open for me to follow, and I looked around curiously as I walked into the sitting room of a large suite, much fancier than the room Holly and I had, though still equally lacking in personality. A deep, plush sofa and two matching armchairs surrounded a solid coffee table. A large-screen TV hung on one wall, with a small kitchen area to one side and a desk and working space on the other. Separate doors led to the bathroom and bedroom beyond.

Cole walked further into the room, still looking completely in control as he removed his suit jacket and draped it over the sofa, his eyes never leaving me. "I assume you'll want to discuss business first."

"Business?" I repeated curiously, dropping my clutch on the table by the door. The only kind of business that concerned me at the moment involved getting him out of the rest of that suit as quickly as possible.

"Do you call it something else here?" he asked, loosening his tie. "I just meant that we should set out the terms."

I didn't have a clue what he meant and I was losing the ability to focus, watching his muscles tense beneath his dress shirt as he pulled his tie off.

Concentrate, Gemma, I admonished myself. What had he said? Something about 'terms'? His words beneath the mistletoe came back to me, how he said he wanted me to do whatever he told me to. Maybe the 'terms' had something to do with that. Did he want to know how far I would be willing to go?

"Can we just see how things go?" I suggested tentatively. I didn't really have any idea what he had in mind, and I didn't want to sound foolish by expecting too much or too little.

His brow furrowed, looking unsatisfied with that response. "I'd prefer to get it settled up front."

Desperate to get the talking over with, I decided to put the ball back in his court. "Well, what would you suggest?"

His eyebrows raised but I couldn't read the expression in his eyes. He appeared to be thinking things over as he removed his cufflinks, staying silent until he made up his mind.

"If you're staying the whole night, how about £2000?"

The mention of money threw me completely off and I stared at him blankly for a long moment, trying to make sense of it. Why were we talking about money?

Suddenly, it hit me, reality sinking in as I put the pieces together. *Oh, my God.* He thought I was a hooker.

~Cole~

Although I never liked making the first offer in any kind of business arrangement, this whole evening had already been unorthodox, nothing following my usual plan. So, when Gemma asked for my input, I decided to throw a figure out, eager to move this along. Two thousand pounds felt more than generous, especially when she didn't seem to have any other plans for the evening, considering that she dropped everything to come with me before agreeing on a price. I'd just made her whole night a lot more profitable, and I didn't expect any resistance.

To my surprise, however, Gemma's body language completely changed once the words were out of my mouth.

She took a step back, her eyes wide, as if I had genuinely taken her by surprise, and a moment later, she started to laugh.

My fingers paused over the shirt buttons I had just started to undo, and the corners of my lips pulled down into a frown. What did she find so funny? My offer had been perfectly reasonable. Maybe this was some kind of negotiating tactic?

"I'm willing to hear a counter-offer," I told her, trying to move this along. I had been rock hard ever since the hallway, ever since I felt just how wet she was. No matter how much of a professional she might be, she couldn't fake being that turned on, and it excited me in turn to know that she wanted me so badly. I couldn't wait to get my pants off and get my dick into something considerably more appealing.

Gemma shook her head, her expression a mixture of amusement and annoyance. "I'm sorry, Cole. I think there's been a mix-up."

Turning back to the door, she picked up her purse from the table where she'd dropped it, and my lips tightened at this new ploy. I should have guessed: she must be pretending to leave to try to drive the price up. I couldn't be less in the mood for this, and it perfectly illustrated why I preferred to always have things settled in advance. "Name your price, Gemma. I don't want to play games."

Her shoulders tensed before she turned back to me with a new look on her face, but this one, I couldn't decipher at all. "Neither do I. Merry Christmas, Cole."

Before I could say anything else, she let herself out, the door swinging shut behind her.

What the fuck?

A minute ago, she had practically been begging for it, and now she wouldn't even make me an offer? This must be some new trick I hadn't encountered before. She would probably give it a minute or two and then come back, claiming to have forgotten something, and check if my offer had gone up. Annoyed but still interested, I poured myself a drink and sat down to wait.

Five minutes went by, and then ten. Eventually, my erection softened and I had to admit that it didn't look like she was coming back. Apparently, I wouldn't be getting laid after all. *Fuck.* I had actually been really excited about the thought of being with her, and I had no idea what had gone wrong. Sure, I hadn't done my research on current rates in London before I arrived, mainly because I never expected to have to throw out a figure, but I couldn't have been *that* far off.

Nearly three years had passed since I'd slept with any woman who hadn't been paid in advance, but usually, the details were all handled through a third party. Negotiating directly with the woman had never been my style, and I only made an exception in this case because Gemma had been so exceptional in the first place.

Muttering to myself in frustration, I stripped off the rest of my clothes and climbed into bed alone. No matter how much I tried to turn off my brain, however, my memory kept drifting back to the sight of Gemma in her dress, the feel of her lips on mine and the way her tight, wet pussy felt wrapped around my finger. Just the thought of it had me growing harder until, with an unhappy sigh, I hauled myself back out of bed and went into the bathroom.

When the water had warmed up, I stepped inside the large walk-in shower and let the water run over me, stroking myself slowly with my hand as I brought the picture of Gemma back to the front of my mind. When I pictured her plump red lips wrapped around my dick, it made me so dizzy with pleasure that I had to put my other hand on the shower wall to keep my balance. Pumping faster, I imagined her red hair splayed out on the pillow of my bed, her eyes closed in bliss as she orgasmed beneath me, and those images alone were enough to get me off, panting in the steamy shower while the water washed all the evidence of my arousal down the drain.

With my mind a bit clearer, I returned to bed with a new sense of conviction. I still wanted her, and what I wanted, I always got. There had to be some way to find her. Apparently, I insulted her with my offer, but if I found out who she worked for, I could ascertain her usual price and find out how to get in touch with her. Despite the setback, I could still find a way to have her and make those visions in my head a reality.

The hotel manager should be able to tell me about the party she'd been working at, which would be a good place to start. He should have access to the name of the company that had provided the entertainment, or at least the information about the company that had thrown the party, and I could take it from there. Once I'd settled on that plan of action, my body finally began to settle, allowing me to close my eyes and get some sleep.

~Gemma~

My disbelief and amusement over the way things had played out with Cole followed me back to my room, two floors below his. Holly hadn't returned yet, which meant the party must still be going on, but I didn't feel like going back downstairs. The pleasant buzz I'd been floating on all night had died, killed off by the shock of what had just happened.

Standing in front of the mirror, I replayed the events of the night in my head as I examined my appearance, trying to decide what had given Cole the impression that I was a prostitute. While I thought we were flirting under the mistletoe, he had apparently been speaking literally. As I remembered him asking how much a kiss would cost and the way he said he wanted 'the whole package', my cheeks flamed red with embarrassment. Had I honestly thrown myself at him so hard that the only logical conclusion he could come to was that I wanted to be paid? I must be coming across as more desperate than I thought.

I had to admit I also felt desperately disappointed as I peeled off my dress and stepped into the shower, trying to wash the whole night off of me. Cole excited me more than any man ever had, more than I thought possible, and now, I had to face the fact that our entire chemistry had been based on a misunderstanding. Maybe I should have stayed and taken his money. At least then I would have gotten to shag him, and I felt pretty certain it would be a memory worth having.

His dark, brooding face flashed in front of my eyes, and I could almost feel the intensity of his gaze again while my hand moved down across my body, over my hard nipple and lower. I could almost feel Cole's hands on my thighs again, moving up until...

As I got to the part of my memory where he thrust his finger inside me, I let my own fingers follow. A low moan echoed in my throat, echoing into the bathroom air while I imagined his big, strong hand working me over, plunging my hand in as deeply as I could. I hadn't even had a glimpse of what hid beneath his suit trousers, but even the thought of it, and what he might do with it, had me panting. With hardly any effort at all, I could picture him hovering over me, his body moving against mine, and my knees buckled as I came, the water from the showerhead still pouring over me.

Fuck, that didn't take long at all. My orgasms were usually a lot harder to come by.

Taking a deep breath, I regained my balance and turned the water off. After drying off and putting on my comfortable pajamas, I climbed into bed, trying to think about things more objectively. As good as the imaginary sex might be, did I really want to be with someone who judged any woman so quickly based on what she wore, or who assumed that I could be bought? Definitely not. He must be wealthy, based on his suit and his hotel room, so he was probably the type who thought his money could get him anything he wanted. I had spent my whole life surrounded by, and avoiding, those types of men.

Cole wasn't worth my regret, I decided. I could chalk the whole thing up as a learning experience and move on, as he no doubt would himself, and with that thought in my head, I went to sleep.

The next day, Holly and I had a lazy morning followed by a room-service lunch. When I told her the story of what had happened with Cole the night before, she nearly fell off the bed laughing.

"Oh, Gem, I wish I could have seen the look on your face when he offered to pay you! What did you say?"

"I just told him there'd been a mix-up, but to be honest, I was really disappointed. I bet it would have been good."

"That is too bad," Holly agreed sympathetically. She knew just how long it had been since I'd had anyone exciting in my bed. "Why are the hot ones always such jerks?"

"Not just the hot ones," I reminded her. I was beginning to think there weren't *any* men out there who weren't defective in some way. The two of us certainly hadn't found any.

She tapped a finger against her cheek thoughtfully. "But, hang on, you didn't actually tell him that you weren't a hooker?"

I shook my head. "Not in so many words, but I'm sure he figured it out."

Holly looked unconvinced. "It sounds like he's not the brightest bulb on the tree. Maybe you should have spelled it out for him."

"It's not like it matters. I'm never going to see him again."

"True, but at least maybe he'd think twice before he made the same assumption about someone else."

"You're saying I should have taken one for the team?" I clarified, and she wrinkled her nose at me.

"Well, *someone* will have to put him in his place sooner or later. It might as well have been you. I would have loved to see you go all high-class on him."

When she'd finally finished laughing at me, we headed out to do some early Christmas shopping, returning to the hotel in time to get ready for our event later that afternoon.

Though I had been trying not to dwell on it too much to keep my nerves in check, this event was a very big deal for us. An upscale West End hotel would be celebrating their grand reopening, a hotel that Holly and I had been working on for the better part of the last year. Together, we had completely redesigned the whole ground floor, giving it a brand new look, and Holly had spruced up the guest rooms with her unique flair. We were excited for people to see our work and we were hoping a lot of new interest in our business would follow.

The two of us started Anchor Design three years ago, just out of university, and this hotel project had been our biggest one so far. Holly and I made a great team: I oversaw the architecture side of things while Holly handled all the interior design. She served as the managing director of Anchor, while I owned and funded the business, though there weren't many people who actually knew that detail. I preferred if the other staff thought of me as one of them and that our clients weren't aware of my family connections. That also explained why I'd taken Sudlow, my mother's maiden name, as my professional name. My father and his position played no part in our business.

Compared to the party the night before, our event that evening would be a much more restrained affair, and we dressed to match. Holly wore a pretty pink wrap dress with gold jewellery that beautifully complemented her tanned skin and blonde hair, while I went with an emerald green A-line midi dress and matching heels. The green shade brought out my eyes and contrasted vividly with my red hair, making it one of my favourite colours to wear. Forgettable was one word I never wanted applied to me or our designs. I would much rather stand out from a crowd.

Once we were ready, we walked the few blocks over to the hotel where the owner, a handsome Italian billionaire in his 50s named Alberto Morelli, whom we had only met once before, came over to greet us.

"Ms Sudlow, Ms Chapman, it is wonderful to see you again." He gave us both kisses on the cheek as if we were old friends. "Everything looks wonderful, I think you will agree."

Satisfaction flowed through me as I looked around the entrance area. Holly had been handling most of the on-site consultations, so this was the first time I'd seen it in person since work finished, and it more than lived up to my expectations. Sometimes, it amazed me to consider how something that started out as an idea in our heads could become reality like this. Design could be truly magical.

Signor Morelli ran us through the plan for the event. "Once everyone has arrived and had a drink or two, I will make a short speech and bring you both up to introduce you and your company. Afterwards, we'll have dinner in the restaurant." He gestured toward the dining space that we had also redesigned. "Everyone will love it. You should know that I have invited several of my top competitors here tonight, and I have no doubt that they will try to tempt you away from me. But I hope that before you take on too many new clients, you will consider my offer to redo my hotel in Milan."

"You're at the top of our list, Signor Morelli," I promised him. "We'll be in touch with your office soon."

He hurried off to greet the next guests while Holly rolled her eyes at me behind his back. "Please tell me we're not actually considering working for him again." Despite how well the hotel had turned out, the whole project had been one headache after another. The project manager had tried to cut corners at every turn and Holly had fought tooth and nail to keep our original vision intact.

"Of course not," I agreed quietly. "But he doesn't need to know that, and neither do any of his competitors. The more in demand they think we are, the better for us. Now, let's go get ourselves a drink and see what other potential clients might be lurking around. This night is going to lead to big things for us. I can feel it."

~Cole~

Jackson knocked on my door at nine o'clock in the morning, precisely, just as I'd told him to. As soon as I let him in, he peered around the suite's living area with interest. "Am I in time to say hello, or has she already gone?"

When I went back to the party the night before to tell him I'd be leaving with the woman in the Santa dress, he had been more than a little jealous. "You lucky bastard. You know she's basically my dream girl, right?"

I shrugged, feeling rather pleased with myself, but I threw him a bone too. "It's not like we're getting married. If you put up the cash, I'm sure you could get her for yourself another time."

Jackson's mouth dropped open in surprise as he leaned closer to whisper to me. "She's a call girl?"

"Of course. You saw her."

"I did," he agreed, knitting his brows. "And I didn't get that vibe at all."

"Which is why I got her first," I concluded with a smirk. "I'll see you in the morning."

Now, he stood here looking around my suite as if she might suddenly appear out of the woodwork.

I kept my reply short and to the point as I took a seat on the couch. "She's not here. Let's get to work."

I had some paperwork for the new hotel that I wanted to review, along with some documents my board had sent me for some of our other properties.

"You've got to give me more than that," Jackson grumbled as he sat down in one of the chairs across from me, pulling out his own laptop. "Did she look as good out of that dress as she did in it?"

For a moment, I almost considered lying to him by pretending she had spent the night, looking to cover my bruised ego, but since I might need his help to track her down, it would be better to be honest. "I don't know. Nothing happened."

"What?" He couldn't have looked more shocked if I had told him aliens had landed during the night. "Why not?"

I sighed, frustrated both by this conversation and by the events of the previous night. "Apparently, I didn't make her a good enough offer."

Jackson gave a low whistle. "Well, if you can't afford her, I don't know who could. How much did she want?"

"I don't know," I repeated, my jaw clenched. "She didn't say."

Confusion flashed across his face, and I couldn't blame him for it. I still felt confused too. "Exactly what happened, Cole?"

As briefly as possible, I gave him a summary of my conversation with Gemma once we got back to my suite. Though he tried to hide the smile on his face as I finished speaking, he wasn't quite quick enough, and it only made me grumpier. "What?"

"You're an idiot." His grin broke through as he tried, and failed, to keep from laughing.

"Me? She's the one who went from hot to cold in two seconds."

"Because you insulted her."

What did he see that I didn't? "My offer was reasonable."

"No, you moron!" Jackson shook his head in disbelief. "It has nothing to do with the amount you offered; she obviously wasn't a prostitute at all. She simply wanted to spend the night with you."

I should have expected that from him. He still believed in love at first sight and other kinds of similar nonsense, so I scoffed at his conclusion. "That's not true. She said..."

I trailed off, trying to remember exactly what she had said when she kissed me under the mistletoe. We hadn't discussed any amounts, of course, but I thought we were both clear on the nature of the situation.

However, as I reviewed the conversation in my head, I began to see that perhaps I assumed too much. I wanted it to be true, so I heard what I wanted to hear, and a fresh wave of disappointment washed over me as I realized Jackson might actually be right. And if she really wasn't a hooker, then trying to track her down would be pointless. Even if I found her, I couldn't sleep with her after all.

Fuck.

When I didn't finish my thought, Jackson couldn't help gloating. "You see? You're a moron."

"Shut up," I growled, more frustrated with myself than with him. "Maybe you're right, but if that's the case, then I had a lucky escape. You know I don't do that."

"You don't take a beautiful woman to bed unless you can pay her for it," he clarified. "Because that makes sense."

To me, it did. "I'll end up paying for it one way or another. Better to get it over with up front."

He shook his head again, but this time with a hint of pity. "Not all women are like Samantha, you know."

"And this conversation is officially over," I declared. "Let's do some work, please."

We spent a couple of hours going over things and had lunch delivered to the room. After we'd eaten, he excused himself to go start looking for more local design firms for the new hotel. "And don't forget, we've got that reception at Morelli's hotel later," he added on his way out the door.

I still needed to arrange a woman to attend that with me, which would help avoid a repeat of the previous night's mess, so I made a few calls to set everything up before getting back to work. A few hours later, I met Jackson and the woman I'd hired in the lobby and we took a car over to the Mayfair Mews Inn.

Alberto Morelli had long been one of my main competitors in Europe with a chain of hotels that rivalled my own. The fact that he had invited me to the reopening of his central London hotel meant that he felt confident I'd be impressed by whatever he had done to it.

From the outside, the hotel looked like a typical Georgian building, blending in with the residences around it on a typical Mayfair street, but the moment we stepped inside, I had to clench my jaw to keep it from dropping.

The entire ground floor had been reimagined. Open and airy with various shades of greens and browns, it felt like a forest mirage in the middle of the city. Water cascaded down one wall of the lobby while plants climbed up another. In the wrong hands, it could easily have been garish, but here, it felt calming and classy, and completely unique. I'd never seen anything like it. The fact that they had been able to do this to an existing building while maintaining the structure made it even more unbelievable.

With the practice of experience, I kept my face carefully neutral in case Morelli or any of his cronies happened to be watching, but inside, my mind raced. Who designed this for him? More importantly, how could I steal them from him? This was exactly the kind of imaginative thinking I'd been looking for.

"Ah, Mr Stamer, I'm so delighted you could join us." Alberto Morelli headed towards me with a pleasant smile on his face, but I could see the hint of triumph in his eyes. He knew exactly what a winner he had here.

"Signor Morelli." I greeted him coolly in return, offering my hand. "Thank you for having us. This is Jackson Hanmer, my acquisitions director."

Jackson and Alberto shook hands before the Italian man turned to the woman on my arm. "And this beautiful lady is…?"

"Vanessa." I didn't know her last name, nor did I care. Vanessa probably wasn't even her real first name, but she was exactly the sort of woman I liked to take to these events: beautiful, well-spoken and completely uninterested in me beyond this evening.

"Ah, cara mia, welcome to my hotel," Alberto carried on, taking Vanessa's hand and kissing it. "Do you like it?"

"It's beautiful," she answered with a practiced smile. "You must be very pleased with it."

"Very." He gave me a wink while I gritted my teeth, trying not to show my envy.

Thankfully, I didn't have to lower myself by asking for the designer's details, since Jackson did it for me. "Who designed it, Signor?"

Alberto smiled in satisfaction. "A small London firm I discovered. Very talented and *very* exclusive. I'm afraid that any work you might be thinking of for them will have to wait until my other projects are completed."

We would see about that. "What's the name of the firm?" I tried to make it sound like I asked to be polite and not because I desperately wanted to know.

"Anchor Design. The main architect and designer are here tonight, I will be introducing them shortly. Now, please excuse me gentlemen, more guests are arriving." He wandered away from us to rub his success in someone else's face.

Anchor Design. Why did that sound familiar? "Have you heard of them?" I asked Jackson, keeping my voice low in case anyone else might be listening.

He shook his head. "No, but if they're here, we'll find them."

We joined the small line-up for the bar as I continued to look around the lobby. With each new detail I noticed, my admiration grew, and it made me furious that we hadn't found this design firm first. I wanted to see more of their work, and I wanted to see what they could come up with for me. As my eyes scanned the room, a memory tugged at the back of my mind, something to do with Anchor Design, but I couldn't quite place it.

Chapter Three

WE MEET AGAIN

~Gemma~

The bartender placed a lychee martini down in front of me and a chocolate one for Holly. "To our success?" I suggested as a toast, holding my glass up.

"Absolutely," she agreed, clinking my glass with hers and taking a long sip. "Now, let's go mingle with the super-rich and design-challenged."

Turning back to the room, we shimmied past the other people queuing for the bar and had just made our way through the crowd when a deep voice called out my name.

"Gemma?"

The sound sent a shiver through me, but I refused to believe my ears. It couldn't be him, could it? Why on earth would he be here? I must be imagining things.

Yet, when I turned around, Cole stood there, staring at me in surprise. He had his friend, Jackson, on one side, and a very elegant brunette on his other arm. He wore a different suit from the night before, but it fit him just as well and looked just as expensive.

To my frustration, he looked just as sexy as I remembered. I had almost hoped that the alcohol had clouded my judgement the night before and made him better-looking in my mind than he had been in real life, but unfortunately, that didn't seem to be the case.

All the resolutions I'd made the night before about not regretting the quick way things had ended between us flew right out the window, and I wanted nothing more than to feel his lips on me again and to hear him whispering dirty things in my ear.

"Hello, Cole," I said politely, trying to keep my voice steady and cover for the way my heart pounded in my chest. "Nice to see you again. And Jackson, right?" I addressed myself to the other man so that I wouldn't have to look directly at Cole's intense gaze. I had no idea why they would be here, but I needed to remain professional. We had too much riding on the party to let my hormones take over.

Jackson gave me the same warm, genuine smile he had the night before. "What a lovely surprise. Gemma, is it?"

I nodded in confirmation, remembering that we hadn't been properly introduced the night before. "That's right, and this is my friend and colleague, Holly."

Jackson's eyes widened for a second as he looked over at my companion and held his hand out to her. "A pleasure. I have to admit, I thought Gemma was kidding about having a friend named Holly, but I've never been more happy to be wrong."

His smooth flirting made me smile as I turned to the woman next to Cole, waiting for him to introduce her next. However, he said nothing, continuing to stare at me, looking almost as stunned as I felt.

"And you are?" I finally asked her directly, when the silence grew slightly too long.

"Vanessa," she introduced herself, shaking my hand confidently. "Lovely to meet you."

"And you." As I turned back to Cole, waiting for him to say something that might explain his presence, I remembered he had been attending the Lytton Hotel staff party the night before. At the time, I thought he might be a manager there or something, and Signor Morelli had just told us he'd invited some of his competitors. That might explain the connection, but before I could ask, he finally spoke again.

"Who are you here with?" he asked, looking around as if there must be a man somewhere nearby, and I had to refrain from rolling my eyes.

"I'm here with Holly." As I glanced over at her, I could see the questions in her eyes, wanting to know exactly who these men were, but those answers would have to wait, mostly because I still didn't really know.

However, this would be a good opportunity to get some unbiased feedback on our work, since they didn't seem to have any idea who Holly and I were either.

"What do you think of the hotel redesign?" I asked, taking a sip from my martini. The tart sweetness of the lychee and the warmth of the vodka helped me to focus on something other than the disorientation brought on by Cole's reappearance. Although I addressed the question to both of them, I kept my eyes on Jackson. I could feel Cole watching me, but if I made eye contact, it would be too easy to forget everything else in the heat that seemed to pass between us.

"It's exceptional," Jackson replied sincerely, and I had to fight to keep from smiling. "We were just saying we'd love to work with the designers."

"For the Lytton?" That surprised me. Although the decoration hadn't been to my taste, it all looked quite new and in good shape. I hadn't noticed anything there in need of renovation.

He gave me a slightly funny look in reply. "No, for a new project we're working on."

That piqued my interest, and I shifted slightly closer to him. "Forgive me. Because you were at the Lytton party last night, I thought you must work for the hotel, but I suppose I should know better than to make any assumptions about a person's line of work without asking."

My eyes flicked over to Cole and his lips tightened, letting me know he definitely caught my double meaning.

Jackson brushed off my apology. "No, that's our fault, we should have introduced ourselves properly. We're with Stamer Hotels."

Before I could stop them, my eyes widened in surprise. Of course I knew the name, since Stamer Hotels was a massive international hotel chain. If they really did have a new project they were working on, that could be a huge opportunity for us.

"I'm Jackson Hanmer," he continued. "And this is Cole Stamer."

Wait... did he just say Cole was Cole *Stamer*? From the Stamer family who owned the whole chain? No wonder he dressed so well. His bank account probably rivalled Signor Morelli's billions.

I had a whole host of new questions, but I tried my best to smile as though none of that surprised me. "It's lovely to meet you both. What brings you gentlemen to London?"

Jackson returned my smile easily, just as comfortable with business discussions as with small talk. "A new hotel, which is what we're hoping to discuss with the firm that designed this place. What about you? What brings you here tonight?"

Holly and I exchanged glances again, and she nodded to tell me to reply, that she'd follow my lead. I decided to keep things vague a little longer. "Actually, we know the design firm. Quite well. I imagine they're going to have a lot of offers after tonight."

"I'm confident we can convince them to work with us," Jackson replied, giving me another charming smile. He really was quite handsome, in a completely different way than Cole, but he didn't make my pulse race the way Cole did.

And speaking of Cole... a wicked thought crossed my mind, and before I could stop myself, I turned to him with the most innocent expression I could muster. "So, you're saying that people usually find your offers impressive?"

~Cole~

Jackson tried not to laugh as Gemma posed her question, all faux innocence and sweetness. He knew exactly what she meant by it, and so did I.

What was she doing here? She still hadn't told us her full name or why she had come to this party. Jackson said she must not have been an escort after all, but I still couldn't be certain. At a party like this, looking as polished and put together as she did, she could easily be a high-end girl on the arm of someone like Morelli. Or maybe she worked with one of my competitors? Was the whole thing a set-up to try to get close to me? My mind raced furiously as I tried to figure it all out.

Suddenly, in a flash, it came back to me: Anchor Design had been the name on the door of the party she'd been at. She must be here with someone from the design firm. After all, she just said she knew them quite well, and since she had been willing to go to my room with me, it seemed more likely that she wouldn't be in a relationship. She must be a working girl after all. Fuck, I really hoped so.

And now, she had just mocked the offer I made her, though I still didn't understand what was wrong with it. I'd paid less than that for Vanessa and she would not only attend this party with me but join me for an hour back at the hotel afterwards.

Vanessa was beautiful, no question, but looking at her next to Gemma, I couldn't help thinking I'd rather take Gemma back to the hotel with me that evening. Something about the sparkle in her eyes and her rather unusual mix of confidence and submissiveness appealed to me more than I could explain. But if my calculations were correct, I should still have a chance. If I could find out who she was here with, I would find out what they were paying her and I would better it. Somehow, I could still turn this to my advantage.

So when she asked if people generally found my offers impressive, I leaned closer to her, keeping my voice low enough that even the others in our small group couldn't hear it. "I promise you, Gemma: when there's something I really want, I get it."

Her lips twitched as she looked back at me, her eyes sparkling in an amused challenge. "I guess we'll just have to see about that."

Before we could go any further, the squeal of a microphone echoed through the room and everyone turned to find the source of the noise. Alberto Morelli stood on the staircase, a few steps up so everyone could see him, beaming as he addressed the crowd.

"Thank you all for coming to the reopening of the Mayfair Mews Inn."

He launched into the usual spiel about the importance of his hotel, and I couldn't stop my mind from wandering as he continued speaking. Gemma still stood in front of me but she had turned around to listen to Alberto, giving me a view of her back. The dress she wore was obviously a lot more tasteful than the one she'd had on the night before, but it still showed off her figure beautifully, and I had an almost overwhelming urge to gather her hair to one side and kiss my way down her neck. I desperately wanted to hear her whimper again the same way she had under the mistletoe. Fuck, I wanted her badly. I honestly couldn't remember the last time I'd been this attracted to someone.

When Alberto started talking about Anchor Design, I forced myself to concentrate back on his words. This could be important. I needed to find out who the people were that I would need to win over to get this firm to work with me.

"I'm sure you can all agree that there is nowhere else like this in London," Alberto gloated with a smug smile on his face. "I am delighted to introduce you all to the women behind Anchor, the creative team in charge of this stunning transformation: Ms Holly Chapman and Ms Gemma Sudlow."

Wait... *what* did he just say?

Gemma turned back to me and gave me a wink. "That's my cue. Would you hold this for me?"

Before I could even register what just happened, she handed her martini to me. I took it out of reflex more than through any conscious decision, watching in disbelief as she and Holly made their way through the crowd to join Alberto on the stairs.

Fuck. Jackson had it right: I had, in fact, completely misjudged her. Rather than being here with someone from the design firm, she worked for them. Not just worked for them; by the looks of it, she must be one of the main designers.

My instincts rarely let me down that badly. How had I read her so completely wrong?

As I tried to make sense of it all, Gemma and Holly took turns speaking about the inspiration for the designs. They were both well spoken and charming, their passion for the project evident in the way they talked about it. Looking around the room, I could see several of our other competitors listening carefully, some of them whispering to each other. Obviously, we wouldn't be the only ones interested in hiring them.

When they had finished, I turned back to Jackson who grinned at me in delight, not even trying to hide his amusement. "You should have seen your face when they called their names," he crowed. "Tough break, Cole. You really think they're going to want to work with you now?"

I'd suffered a setback, I had to admit, but I wasn't giving up just yet. "You should know better than to underestimate me," I reminded him. "Everyone's got a price. There's something she wants; I just have to figure out what it is and give it to her."

~Gemma~

After Signor Morelli finished speaking, he invited everyone to the restaurant for dinner. Holly and I had barely taken two steps before being swarmed by other guests wanting to compliment us on our work and talk to us about their future projects.

As I chatted with them all, I did my best to remain calm and not let my excitement show. So far, this had all turned out exactly as we'd hoped it would.

Well, *almost* exactly. I still couldn't quite believe that Cole had turned up here or that he was... well, who he was. Even though I promised myself I wouldn't look for him, I could swear that his eyes were on me from across the room.

After what happened the night before, I shouldn't want anything to do with him, but my body disagreed. I couldn't stop thinking about him, and more specifically, what it would be like to be with him.

Now that I knew who he was, what happened between us made even less sense to me. Why had he assumed I wanted to be paid? I hadn't mentioned anything about money at all; he brought it up all on his own. Surely, a man so attractive *and* rich would be used to women wanting to be with him without expecting to be compensated for it.

Complicating matters even further was the business side of things. Jackson said they were here about a hotel and that they wanted to speak to Anchor about designing it, which meant they wanted to talk to me. That would be an amazing opportunity for us. As much as I had enjoyed the refurb on this hotel, designing from scratch and having complete freedom to create something from nothing appealed to me even more. From everything I'd ever heard about Stamer Hotels, I didn't imagine we'd have to worry about scaling back our designs either.

However, would Cole still want to work with us now that he knew about my involvement? And if he did, could we really move past the awkwardness of our initial meeting?

And even if the answer to both of those questions was yes, could I work with him? Could I really stand being in the same room with him, pretending I didn't remember the feel of his body against mine?

Eventually, the crowd around us thinned as people drifted towards the restaurant, leaving Holly and me free to make our own way there. We expected to be sitting at a table with Signor Morelli himself, but as we got closer, we could see that there were no available seats.

Before we could look for someone to ask where we were meant to be, Jackson appeared next to Holly. "I believe you ladies are with us," he told us with a smile, gesturing towards a nearby table with two empty chairs, across from Cole and Vanessa who were already seated, their backs to us. When I gave him a suspicious look, he chuckled. "Cole wasn't kidding about getting what he wants, and what he'd like right now is to get to know more about the two of you and your business. Won't you please join us?"

A quick look around the room told me that all the other seats had been assigned. Cole must have somehow changed the seating plan, though I couldn't imagine how he had done that at someone else's party, and so quickly. When I looked to Holly for help, she simply shrugged. We hadn't had a chance to speak about Cole at all yet since we ran into him, and though I would have preferred to come up with a game plan with her before we spoke to him, it didn't look like that would be an option.

As gracefully as I could, I slid into the seat across from Cole with Holly beside me while Jackson sat at the head of the table, between me and Cole. Cole's eyes locked on me the moment I sat down, but I avoided looking at him, taking a drink from my glass and looking around the room. For a moment, no one spoke. Jackson seemed to be waiting for Cole to take the lead, but when he finally opened his mouth to say something, I quickly jumped in before he had a chance. I needed to try to keep some control over the situation if I wanted to have any chance of keeping it together for the rest of the evening.

"So, Vanessa, do you also work with Stamer Hotels?"

I fixed a friendly smile on her as I asked the question. Obviously, she was here as Cole's date, but that could mean any number of things. Were they colleagues? Dating? Maybe that explained why he'd been looking for a woman he could pay, so that it didn't get back to his girlfriend that he'd been with someone else?

Vanessa gave me a polite, calm smile in return. "No, I'm just a friend of Mr Stamer."

'Mr Stamer'? Apparently, they weren't all that close. "So, what do you do, then?"

"I'm an actress and model," she replied, glancing over at Cole as if looking for direction.

"And professional escort," Cole supplied, sounding completely un-bothered by the fact. "If that's what you were getting at."

If nothing else, I had to give him credit for owning it. "I hadn't reached that conclusion, but thank you for making things clear."

So, he brought a woman with him whom he paid to be here. Did that mean he did this regularly? I couldn't tell if that made me feel better or not. If those were the kind of women he usually spent time with, perhaps it made a little more sense that he had thought I would be the same.

"I don't believe in making things unnecessarily complicated," Cole said. When I finally met his eyes, I couldn't see any trace of embarrass-ment or guilt there, only confidence and determination. "I apologize if we got off on the wrong foot last night, but I would like to focus on business now."

So, he was going to acknowledge what happened between us, sort of. Holly nudged me under the table, and understanding her unspoken question, I gave her a small nod. When her eyes widened, I knew that she got the message: the man across from us and the man I had told her about this morning were one and the same.

I gave him a polite but determined smile of my own. "Well, in case you hadn't noticed, Mr Stamer, this isn't a business meeting. If you call our office on Monday, we'll be pleased to set up an appointment for you."

"We're all here now," Cole pointed out. "I'm sure you have access to your portfolio on your phone. You could start by showing us some of your work."

I couldn't fault his persistence, but I had no intention of giving in that easily. "My phone doesn't really do justice to our work. At our office, we have models and high-res photos we can show you. It will give you a much better idea of what we're capable of."

"Of course," Jackson agreed, shooting a look at Cole that looked to me like a warning. "We'd be delighted to make an appointment but we're only in town for a couple of weeks. We go back to the States on the 15th."

That gave me a perfect opportunity to try to move the discussion away from work until Holly and I had a chance to regroup. "What do you have planned for your stay in London? It's a great place to be, especially just before Christmas. Do you visit often?"

Acting like I hadn't spoken, Cole looked up at the ceiling above us. "How were you able to take out the wall that used to be here? It must have been load-bearing."

It surprised me that he knew there had been a wall there, and I couldn't help glancing up to see if we had left any tell-tale signs, but the cover-up looked as smooth as I expected it to be. Had he been in the hotel before the renovation, or did he actually know enough about architecture to know that there would have been a wall here in the original design?

Jackson shook his head apologetically. "You'll have to forgive him. He's not really much for small talk."

I couldn't help remembering how quickly Cole and I had jumped from standing under the mistletoe to having his finger inside me. No small talk, indeed.

I flashed Jackson a cheeky smile. "Well, since he's the one who changed our seating assignments, he's just going to have to grin and bear it."

Jackson rewarded me with a charming smile of his own. "I completely agree. And to answer your question: we've been to London a few times on business, but we've never really spent much time just seeing the city. What would you recommend?"

"I would need to know a bit more about you before I make any recommendations."

I dialled up my flirt factor just a touch as I leaned closer to him, and Cole tensed, giving me a little thrill of satisfaction. Did it bother him to see me flirting with his friend? I had to admit that the idea of him being jealous appealed to me, though I couldn't fully explain why.

Playing into it, I leaned even closer to Jackson and lowered my voice. "For example, it's no use telling you to spend the day checking out the churches in the City if you'd rather be at the Museum of Sex Objects."

As Cole's eyebrows raised, I kept my face as neutral as possible, blinking innocently.

"Does that really exist?" Jackson asked, his grin getting even wider.

I nodded as I leaned back and took another drink. "Of course. Anything you want, you'll find here. As the saying goes: if you're tired of London, you're tired of life. So, before I tell you what you should do, I just need to know..." I shifted my gaze back to Cole as I asked the question, challenging him once again. "What is it you're looking for?"

~Cole~

Even though I knew full well that Gemma was trying to get a rise out of me, she managed to succeed anyway.

No matter how much I wanted her, she was off-limits to me now; I understood that as soon as I realized exactly who she was. I couldn't pay her for sex, and I didn't get involved with anyone that wanted anything else. It wouldn't be worth it in the end. On top of that, I wanted to do business with her, which brought a whole other level of complexity to the situation.

My personal desires were just going to have to take a back seat, as frustrating as that might be.

I'd managed to get Gemma and Holly seated with us so that we could talk to them about my new hotel, but so far, things weren't going to plan there either. From the way her eyes widened when Jackson introduced us, I could tell Gemma understood the significance of my company, and she would have to know the resources that we had to put towards a new building. Normally, designers would be falling over themselves for a chance to work on a project like this, and yet, she seemed determined to play hard-to-get.

"If you want Christmas ideas specifically, I'm definitely the one to ask." Gemma continued to talk about sightseeing in London as if it had any relevance to my life whatsoever.

Jackson shot me an apologetic look before turning his attention back to Gemma. "Actually, that won't be on our agenda. As I mentioned last night, Cole's a bit of a Scrooge. I'm afraid he hates Christmas."

Gemma's green eyes widened in disbelief as she looked over at me. "Seriously? How can you hate Christmas?"

It felt like pure electricity every time her eyes met mine, but I forced myself to ignore it. Instead, my mouth formed a thin, hard line as I pushed away the memories of why this season brought out the worst in me. "It's fine for children. For adults, it's an overly sentimental, commercialized cash grab. I may have liked it at one time, but I've grown up since then."

In her eyes, a hint of sympathy appeared that hadn't been there before. "Well, maybe you've just never done it right, then."

To my relief, our food arrived and the conversation moved on to other topics. Jackson did manage to bring up the subject of our new hotel again, and I didn't miss the interest in Gemma's eyes when he did. She might be playing coy about working with us, but I felt certain we'd find a way to make it happen.

Once dinner had finished, Gemma and Holly left us to circulate around the room, joining Alberto again as he showed them off to his investors. We also made our way around the room, speaking to several of the men we knew, but my attention kept getting drawn back to Gemma against my will. Her striking emerald dress and the way it contrasted with her fiery red hair made it impossible to ignore her.

"You're staring again," Jackson pointed out as he followed my gaze.

Averting my eyes, I grunted in acknowledgement. "I'm just thinking about the hotel."

"Of course," he laughed, clearly not buying it.

Once we'd connected with everyone we needed to, Jackson called for a car to take him, Vanessa and me back to the hotel. When we arrived, Vanessa unbuckled her seat belt, but I held out a hand to stop her. "You can have the driver take you home."

She looked up at me in uncertainty. "I thought you wanted some company upstairs too?"

"I've changed my mind. I have work to do, but you'll still receive your full fee."

With a shrug, she leaned back in her seat and rebuckled the belt. "As you like. Have a good evening, Mr Stamer."

I ignored Jackson's curious look as the car pulled away with Vanessa still inside. There would be no easy way to explain to him that after seeing Gemma again, Vanessa didn't appeal to me anymore. I could barely understand it myself.

As I always did in these situations, I focused on work instead. "I'm going to learn everything I can about Anchor Design. There's no need to waste any more time. We know what we want now, so let's make sure we get it."

By Monday morning, I'd decided on a strategy. The Anchor offices opened at eight, so Jackson and I would go there in person, first thing. It would be hard for them to put us off if we were standing right in front of them.

Dressed in our freshly pressed suits, we fit right in with the other people out in the early morning on the streets of St James's. The sun had just started to rise, tinting the sky a pinkish hue that reflected off the old stone buildings, making everything feel a little bit warmer than the temperature suggested. As I told Jackson I would, I had done my research into Anchor Design and had been surprised that such a new and small-scale firm would have an office in this part of the city, surrounded by art galleries, wine merchants, high-end tailors and auction houses. The whole place felt slightly staid and reeked of old money, and it didn't seem to fit with Gemma and Holly and their vibrant style, not to mention that the rent must be exorbitant. It seemed an odd choice all around.

The entrance to the Anchor office sat inside a small courtyard, hidden behind other buildings. We entered the courtyard through a side passage beside a pub and arrived at the door at the same time that Holly arrived from the other direction, dressed warmly and professionally. Half an hour before they officially opened, she obviously didn't expect to see anyone yet, and her steps faltered as she recognized us.

"Good morning, gentlemen," she greeted us, covering her surprise well. "What brings you out so early in the morning?"

"You said we needed an appointment," I reminded her. "We're here to make one."

My research had told me that Holly served as managing director and chief interior designer for the firm while Gemma oversaw the architectural design end. So far, I had only been able to find out they were owned by an offshore holding company, but I'd had no luck determining the identity of the business' ultimate owner.

Holly entered the office through the already-unlocked door, and held the door open for us to follow. "You could have rung us for an appointment," she pointed out. "I'm sure you have better things to be doing with your time."

"This is important. We'll wait until someone's available." I looked around curiously as we followed her into a pleasant, open-plan working area, with a few desks, some meeting tables, and a small waiting area by a receptionist's desk. The whole space had been optimized, making it appear larger than it actually was, and I suspected they must have designed it themselves.

"Hols? Is that you?" Gemma's voice rang out from one of the open office doors along the back wall. "I wanted to go over some strategy before we hear from Cole or Jackson, so we can make sure to..."

She trailed off as she appeared in the doorway and saw Jackson and I standing there, while I took a moment to appreciate her white blouse and black pencil skirt and heels, her red hair pulled back in a French twist, the picture of professionalism. She looked so put together, but I couldn't help imagining how easily I could make her come undone.

Catching her off guard gave me a great deal of satisfaction, and I couldn't help smirking as I nodded at her in greeting. "I'm afraid it's too late for that, but I'm quite good at strategy. Maybe we can work something out together."

Chapter Four

An Agreement

~Gemma~

With a great deal of effort, I forced myself not to react to Cole's statement or to show my surprise at seeing him standing in our office before we were even open for the day. That proved a challenge, mostly because I could barely concentrate on anything other than how good he looked. The suit he wore, another different suit, had obviously been tailored just for him, just like the others. Every inch highlighted his body, showing off the long, lean lines of his frame, making him look powerful and in control, and his dark eyes and the hint of a smile on his lips betrayed his satisfaction at having caught me off guard this morning.

After seeing him at the hotel opening on Saturday, I went home and tried to put him out of my mind. Yet, for some reason, I kept thinking about Vanessa, the woman who attended the party with him. The woman he had paid to be there, and who had almost certainly gone back to his hotel with him that evening. I couldn't help imagining what it would be like to be in her shoes, what it would be like to be with Cole if he had paid me to be with him. If I had no choice but to do whatever he told me to.

I had no idea where these fantasies had come from. Those kinds of thoughts had never crossed my mind before, but now, faced with his commanding presence in my office this morning, they immediately jumped back to the front of my mind again. Swallowing hard, I forced myself to remember where we were and what he had come here for.

"Mr Stamer." I greeted him formally and turned to Jackson, who at least had the decency to look a little apologetic for the early intrusion. "Mr Hanmer. I don't believe you have an appointment."

"Not yet," Cole replied with that same smug half-smile still on his lips. "That's why we're here."

"Well, I'm afraid we're very busy..." I started to say, crossing my arms and leaning against the door frame, trying to look just as casual and in control as he did.

However, I hadn't even got the sentence out before he cut me off, his dark eyes looking between Holly and me. "It's the first morning back after the opening of the Mayfair Mews, so I'm guessing you have at least half an hour set aside to discuss how it went and review the criteria you'll use to determine which projects to take on from the dozens of offers that are bound to come your way."

I pursed my lips, refusing to admit that he'd just accurately outlined my entire plan.

"If you give that half hour to us instead, I'm sure we can convince you that your next projects should be for Stamer Hotels. That will save you and your staff a lot of time in the long run."

"I assume you've had other firms put in tenders for your new hotel?" I asked, trying to maintain some control over the situation. "We'd be happy to do the same if you provide us with the brief."

"I don't think you understand me, Ms Sudlow. I'm not asking you to bid on one hotel. I'd like to sign an exclusive contract with you to handle all of our design needs in the UK and across Europe."

None of us could miss Holly's gasp from the other side of the room, and my stomach fluttered in both excitement and disbelief. What he had just suggested was practically unheard of, especially for a firm as new as ours. How could he possibly be talking about that kind of arrangement based on seeing one hotel lobby?

"You haven't even seen our portfolio," I heard myself mumbling, though I hadn't even really meant to say the words out loud.

Jackson stepped in, putting his hands in his pocket sheepishly. "Actually, we've seen everything you've done, including the projects both of you were involved in prior to this firm. We've even seen some of Ms Chapman's university projects."

This time, I couldn't hide my surprise. How had they managed all of that? None of that was easily available to the general public, though I did notice that he only said they'd seen *Holly's* uni projects and not mine, which must mean they hadn't figured out my legal name yet.

"There's not much I can't do with the time and inclination, Ms Sudlow." Cole's dark eyes seemed to be even more piercing than usual as he put the ball firmly back in my court.

With each word, it became more obvious there wouldn't be an easy way to put them off and, truth be told, after that build up, I wanted to hear their proposal. Based on the amount of research they'd already done, they were obviously taking it seriously. Surely, I could handle being in the same room with Cole for half an hour without losing all my self-restraint.

"Let's dispense with the titles, shall we?" I uncrossed my arms and stepped clear of the door to my office to let them in. "Call me Gemma. You've got thirty minutes, so let's hear what you've got to say."

Half an hour later, I called out to my assistant, Denise, to take Cole and Jackson back out to the waiting area and get them some tea. As soon as the door closed behind them, Holly turned to me, her eyes wide as saucers.

"Holy fuck."

Although I wouldn't have put it in quite those terms, I felt just the same. Cole hadn't been joking: they already had a contract drawn up, offering us a three-year deal to work on their European projects, with an option to extend at the end of it if both parties agreed. The amount they were offering exceeded what we would earn by taking on individual projects, and would save us the time required to procure those assignments.

We would be crazy to turn it down, wouldn't we? And yet, as I bit my lip and flipped through the pages of the contract that they'd left behind for us to look over, I hesitated anyway.

"What's wrong?" Holly often knew me better than I knew myself, and she could see straight away that my enthusiasm didn't match hers.

"It wouldn't leave us time to do very much else," I pointed out, still trying to put my finger on the exact reason for my reluctance. "If this was a year or two ago, when we were completely new, then I'd jump at it. But right now, we have the chance to branch out a bit and I'm not sure that signing on with one company like this is the best thing for us creatively."

"For the amount they want to pay us, we could hire more staff," Holly countered. "We could have a whole team devoted to this contract and a separate team for other work."

"But it stipulates that you and I have to be personally involved," I reminded her, pointing at the applicable section in the contract, spelled out in black and white. "A lot of our time is going to be tied up in this."

"And that's a problem because...?" she prompted.

My finger slid over the words on the page, looking for an answer, when Holly snickered.

"Oh my God. It's because of Cole, isn't it? You still want him."

Immediately, my eyes snapped up to her. "What? Of course not."

Her expression melted into something disturbingly close to pity. "Oh, Gem. I didn't realize. I thought you were over it after he propositioned you, but clearly, you're not."

I opened my mouth to protest, but closed it again nearly as quickly. As much as I hated to admit it, she had a point. "If we're working with him, then he's completely off-limits. That shouldn't bother me, but..."

"You still want him," she repeated, filling in the rather obvious blank as she leaned closer to me, trying to read my thoughts in my face. "I mean, I get it. The man is fit, even if the broody ones aren't really my type. Are you actually interested in him, or is this just a physical thing?"

Again, I had no easy answer for that. "I don't really know anything about him, and he obviously doesn't know anything about me either, which, after this year, is a nice change."

"So, you want to date him?"

"No." I quickly brushed that thought aside. Right now, I had no intention of jumping back into a relationship. "But I *am* attracted to him, and it's hard to imagine working with him when these other thoughts keep running through my head."

"Well, we haven't started working with him yet." Holly rested her chin on her hand, thinking things over. "If you want to make a move, this is your chance. Just tell him you want to shag him and get rid of the sexual tension before we sign on the dotted line. I can't imagine he'd say no. Look at you!"

As always, her fierce loyalty made me smile, but the smile quickly faded as I leaned back in my chair with a sigh. "You make it sound so easy."

"It *is* easy," she promised. "I've seen the way he looks at you. He wants it too, trust me. You can do this, Gem, and you deserve to have some fun. Just make him an offer he can't refuse."

~Cole~

I didn't expect it to take long for Gemma and Holly to make a decision. The offer I had put together was almost too good to be true, especially for a small business like theirs. They probably would have agreed to less, but I didn't see the point in beating around the bush: I wanted what they were selling and I was willing to pay for it, simple as that.

I lived my whole life that way, and it hadn't let me down so far.

So, when Holly came out to the reception area where Jackson and I sat, I assumed we were being called back in to shake hands and agree in principle. Instead, she said Gemma would like to speak with me privately. A quick glance over at Jackson didn't make things any clearer; he simply raised his eyebrows curiously. He didn't know what this meant any more than I did, and it seemed the only way to find out would be to go and speak with her.

Placing my coffee down on the table, I got to my feet and made my way back to Gemma's office. The rest of their staff had arrived for the day by now and several pairs of curious eyes followed me as I made my way inside and closed the door behind me. Gemma hadn't moved from the small table where we all sat earlier, so I joined her back there.

Though she gave me a smile as I sat down, I could see telltale signs of nerves in the way her fingers pressed together and how she swallowed, and it confused me. She hadn't been nervous earlier when discussing the contract. However, Holly and Jackson had been here then, and now, we were alone for the first time since she left my hotel room on Friday night, and the air between us seemed to crackle with electricity. Could she feel it too?

As if she'd read my mind, Gemma dove right in. "I wanted to talk to you about the other night. The night we met."

I probably should have guessed that was the reason she'd called me in. "I've already apologized for that," I reminded her. If she knew how rarely I apologized for anything, it might have made more of an impression on her.

"You did," she agreed. "But I just wanted to make sure things weren't going to be awkward between us because of it. I mean, if we agree to work together."

"I'm a professional, Gemma. I'm sure you are too. There's no reason for either of us to be uncomfortable over a simple misunderstanding. We can pretend it never happened."

Her lips pursed, almost as if she'd been hoping for a different response. "Before we forget all about it, can I ask you something? What exactly did I do that night to make you think I wanted to be paid?"

The question made me wince, since I would rather not get into my thought process with her, or with anyone. My rules were personal, and she had it right when she said it would be better to keep things professional. On the other hand, I didn't want her to think I had insulted her in any way, since I certainly hadn't meant it as an insult. Judging by her expression, she didn't seem upset so much as curious, so perhaps it would be best to try to satisfy her curiosity so we could move on.

"It had nothing to do with anything you did or didn't do. I simply let myself be swayed by what I wanted to be true rather than what I actually saw. That's a mistake I don't make often."

In truth, I prided myself on my ability to read people and to size them up quickly. Making such a large error very rarely happened.

Gemma still looked confused. "So, you're saying that you *wanted* me to be a prostitute?"

I couldn't stop the corners of my mouth from turning up at the thought of how that night would have ended if that had been the case. "Very much."

Gemma's teeth dragged across her bottom lip in response to my tone, making my smile grow wider. Very interesting. I had assumed that any initial attraction she had to me dissipated after our misunderstanding, but perhaps I'd been mistaken. The subtle signs her body gave me right now suggested that she was still interested, and I sure as hell was too.

Unfortunately, we couldn't do anything about it, so I tried to put the thought out of my mind again.

Gemma, however, still had more questions. "What exactly did you have in mind that you thought I wouldn't do unless you paid me to?"

Despite myself, I let out an uncharacteristic laugh. Had she really been thinking that?

I answered her with a smirk, still feeling amused. "I kind of like you thinking that I have some unusual fetish or that I'm some kind of deviant."

Gemma grinned in reply, her eyes sparkling as she saw we could both speak freely. "Well, maybe you are. Should I guess?" She tapped her finger against her lips as she thought it over, and I couldn't help staring at her mouth as she did it, even though she hadn't done it on purpose. Her next words, however, drew my attention back to her eyes. "Something involving clowns?"

I shuddered involuntarily. "God, no. That's just terrifying."

"Are you afraid of clowns?" A hint of glee snuck into her tone, sounding pleased that she might have discovered a weakness of mine.

"Not afraid, exactly. I just don't see the point of them."

"So, you hate clowns and Christmas," she mused. "Maybe you just don't like fun."

As much as I enjoyed her teasing, I couldn't stop myself from leaning closer to her and lowering my voice, noting the way her eyes widened as I did. "I have plenty of fun. It just has to be the right kind."

Gemma shifted in her seat and my lips twitched upward again. I could guess the reason for the movement: she was getting a bit turned on, just as I was. We had a definite chemistry between us, something I hadn't experienced in a long time, and although I would love to see how it translated to the bedroom, there were several reasons that I couldn't.

Fuck, this was frustrating.

Suddenly, Gemma seemed to realize that I hadn't answered her original question, so she returned to it now. "None of that explains why you wanted me to be a hooker."

The humour slowly drained from my body as I tried to figure out how to explain it without going into too many details. "I already told you that I don't like unnecessary complications. That's true in my personal life as well as in business. It's better if everyone knows in advance what the expectations are and what they're going to get out of it."

"Life doesn't always work that way," she pointed out, sounding like someone speaking from experience.

"It can if you keep things clear and transparent up front," I argued back. My rules for myself were based on that belief. It formed the basis for the way I'd lived my life ever since Samantha.

Gemma took a deep breath, as if steeling herself for something challenging. "Okay, then, Cole. For the sake of being clear and transparent, I have to tell you that I haven't been able to stop thinking about what happened the other night."

A groan of frustration almost escaped me but I caught it at the last second. "It's crossed my mind too, but now..." I spread my hands out to indicate the contract on the table and her office in general, "things are even more complicated."

"Then let's uncomplicate them." Gemma's words were direct and her gaze even more so.

She had my attention, and I raised an eyebrow at her in curiosity. "And how, exactly, do you propose we do that?"

Her eyes never left mine. "By spending the night together. Tonight."

~Gemma~

My suggestion obviously caught Cole off guard, and to be honest, it surprised me too. I hadn't even really meant to say it. I had called him into my office to clear the air about what happened between us so we didn't feel like we needed to tiptoe around it. And somehow, between the flirting and the way my body lit up through his sheer proximity, I ended up telling him that I wanted to sleep with him.

When he didn't immediately turn me down, taking a moment to think it over, I assumed that meant he must still be interested, and I couldn't stop the hope and excitement that rose up inside me.

His voice sounded low and restrained when he did reply, as if he were struggling to keep control. "I'd like to, Gemma. God knows I would, but I'm afraid it's just not something I can do."

What did he mean by that? "We haven't signed anything yet," I reminded him. "So, if you're worried about mixing business and pleasure..."

"That's not it."

The tightness of his face told me he meant it, that it had nothing to do with not wanting me, but that still left me clueless about what the sticking point might be.

"What is it, then?"

"I don't want..." He trailed off for a moment in a hesitant uncertainty that seemed out of character for him, before deciding on an answer. "I don't want to owe you anything."

Owe me? What the hell did that mean?

As I tried to figure it out, my mind flashed back to how things had gone at the hotel the other night and how he had been insistent on settling the 'terms' before anything happened between us.

"So, you'd be more comfortable with some kind of payment involved?" I guessed, wanting to be sure I understood.

With his nod, the aching between my legs grew even stronger than before, taking me completely by surprise. Why did I *like* the idea of him paying me? I had no idea, but obviously, I did. My body's reaction couldn't be denied.

Taking another deep breath to steady myself, I made my own proposal. "In that case, let's agree on a payment."

His eyes widened in surprise, looking even more startled now than he had when I'd asked him to spend the night with me. "I assume you're not talking about money?"

I had no interest in his money, and I told him so. "No. I have enough money."

That made him laugh again, a genuine laugh that lit up his whole face, and I liked the way his dark eyes shone when it did. His usual smouldering look was sexy as hell, but when he laughed, I could glimpse something sweet and almost innocent about him.

He shook his head in amusement. "No one has ever said that to me before."

With a shrug, I smiled back at him. "I'm sure you have more money than I do, but that's not what I'm interested in."

Cole's eyes scanned me curiously, trying to determine how serious I might be. "What do you want out of it, then?"

The ridiculousness of his question almost made me laugh. All I really wanted was to spend the night with him, but it seemed like in his head, that would only benefit him. Apparently, I would have to think of something else to ask for.

What could I request instead? As I looked around the room, trying to think of something that would work, my eyes fell on the calendar on my wall. When I'd flipped it over to December on Friday morning, my stomach sank at the sight of all the green and red-coloured events written in. I'd filled it all out at the beginning of the year, back when I still thought I would be getting married this Christmas. I still had tickets for most of the events, but I hadn't been sure if I would still go to them.

That night, Edwin and I had been planning to take his best man, Robert, and my maid of honour, Holly, to the annual Winter Wonderland at Hyde Park. Holly and I were still planning to go and enjoy ourselves, but that left two extra tickets. Maybe it would be fun to bring Cole and Jackson with us? It would be nice to have people there who didn't know about the messiness of my personal life, giving me something else to focus on rather than thinking about what might have been.

With my mind made up, I turned back to Cole. "I have some extra tickets tonight for a Christmas event. Come with me."

The mere mention of Christmas made his expression darken, which in turn made me even more curious. He hadn't been kidding: he really didn't like Christmas, and I couldn't help wondering why. There had to be more to it than what he'd said the other night. I could understand finding it mildly annoying, but what I saw on his face right now was outright dislike.

His reply sounded suspicious and cautious. "What kind of an event? I'm not going to help you chop down a tree or anything."

The idea of Cole standing in a field of trees in his expensive suit made me laugh. "This is England, not New England. We don't have fields of Christmas trees around every corner. I have an artificial tree and it suits me just fine."

His lips twitched, but he quickly pulled the smile back. "What did you have in mind, then?"

"Holly and I are going to the Hyde Park Winter Wonderland. You and Jackson could come with us."

"And then what?" he asked, clearly trying to lay out the terms of my proposal in his head.

"If we have a good time and you aren't a total killjoy, you and I can go back to your hotel afterwards. You spend a couple of hours with me, I spend a couple of hours with you. That's it. No further complications."

As he looked away from me, I could almost see the wheels in his brain turning, trying to calculate the risks, and I couldn't help wondering what had happened to him to make him so guarded about even casual sex. I hadn't asked him for any kind of commitment and I had no plans to.

"I suppose until you sign the contract, we're not actually working together." He said the words thoughtfully, still thinking it over.

"Right. We need to have our lawyers look things over anyway. By the time we're ready to sign, this will be over and done with. We'll have got... whatever this is... out of our systems."

He nodded, making it clear he also thought it would be simply a matter of breaking the sexual tension so things could be normal between us.

"What happens at this Wonderland?"

Cole leaned back in his chair as a thrill of anticipation ran through me. Did that mean he would accept my offer? I tried not to show my excitement at that prospect and simply answer his question instead. "It's kind of like a carnival. There are rides and food and a market. It's a lot of fun, actually."

"We've already established that you and I have different ideas about what's considered fun." His dark eyes glinted dangerously and my stomach flipped in response. How did he make me want him so badly with just his tone of voice?

Yet again, I forced myself to keep calm and to keep my eyes on him as I replied. "Well, if all goes well, we'll both be satisfied tonight."

His lips twisted into a smile, one that made me bite my lip in longing. I really couldn't wait to feel those lips on me again, and the idea that it might actually happen had my whole body throbbing in excitement.

"Very well, Gemma. I think we have a deal."

~Cole~

This meeting hadn't turned out as I expected at all, but I couldn't be more pleased with the direction it had taken. The proposal Gemma made wasn't my usual arrangement, not by any means, but in the end, I would still get what I wanted: Gemma in my bed by the end of the day, and I couldn't wait.

If I had to endure a little Christmas foolishness before then, it seemed a small enough price to pay. And she had agreed it *would* be a payment, ensuring that once this evening ended, no further obligation would exist between us on either side, just the way I liked it.

Our business concluded, Gemma and I left her office together and found Jackson and Holly deep in conversation in their office waiting area. Holly was also an attractive woman, and I could see Jackson's interest in her, so having them along shouldn't be a problem. They would keep each other occupied, and maybe Gemma and I could slip away a little early.

As Gemma explained our plans to attend this carnival this evening, Jackson glanced over at me in surprise and I could practically hear his thoughts. We never spent our time on these types of trips on pointless entertainment, and certainly nothing Christmas-related. However, once he got past his initial incredulity, he grew progressively more enthusiastic as Gemma and Holly explained to him what the evening would involve.

"Do we need to wear anything special?" he asked.

"I am not dressing up," I quickly informed them all, trying to imagine what else might be involved that I didn't want to do. "Or singing."

"You have a lot of rules," Gemma complained good-naturedly, her green eyes sparkling again. All of her earlier nerves had disappeared and she looked confident and cool again while I smirked back at her. She had no idea of the extent of my rules. "But no, there's no fancy dress required. Just wear something warm."

"To be clear, I am happy to both dress up and sing should the need arise," Jackson offered, giving them both his most charming smile as I rolled my eyes.

As soon as we were out the door of their building, I silenced Jackson immediately. "I don't want to talk about it."

"Alright, I won't ask about our double date."

"It's not a date," I growled back. "It's a business meeting. We're getting to know them better before we enter into the contract."

"Whatever you say," he agreed with a laugh.

I ignored him as we made our way to our next scheduled meeting. Over the rest of the day, the idea of having Gemma and Holly design our new hotel made a significant improvement to my mood, not to mention the prospect of having Gemma in my hotel room later on. More than once, I found my mind drifting from the business at hand to the things I'd like to do to her when we were alone.

When work finally finished, we returned to the hotel to change. Jackson dressed down in jeans and a sweater, but I had only brought suits with me for this trip. Luckily, London wasn't too cold in December, so I should still be comfortable, especially once I threw on my black cashmere peacoat and my scarf and gloves. Stealing a glance in the mirror as I left the suite, I had to admit I looked more like someone heading to a night at the symphony than to a funfair, but I didn't really care. I didn't need to impress anyone. The way this night would end had already been determined.

The city's Christmas lights twinkled above us as we took a taxi to Hyde Park, but I kept my eyes on the road, focused on the evening ahead of me. When we arrived, we found the entrance to the Winter Wonderland with no trouble, and Holly and Gemma were waiting for us there, as promised. I couldn't stop my eyes from devouring Gemma as she turned to greet us. Even in her warm winter gear, she was a sight to behold. A white knit hat made the red of her hair and the green of her eyes stand out even more while her black coat hugged the curves of her waist and hips, and her fake fur-lined boots came far enough up her calf to draw attention to her gorgeous legs in her skinny jeans. She must have changed out of the skirt she'd worn earlier to help keep warm.

Fuck, this evening could not go quickly enough. I couldn't wait to get her back to my room and peel each and every layer from her.

"You are both looking lovely this evening," Jackson greeted them, giving Gemma a friendly smile and Holly a kiss on the cheek. "So, what are we doing first?"

"First up is mulled wine," Holly instructed, taking his arm. "That'll keep us warm."

"Lead the way," he invited.

We joined the queue of people to get in and I couldn't help noticing all the young couples around us, holding on to each other, and an unexpected nostalgia washed over me. I could almost see younger versions of myself and Samantha at a place like this, back when I had cared about having fun with someone.

"What are you thinking?" Gemma's soft voice cut into my thoughts, and I glanced down to find her looking up at me. "Not as bad as you feared?"

Quickly and firmly, I banished all thoughts of the past and moved on to cold calculation. "That remains to be seen. I was just trying to figure out where all these people are staying tonight, which hotels are closest."

Jackson groaned. "Please, can we go one night without talking about work? Gemma, back me up here?"

"Gladly," she agreed. "This evening is a work-free zone."

Before I could protest, we made it to the front of the queue and Holly and Gemma stepped to the side for the security guards to check their bags. Once we were in, temporary pathways stretched out in front of us through the park, leading past fairground rides, food stalls and market stalls.

As she'd suggested, Holly made a beeline for the mulled wine. Gemma and I hung back while Holly and Jackson joined the queue.

"So, I don't actually know anything about you," Gemma admitted. "Other than that you're in the hotel business, of course. Where is home for you?"

Though I didn't want to get into too many personal details, that particular question seemed harmless enough. "New York. Whenever I'm there, anyway." I hadn't really thought of any place as 'home' in a long time.

"You travel a lot?" she guessed.

I nodded curtly. "We've been focused on expanding outside the US this year which has meant a lot of time abroad, but you said you didn't want to talk about work."

"It depends on the context," she clarified. "In this case, since it related to a personal question, I'll let it slide. It's a grey area."

I simply raised an eyebrow at her. "I don't do grey areas."

My tone made her shiver, no matter how she tried to hide it. "I'll keep that in mind, Cole."

Holly and Jackson returned with drinks for all of us and we wandered further into the park. Around the bend, a choir sang Christmas carols, so we stopped and listened for a few minutes. Jackson had his arm around Holly casually, but Gemma and I kept a careful distance from each other. Public displays of affection hadn't been part of the terms.

When the performance finished, we carried on walking, and just as I thought this might not be so bad, we turned a corner and a skating rink appeared in front of us. For years, I had done my best to avoid this particular memory, but suddenly, without warning, it hit me hard.

I could almost smell the fresh winter air in Central Park on that day four years ago and feel the ice beneath me, the wetness of it soaking through the fabric of my jeans as I got down on one knee in the centre of the rink. I could still see the way hands shook and feel the nervous beating of my heart as I held out the ring to Samantha. I could hear the cheers of the other skaters around us when she said yes.

At the time, I believed it to be the happiest moment of my life.

"Cole?" Gemma's voice pulled me back to the present, and I looked over to see her giving me a curious look. I must have stopped walking, my gaze still focused on the rink in front of me, and I blinked quickly to try to erase any trace of the memories that had just engulfed me. Showing weakness definitely went against my rules.

But before I got a chance to offer an explanation, or before she could ask any follow-up questions, a new voice joined us.

"Gemma? Is that you?"

Chapter Five

OFF BALANCE

~**Gemma**~

Before I had a chance to figure out what caused the colour to drain from Cole's face, my ears were assaulted by the last voice I could possibly want to hear right now; or ever, for that matter.

"It *is* you! We haven't seen you in so long." The bleached blonde woman sailed past the rest of the group and came right up to me, putting her arms on my shoulders and giving me an air kiss while I stiffened at her touch, making no move to reciprocate her blatantly phony greeting.

"Why the hell would she want to see you, Annabel?" Holly came up beside me, ready to jump to my defense as Annabel took a step back.

Annabel looked between me and Holly with wide-eyed innocence. "Oh, we're past all of that, surely. It's good to see you too, Holly. You've both been such strangers lately."

The icy shock of seeing her quickly started to thaw as my blood began to boil. *We're past all of that?* How dare she suggest that when she had never even bothered to apologize, never made any effort to speak to me about it at all? I could only hope that she was here on her own or with some girlfriends, that she was here with anyone but...

"Bel!" Edwin's voice called from a few feet away, and I went even more rigid, my body freezing in disbelief.

"You've got to be fucking kidding me," Holly swore under her breath.

Knowing she had my back made it a little better, but I still didn't feel ready for this. I hadn't seen him since we broke up, and though I inevitably would have to, I hadn't planned on it happening right that moment. Unfortunately, it looked about to happen whether I wanted it to or not.

In the next moment, Edwin appeared next to Annabel, taking her hand and not even glancing at the rest of us. He looked just the same as always: the slicked back hair, the long, elegant nose, the slightly pouty lips; classic, unintimidating good looks that were pleasant to look at but ultimately forgettable. His face had never lingered in my mind the way Cole's did.

"You can't get away from me that easily," he teased, pulling her back the way they had come. Only when she resisted did he finally look over in my direction, and the moment that he actually saw and recognized me couldn't have been more obvious. The smile on his face disappeared immediately as he swallowed hard. At least he had the decency to look embarrassed, unlike Annabel. "Gemma? What.... uh, what are you doing here?"

"We're performing heart surgery," Holly spat at him. "What does it look like?"

From the corner of my eye, I could see the look that Cole and Jackson exchanged, and my heart sank. This hadn't been part of my plan for this evening at all. I had just one night with Cole, one night to see just how hot things could be between us, and the last thing I wanted was for him to see me as the sad, rejected fiancée that everyone else in the whole damn country saw me as.

Taking a deep breath to steady myself, I racked my brain for the quickest way to salvage this situation. One thing I knew about Edwin was that he didn't handle confrontation well. If I gave him an easy out, he would definitely take it.

With that in mind, I put on an unnaturally cheery voice and answered his question as if Holly hadn't said anything. "You know me, I love Christmas stuff. I wouldn't miss Winter Wonderland."

Had he remembered that we planned to come here together? Did he still have it in his calendar too? Or had he forgotten all about it, and they had chosen that night to attend by complete coincidence?

Whatever the case, my answer seemed to relax him. As I'd expected, and as he always had, he would believe whatever I said so long as it made his life easier.

"That's great. I hope you enjoy it." That seemed to settle everything as far as he was concerned, and Edwin finally looked away from me, nodding to Holly before taking in the sight of Jackson and Cole beside us.

To my surprise, Cole took the initiative and introduced himself, sticking out his hand. "Cole Stamer."

"Edwin Matheson." Edwin shook Cole's hand as his eyes moved back and forth between me and Cole curiously. "You're a friend of Gemma's?"

Meanwhile, Annabel had also taken her first proper look at Cole, and her jaw dropped. "Cole Stamer?" she squeaked before Cole could answer Edwin's question, and I had to refrain from rolling my eyes. Of course she would recognize Cole's name if not his face. I could practically see the dollar signs dancing in her eyes as she looked at him.

"That's right," he confirmed. "And yes, I'm here with Gemma." Giving me a wink, he stepped closer to me and slung his arm around my shoulder, right there in front of everyone, as I blinked up at him in surprise.

What was he doing? He hadn't touched me all night, hadn't even tried, and now, suddenly, he started acting like we were here on a date? He offered no explanation, simply giving me a supportive squeeze before turning back to look at Edwin and Annabel with his usual cool indifference.

Annabel's eyes narrowed as she watched us, and I could almost see the calculations taking place in her head, trying to figure out what this might mean for her. She never cared about anything else. "Well, isn't that exciting," she exclaimed insincerely. "Gem, we'll have to catch up soon and you can tell me all about it. Let's go, babe."

Looping her arm through Edwin's, she attempted to steer him away from us but he resisted for just a minute, his eyes still cycling between me and Cole and his arm around me. "It was good to see you," he mumbled, his expression full of uncertainty, before they finally turned away and left.

As soon as they were out of earshot, Holly let out a string of expletives, making Jackson and Cole both smile.

"Hols, it's fine," I assured her. Now that they were gone, I couldn't wait to move on myself. "Let's forget it, okay? We're here to have a good time."

"Time for a beer?" Jackson suggested.

That sounded like something I would definitely want before long, but for right now, I shook my head.

"The Giant Wheel's just up ahead. Let's do that first before we have too much alcohol. We wouldn't want to vomit on anyone waiting below." The joke might be weak, but I gave them all a smile that I hoped looked genuine, and they all indulged me by smiling back.

As we all started walking again, with Jackson and Holly arguing about where the highest ferris wheel in the world was found, Cole's arm slipped from my shoulder, but he stayed close to me as we walked, almost touching. "So, those were friends of yours?" he asked me quietly, keeping his voice low so Holly and Jackson wouldn't hear.

"Not really." I honestly hadn't expected him to stick up for me as he had, and I couldn't imagine what he thought about the whole scene. "I'm sorry about all that. Personal drama, as I'm sure you guessed. Thanks for stepping in, but I should warn you, there might be some gossip that comes from it."

He shrugged in that casual, unflappable way of his. "I didn't say anything incriminating. If Posh Barbie chooses to make an assumption about our relationship, that's on her."

My laugh spilled from my lips before I could stop it. Cole's dismissive nickname for Annabel struck me as perfect; he'd obviously sized her up pretty accurately very quickly, identifying her as something polished and beautiful, but fake. "Well, thanks anyway. You didn't have to get involved."

Though I didn't know why he'd pretended to be interested in me in front of them, I appreciated it all the same. The look on Annabel's face when she heard Cole's name and realized that I might be dating him had brought me way more satisfaction than it should have. I only hoped it wouldn't backfire on him.

More than that, though, I had to admit that I liked the feel of Cole's arm around me. Firm, possessive and supportive all at the same time, it sent tingles down my spine in a way that Edwin's touch never had. Although this part of the evening counted as my 'payment', my mind kept jumping ahead to what might happen back at his hotel afterwards, and it had my whole body humming in anticipation.

~Cole~

Wham's 'Last Christmas' blared from the speakers as we got close to the front of the line for the Giant Wheel, the bright multi-coloured lights of the ride reflecting on Gemma's face as I looked down at her. I didn't know the exact nature of the situation between her and the couple we'd encountered, and I had no plans to push her to share anything. It was her business, not mine, and normally, I would have stayed out of it entirely. But clearly, it had been unpleasant for her, and something about seeing her so defensive made my protective instincts kick in, instincts that I hadn't used in a very long time. I couldn't fully explain it, but I didn't regret doing it either.

Holly and Jackson were directly in front of us in the line and they stepped forward when the next open cabin came around. Holly linked her arm through Jackson's, turning around to give Gemma a wink. "We'll take this one and you guys can have the next one."

Gemma and I both watched as Jackson put his arm around Holly as they sat down. "Should I be worried about that?" Gemma asked me, gesturing to our cozy-looking friends.

A smile tugged at one corner of my mouth. Jackson was a flirt, no question, but he also had a healthy respect for women. He wouldn't make a move unless she wanted him to, and I had never heard him bragging about any of his conquests, though he must have plenty. Gemma didn't need to worry, but I offered my assessment of her friend instead: "Holly looks like she can take care of herself."

Gemma chuckled warmly. "I agree, but I'm curious what makes you say that? You don't know anything about her."

The teenager working the front of the line called us forward to get in the next cabin and I held Gemma steady as she stepped in before sitting down beside her. Almost instinctively, we sat close together, our legs touching, and she didn't make any effort to pull away as the wheel began to move, lifting us higher off the ground. Since I'd put my arm around her earlier, we'd hardly had an inch of space between us and I had to admit I didn't mind. It made me look forward to the rest of this evening even more.

I returned to our interrupted conversation, answering Gemma's question matter-of-factly. "I'm good at reading people and I'm usually right.

"Not always," she reminded me, raising an eyebrow in challenge to make it clear that she was referring to the night we met. I had to concede that point, but thankfully, she left it at that. "You've got me curious now: what's your impression of Holly?"

I took a moment to consider all the things I'd seen at the hotel reception the day before and in their office that morning, plus what had just happened, before formulating my response. "She's talented, obviously, and hard-working, but she knows how to separate work and play. She's a loyal friend and protective of those she cares about. She's got a bit of an inferiority complex when it comes to people of a higher social class, but she covers it well. And she hasn't had a serious boyfriend for... I'm guessing, two years?"

When Gemma couldn't hide the look of shock on her face, I knew that I had nailed it. "Two and a half years, actually. That's... you... how did you do that?"

Though I tried not to smile, the corners of my mouth twitched upward anyway. They seemed to do that a lot around Gemma. "In my work, I meet a lot of people, and it helps to be able to size them up quickly. People give you all kinds of clues about themselves if you know where to look."

The wheel moved again, just a few feet before stopping to let more people get on.

"How do I know you didn't just do some research on her?" Gemma asked suspiciously. "You knew a lot about our company too, so maybe you just have some private investigators working for you."

Genuine amusement filled my chest as I smirked over at her. "You really think I've had you both investigated?"

She shrugged, but she couldn't hold back her smile either. "I honestly don't know what to think with you, Cole."

The wheel began moving again, bringing us almost to the top. High above the ground in the chilly night air, no one else could see us now. From our vantage point, we could see the London Eye in the distance, Big Ben and the Shard, but all I could focus on was Gemma. The closeness of her body to mine, the smell of her perfume and the pink of her lips suddenly felt overwhelming, and waiting until we got to the hotel seemed impossible. I needed to taste her again now.

"That's the way I like it, Gemma," I told her, leaning down to whisper in her ear. "You never know what you're going to get with me."

My lips brushed against her ear and down her neck, pushing her scarf aside, and in return, her body gave me all the signs I hoped for. Her intake of breath and the way she tilted her head to give me better access to her neck made it clear that she wanted this too.

"Maybe..." Her voice trailed off as I snaked my arm behind her, my hand coming up beneath her coat to rest on her hip. With a shuddering breath, she tried again. "Maybe you could give me some idea what I might get?"

My smile widened, my lips still pressed against her neck. She wanted a preview, did she? That could certainly be arranged, and I brought my mouth back up to her ear, the sweet scent of her perfume still filling my nose. "You want to know what I'm going to do to you later?"

She exhaled, her lips parting, letting me know that was exactly what she meant.

"First, I'm going to get you out of these clothes. You're wearing far too much tonight, Gemma. I'll take off your scarf..." My fingers trailed along the top of it so she could imagine it, and she shivered in response. "And your coat. I'll run my hands down over your shirt, feeling every swell and curve, before I take the bottom of it and lift it up over your head."

The wheel had come back around to the ground now, but we were still moving, heading back up again into the night sky, the stars bright above us.

"I'll take a moment to enjoy the sight of you standing in my room with only your bra between me and your beautiful breasts. I'm guessing your bra is white today since you were wearing that white blouse earlier. Am I right, Gorgeous?"

"Yes." Her reply was barely even a whisper but the sound of it made my dick twitch forcefully in my pants. My imagination had been doing a good enough job of getting me hard in the first place, and hearing her reaction to my words didn't help me cool down any. Fuck, maybe this hadn't been such a good idea when we had to stand up and walk out of here in a couple of minutes, but I couldn't stop now.

"Then I'm going to undo the button on these tight jeans of yours, my fingers pressing down against your skin as I pull down the zipper and slowly pull them down, peeling them off you, letting me see your pretty white panties that match your bra. I bet they're going to be so wet that they're nearly see-through."

Gemma whimpered against me, that same fucking sexy sound she had made under the mistletoe, and I groaned in response. My hand on her waist found the edge of her waistband as I spoke, my fingers running along it to tease her, and she leaned further into me, her hand on my thigh, squeezing gently. Each movement felt electric, and I couldn't remember the last time I'd been this turned on while still fully clothed.

"Now, you're standing there in just your underwear, waiting to do whatever I tell you to do. You will, won't you, Gemma? You'll do whatever I say."

"What..." Her words came out short and laboured as I nipped down her neck again, my breath hot against her skin, contrasting with the cool evening air. "What would you tell me to do?"

The way she phrased that immediately caught my attention. Just as it had on the night we'd met, the idea of me controlling her seemed to work for her. Since it worked for me too, I leaned into it, fully taking charge.

"There are so many possibilities," I told her, the words both a promise and a warning. "Maybe I'll tell you to take your panties off and lie down on the bed, open your legs for me and show me how you make yourself come."

I could feel the movement as Gemma's thighs pressed closer together, trying to find some relief against the pressure I knew she must be feeling, assuming she was even half as turned on as I was.

"Or maybe I'll have you drop to your knees, undo my pants, and let you play with my dick for a bit before I fuck your mouth."

Another whimper escaped Gemma's lips, and I couldn't take it any longer. Grabbing a fistful of her red hair, I pulled her head back and kissed her, devouring her lips with mine, with a hunger that felt insatiable. Her hand moved higher on my leg until her palm ran across my hard dick and I groaned again into her mouth. It felt like fire when our tongues connected, a scorching heat that fueled my desire even more.

I completely lost track of where we were and how we had got there, and anything other than the feel of her. The movement of the ferris wheel only added to the feeling of falling into her, of being off balance and of losing myself in the warmth of her kiss. I had no intention of stopping until we heard someone clear their throat in an exaggerated, embarrassed way, and I realized that we had stopped moving.

"Um, folks? The ride's over."

~Gemma~

As quickly as I could, I disentangled myself from Cole and turned to the poor ride attendant whose gaze seemed to be focused everywhere but directly at us. Somehow, we were back at the bottom of the wheel where the next people in the queue were waiting to get on.

"Sorry," I mumbled as I staggered to my feet, my cheeks flushing red partly from embarrassment and partly from how turned on I was. My legs felt like jelly as I stepped out of the cabin, but Cole's hand on my waist helped to steady me.

Jackson and Holly waited for us at the bottom of the steps and the grins on their faces made it clear that they had caught at least a glimpse of our... display.

Shit, I needed to get myself back under control. My whole body was throbbing, aching with need, and I wanted nothing more than to get back to Cole's room and make everything he had just described to me a reality. How did he manage to get me so worked up with just his words? I had spent whole nights in bed with a man without being as close to orgasm as I felt right now.

"So, where to next?" Holly asked smugly, her arm still linked through Jackson's. "Or are you two ready to call it a night?"

I did my best to ignore her suggestive teasing. Realistically, we needed to stay here for a little longer. Cole insisted on paying me with this outing, so I wanted to make sure we spent enough time here that we could have equal time in his room later, not to mention that I'd never hear the end of it from Holly if I disappeared with Cole right now.

"I think it's time for that beer, then we can check out some of the market stalls."

We spent another hour walking around the park, drinking our pints and visiting the market. From the outside, it would have looked like any regular double date, and sometimes, it even felt that way too. Conversation flowed easily enough and Cole's hand often found its way to my waist, just a light touch, but I was always aware of it even through the layers of clothing.

Not having eaten anything yet that evening, Holly and I split an order of churros while Cole and Jackson each got a bratwurst. I thought about asking Cole if I could have a taste of his sausage, but I managed to hold my tongue. I couldn't even imagine what he'd say to me if I gave him an opening like that.

"You are physically incapable of walking by one of these booths without taking a look, aren't you?" Cole's tone betrayed a mixture of exasperation and amusement as I stopped at yet another craft stall.

"I'm a designer," I reminded him. "I'm always on the lookout for something that's going to inspire my next project."

"Your next project meaning my hotel?" he clarified.

"Maybe." I gave him a cheeky smile as I picked up a truly hideous driftwood sculpture and held it up for him. "What if we built the whole thing around something like this?"

His eyes widened in alarm for just a second before he realized I was teasing him, and he shook his head, his eyes gleaming at me. "I'm going to have to keep a close eye on you, aren't I?"

"I would suggest it." With a wink, I turned back to place the sculpture back on the table.

Cole stepped closer to me, the warmth of his body pressing against my back as he murmured in my ear. "It's a good thing you're so much fun to look at, then."

Fuck. I couldn't take it when his voice got all low and gravelly like that, and it instantly took me back to the things he'd said to me on the ferris wheel and the way he'd made me feel.

"You know, I think I've probably seen enough here for tonight," I said, trying to sound casual and unconcerned and not at all like I was desperate to start ripping his clothes off.

It didn't make any difference. Cole knew exactly what I was getting at anyway, his hands coming to my waist and pulling me back against him even more firmly. "Are you saying I've fulfilled my end of our deal?"

"You've done pretty well," I admitted, stepping away from him before I melted entirely. With my body trembling in anticipation, I led him away from the booth and over to where Holly and Jackson were waiting. "You didn't make any children cry with your Grinch-like spirit, so I'll count it as a win."

"He hasn't made any children cry *yet*," Jackson amended, having overheard the last part of our conversation. "We still have to get out of the park, there's still time."

Although Cole glared at him, Jackson didn't seem bothered in the least, and the dynamic between the two of them made me smile. Clearly, Jackson didn't take himself or Cole too seriously, and despite outward appearances, I got the feeling Cole appreciated it.

We set off towards the exit and the taxi rank at the edge of the park. "How long have you known Jackson?" I asked Cole once we had fallen back to walking two-by-two, Jackson and Holly in front of us, chatting to each other.

As his gaze moved over to the back of Jackson's head, I could spot the true affection that he had for his friend. "Since high school. Back then, he was one of the few people not intimidated by or jealous of my family's status. He's always called me on my bullshit, and that's only gotten more important to me as time's gone by."

I definitely understood the value of a true and honest friend. "Has he always worked for you?"

"He would say he works *with* me and not *for* me." Cole sounded amused by the distinction. "But no, actually. He went to college and got a business degree, and then he did a few years at another company, and when a spot came open at Stamer, he applied for it like anyone else. He didn't want people thinking he only got to where he is because he knew me."

I could certainly appreciate that too, and it made me respect both of them even more. "And what about you? Did you work anywhere else?"

Cole gave an amused snort. "No. My dad started grooming me to take over the business as soon as I started to talk. I went to college too, but only to get the piece of paper. I always knew this is what I would do."

"Do you like it, at least?" It would be a lot of responsibility for not much return if he didn't even enjoy it.

Thankfully, he reassured me on that point. "I do. Hotels are special places, and I want people to feel that when they stay at one of our places. That's where you come in, Gemma. You're going to make our new London hotel very special."

"Don't think I missed what you did there," I warned him. "We're not talking about work, remember?"

Rather than arguing, Cole put up his hands in a gesture of surrender. We had no time to discuss it further anyway since we'd arrived at the edge of the park where a line of taxis waited at the rank, and Jackson and Holly turned back to us. "We were just talking about going for a drink," Holly informed us. "Do you two want to join us?"

I hadn't told Holly anything about the deal that Cole and I made, and I assumed Cole hadn't told Jackson either. It might seem suspicious if we blew them off now, but I knew the only thing I wanted to do right now was to get back to his hotel.

Cole was obviously on the same page. "I've actually got some work I need to review this evening," he lied, stealing my excuse.

"And I've got some... uh, phone calls to make," I added lamely. Holly's raised eyebrows made it clear she had her doubts, but she didn't call me out on it. I turned away from her questioning look and back to Cole, trying to sound as if the thought had just occurred to me. "Are you heading back to the Lytton? We could share a taxi and I can get on the tube from there."

"Sure."

We said goodnight to Jackson and Holly, and Cole held the taxi door open for me.

"Do you think we fooled them?" I asked him as he got in and closed the door behind him.

"Not at all," he said, pulling me close to him. "Do you care?"

"Not at all," I murmured in reply as his lips found mine again.

~Cole~

At last. This evening hadn't been as bad as I feared it might be, but each minute that I had to wait to get Gemma alone had still been painful. Now, we were making out in the back of the taxi like horny teenagers rather than two professional, rational adults. I couldn't keep my hands off her for another second.

There were still way too many clothes in the way, but I managed to find a bit of skin on Gemma's back when I put my arms around her.

My fingers traced the waist of her jeans on the back and she shivered beneath my touch.

"Your hands are cold," she laughed, breaking the kiss long enough to admonish me before pressing herself to me again.

"And your skin is very sensitive," I murmured back, the words coming out as almost a growl in my desperation. "Fortunately for me."

My hand slipped down the back of her jeans, beneath her panties, and she gasped into my mouth, letting my tongue in deeper. The lingering sweetness of the food she'd had at the park mingled with her own sweet taste, and it only made me hungry for more. There wasn't an inch of her I didn't want to taste.

Much too quickly and yet not quickly enough, the taxi pulled up outside my hotel. As fast as humanly possible, I paid the driver and got out of the car, holding my arm out to help Gemma exit.

As soon as she did, flashbulbs started to go off around us, throwing me completely off balance. Ovals of light danced in front of my eyes as I tried to figure out what was happening. Gemma instinctively turned away to shield her eyes from the brightness while I scowled at the photographers. Even through the bursts of light, I could see three of them and they'd clearly been waiting for us. For me, at least. One of them called my name, trying to get me to look over at him.

Putting my arm around Gemma, I led her inside as quickly as I could.

"What is that about?" she asked once we were in the lobby and out of reach of the cameras.

My lips tightened into a frown, not really sure what to tell her. "I don't know. I haven't had paparazzi interested in me in years, not since I stopped dating."

"You stopped dating? Why?"

I hadn't expected her to focus on that part of what I'd said, and I really didn't want to talk about other women right now. "It doesn't matter. Are you okay?"

"I'm fine. It just surprised me. You're alright?"

"Fine. Let's go upstairs."

As we got in the elevator, I pulled out my phone to send a text to my office in New York, and Gemma kept her distance while I typed my message. She still looked a little thrown off by what had just happened, and honestly, I felt that way too. I really couldn't figure out why the paparazzi were suddenly interested in me, and here in London of all places. I had never been a household name over here.

"Do you want a drink?" I asked once we were in my room, taking off my coat and scarf. "I'm just waiting for a call from my publicist to see if she's heard anything that might explain the photographers."

"Sure." Gemma also removed her outer layers while I poured her a glass of wine in the small kitchen of my suite. As I handed it to her, my phone rang and I had a quick conversation with my publicist, Nellie. However, the sudden attention surprised her as much as it did me, which didn't make things any clearer.

By the time I hung up and sat down beside her, Gemma had almost emptied her glass, and she gave me an apologetic half-smile. "I'm afraid the paparazzi might be my fault, actually."

I had no idea what she meant. "Your fault? How?"

"Because of the woman we ran into earlier tonight at the park," she explained. "The blonde one. Her name is Annabel Clarkson and she's a minor celebrity over here. Very minor. A reality TV star, one of those people who's famous for being famous."

I still wasn't following. "And?"

"And she recognized you," Gemma reminded me. "And you told her you were with me. So, if she mentioned something on her social media..."

"The tabloids would have picked it up," I concluded. Well, that did partially explain things. From there, it would have been easy enough to guess where I would be staying since my company owned part of this hotel, but I still had questions about why the idea of me dating Gemma would be of interest to anyone. Could it simply be because I hadn't been in a relationship for so long? I really didn't think anyone cared that much about my love life.

Unaware of my train of thought, Gemma nodded in agreement with what I'd said out loud. "I didn't expect news to travel quite so fast, and I'm sorry if this causes you any trouble."

I couldn't deny it would be an annoyance, but at the moment, I had other things on my mind, things that had been pushed to the side for far too long already.

"Well, if I'm going to have paparazzi tailing me for the rest of my stay in London, then the rest of this evening better make it worth the trouble."

Colour immediately rose in Gemma's cheeks as she realized what I meant. In all the confusion, she had almost forgotten, as had I, that we were now, finally, alone in my suite, back where we had been three nights ago. That night, I wouldn't have thought I could possibly want her any more than I did then, but now that we'd had to wait the extra days, it would be even more satisfying to finally have her.

Our interaction on the ferris wheel earlier had only added to the enticement, showing me just how much the idea of me telling her what to do turned her on, and I planned to take full advantage of that fact. In her professional life, she was in control and she liked it that way, but behind closed doors, I had a feeling she didn't want that at all. Everything about her reactions to me suggested that she wanted to be dominated, whether she knew it or not, and I would be more than happy to oblige.

Since she still hadn't answered me, I leaned in closer to her. "What do you think, Gemma? Are you going to make it worth my while?"

Draining the rest of her wine glass, Gemma put it aside and looked back at me, her eyes bright with anticipation. "How would you like me to do that?"

Her reply, breathy and full of need, was exactly the answer I'd hoped for. She leaned towards me, eager for my touch, but instead of closing the gap like she expected, I leaned back, spreading my arms over the back of the couch and making myself comfortable.

"You're going to start by showing me what I've paid for. I want to see it all and I want you to show it to me."

When she hesitated, looking uncertain, I spelled it out even further, letting her know exactly what I wanted.

"You're going to strip for me, Gemma. Now."

Chapter Six

A NIGHT TO REMEMBER

~Gemma~

Cole's words sent a shockwave straight to my core. He wanted me to strip for him? I had never stripped for anyone. I'd taken my clothes off, obviously, but not in the way he meant. Not like I was giving a performance, and every nerve in my body tingled as I realized he intended to treat me just like a hired woman, just as I had fantasized, and surprisingly, it turned me on just as much in real life as it had in my imagination.

Logically, I knew that I should back up a step and explain to him exactly why the paparazzi would be interested in me and him being together, but at the moment, I couldn't focus on that at all. All I could think about was his strong, demanding tone and the casual way he sat there, his eyes challenging me as he waited for me to entertain him. It didn't look like he had any doubt that I would do it. He looked completely in control, which made me even hotter, my whole body crying out for his approval.

I wanted nothing more than to please him. Despite never having done this before, despite not having a clue what to do, I would do it simply because he wanted me to, and my legs shook in anticipation as I pulled myself to my feet.

Would this be better with music, I wondered? He hadn't said anything about music and where would I get music from anyway? My thoughts seemed to be all over the place, and I tried to focus and remain calm as I took a couple of steps away from the sofa before turning back to face Cole. The pounding of my heart sent my pulse racing throughout my body, but especially between my legs. Every part of me felt more sensitive and alive as Cole's eyes tracked my movements.

To start, I raised my hands to the back of my neck, gripping onto it while I rolled my head back, pushing my chest forward at the same time. Even my own touch made my skin react, I was so primed for any kind of stimulation. With my right hand, I reached up and pulled the clip out of my hair, releasing it from its twist so it tumbled down over my shoulders.

Cole shifted in his seat and my gaze immediately fell to his trousers as I wondered if he felt anywhere near as turned on as I did. Judging by the stretch of the fabric there, It looked like I might be on the right track, but I wanted to know more about what he wanted and how he wanted me to do it.

I wanted him to tell me exactly what to do.

"Would you prefer me to go fast or slow, Mr Stamer?"

I lingered slightly on his surname, something about referring to him that way making me feel even naughtier. Vanessa had called him Mr Stamer the other night, as if she didn't know him well enough to use his first name, so when I said it, it helped support the illusion that he had simply hired me for the night. From the way his eyes darkened, it seemed that he liked it too.

"Nice and slow, Gemma." Cole's eyes never left mine. "Like I'm paying you by the hour."

My thighs clenched at his words, a jolt of longing running through my whole body. Fuck, why did that turn me on so much? Since my mouth felt too dry to reply, I simply nodded in agreement.

With slow, deliberate movements, I undid the buttons of my blouse, one by one. Cole's eyes followed my hands, his jaw clenching as my fingers skimmed over my bra, and a moment of clarity hit me. No matter how cool he played it, we were both equally invested in this, and even though I might let him call the shots, I still had a lot of the power. I'd never explored this dynamic before, never had a partner who showed any interest, but between me and Cole, it seemed entirely natural.

When all the buttons were undone, my fingers found the edges of each side and slowly, inch by inch, I pulled them apart, revealing my white, lacy bra to him. My breath had grown so short that my chest heaved more than usual, moving up and down with each intake and exhale, but I had a feeling he didn't mind. He also seemed to be having a little trouble catching his breath.

Pulling the blouse down my arms, I let it fall to the floor, the silky white fabric pooling at my feet. My nipples were already hard against the fabric of my bra and they seemed to grow even harder as his eyes moved over me. When he looked up at my face, I had to bite my lip to keep from moaning at the stormy look I could see in his eyes. No one had ever looked at me that way before.

"Keep going." His voice sounded hoarser than it had been, but still as commanding and dominant.

My hands dropped to the waist of my jeans and I undid the button and pulled the zipper down, spreading the fabric so he could get a glimpse of the lacy trim of my panties. Turning my back to him, I closed my eyes and took a deep breath while he couldn't see my face, revelling in the way my body throbbed. He hadn't even touched me and my arousal was as strong as it had ever been, the fantasy and the dynamic between us working wonders with my body.

Still facing away from him, I pulled my jeans down, gradually revealing myself as I peeled the tight denim from my skin, down my thighs and bending over to pull them all the way down. From Cole's sharp intake of breath behind me, I could tell just how much he enjoyed the view, and I wondered if he could see the damp spot between my legs. Did he know just how wet he'd made me?

Now, I wore only my bra and panties, and I stood back up, keeping my back to him and shaking my hair out down the back, wiggling my hips at the same time. The sofa creaked as he shifted again, and knowing I was getting to him just made my own need stronger.

When I raised my hands to the back of my bra, ready to undo it, Cole's voice stopped me. "Not yet. Turn around, Gemma. Let me see you."

Obediently, my hands fell back to my side and I turned slowly, watching as his eyes devoured me from head to toe. Every part of me ached for his touch, to feel his body on me and not just his gaze. His arms were still spread over the back of the sofa, but I could see that his hands were gripping it tighter than they had been, the only real physical manifestation of the fire I could see in his eyes.

"Touch yourself," he ordered, the words rocking me once again. "Your left hand on your bra, your right hand on your panties. Feel yourself through the fabric."

My fingers trembled as I did as he said. I already knew how turned on I was, but the physical evidence of it couldn't be denied: my nipples were stiff beneath my hand and my panties were soaked through. My mouth opened and a moan escaped my lips as I pressed harder between my legs.

"Fuck."

I may have been thinking it, but Cole was the one who said it out loud. His nostrils flared as he tried to control his breathing, and I had a sudden urge to push his buttons a little further, teasing him just as I had at the party the other night, seeing how long it would take him to lose control.

"Are you happy with your purchase, Mr Stamer?" My voice hardly even sounded like me. Need flooded through every word, and I felt certain that Cole could hear it too.

In fact, his lips twitched as he tried to keep his expression neutral. "My purchase looks very good on the shelf, but we'll have to see how it performs under pressure."

Just the word made my knees press together, trying to alleviate the ache between my legs. "What kind of pressure?"

His eyes dropped to the bulge I could now clearly see beneath his trousers. "Come over here and find out."

Though my knees nearly buckled, I managed to keep my balance and walk over to him. As I drew close, I expected him to reach for me, to touch me, finally, but he kept his hands where they were, just watching me.

"What do you want me to do?" I asked, desperate for his instruction.

"You're going to straddle me. Climb up on my lap and grind against me until you make yourself come. I want you to use me to get off, Gemma. I want to watch you do it."

Oh, *fuck.*

~Cole~

My fingers gripped the edge of the sofa harder as Gemma whimpered in front of me. The sight of her in her lacy white lingerie and the way her chest moved as she breathed heavily had my hands itching to touch her and my dick aching with need. However, as soon as I got inside her, I wouldn't be able to hold back for long, so I would use whatever self-control I had to draw this out as long as I could before we got to that point. It had taken days for us to get here, and I had no intention of rushing a second of it.

Just as I'd told her to, Gemma lowered herself onto my lap, her knees on either side of me. The pressure of her pussy against my hard dick felt exquisite, and I couldn't keep from exhaling sharply as she adjusted herself, finding the perfect spot where my hardness pressed against her just where she needed it most.

Her hands went to my chest as she began to move against me, but I shook my head. "Don't touch me. Touch yourself, Gorgeous. Let me see you do it."

She immediately obeyed, removing her hands from my shirt and moving them to her chest instead, her fingers skimming over her bra and making the fabric rub against her nipples that I could see straining against the lace.

"Can I take my bra off?" Her whispered voice couldn't be any more full of need, full of longing, and my dick twitched beneath her at the sound of it. I loved that she asked my permission. I loved that the beautiful, confident woman who had charmed everyone at the hotel opening the other night would submit to me like this. It had to be the hottest thing I had ever seen.

"Slowly," I agreed, struggling to keep my hips still as she continued to work herself back and forth on my lap.

Keeping her eyes on me, she reached behind her back and undid the clasp. Holding the fabric against her chest with one hand, she used the other to slide the straps down her arms before, agonizingly slowly, she pulled it away from her completely.

My eyes immediately dropped to her chest, to her beautiful, rounded breasts that bounced perfectly while her hips grinded against me, her pace increasing with each passing second. As I watched, she brushed both hands over her hardened nipples and then took them in her fingers, one in each hand, pinching and gently twisting them.

I'd been trying hard to stay silent but I couldn't help groaning now, watching her writhe on my lap, touching herself as her hips moved against me, desperately seeking the friction she needed. Everything about her was amazingly sexy. My hands tensed against the sofa again, wanting to touch her in spite of how much I was enjoying the show. I wanted to watch and I wanted to take part. I wanted it all.

"Are you close, Gemma?" The sound of my own voice surprised me, thick with lust. I truly didn't know how much longer I could wait.

"Yes," she whispered, her eyes closing as she focused on the different sensations assaulting her body. "So close, Cole..."

I liked when she called me 'Mr Stamer', but hearing her say my name now damn near killed me. My hips bucked up against her involuntarily and she moaned in reply, pushing back against me with increased force.

"Come for me, Gemma. Let me see your face as you come."

She let out a cry at my words as her body tensed, her legs quivering around me. "Yes, Cole, fuck, yes!"

Looking just as good as I'd imagined it would, her body convulsed on top of me, shuddering a moment before she collapsed against me, overwhelmed by pleasure. Finally, I put my arms around her, holding her to me while she recovered, and once she had, I captured her mouth against mine, ready to devour her. Gemma responded immediately, her lips opening for me, and I pulled the bottom one into my mouth, biting down on it just hard enough. She moaned again, the sound making me even harder, which shouldn't have been possible by that point. Fuck, I needed to get out of my pants.

With her still on top of me, I twisted around and lay down on the sofa, Gemma's body following me down so she ended up hovering above me. "Unzip my pants."

She laughed, a small, breathy laugh, as she couldn't resist correcting me. "We call them trousers here."

I was in no mood for being teased as I narrowed my eyes at her to remind her who was in charge. "It doesn't matter what you call them. Open them."

She got the message. Biting her lip, Gemma moved down my body, shifting her weight off me so she had access to the zipper. Her hand brushed against my dick as she pulled it down, and I exhaled again, barely holding it together, while Gemma looked back up at me, waiting for my next command.

"Don't stop now. Set me free."

With a quick tug at my briefs, I could finally breathe again. As Gemma got her first look at me, I could hear her sharp intake of breath, and I had to stifle another groan. Every single thing she did turned me on, each delightful contradiction combining to nearly kill me with desire.

"You like the look of it, Gorgeous?" Her eyes hadn't moved from my dick, devouring its long, hard length with her gaze, but when I asked the question, she glanced up at me and nodded, almost shyly. Fuck, how did she manage to seem both innocent and utterly provocative at the same time? "Why don't you see how it tastes?"

The sound of that amazing whimper of hers went straight to my dick, as did her lips. Leaning down over me, her eyes still locked on mine, she licked me from the base of my shaft all the way to the tip and back down again.

"Fuck." I couldn't stop the word from escaping, my self-control slipping a little more with each movement of her tongue. Nothing about this was new, I had done it countless times before, and yet, it somehow felt completely different.

Without using her hands, she drew her tongue back up my shaft again, and as my head jumped beneath her touch, she caught it in her lips, taking me into her mouth. I took a shaky breath, trying to keep my eyes open to watch her even as the sensation threatened to overwhelm me. It didn't get any easier when I hit the back of her throat as she took me in as far as she could, and she moaned, her mouth humming around me, sending the vibrations through my dick and my whole body.

If she didn't stop, I was going to come in her mouth right there and then.

"That's enough." The words sounded harsher than I meant them to, but I couldn't have spoken normally if my life depended on it. "There's a condom in the bedside table. Go get it."

Obeying me immediately, Gemma lifted herself from the sofa and hurried away as I pulled my pants and underwear down further. I still had my suit jacket on, was still fully clothed other than my painfully hard dick, a testament to just how little control I actually had over the situation. My need for her was in control now, not me.

As soon as she returned, she opened the package and rolled the condom onto me, guessing correctly that I wanted it. "That's it. Now, take off your panties and lower yourself onto me. You're going to come on top of me again, this time with me inside you."

Without complaint, Gemma slid out of her underwear and climbed on to me eagerly, lining her hips up with my dick between them before pushing them down and taking me inside her as we both moaned in unison. She felt incredible, and judging by her reaction, she enjoyed the feel of me too. When she had taken me all the way in, she paused for a moment, her eyes closed as she rested on top of me.

"You doing okay, Gorgeous?"

With a sweet, satisfied smile, she opened her eyes again. "You're pretty big. I'm just getting used to it."

Fuck. Women said that kind of thing to me often enough, because they thought I wanted to hear it, but when Gemma said it, it sounded completely sincere and unlike anything I'd heard before.

"Take your time." I put my hands behind my head to help resist the urge to touch her. "When you're ready, you can ride me. Nice and slow to start with, Gemma."

Placing her hands on my stomach, over my shirt, to steady herself, she lifted herself up inch by inch and slowly lowered herself back down, rolling her hips as she reached my base to give her clit the friction it wanted.

As my dick filled her, I groaned again, unable to hold it back any longer. "That's perfect, Gemma. Just like that."

Encouraged by my praise, she lifted herself again and sank back down, over and over, her eyes locked onto mine and her lips parted. When her pace began to increase, I didn't slow her down. I didn't want to. I'd waited long enough. We were both breathing faster now and my finish was approaching fast, so I tried to bring her along with me.

"Touch yourself, Gorgeous. Make yourself come while you fuck yourself with my dick."

With another little whimper, her hand reached down to her clit, circling it while her hips continued to move against mine.

"Oh, God, Cole..." She trailed off, her eyes closing and her head falling back as her orgasm claimed her, looking just as fucking perfect as the first one.

That sight gave me the final push I needed to reach my tipping point, and I stopped trying to fight it, surrendering to the pleasure that rushed through my body as my dick pumped inside her and Gemma collapsed against me.

Reaching down, I wrapped my arms around her, feeling the pounding of her heart as she rested against me, a rhythmic thumping that mirrored the heavy thuds in my own chest. That whole experience had been incredible, and I hadn't even touched her yet.

That particular pleasure was still to come.

~Gemma~

My mind reeled with residual pleasure as I lay against Cole's chest on the sofa, trying to make sense of what just happened. It had been easily the most intense orgasm of my life, I knew that much, and Cole hadn't even touched me. Still nearly fully dressed, he really hadn't done anything other than speak to me and let me use his body. Somehow, he seemed to know me better than I knew myself, understanding just what I needed to hear to turn me on faster and harder than anyone ever had before.

The next words out of his mouth, however, were completely unexpected. "Are you hungry? You didn't eat much at the park."

Cole's voice had lost its domineering edge. He still sounded calm and controlled, but the sudden switch to talking about food while still inside me felt like it came out of nowhere.

Shakily, I pushed myself back up so I could see his face. "No, I'm okay."

"Are you sure? I'm going to order something." He slid his hand down between his leg and mine, retrieving his phone from the pocket of his trousers before holding it up in front of his face as he pulled up an app.

Even more confused, I lifted myself off of him. He didn't even glance up from his phone as I got up, or when my gaze moved to the full condom still encasing his cock. Did he expect me to do something about that? He didn't seem bothered by it.

"I'm going to get a sandwich and some chips," he told me absent-mindedly as he scrolled through the images on his screen. "You sure you don't want anything?"

"No, thanks." Standing beside the sofa, completely naked, I felt more and more unsure by the second about exactly what was happening now. Finally, I reached down and slid the condom off of him, but besides a slight wince, he didn't react at all.

Was that really it? He had his orgasm and I was of no further interest?

Suddenly, embarrassment began to take over. As the endorphins left my body, shame took their place, shame over the way I'd acted since we got here and the way I'd suggested this whole arrangement to him this morning. Of course he would treat me as if I were disposable. What had I done to suggest anything else to him?

Moving quickly and deliberately while Cole continued to stare at his phone, I gathered my clothes and took them into the bathroom with me, tossing the condom in the rubbish bin. Once I had my clothes back on, I took a deep breath as I looked at myself in the mirror. My eyes had a slightly wild look to them and my cheeks were flushed; I definitely looked like someone who had just been fucked.

But I hadn't been, really, had I? I had fucked him. He hadn't done anything at all.

What was I even doing here?

Shaking my head at myself, I left the bathroom, determined to grab my coat and get out of there as quickly as possible. The memory of the paparazzi outside crossed my mind, but hopefully, they would be gone by now. Being photographed like this would be the perfect topper to the most exciting but ultimately confusing experience of my life.

While I'd been away, Cole had sat up and done up his trousers, his cock tucked back out of sight, but he still had his phone out. He glanced up as I reappeared and his brow furrowed at the sight of me.

"You didn't need to get dressed. I can answer the door when the food gets here."

My steps faltered at the disapproval in his tone, knocking me off balance once again. "I thought we were finished."

He raised an eyebrow, his attention fully back on me. "Trust me, Gemma. You'll know when we're done."

Colour rose in my cheeks, but I stood my ground. Why did he make it sound like I was the one behaving strangely here? "Then why are you ordering food?"

With all the restrained strength of a wild animal, Cole stood up, stepping closer to me. As his body crossed into my space, my pulse rate increased again, against my will. "I'm ordering food because I'm hungry. Because I need more energy for what comes next, but believe me when I tell you, I'm not anywhere near finished with you yet."

My mouth went dry with his words and my resistance completely evaporated. Just like that, he had me ready to do whatever he told me to again. What the hell was wrong with me?

"There are some robes in the bathroom," he added. "Why don't you take your clothes off again and put one of those on? It'll be a lot more comfortable."

Taking a step back, he looked down at me with those dark eyes for just a second, checking that he had my agreement before sitting back down on the sofa and turning his attention back to the phone as if he had never got up at all.

I stood my ground for a moment longer, fighting against the almost overwhelming urge to give in to him, but in the end, my efforts were useless. I *wanted* to give in. Returning to the bathroom, I took off my clothes again, folding them on the counter, and put on one of the soft white robes instead, tying the belt tight around my waist.

When I came back out again, Cole was still looking at his phone but he patted the seat beside him on the sofa. "Come and sit. I just need to take care of something for work, it won't take long."

I did as he asked and he put an arm around me, pulling me closer to him. Though the gesture wasn't anything particularly special, it somehow made me feel safe and protected. I really couldn't understand myself right now, and I was getting tired of trying. It seemed easier to just let myself go and feel what I wanted to feel.

With his free hand, Cole made a call. I could hear the person on the other end speaking to him with an American accent, going through the details of some kind of marketing plan. It meant nothing to me, so I stopped listening to his words and focused on the vibration of his chest as he spoke. His deep voice comforted me in a way I couldn't explain, and I reached over and undid one of the buttons of his shirt, sliding my hand through the opening to rest against his skin. His breath caught as I did it, but he didn't stop me and he didn't stop talking either.

Before he had finished, room service knocked on the door. I pulled my hand back and out from his shirt, starting to stand up to answer the door, but he held out his hand to me and stood and answered it himself, still talking on the phone. Soon, he returned with a tray, setting it on the coffee table as he sat back down and put his arm back around me as he wrapped up his call. Everything he did felt so unhurried, so completely sure of himself, and so different from anyone I had been with before.

When he finally hung up, he placed his phone down on the end table and pulled the lid off the room service tray, revealing some kind of multi-layered sandwich and a couple of bags of crisps.

"I thought you were getting chips?" I asked, realizing as I saw the food that I might be hungrier than I'd realized, and the thought of a few warm, salty chips actually appealed to me quite a lot.

Cole gave me a funny look as he held up one of the crisp bags. "What do you call these?"

Realizing where the confusion lay, I laughed. "Those are crisps. I thought you meant chips, like French fries."

"No, I meant chips, like chips." He shook his head as his lips twitched in amusement. "Does that mean you don't want any?"

"No, thanks. Next time, I'll remember I'm talking to an American."

He freed his arm from me to start eating his sandwich, and I shuffled back to give him more space. "Have you spent much time in the US?" he asked.

"A little bit. In uni, I took part in an exchange program where I got to do a term at Columbia. I enjoyed that a lot."

"You lived in New York?" He sounded genuinely curious as he turned on the sofa to see me better.

"Just for four months." The memory of it seemed bittersweet now. Although I had enjoyed it, I also spent half the time feeling bad about leaving Edwin behind and keeping in touch with him. If I'd only known then what I knew now, I would have made more of an effort to focus on myself and what I wanted. In any case, Cole didn't need to know any of that, so I kept my response more general. "I really liked the classes and the city, even though it's very different from London."

"What was your favourite building?"

Cole's question made me smile; the perfect question for an architect, it reminded me how he asked me about the wall we'd removed at the Mayfair Mews. He seemed to have more than a passing interest in architecture himself, which not all developers did.

"It's cliché, but probably the public library. It's so beautiful and beautifully in line with its purpose." His nod of approval sent a small ripple of warmth through me. "What about you?"

He gave his reply some real thought. "It changes regularly, but as you say, anything that's functional and beautiful. Was VIA 57 West completed when you were there? It's a great example."

I knew of the residential building, but I'd never seen it in person. "No, they were still working on it."

We chatted more about buildings in New York and here in London until his plate was empty, and I almost couldn't believe how comfortable it felt. While at first, I had been thrown off by his abrupt switch from sex to companionable chatter, now, it actually boosted my confidence. Asking me questions and showing genuine interest in my answers, Cole wasn't treating me even a little bit differently because of the way I had 'performed' for him, and that appealed to me more than I realized it would.

It made me believe that we could go back to a professional relationship after all of this without things being awkward. Maybe that was what he'd been trying to show me?

But just as I'd started to feel almost too relaxed, he reminded me that this evening wasn't over just yet as he leaned closer to me, his eyes locked on me just as intensely as before.

"Well, Gemma, now that I've got my energy back, let's see if we can find a way to use it all up again."

~Cole~

Gemma's whole demeanour changed with the words I spoke. She'd returned to her confident, charismatic self while we'd been talking, but as soon as I made it clear I was ready to continue our earlier activity, I could almost see the meekness wash over her. She looked completely ready to follow my commands again, ready for me to take full control.

For me, that was an incredible turn-on.

I'd had plenty of women pretend to be submissive for me, but never anyone who'd done it so instinctively, so naturally. She obviously liked it too, and I couldn't help wondering about her previous relationships and whether the men she'd been with before had dominated her too. From the confrontation I'd witnessed in the park earlier, I figured she'd dated the man we ran into there, and he didn't seem like a good fit for her at all. The blonde woman he was with now clearly called the shots between them, so I couldn't see that he and Gemma in the bedroom would have led to many sparks for either of them.

At any rate, I couldn't care less about her former lovers at this point. By the time I finished with her, I wanted her to have a new standard to measure any future lovers against.

Standing up, I pulled Gemma up with me and led her to the bedroom without another word while she followed behind me unquestioningly. Once we were in front of the bed, I dropped her hand and finally began removing my own clothes at a deliberate, unhurried pace.

"Take off the robe and climb on the bed," I commanded as I pulled off my tie and started undoing the buttons of my shirt. Her hips swayed as she crawled up to the middle of the large bed and sat down, turning back to me to wait for further instruction.

My shirt came off and my pants quickly followed. At last, we were both naked, and I couldn't wait to finally feel her skin against mine.

"Lie down."

Obediently, she leaned back, still in the centre of the bed, resting her head against the pillows.

"Spread your legs for me, Gorgeous."

Once again, she obeyed me without question, her knees dropping open as she watched me through half-opened eyelids. Climbing onto the bed after her, I ran my hands over her body, starting at her ankles and working my way up her legs, over her hips, to her breasts. As much as I enjoyed watching her play with them earlier, I couldn't wait to touch them myself.

Gemma's back arched up beneath my touch, trying to get more pressure as I lightly brushed the tips of her nipples with my fingers.

"Someone's eager," I observed, moving my hands down to her waist instead, tracing the curves of her hips.

"Cole, please," she begged as my fingers moved lower, skimming across her folds with a feather-light touch.

I continued to tease her, feigning ignorance. "Please what? This?"

With one quick motion, I thrust a finger into her, causing her hips to leave the mattress as she rose to meet me. The moan she let out was better than anything I had been imagining in the last three nights I'd spent alone, and I wanted to hear it again, and again, and again. Covering Gemma's body with mine, I kissed her neck before moving my lips down to her breasts, rolling her nipple around with my tongue while my fingers continued working her, pumping in and out as my thumb rolled over her clit.

Gemma squirmed beneath me, her little moans and groans punctuated by breathy whispers of my name and the odd swear word. My body reacted to the sound of her almost as much as the sight; I loved to hear her and loved to have her completely at my mercy, so beautiful and so sensitive to my touch. When she came, her core clamping around my fingers and her legs trembling beneath me, it filled me with both a deep satisfaction and an even deeper desire to possess her more completely.

All the plans I'd had for what I wanted to do with her went out of my head as one thought replaced all the others in my mind: I needed to be inside her, now. Grabbing another condom as quickly as I could, I was back on top of her before she'd even opened her eyes, pressing up against her entrance with the tip of my dick. As I slid into her, the motion smooth and easy because of how wet she was, her head rolled back, her red hair spread against the white hotel pillows, looking just as magnificent as I had pictured it that first night we had met.

"I'm going to fuck you hard, Gorgeous," I warned her. "I'm going to sink myself into you so deeply, you'll be feeling me the rest of the week."

Her eyes opened to find mine, the green depths of them full of wanting. "Yes, Cole, please."

Her eagerness sparked an even stronger fire within me. With a low groan that was almost a growl, I took her, over and over, the pace punishing, my body slamming into hers with a force that was anything but gentle. I wasn't usually so rough, but something about her made it seem natural, and there were no complaints from her side.

All too soon, she came again, and the feel of it pushed me over too. I came hard, roaring out her name as I continued pumping for a few more thrusts, not wanting it to end. It had to eventually, though; finally, I was spent and I collapsed down on the bed next to her, my heart racing from both the exertion and the pleasure she's given me. Silence filled the room, broken only by the sound of our breathing, heavy and ragged as we both came down from our high.

That was... something else. Things didn't usually go this way with the women I hired. That normally went more like the first part of our evening, with me telling them what to do and them working for my pleasure. It had never been like that with Samantha either; I had never been that rough with her. I didn't know what it was about Gemma that made me feel like I wanted to both have her and be had by her, to give her everything and take it all back, but fuck, it felt amazing.

With one arm, I reached out and pulled Gemma to me, feeling her body mould naturally to mine. "Are you alright?"

As certain as I felt that she had enjoyed that as much as I had in the heat of the moment, I also wondered if she might feel differently once reality set back in. I wanted to make it completely clear to her that I still fully respected her. If anything, I respected her more for being able to let herself go like she had. Not everyone could give up control like that.

Her reply was just a murmur. "I'm good, but I should probably go."

"There's no rush. You can rest for a bit or have a bath or a shower. Whatever you want."

For some reason, I wanted to make sure she felt good even now that we'd finished. I wanted to take care of her, which was something else I never did with the women I hired, but this felt different. She was different.

"I appreciate that, but I really should go. I've got a busy day tomorrow."

Since she sounded like she'd made up her mind, I didn't press the issue. "Do you want me to call a car for you?"

"Sure, that would be great."

The bed moved beside me as Gemma sat up and got to her feet, and I watched her leave the room, trying to ignore the feelings of regret and disappointment at the idea that I would never get to see her this way again. I didn't want that to be the case, but I didn't see how else this could go if I wanted to stick to my own rules.

Our deal had only been for one night and, if I was being honest with myself, it had been a pretty flimsy deal in the first place. Me going with her to the park hadn't been much of a payment. I pretended it was because I wanted to have her, but I couldn't just ask to see her again. That would be crossing a line that I wasn't willing to cross. My rules existed for a reason, and the fact that she made me want to break them was the strongest reason why I shouldn't.

There was something between us, I couldn't deny that, but I also couldn't take the risk of fanning the flames. With so many sparks flying around, it seemed impossible that I could step further into the fire without getting burned.

Chapter Seven

REALITY TV

~Gemma~

My legs continued to tremble as I got redressed in the hotel bathroom. After fantasizing about Cole for the previous three nights, I'd come into the evening with pretty high expectations and he still managed to exceed anything I had imagined. No one had ever made me feel that way before, and I couldn't completely silence the little voice in my head that suggested no one ever would again.

When we made our agreement, I had hoped that we could have sex and move on, but already, I knew it wouldn't be that easy. The experience we just shared would be living rent-free in my head for a long time to come.

When I stepped back out into the main room of the suite, Cole had put on the robe that I'd discarded in his room. It shouldn't have been sexy on him, but somehow, he made it work. Knowing that he was naked beneath it, knowing just how perfect his body looked unclothed, didn't make my goal of moving on any easier.

"The car will be waiting for you downstairs," he told me.

"Thanks."

For a few seconds, we both stood there awkwardly, just looking at each other, and frustration coursed through me. I didn't want things to be awkward. The whole point of what we'd just done had been to get rid of the tension between us, not to create more.

With that in mind, I tried to lighten the mood. "Well, it was a pleasure doing business with you, Cole."

His dark eyes flashed, indicating that he had a few things to say about that, but he held himself to a single-word answer: "Likewise."

Walking to the door, I put my boots back on and grabbed my coat. As I wrapped my scarf around my neck, Cole spoke again.

"Gemma."

He only said the one word, just my name, but it stopped me in my tracks. "Yes?"

Turning back to him, I watched as his lips grew tighter and tighter, some kind of internal battle going on inside him, until he finally seemed to gain the upper hand and took a deep breath, making a visible effort to relax.

"Is there anything else on your calendar this week that you need some company for?"

Immediately, hope spiked within me. I knew exactly what he meant: he wanted to repeat this evening, and I couldn't even pretend I didn't want it too. My body reacted instantly, with the aching that had only recently subsided coming back in full force. I had literally just been satisfied completely, and already, I wanted him again.

"Actually, I do." I had planned a full-on schedule of activities for me and Edwin over the next three weeks, but Cole didn't need to know that. I offered him a casual, flirty smile instead. "Can you handle more Christmas fun?"

That now-familiar smirk of his reappeared on his face. "If tonight has been any indication, I think the reward will be sufficient."

So, he clearly enjoyed himself as much as I had. Maybe one more time wouldn't hurt. Maybe one more time would be what it took to satisfy the need in me.

I grabbed my phone from my pocket and held it out to him. "Give me your number and I'll send you the next thing on my schedule. You can let me know if it works for you."

As calm and cool as always, Cole came over and took the phone, standing next to me while he entered his number. Just being next to him again, smelling his cologne and watching each tiny movement of his muscles, almost made me want to tear my clothes off again right there and then. When he handed the phone back to me, he leaned over and brushed his lips against my cheek, barely touching it. "I'll look forward to hearing from you soon."

Swallowing hard, I forced myself to pull away. "Goodnight, Cole."

I left the room while I still could, while I still had any willpower left.

Only when I had settled in the back of the car, watching the streets of London go by, did I remember Annabel and the paparazzi. *Fuck.* I really should have given Cole more details about that while we were in the same room, but my distraction hadn't been entirely my fault. Now that the distraction had disappeared, reality started to sink back in.

With dread pooling in my stomach, I pulled up Annabel's Instagram account. Unsurprisingly, it featured a bunch of photos of her at the Winter Wonderland, including one of her with Edwin's arm around her as he gazed at her adoringly, reminding me why I made a point of never looking at her posts. In the past, seeing this kind of thing would always send me into a spiral of doubt and bitterness, but at that moment, instead of the usual agonizing self-loathing that would accompany any thoughts of Edwin and Annabel, the sight left me curiously unaffected. Maybe finally getting laid had helped to soothe my resentment? That would be a nice side-effect.

Finally, I found the post I was looking for.

Spotted tonight in the Park: a certain super-rich American hotel exec (CS) looking cozy with Eddie's ex!

'Eddie'? Edwin had always told me he hated when people called him that.

The post already had thousands of likes and comments. Though I knew I shouldn't look, my eyes strayed to the first few comments anyway. Most of them were about Cole; people had guessed immediately that the post referred to him, since she hadn't been subtle. After that, it didn't take long for the comments I expected to appear.

He must not watch LOK.

Sounds like he's in for a massive letdown.

Wow, would have thought someone that loaded could do better.

My jaw clenched as I quickly turned the screen off, my gaze returning to the city outside the taxi window instead, though I didn't actually see a thing. No matter how much I tried to fight it, my heart pounded as the familiar feelings of shame and self-doubt washed over me. Having my fiancé break up with me had been one thing, but it was another thing entirely to have complete strangers speculating about the reasons he'd left and the reasons no other man would ever want me.

Cole would see those comments. He had a publicist, which I'd learned earlier, and if she was any good at her job, she'd find out about all of this in no time. Not to mention the pictures that were bound to appear in the tabloids tomorrow morning, along with a rehash of the whole situation. He'd see everything that people had said, and he'd know everything that had happened.

The chances of a second night with him seemed to be fading by the second, so before I lost my nerve, I sent him a quick text inviting him to the event I had in my calendar for the next evening. If he wanted to blow me off, at least he'd have to give me an excuse.

With that done, I took a deep breath, letting all the negative feelings flow out of me. I couldn't do anything else about it now, and I wouldn't let this bring me down like it had before. If nothing else, I had the memories of that night with Cole, and they were good enough to keep me going for quite a while.

What would Edwin think if he could have seen the way I'd behaved with Cole? The way Cole had brought me to climax, the way I had come for him, over and over again. It would be enough to make Edwin take back everything he'd said about me.

Maybe the problem had never been me at all. Maybe the problem had simply been that he'd never known what to do with me.

~Cole~

After Gemma left, I pulled out my laptop, still wearing only the bathrobe that she'd previously had on. It still smelled of her, and the scent managed to keep me semi-hard even as I tried to concentrate on my work.

Only a few minutes later, my phone buzzed, and as Gemma's name appeared, I quickly snatched it from the table. Her message invited me to go to some house with her tomorrow, and I didn't even bother to look at the details. After the evening we'd just shared, I'd go anywhere and do pretty much anything for another night with her. No price was too high.

I really hadn't even meant to ask her for another night. She had come so close to walking out the door without the words coming out of my mouth, but now that they'd been said, I didn't regret it. I would regret it more if I never had her in my bed again.

So what if this would be the first time the same woman had been in my bed for more than one night since Samantha? Since that Christmas Eve? It didn't mean anything, I told myself. The whole thing was still just a business deal, just like always. The terms might be different, but they were still clear: I would keep her company and she would keep me company. We owed each other nothing beyond that.

*I'm free tomorrow. Text me the details of where and when to meet you.
C*

With my reply sent, I turned back to my laptop screen and got back to work.

About an hour passed before Nellie phoned me again.

"Nellie." I answered the phone with just her name, putting her on speaker phone. She had a habit of diving right into whatever she had to tell me, which I appreciated, and she did it that time too.

"I've found the source of the rumours that interested the paparazzi, but before we get to that, let me ask you: exactly how much did you know about Gemma Redvers before you started seeing her?"

I frowned down at the phone, though she couldn't see me. "First, I'm not 'seeing' anyone. Second, the woman I was photographed with tonight is named Gemma Sudlow."

"So, you knew nothing." Nellie sighed, sounding disappointed in me. "Are you going to be seeing her again?"

I bristled both at the implication that I didn't know something that I should, and at Nellie's newfound interest in my personal life. "Explain to me how that's your business."

"It's my business because I need to know if I should work on killing the story or if you're going to get photographed together again. Am I saying this was a business thing, or will you be taking taxis back to your hotel together regularly?"

I'd certainly been planning on doing it again the following evening. "Back up a second. Why did you call her... whatever you called her?"

"Redvers," Nellie repeated. "That's her legal name. It sounds like she hasn't told you who her father is."

Each word put my back up a little more. Why would she suggest that Gemma had hidden something from me? I had done a basic background check on her and Holly, and nothing came up about her having a different name. As far as I'd been able to tell, they were both regular, middle-class, working women. The only thing that had been unusual was that we hadn't been able to find any record of where Gemma had gone to school, but I assumed she must have gone somewhere abroad. She'd confirmed as much to me that evening when she said she'd spent some time in New York, so I hadn't thought anything further of it.

"Just tell me." I hated guessing games.

"Her father's name is Andrew Redvers. His *title* is the Earl of Totnes."

Her father being an earl was interesting, I supposed, but ranks of nobility had never particularly interested me. I didn't see how it made any significant difference to my life. "Is that supposed to mean something to me?"

Nellie sighed, like she was dealing with a child who refused to pay attention. "It means she's from a very old, very wealthy family."

The fact that she came from money did surprise me, but she probably had her reasons for wanting to separate herself from that. It really didn't concern me. "So, that's why the press cares that I was seen with her?" I tried to guess.

"No."

My stress level getting higher with each passing second, I rubbed my forehead with my hand to try to release some tension. "Get to the point, Nellie. Why are they interested?"

"Have you heard of a TV show called *Ladies of Knightsbridge*?"

"Does that sound like something I would know about?" I snapped back. My patience was wearing thin.

"Fine, stupid question. It's a reality show following young women from old noble families as they fritter their time away, shopping and socializing. It's got a big following in the UK."

"And Gemma is on this show?" Of all the things she'd said, that surprised me the most by far. I couldn't imagine Gemma doing something like that.

"No," she quickly corrected me. "She wasn't on it directly, but she was... a bit of a plot point last season, for lack of a better description."

"I have no idea what you're talking about." When would she stop dancing around the issue? I still didn't understand what the point of any of this was.

"Okay, let me spell it out. Gemma used to be engaged to a man named Edwin Matheson, who's the son of another Earl. Not quite an arranged marriage, but close enough. They were engaged for six years."

Six years? That seemed like a ridiculously long engagement, and Gemma couldn't be much more than twenty-five. They must have gotten together very young, and I recognized the name: Edwin Matheson was the man we ran into at the park earlier. Finally, things were starting to come together.

"Used to be engaged," I repeated. "Fine. Then what?"

"He had an affair with one of the women on this *Knightsbridge* show, a Lady Annabel Clarkson. The whole thing was documented on the show. The whole country watched Gemma's fiancé complain about their sex life on national TV, cheat on her, and eventually dump her."

That protective urge that had hit me back in the park suddenly returned with full force. Had Gemma really gone through that? It seemed almost impossible to imagine the vibrant woman I had gotten to know being treated that way, and I wanted to spare her from it, even though it had already happened. I wanted to make anyone who had hurt her pay for it.

Where the fuck did all of those feelings come from?

"That's why they care, Cole," Nellie concluded. "The press painted her as an uptight, sexually unadventurous prude, and now, they think you're dating her."

~Gemma~

When I got home, I had a consultation over the phone with Holly to try to decide how to handle the potential fallout from the tabloid stories. She had also just walked in the door when I called, fresh from her drinks with Jackson. They enjoyed each other's company at the pub, but it hadn't gone any further than that, at least not that night. She certainly didn't seem opposed to the idea that it might eventually.

As for the press, I wasn't sure what we should do. When the whole Annabel/Edwin story had broken earlier that year, we managed to avoid any association with our business. Our friends and colleagues knew about it, but the general public never made the association. Most of the papers stuck to referring to me as Edwin's rejected ex; or, if they did use my name, they used my legal name. That helped sell the story anyway: the fact that they got to humiliate the daughter of one of the country's oldest families along the way. Thankfully, none of them seemed to care about my business.

I had never been so happy with my decision to take a separate name for my professional career.

However, if any of the paparazzi had actually gotten a decent picture of me, people might recognize me as not just Gemma Redvers, but also as Gemma Sudlow, architect with Anchor Design, right as our star was rising thanks to the Mayfair Mews opening. And although Holly argued that there was no such thing as bad publicity, I would rather do without it.

I still didn't tell Holly that I'd gone to Cole's room, telling her only that we had been photographed getting out of the taxi together. I couldn't really explain why I didn't want to tell her. Usually, we shared almost everything, and she knew all about my attraction to him. After all, she had been the one who encouraged me to pursue him. And I certainly didn't feel any embarrassment over the fact that we had slept together.

When I tried to pin down the reason for my reluctance, I supposed it simply came down to the fact that our whole connection, the time

Cole and I had shared, was something so fragile, so unstable, that if I told anyone else about it, it might just shatter entirely.

"Is there any chance we can borrow Cole's publicist?" she asked, only half-joking.

"I doubt it, but maybe we should look at hiring someone for some freelance PR work, just in case?"

We agreed to look into it first thing in the morning, and after I'd hung up, I quickly checked my phone for any other messages. Cole had replied to me when I was still in the car, telling me that he would be available the next night for my planned activity, with the implied understanding that I would return to his hotel again. Would he change his mind once he found out about all of my drama? It actually surprised me that he hadn't found out already. I kept waiting for my phone to buzz with his cancellation.

When I finally crawled into my own bed, I expected the swirling thoughts in my head to keep me up half the night. Instead, I thought back to my time with Cole, and remembering the soothing, blissful feeling of surrendering to him helped me to relax. Before I knew it, my alarm buzzed in my ear, urging me to get ready and face another day.

The first thing I had to do was check on the damage that had been done. Seeing no point in putting it off, I grabbed my phone while I was still in bed, my fingers trembling as I brought up a search for Gemma Redvers. Sure enough, there were photos of Cole and I the night before, but to my immense relief, none of them got a clear shot of me. From one angle, I had my face turned away from the camera, and in another, Cole's arm was around me, shielding me from view. Looking at the photo, I could almost feel his arm encircling me again, and it made me feel safe, like he'd protected me even though he hadn't had any idea what he needed to protect me from.

As I scrolled through the story, a text popped up on my phone, and my stomach dropped. Speak of the devil: there was Cole, texting me at six in the morning. Obviously, he had seen the photos, so his message would likely be the cancellation I had been expecting.

I closed my eyes briefly to steel myself before opening the text, but to my surprise, he wasn't cancelling. Instead, his message was brief and to the point.

Meet me for breakfast? C

Breakfast had never come up before, so I could only guess that he wanted to talk to me about everything, and I couldn't blame him. We should get it all out in the open.

I'm up now, I responded. *Where and when?*

Your office. Whenever you're ready.

The suggestion surprised me, but I suppose any other location might be risky. Going out somewhere in public meant that we might be seen.

I'll text you when I'm nearly there.

Although I would have liked to spend a bit more time getting ready for the day, I didn't want to put the conversation off any longer than necessary. I couldn't imagine that it would be particularly pleasant. As quickly as I reasonably could, I got ready and called myself a taxi to the Anchor offices. When I was ten minutes away, I texted Cole to let him know and he replied that he would leave the Lytton in a few minutes and be with me soon.

After the taxi dropped me off, I stopped at Pret to pick up some things for breakfast, and set about making some tea when I arrived at the office. No sooner had the kettle boiled than my phone buzzed one more time.

I'm outside.

Abandoning the tea, I headed for the door.

Cole stood just outside, as devastatingly handsome as always. His suit that day was a pinstripe grey, just visible beneath his overcoat. With some trepidation, I searched his face for any signs of anger or disapproval, but there were none to be found; just his usual unhurried, unbothered gracefulness, and maybe even the hint of a smile in his eyes.

As he entered, I took a peek out into the courtyard around him, just in case there might be more photographers lurking. He obviously knew exactly what I was doing because he smiled ruefully. "No one followed me. I took a back exit from the hotel, just in case."

Swallowing all my anxiety, I led him to my office and offered him the tea and breakfast. When we were finally set up, I sat down at the table with him, looked him in the eye, and offered my apology. "I'm sorry, Cole. I should have told you."

He shrugged, seeming unconcerned. "You *could* have told me. I don't know if you *should* have."

Was he serious? Why wouldn't he be furious about this? I had certainly made his life more difficult for the next couple of weeks, if nothing else. Even though it had been unintentional, he still had a right to be annoyed with me. Edwin certainly would have been, though he would have stewed over it in silence rather than telling me how he felt.

"I'll tell you anything you want to know now," I offered. "I'm not sure how much you've heard already."

"Nellie filled me in on some of the basics." He took a sip of his hot tea, his eyes meeting mine over the rim of the cup with a bit of curiosity but no judgement. "I imagine your version of it is different. I'm willing to hear whatever you want to tell me, but if you'd rather not say anything, that's fine too."

I really didn't understand his drama-free reaction. "What does this mean for our contract?" I couldn't help asking.

"It's got nothing to do with this."

"And tonight?" The hopeful tone of my own voice made me wince. Sounding slightly desperate, it would leave him in no doubt of how much I wanted to see him again.

"Separate."

I took a deep breath as I tried to understand. "So, you're not asking me about the situation as a business partner, or as a lover."

He huffed through his nose, sounding amused by my assessment. "No. I'm happy for you to be both of those things, as we've already discussed, but that's not why I'm here right now."

"Why are you here, then?"

Those dark eyes glimmered with an emotion I hadn't seen in them before. It almost looked like empathy. "I'm here as a friend."

~Cole~

If someone had asked me before I arrived in Gemma's office that morning if we were friends, I wouldn't have known how to answer the question. I never threw that label around lightly. My true friends could be counted on one hand, and they were all people I had known for years, people who had earned my trust through repeated loyalty.

With Gemma, I had only known her for four days, and only had a handful of real conversations with her. And yet, when she asked me in what capacity I had come there, it seemed completely natural to call myself her friend.

The press wouldn't be interested in me if not for her, that much was true, but they also wouldn't be interested in her if not for me. Her own 'scandal' had faded from the public consciousness months ago. The only reason it had come back into the spotlight was because she'd been seen with me. The situation was unfortunate, but neither of us were to blame, and I didn't see why we couldn't help each other through it.

In the last twelve hours, I'd learned a lot about her and it only made me want to know more. As far as I could tell, we were two people who grew up around wealth and power, who enjoyed their work and were good at it, and who had failed at their personal relationships in a rather spectacular manner. We had much more in common than I would have ever suspected the night we met under the mistletoe.

It only made sense to me that we face this together.

Despite my conviction, the look on Gemma's face tended towards disbelief. "I appreciate your support, Cole, more than I can say, but I want to make sure first that you fully understand the situation."

I meant it when I said she didn't have to tell me anything, but if she wanted to, I wouldn't stop her. "Okay. Tell me."

She took a long sip of her tea before setting it down and folding her hands in front of her. "So, the man you met last night in the park, Edwin, was my fiancé. I assume you know that."

I nodded.

"Our fathers were best friends and business partners. On the day I was born, they joked that if we were living a few hundred years ago, they would betroth me to Edwin on the spot. At least, they claimed they were joking. I never felt completely certain. For as long as I can remember, Edwin and I were pushed together, told over and over again what a perfect match we would be to combine our families and our families' business interests."

"No pressure, then," I observed mildly.

Gemma gave me a rueful smile. "Right. I didn't like the idea on principle, but in reality, I couldn't find fault with Edwin. He was a respectful, intelligent, successful young man; everything that a girl in my position should be looking for."

Although I had some curiosity about her 'position' and the aristocracy she'd been raised in, I didn't want to interrupt the flow of her story. Those questions could wait for later.

"We started 'dating', for lack of a better word, when I was 15 and he was 16. We'd go to society events together. He attended a boarding school out in the country, and he told me that he did see other girls there, but that it would never be anything serious. He told me he didn't mind if I did the same."

"Did you?"

She smiled again, a smile tinged with regret. "I went on a few dates, but they were all pretty innocent. Edwin went to Cambridge for university and I followed him a year later. At that point, he decided that if we were serious about things, we should become exclusive. He proposed to me the day he graduated so that he could tell his parents when they attended his degree ceremony. It would prove to them that he had his life completely under control."

"You had a very long engagement." That had been my first thought when Nellie had told me about it, and I was curious to hear the reasons why.

"We did," Gemma agreed. "Getting engaged made everyone happy, but whenever the subject of actually getting married came up, we'd always find a reason to put it off. Finally, last year, our parents started to get impatient, so we set a date."

"And then he panicked?"

"I suppose. I don't know if I ever thought of it in quite those terms before, but yes, as soon as we had the date, things changed. Little things that hadn't seemed such a big deal before just got bigger. And the big things... well, they became mountains that we couldn't see over."

She took another drink of her tea, looking down at the cup in her hands as if she was afraid to meet my eye.

"Did you... have you seen the show? The episode where he talks about me?"

Completely out of character, I reached out and put my hand on hers, pulling her attention back to me. "No. And I don't intend to."

"I can understand if you want to..."

"No, Gemma." I squeezed her hand as I cut her off. "I don't want to hear what he said. I want to hear it from you."

For a moment, I thought her eyes might be watering, but she blinked and they were back to normal. "Well, the short story is that Annabel was a friend of mine. Not a close friend, but someone in my family's social circle who we saw regularly at events. When Edwin and I visited the venue where we were planning to have our wedding, she was there making arrangements for some kind of charity event. She and Edwin had known each other when they were younger too, though I didn't realize at the time exactly how well they had been acquainted. That day was the first time they'd seen each other in years, and while I stood there talking to the wedding planner about seating arrangements, Edwin and Annabel snuck off to a back room and had sex."

My jaw clenched at the thought of anyone treating Gemma that way, but I knew the worst was still to come. The fact that it happened was bad enough, but the real problem was how publicly it happened.

"Annabel had just started filming *Ladies of Knightsbridge,* and the camera crew was there that day. They were filming her preparations for her event, and they caught enough on camera to make it clear exactly what had happened. Over the next couple of weeks, she and Edwin met regularly, to sleep together but also to talk about all the ways in which she was a better lover than me. All in front of the cameras."

That all squared away with what Nellie had told me. "Did he realize that the footage would be used?"

She nodded, her face tight. "He signed a release."

"And he didn't tell you in advance?"

"No. I only found out when the rest of the world did, but he obviously knew it was coming since he moved out of our flat the day before it aired."

I exhaled loudly, trying to dispel the anger that filled me on her behalf. "Well, he's clearly a bastard. You don't need me to tell you that."

A quick smile crossed her face at my words, but I could glimpse the pain that lay behind it. "I don't need you to, but it's always nice to get the confirmation anyway."

We both fell silent for a moment, drinking our tea as I thought over what she'd said. "Are they actually in love?"

Gemma shrugged. "I guess so. They're still together, anyway. They had a sexual relationship as teenagers, and they just picked it right back up when they reconnected. Obviously, they're more attracted to each other than Edwin and I ever were. I might even have been able to be happy for them that they found each other, if it weren't for the way they'd gone about it."

I had to agree. There were definitely good ways and bad ways to end an engagement, and that had to be one of the worst I had heard. It might even be worse than the way my own had ended.

"There's still one thing I really don't understand, Gemma."

She swallowed, as if preparing herself for a challenge. "Sure. What is it?"

I leaned forward, looking straight into her eyes. "If he thought there was something wrong with you in bed, what the fuck is wrong with him?"

~Gemma~

Though I wanted to laugh in response to Cole's question, I couldn't. The heat coming off his stare told me he didn't mean it as a joke. He looked deadly serious; he honestly didn't believe anyone could be unsatisfied with me, and the passion and the defensiveness in his gaze, defensiveness on my behalf, stopped my laughter before it could start.

I managed a shaky smile instead. "Well, last night wasn't exactly representative of the way things were between me and Edwin."

That must have been the understatement of the century.

"How were they?" The question was straightforward and almost clinical. He wasn't looking for me to praise him in comparison; he just wanted an honest assessment.

Still, I couldn't help feeling awkward talking about it. I liked the fact that Cole seemed to think of me as some kind of goddess in the bedroom and I didn't want to lose the esteem he held me in. However, I had promised to answer his questions honestly, and Edwin's version of events was hardly a secret. I might as well be up front.

"We were together for eight years and I can count the orgasms he gave me on one hand."

Cole's mouth dropped open in disbelief. I had never seen him lost for words, and it would have struck me as comical if the whole situation wasn't so ridiculously sad. His lips moved as if to form a question, but then he stopped himself. He looked at me, then looked away, then back at me again. Finally, he seemed to decide what he wanted to say: "You can't be serious."

"I wish I wasn't. I mean, sometimes I could get there if I helped him along, but in terms of what he did on his own... that was about it."

"I don't understand." He looked so bewildered that again, I had the urge to laugh. Of course he didn't understand. With the skills he had, I couldn't imagine he had ever been in that kind of situation. "Why were you even together, then?"

"As I said, our actual feelings were secondary to the other benefits of our relationship. And, to be fair to Edwin, he didn't know how bad it was for a long time."

Cole's brow furrowed in confusion. "How could he not know?"

I grimaced, looking down in shame. "Well, I didn't want him to feel bad, so... I faked it. A lot."

The way he shook his head in disappointment had me feeling even more embarrassed.

"I know now that it didn't help matters at all. It was a stupid thing to do, but he would get frustrated that nothing happened, and I didn't want him to feel bad."

"He should have felt bad." Cole's response was as blunt as always.

"Well, I was young and inexperienced and I didn't want to blame him. And when I got tired of pretending, he assumed that something had changed. Eventually, we spent less and less time together in bed since it ended up being a frustrating experience for both of us. So, in the end, it's not really that shocking that he left me for someone who was more sexually compatible with him. I just wish he'd gone about it differently."

"And he talked about your... lack of response on the show?" Cole guessed.

"Right. He pretty much said that he had done everything humanly possible, and I was simply incapable of being aroused."

Cole snorted in disbelief. "And Posh Barbie is more his speed?"

The fact that Cole remembered and repeated his nickname for Annabel made me smile. "Apparently so. From what I gathered from comments that were made, she likes to be in charge in the bedroom, and I guess that works for him. We never really tried that."

The expression on Cole's face morphed into a sly smile, his eyes taking on the hard, commanding edge that made me weak. "Of course you didn't, and it wouldn't have worked for you even if you did. That's not what you need, Gemma."

The certainty in his voice, the complete conviction that he knew *exactly* what I needed, set off tingles through my whole body.

As quickly as it had come on, his dominating side fell away. "I appreciate you telling me all this. But for right now, all we really need to decide is how you want to approach tonight."

"Tonight?" To my embarrassment, my voice squeaked on the word, my heart still racing from the reaction he'd just caused in me.

Thankfully, Cole pretended he hadn't noticed it. "With the paparazzi, I mean. They didn't get a good shot last night so I imagine they'll try again. And since I *do* intend to go out with you tonight and bring you back to my room, we just need to decide how you want to play it."

As covertly as possible, I let out a sigh of relief at the news that he still wanted to spend the night with me. Although I really appreciated his support and the idea of having him as a friend, that definitely wasn't all I wanted from him. "What are our options?"

"I think we have two main ones. First, we could try to keep things secret. I have access to all the entrances of the Lytton so we don't need to use the main doors. I could hire security to keep the press away when we go out. Or, the second option is that we can act like we don't care and allow the photographs to be taken. The tabloids only really care about this because they think it's a secret, so we make them think there's nothing there, or we're open enough that it's no secret. Either way, they'll lose interest."

His certainty and confidence was incredibly appealing. "If we went with the open option, people would assume we're in an actual relationship," I pointed out. "That doesn't bother you?"

He gave me what I was quickly starting to think of as his trademark smirk. "There are worse things in the world than people thinking I'm dating a beautiful woman. As long as you and I are clear what the situation is, I don't give a rat's ass what anyone else thinks."

After so many months of being crushed by everyone else's judgement, the idea of parading around town on Cole's arm and having everyone think I'd landed myself a much bigger catch than Edwin had ever been sounded more than a little tempting. "In that case, I think I'd prefer to do that. I'm tired of being ashamed."

Cole's eyes flashed dangerously. "You have nothing to be ashamed of, Gemma. You're a smart, successful woman who just happened to waste your time on a man who didn't match your needs and didn't deserve you."

How did he always know just what I needed to hear?

"But if you want to be open, for your own sake and not for anyone else, that's what we'll do. Come to the Lytton when you're finished work and I'll take you to dinner before we visit this house of yours. We'll go somewhere that everyone will see us."

As wonderful as that sounded, I couldn't help looking down at the outfit I had chosen for the day. In my rush to meet with Cole that morning, I certainly hadn't put the effort I could have into looking my best, not to the level required if we were planning to pose for photographs like he had suggested.

From that simple gesture, Cole immediately knew what I was thinking. "I'll have something sent for you to wear."

"You don't need to buy me things, Cole." I said it with a smile, but I wanted to make it clear that I meant it. "I don't need your money. That's not our price, remember?"

His eyes flashed once more with that gleam that turned me to putty. "I remember. But I also remember that you like doing what I tell you to, don't you, Gemma?"

Of course I did. He made it feel exciting and dangerous and safe all at the same time. But could we really go back to that? If we were going to be friends and business partners, if he was going to keep being as supportive as he had been that morning, could we really also keep the same dynamic in private as we'd had the night before? How would that even work?

Whatever doubts I had, Cole didn't seem to share them. As he leaned towards me again, my breath caught in my throat.

"What I'm telling you right now is that you are going to dress in whatever I send you. And all night, while you're wearing it, you're going to remember that it belongs to me. I paid for it, just like I paid for every inch of you underneath it. Tonight, you belong entirely to me."

Chapter Eight

SECOND NIGHT

~Cole~

The clock had only just reached 8:30 when I returned to the Lytton after having breakfast with Gemma, leaving me plenty of time to make some calls and put a few plans in place for that evening before I started work for the day. My suggestion to send Gemma a dress to wear for dinner had been completely impulsive, but the more I thought about it, the more I liked the idea. Even better, I knew she liked it too. Wearing the dress I chose and bought for her would turn her on all night, just like it would for me to see her in it, heightening the anticipation for both of us until we were back in my room again.

With the cat already out of the bag thanks to that morning's papers, I filled Jackson in on everything that had happened with Gemma, at least so far as our general arrangement and the tabloids were concerned. In particular, I told him about my plans for the evening so he knew I'd be unavailable.

"You're actually going to be seen in public with her," he repeated after I'd finished speaking, looking shell-shocked as he leaned back in his seat. "On a date. On purpose."

"It's not a real date," I reminded him. "But yes, I'm going to make sure that we're seen. The press can think what they like. Gemma and I are clear on what this is, so it's no different from me taking any other escort to any other event."

"Except she's not an escort," he pointed out.

"For the purposes of our deal, she is." In my mind, the distinction was completely clear.

"That's bullshit, Cole, and you know it. She's got her own money, right? She's not after yours. You like her as a person and you're attracted to her, so what am I missing? Why not see if there's something more there? Why insist that it has to be a transaction?"

"It's not just about the money." I shouldn't have to explain that to him, of all people. Although money had been the catalyst for what happened with Samantha, the heart of the issue had always been something else, and he'd been there with me through it all. "It's about trust."

"And why don't you trust Gemma?"

As I opened my mouth to reply, I realized I had no real answer to that. Gemma hadn't given me any reason not to trust her, at least not yet, so I kept my response more general. "It's not her, specifically. I don't trust anyone."

He simply shook his head, looking disappointed in me. "It sounds to me like you're in serious denial. Both of you, if she's agreeing to this madness."

"I don't remember asking for your opinion."

"You didn't, but I'd like to go on the record now, so that once you finally figure it out, I get to be the one to say I told you so."

Giving him a stern look, I changed the subject to work and we moved on. However, I couldn't ignore that as the day went on, my eyes strayed to the clock much more frequently than usual. My impatience grew with each passing hour until I couldn't wait to be finished with the day's work and to see Gemma come in the door wearing the dress I had sent her.

Finally, five o'clock arrived, and shortly afterwards, I received a text.

Followed all your instructions. I'm on my way now, should be there in ten minutes. G

A thrill of anticipation shivered down my spine at her choice of words. If she'd followed *all* my instructions, she would be arriving in the items I had picked out for her and nothing else. That thought had blood rushing to my dick almost immediately.

When I made my way down to the lobby, I could see the photographers on the sidewalk outside, as planned. Nellie had given them an 'anonymous' tip to let them know they would have a good chance of catching Gemma and I together either here or at the restaurant. A few already lingered outside and I suspected there would be more at the restaurant too. We shouldn't be missed.

Sure enough, a couple of flashes went off to warn me of Gemma's arrival before I laid eyes on her for myself. As she walked through the door with her head held high and a mischievous, satisfied smile on her face, not a single person in the lobby could keep from staring at her. She looked absolutely incredible.

Her red hair had been swept up elegantly into a twisted bun. The dress I had chosen was a deep, rusty red, just a shade or two darker than her hair, with spaghetti straps, a square neck, a form-fitting bodice that hugged every inch of her curves, and a deep slit up one side of the floor length skirt, revealing almost her entire left leg and the high silver heels she wore. A rented diamond necklace reflected the light as she moved, but even its reflection paled in comparison to the sparkle in her gorgeous green eyes.

The slit of her skirt went so high that it wouldn't take much of a move in the wrong direction to reveal that she had nothing on beneath it. She held her winter coat over her arm to make sure none of the effect of the dress was lost on the waiting cameras.

"I think this might be a little too much," she whispered as she came up to kiss my cheek in greeting, her eyes shining with good humour, and my chest filled with warmth at the idea that my actions had caused that spark of happiness.

"Nothing is too much on you," I assured her, the words coming out almost as a growl. If we didn't have the paparazzi waiting for us, I would have been tempted to forget the rest of the evening and take her straight upstairs right there and then.

However, not only were the press and dinner waiting for us, we also had the house we were meant to visit, which would count as my payment for the evening. If we skipped that, we would just be spending the night together for no reason, and that went against my rules. Therefore, we still had to go out, whether I wanted to or not.

"Shall we?" I offered my arm to Gemma and she took it before we walked together out the automatic doors of the hotel lobby.

The group of photographers exceeded the number who had been there the night before, ranging somewhere between five and ten. Though I didn't smile, I also didn't look away, and I kept Gemma's arm linked tightly through mine as we walked slowly enough to the waiting car that everyone could get at least a few shots.

Gemma laughed once I had closed the car door behind us. "Remind me never to become really famous. This is crazy."

"You haven't done many red carpet events, then?"

She gave me a curious look. "No, not at all. Have you?"

"A few." Though I didn't particularly enjoy it, networking for the business sometimes meant attending those kinds of gala events.

She asked me about the famous people I'd met, and we chatted easily until the car pulled up outside the Michelin-starred restaurant in east London that I'd booked for us. As expected, more photographers greeted us there and we repeated the whole charade of pretending that we didn't see them while allowing them to take their photos.

Wanting to ensure that people would see us enjoying ourselves, I'd booked a semi-private booth at the back of the restaurant, positioned so that our heads could still be seen over the back of the booth as we talked and laughed together.

I thought I had thought of everything, but as I looked across the table at Gemma, I realized I had missed one important consideration. How in the world was I going to sit there, just out of arm's reach of her for the entire meal with her looking like that, and not do something about it?

~Gemma~

I couldn't figure out why I didn't feel more nervous. Sitting alone at the table with Cole in a high end restaurant, wearing the beautiful dress and jewellery he'd chosen for me, it felt almost like a date, and I hadn't been on one of those, a *proper* date, in a very, very long time.

Not only that, but people were watching us: the cameras outside and the other people in the restaurant. If I turned my head, I would catch them looking at us. It would have made sense to be nervous, but when I tried to analyze the feelings buzzing around inside me, that one didn't seem to figure into it.

Excited? Yes. Turned on? More than a little. But nervous? No. Not at all.

Maybe it came down to the fact that, despite appearances, we weren't on a real date. There was no uncertainty. We both knew that the night would end in his room and that, unless we mutually agreed to extend the agreement, nothing further would happen past this evening.

The stakes were relatively low, and yet, Cole seemed to be uncomfortable. His fidgeting was the reason I wondered if I should be feeling more nervous in the first place, and I didn't understand the reason for it until after we ordered our drinks and decided on the tasting menu. At that point, Cole placed his wine glass down and looked over at me, his eyes full of that heat that did crazy things to my body.

"I'm having a bit of a dilemma over here, Gemma."

'Over here'? The phrasing made me laugh, since he made it sound like there were miles between us instead of just the width of the table.

"What's the problem?"

"The thought of what's under that dress is driving me a little crazy." He raised an eyebrow as his lips twitched. "Or rather, the thought of what's not under it."

Immediately, my thighs clenched together at the reminder. He had told me not to wear any underwear tonight and I hadn't. I assumed he did it to build the anticipation for later, but with the way he looked at me now, I began to suspect he had something else in mind.

"I know this dinner isn't technically part of our deal, but ... would you let me sit a little closer?"

The fact that he asked for permission told me everything I needed to know. Without him explaining, I understood that if I granted it, if I said yes to him moving closer, I would be giving him control over the situation. I would be giving him carte blanche to do whatever he wanted. On the other hand, if I said no, he would stay where he was. The power to make that decision rested entirely in my hands.

As I contemplated my options, I couldn't help imagining what he might do. What did he usually do with the escorts he took out, women like Vanessa who had been with him just a few nights ago? Had they been doing anything beneath the table when we were all sitting together? I hadn't noticed, but that didn't necessarily mean they hadn't. After all, if he did something to me now, would anybody else know? The long tablecloth would shield us from view.

Anything of that nature would be new territory for me. Edwin and I had certainly never done anything intimate in public. That would have implied that we couldn't keep our hands off each other long enough to wait to be in private, which definitely had not been the case.

Cole's question, however, implied exactly that: he couldn't wait. He wanted to touch me right then and there, and fuck it, I wanted that too.

"You can sit wherever you like, Mr Stamer."

Cole's eyes darkened as I called him by his professional name. After the previous night, we were both completely clear on what that meant: me giving up control to him, just like we both wanted.

In a matter of seconds, he slid around the booth to my side of the table, sitting right beside me with his hand upon my knee, the bare one exposed by the slit of my dress. My legs were crossed, partly to try to control my arousal, and I kept them that way. He would tell me if he wanted me to do something else. Rather than feeling oppressed by him taking control, it actually felt rather freeing to realize I didn't have to make any decisions about what came next. He would make the choices for both of us; all I had to do was obey.

Though I expected Cole to make a move immediately, he didn't. We sat that way for a while, his hand on my knee, his fingers tracing light circles as we talked about other things and drank our wine. He told me about his expansion plans for his hotel chain in Europe and some of the other projects he might want to get Holly and I involved in once we'd finished the London hotel design, while I told him about some of the other offers we had received since the Mayfair Mews event.

Incrementally slowly, his hand began to move higher up my leg. Each time it did, it sent an electric shock straight to my core, the anticipation just as good as the sensation. Part of me wanted to urge him to go faster, but a bigger part liked being at his mercy. He would get to it when he got to it; I could do nothing but wait.

"Have you heard anything from your lawyers yet about our contract?" Cole's professional tone of voice contrasted completely with the roughness of his fingers that inched closer to my hips.

"No, but they've promised to get back to me by Friday."

I suppressed a gasp as Cole slid his whole hand between my legs and began to spread his fingers. Instantly, I understood the silent direction: he wanted my legs open. Trying to make the movement look natural to anyone who might be watching, I uncrossed my legs and spread them, the air feeling cool against my bare skin.

A moment later, the waiter came to bring the first of the seven courses of our tasting menu. He explained what the dish consisted of, some kind of fish, but I had trouble concentrating on anything other than the feel of Cole's fingers brushing gently against my folds.

"Sounds interesting," Cole said after the waiter had left. "Let's try it."

He picked up his fork with his left hand as if it were natural for him and not because his right hand was otherwise occupied. Following his lead, I also cut off a piece of the fish, but as soon as the fork hit my lips, Cole's finger brushed my clit. My mouth immediately clamped down on the fork as I tried not to outwardly react, and Cole also pretended nothing had happened, though I could have sworn the corners of his lips twitched again.

We finished that dish, still talking about work, and when someone came to collect the empty dishes, Cole's finger made contact with me again. This time I did a better job of hiding my reaction, which seemed to please him. As the second dish was brought out, the waiter set my plate down in front of me at the same time that Cole's finger slid into me.

"Th- thank you," I managed to stutter, and the waiter gave me a slightly confused smile before leaving us alone.

Once again, Cole ate with his left hand while his finger swirled inside me, brushing once or twice against my sensitive g-spot and causing my body to flinch involuntarily each time. Though neither of us acknowledged it, he paid careful attention to my body's reactions, dialling back when I squirmed too much and pushing the edge if I started to look too comfortable. The third course added a second finger, and with the fourth, his thumb began working my clit as his fingers moved slowly in and out of me.

My ability to speak coherently began to disappear. Cole continued the conversation on his own as if nothing was happening, speaking genially with the wait staff and with me, while I simply tried not to look as if I was falling apart. My cheeks must have been flushed, but no one seemed to notice. Everyone else carried on as if I weren't being fucked right in front of them.

By the time the waiter set the fifth course in front of me, I could barely think. When I tried to pick up my fork, it fell limply from my hand.

Finally, Cole took pity on me. "This looks like the main course, Gemma. Are you ready for it?"

I could only nod. My body ached, desperate for release, so when he finally increased his pace, his fingers moving in and out forcefully with his thumb pressing down on me, it didn't take me long to reach the edge, agonizingly close to going over.

"Don't make a sound." Cole's voice rumbled deep in my ear as he leaned over to whisper to me. "Come just for me, Gemma."

Biting my lip as hard as I could, I followed his command. Waves of pleasure washed over me and my vision blurred, but somehow, I stayed upright and kept quiet. Not a single person in the entire restaurant seemed to notice a thing.

"Perfect." He continued to whisper, his words meant just for me. "You're fucking perfect. Now, finish your meal."

I let out a shaky laugh as Cole withdrew his fingers, finally letting me focus on my meal. I thought he might move away now that he'd finished, but he didn't. He stayed right beside me, his hand on my knee again while we finished the rest of the meal, with him still eating with his left hand, as if nothing out of the ordinary had happened.

As if he hadn't just turned my whole world upside down once again.

Somehow, he made me feel like a completely different person, and I loved every second of it. The person he saw me as was the person I wanted to be: sexy, confident, comfortable with herself and unconcerned with what anyone else thought.

How could I ever go back to my old life once he'd truly finished with me?

~Cole~

Gemma coming on my hand at the table, trying not to let anyone know, might just have been the single sexiest thing I had ever seen and it left me uncomfortably hard for most of the meal. By the time we'd finished eating and I went to the washroom to clean up, I'd at least managed to think enough unsexy thoughts that I could walk without drawing attention to myself. Even so, I couldn't wait to see what else I could do to her once we got back to the hotel.

I thought my anticipation couldn't get any higher than it had been the night before in the park, but now that I'd actually had her and knew what I had to look forward to, I wanted her even more.

First, however, we still had to fulfill my side of our arrangement.

"What exactly is this place we're visiting?" I asked when I sat back down at the table, flashing my black card at the waiter to let him know we were finished.

Gemma's eyes sparkled as she laughed. "You waited until now to ask me? What if I'm taking you to a house full of clowns?"

I couldn't help smiling back at her, feeling rather pleased that she remembered our earlier conversation about my aversion to clowns. "I trust you a little more than that, Gemma."

The words surprised me as they came out of my mouth, not because they weren't true, but because they were. I did trust her, at least enough that I hadn't even looked up the place that we were going. For me, that was very unusual. Who else would I trust enough to let them take me somewhere without doing any research first? I couldn't think of many others.

"It's called Dennis Severs' House," she explained. "It's a Georgian house here in the east end of the city, bought by an American man about forty years ago. He refurbished it in a way that the whole house tells a story, through a few different time periods. You walk through it in complete silence and there are sounds and smells all the way through to make it seem as if you've walked in just as the people who live there left the room. The whole house is meant to feel alive, not like a museum at all, and at this time of year, they do a special Christmas installation, all by candlelight."

That actually sounded quite interesting and I could see how it appealed to Gemma as a designer. "We can't speak at all?"

She shook her head. "No, they're quite strict about it. I've been to the house several times, but never at Christmas. And tonight, we actually have a private booking. We'll be the only ones there, other than the staff."

I hadn't really thought about why she would already have tickets to this and be in need of a companion, but when she mentioned a private booking, it clicked into place in my head. "You were supposed to be going with Edwin."

"Yes. Last night was meant to be with him too. This whole month, really; we booked things almost every day in the lead-up to our wedding, maybe just to distract ourselves from what lay ahead."

"And you were going to go on your own, before you asked me?" It surprised me that she still wanted to go.

"Yes," she repeated. "I'd been looking forward to some of these things more than the wedding itself, to be honest, and I don't want to let him stop me from doing them. Still, I'm glad to have some company."

I respected the hell out of her for going ahead with her plans anyway, and I felt equally glad that she didn't have to go alone. It seemed our meeting had been lucky in more ways than one.

Once I'd paid the bill, we left the restaurant in the car I called for us. The drive over to the house only took a few minutes, and a woman in 18th-century dress stood outside when we arrived, standing between two Christmas trees and holding a lantern. Her eyes widened at the sight of our rather formal evening attire as we stepped out of the car, and I couldn't blame her. Gemma looked truly stunning. After greeting us, she took a few minutes to explain how the tour would work. As Gemma had already told me, someone would accompany us from room to room but we were expected to remain silent in order to absorb the atmosphere that had been created.

The tour started in the cellar of the house, down a cramped staircase where I had to duck my head to keep from hitting it on the ceiling. From there, we moved into the warmth of the kitchen where the enticing smell of gingerbread filled the air, and a wave of nostalgia hit me: memories of Christmas time with my grandparents in upstate New York, baking gingerbread men and the feeling of belonging that came with it. The potency of the connection caught me completely off guard. I hadn't thought about that memory in years, and definitely not since I had started avoiding Christmas things in general.

That must be the whole point of the place: evoking memories and feelings through the sights, sounds and smells that both rooted us in the moment and pulled us into the past. Since we couldn't speak, we had only our own thoughts for company, giving them even more power over us.

My eyes wandered to Gemma as we entered the third room, the dining room, wondering what thoughts were going through her head. What did the room make her feel? Being unable to ask her about it only made me more curious.

For my part, the sight of the table made me flash back to the table at the restaurant where we had just shared our meal. Specifically, I thought about the way she came for me there, silently, just as silent as we had to be on the tour. Had the fact that she needed to be silent affected her the same way it affected me at that moment? Did it heighten her other senses, making everything feel more intense?

As much as I tried to pay attention to the rest of the tour, I couldn't stop my mind wandering to the different ways we could test out my theory and all the different things I could try on her. By the time the tour finished, my anticipation had reached a new high.

"You did very well," Gemma teased me as we settled back into the car that would take us back to the hotel. "I didn't know if you'd be able to follow someone else's rules."

"I do prefer setting the rules," I admitted, placing my hand on her knee. "But actually, I really enjoyed the house. The whole experience was unusual, and rather inspiring."

"Inspiring?" She seemed surprised at my choice of words. "What kind of inspiration did it give you?"

A wide smile broke out across my face. She couldn't have phrased it any better. "You'll see."

Only one photographer waited for us at the hotel, presumably someone who had missed our earlier appearance. Already, their interest had started to wane now that they had their photos, just as I'd predicted. I took Gemma's hand as we stepped out of the car and held it all the way until we got to the door of my suite, looking calm and controlled on the outside even as my heart raced with excitement and expectation.

As soon as we were inside, I pulled her to me, claiming her mouth in a deep, passionate kiss. I'd been wanting to do that ever since I had laid eyes on her in the lobby, what felt like a million hours ago, but I waited until now, until I knew that we wouldn't have to stop. Because now that we'd begun, I didn't know if I would even be capable of stopping.

The desire to possess her, to have her submitting to me and putting herself entirely in my hands and knowing that she would, couldn't have been a more powerful turn-on.

That night, I owned her, and damn it, I was going to make it count.

~Gemma~

Cole's kiss overwhelmed me. I lost all sense of time and place and direction as his mouth moved against mine, hungrily and possessively. It felt like he wanted to devour me entirely, and I wanted to let it happen. I wanted to give him everything I had.

When he finally pulled away, we were both struggling for breath. He leaned his forehead against mine for just a moment, a gesture that somehow seemed more intimate than everything that had come before, but when he pulled back further, his eyes had taken on that hard, controlling edge that thrilled me so much.

"The bedroom, Gemma. Go."

I didn't hesitate, turning on my heel and making my way to the room where he had taken me so hard the night before. Was that really only twenty-four hours earlier? It felt like so much had changed since then. Cole knew so much more about me than he had, and yet, he wanted me just the same. I could hardly believe it.

When I reached the centre of the room, I turned back to the door, watching Cole enter. He moved with the grace of a jungle cat stalking its prey, his eyes fixed on me.

"Turn around."

I did, and he quickly pulled down the zip of my dress, letting it fall to my feet. As he'd requested, there was nothing at all underneath, leaving me standing there in my high heels and jewellery and nothing else.

"Sit down on the bed."

I could feel his eyes on me as I walked over to the bed. Turning around, I sat down on the edge of it and crossed my legs, flexing my feet to show off the heels while my hand went to the expensive diamond necklace against my collarbone. Highlighting the few things I still wore only made it more obvious that there was nothing else there.

One side of Cole's mouth raised in a satisfied smirk as his eyes raked over me, head to toe. A trail of fire seemed to follow behind them, everywhere his gaze touched. My whole body burned for him.

Methodically, he removed his suit jacket, his shoes and socks before yanking his tie loose and pulling it off. However, instead of putting it down, he stretched the tie out between his hands as a devilish gleam flashed in his eyes.

"Isn't it interesting, Gemma, how when someone tells you not to do something, it's the only thing you can think of? When we couldn't speak at the house, suddenly, I had a million things I wanted to say to you."

I knew exactly what he meant. It had taken all my willpower not to speak to him either, not to point things out to him or ask what he thought about them.

"Not only that, it made everything else seem sharper. The sounds, the smells, the sights; everything felt more intense because I couldn't comment on them."

It truly pleased me that he had got so much out of the experience, and once again, I felt just the same. With nothing else to distract me, I had been even more aware of his body than usual, the heat and the look and the smell of him.

"It made me wonder: if I took away some of your senses now, how much more intense would the experience be for you?"

He pulled the tie tight between his hands, the fabric taut and hard, and my eyes widened as I started to understand what he meant. I still didn't know *exactly* what he had in mind, but God, I wanted to find out. My heart pounded in my chest and wetness pooled between my legs as if he'd found some kind of secret 'on' switch.

"Yes, please." Although the words came out of my mouth, I was barely aware of saying them. I needed him to know that I wanted it too; how I did that made no difference to me.

Cole's gaze grew even more heated with my agreement. "Good. Open your mouth."

I did as he asked without question and he quickly crossed the room, placing the tie in my mouth like a gag and tying it behind my head.

"Is that okay?" Although his tone was still dominant, I could also hear genuine concern in it. The two things should have been at odds with each other, but I was beginning to see how it all formed part of the same package. He wanted to control my pleasure, but to do that, it needed to be pleasurable for me. He wouldn't hurt me; that wasn't what this was about.

In response to his question, I nodded my head, which was all I could do since he'd taken away my ability to speak.

Cole walked to his closet and opened it, pulling out another tie from what I assumed must be an almost unlimited supply. He didn't seem to want for anything.

"Hands."

At his command, I stretched my arms forward, holding my hands next to each other, and he tied my wrists together, the silk soft against my skin despite the strength of the knot.

Another quick trip to the closet and he returned with another tie. "Close your eyes."

Yet again, I did as he said, and the world around me went dark as he wrapped the fabric across my eyes, knotting it tightly behind my head, just above the one that covered my mouth.

"Now, shuffle back to the middle of the bed, and lie down."

Cole's disembodied voice sounded even deeper than it did when I could see his mouth moving. His hands guided me into the position he wanted since I could no longer see to get my bearings, and when I was on my back, he raised my hands up over my head.

"I won't tie them down, but you need to keep them up there. Do you understand?"

I nodded again, swallowing against the fabric holding my tongue down.

"Good. Now spread your legs for me, Gorgeous."

As he requested, I pulled my knees up, placed my shoes flat on the bed, and spread my legs apart as far as I could. In that position, I felt completely exposed and vulnerable, and yet completely safe at the same time. Whatever this incredible man wanted to do to me, I knew it would be no more than what I wanted him to do. I trusted him completely.

Left with only my ears to guide me, I could hear the rustle of fabric and the sound of a zip that I could only assume came from Cole's trousers. He must be removing the rest of his own clothes, but I couldn't see a thing. My skin tingled in anticipation of his touch as my pulse raced, but where would he touch me first? I had no idea.

The bed dipped down beside me, alerting me that he had joined me, and the throbbing between my legs grew even stronger. Goosebumps formed all down my arms and legs and my nipples tightened all on their own. Every inch of me was ready for him.

Something brushed against my breast, and my whole body jolted in response. Cole chuckled, clearly amused by the reaction. His laugh came from the lower end of the bed, suggesting that his head must be down there, but I had no idea what part of him had touched me, or if it had even been him at all. Maybe he had used something else; I couldn't even guess. I could only let myself feel it.

Another touch came, this time on my knee. Then my stomach, and then my inner thigh. There was never any warning, and no pattern I could work out. Suddenly, I felt a long, slow stroke between my legs, over my lower lips, that must have been his tongue. I moaned against the tie in my mouth, pushing my bound hands down into the mattress above me to keep from lifting them.

More points of contact followed, fingers and lips, I guessed, all over my body, and then a warm, firm touch against my clit that I thought had to be his tongue again. I was so primed for him, so sensitive, that my hips bucked up against him as he lazily circled the sensitive spot.

"Don't move." His voice was deep, throaty and compelling, and definitely coming from between my legs now. With his forearms against my thighs, pushing my legs even further apart, he held my hips down with his hands before his mouth was on me again. His tongue tasted and teased me like a cat lapping up cream before plunging deeper, pushing in as far as it could go.

I did my best to hold still, but I couldn't stop the guttural moans that came out of me, obscured by the cloth in my mouth. Just as he'd promised, the feeling was intense with every part of me focused entirely on the sensations his actions created. He didn't let up, his tongue working me over, alternating between deep thrusts and agonizingly light brushes over my clit. Just when I thought I couldn't stand anymore, he finally clamped down, sucking the tender nub forcefully into his mouth, and I came hard, my legs and my arms trembling as my muffled cries filled the room.

Stars filled the darkness before me, slowly fading as I floated back down from my incredible high.

"That tasted better than anything we had at the restaurant." Cole's voice pierced the fog of my consciousness, sounding even farther away than before. "They should put you on the menu, Gorgeous."

Those dirty words conjured an image in my mind, a fantasy I'd never imagined before, where I could see myself at the restaurant, naked like I was now, laid out on the table. Cole hovered between my legs, eating me out while the waiter and the other diners all watched us.

Oh, fuck. My body convulsed again, pleasure rushing through me in an incredible release, followed by the icy shock of disbelief.

Seriously? Did I really just come again simply from his words? I hadn't even known that was a possibility.

How could he do this to me? It felt like there must be a secret owner's manual to my body, one I never even knew existed, and somehow, Cole had read it cover to cover. He was the authority on it. My body belonged to him, completely, and I didn't want him to ever give it back.

~Cole~

A surge of satisfaction flowed through me as Gemma came again. She looked unbelievably gorgeous, restrained and laid out in front of me, completely at my mercy. I loved how she reacted to me and the fact that I could make her come undone with just my words only heightened my own pleasure. This feeling of control over her was definitely an aphrodisiac for me, stronger than I had ever realized it could be. She needed me, and I needed her to need me. Here in my room, we complimented each other perfectly.

I wanted her so fucking badly.

Pushing myself to my feet, I headed back to my closet and grabbed two more ties. Luckily, I had no shortage of ties, though I had never used them in quite this way before. Once I had them in my hands, I surveyed the room, trying to figure out what would work for what I had in mind. The headboard had nothing I could tie anything to, but there was a wall lamp above the bed, so I walked over and gave it a hard tug. It didn't wobble, so hopefully, it should be strong enough.

Gemma's breathing had started to even out but she hadn't moved from where I left her, her continued compliance telling me silently that she could still take more, and I instructed her to move over until she was directly beneath the lamp. With one of the ties, I secured her ankles together, and lifting her legs, I looped the second tie around the restraints holding both her ankles and her wrists, and tied them both to the wall lamp. Still on her back, I'd essentially folded her in half with her legs up over her head and her beautiful pussy on perfect display in front of me.

When everything had been tied in place, I took a step back to assess her positioning, making sure nothing looked painful. Despite the bondage, I wanted to make sure she was comfortable. The last thing I wanted would be to hurt her in any way.

"Can you breathe alright?"

She nodded, her teeth still clenching down onto the tie I had worn tonight, the first one I had put on her.

With her confirmation, I grabbed a condom from the drawer and rolled it on, wincing at how tight it felt. Fuck, I was so hard already, I would have to take this slow if I didn't want it to be over before it really began.

Climbing back onto the bed on my knees, I lined myself up against her entrance and pushed in slowly, inch by inch, watching with satisfaction as my dick disappeared into her dripping hole. Gemma made a low, guttural sound that I knew without a doubt meant pleasure, and it sent another pulse of electricity through me to know that she was enjoying this just as much as I was. When I was fully buried in her, I paused, running my fingertips down the back of her legs that were being held up in front of me, and once again, she shivered in response. The heightened sensations from her blindfold were clearly working for her.

Taking my time, mostly to keep from coming too fast, I pulled out and slowly pushed myself back in, letting myself feel every inch of her on my dick. My fingers ran down her sides, brushing the sides of her breasts and the curve of her waist, and she moaned again, squirming beneath my touch.

"Gemma." My voice was a warning, and she responded to it immediately as she stopped moving. I wanted her immobile, feeling only what I gave her to feel. The more restrained she felt, the more intense it would be.

I continued on that way as long as I could bear it, thrusting slowly and deeply, with light, almost tickling touches down the rest of her body in between. Finally, I couldn't take it any longer; I needed my release too.

My blood pumping through my body in anticipation, I pulled out at the same pace I had been using, before, without warning, I slammed into her hard. Gemma's head tilted backward, another muted sound escaping from beneath her gag. A couple of more times I did it, the slow withdrawal and the quick taking, trying to control it until my control broke. Then, I just took her hard, leaning onto her body, supporting myself on her as she took me in over and over again, her body welcoming me, enveloping me in her warmth and wetness until the world exploded.

My whole body surrendered to the most exquisite release as we both came, her clamping down on me as I pumped within her, our bodies pulsing together in nearly perfect sync.

Fuck, that was amazing. How did it keep getting better, everything I did with her?

When my vision cleared, I pulled out of her, got rid of the condom, and quickly set about removing all Gemma's restraints. I left the blindfold till last, covering her eyes with my hand as I removed it in case the room lights were too bright after her temporary blindness. She blinked tentatively at me and gave me a soft, satisfied smile that sent a rush of pleasure through me.

I had never seen anything more beautiful. It almost felt like I could live off that smile.

Honestly, what was going on in my head? It had been a long time since I'd thought anything like that, and shaking my head at my own foolishness, I gave both of Gemma's eyelids a gentle kiss. "Wait here. I'm just going to grab a few things."

Throwing all the ties in a pile on the floor, I went to the bathroom and got the lotion that the hotel had provided as well as a bottle of water from the mini-fridge in the kitchen. I offered Gemma the water first, helping her sit up to drink it, then I laid her back down and used the lotion to rub everywhere that she had been restrained. The skin on her wrists and around her mouth looked a little red, but not too bad; nothing that shouldn't fade before the morning.

"What else do you need?" I asked her when I had finished.

Gemma shook her head, her eyes full of warmth as she watched me. "Nothing. I feel great. I'll just rest a bit, if that's okay."

"Of course. Take as long as you like."

I lay down beside her, still feeling completely content until a new thought occurred to me and I turned to look at her.

"You would tell me if I pushed you too far, wouldn't you?" I just realized that we had never really discussed how far we would take this and if she had any limits. Perhaps I should have asked her earlier, but it had all just kind of happened naturally. I hadn't preplanned any of this, and I'd never done anything quite like it before so I didn't have any experience to draw on.

Gemma rolled over onto her side to face me. "Of course. You haven't, so far."

I noted the 'so far'. "Maybe we need a safe word or something?"

Amusement sparked in her eyes, giving them that twinkle that I found so damn sexy. "I've never chosen one before. What do you think of 'finial'?"

The word was so unlikely that I couldn't help smiling. "Are you just choosing a random architecture term, or do you find finials unsexy?"

"Hmm, good point. Finials can actually be very sexy. That might not make me want to stop." She pursed her lips as she thought it over. "Maybe 'cantilever'?"

I couldn't help putting my arms around her and pulling her to me. Her sense of humour and her intelligence made her even more sexy to me. "Whatever you want, Gemma."

We were silent for a moment as she lay with her head against my chest, neither of us speaking until she raised her head to look at me curiously. "A safe word would only be necessary if we were doing this again, wouldn't it?"

She had a point there. What exactly was I suggesting? I didn't know, other than that the idea of not having her in my bed again was even more unthinkable now than it had been the night before. I felt like there were still a million different things I wanted to try with her. To do *to* her. To have her do for me.

I decided to be as honest as I could be. "I want to do this again but I still need to have some kind of parameters on it."

When she didn't say anything in reply, I hoped I hadn't offended her and I tried to clarify my statement.

"It's got nothing to do with you personally, Gemma. I'm just not comfortable with something that's undefined."

"What parameters are you suggesting, then?" Thankfully, she sounded merely curious rather than upset.

"Well, I'm only in town for ten more days. Jackson and I go back to New York next Friday."

Gemma nodded slowly. "Okay. So, what's your plan?"

"Why don't we extend our deal to cover that period? I'll give you my schedule and you can fill in any events that you want for when I'm available. Afterwards, you can spend the nights here with me. The whole night, I mean. You can bring your clothes and whatever you need from home. It's close to your office, so it shouldn't be inconvenient for you."

I felt like I was rambling, the words coming out of my mouth before I'd even thought them through, and I had no idea what she would think of my offer. Was it too much? More than she'd been looking for?

To my relief, however, she smiled. "I can agree to that, on one condition."

"What's the condition?" Though I would agree to pretty much anything at that point, I'd been in business too long to not at least ask the question first.

She propped herself up fully onto her elbows, so she could look directly into my eyes. "You have to answer a question for me."

That seemed too easy, so I tried to figure out what the catch was. "What's the question?"

"Why do we have to have a deal? I understand that you do, but I want to understand why. I don't need anything from you, Cole, so why do you need to give me something?"

Chapter Nine

Ten Million

~Gemma~

I hadn't planned in advance to ask Cole to explain himself, but my curiosity got the better of me. Obviously, it mattered to him that he didn't 'owe' me anything, but on the flip side, I had never asked him for anything. Why did he automatically assume that I eventually would? There had to be something behind it, something that had happened to him to make him so insistent on this. Now that he knew nearly everything about me, it only seemed fair that I had some understanding of the things that drove him.

He sat up once I'd asked the question, rubbing his face with his hands, so I sat too, placing my hand gently on his back.

"What difference does it make?" His voice sounded quiet and almost uncertain, not at all like his usual confident self.

"It matters to me because it matters to you. I'd just like to know why. Whatever you say, whatever the reason is, it won't change the fact that I want to do this. You know so much about me; I just want to know you a little bit too."

He turned to face me with a hesitancy in his eyes that I had never seen there before. "I can understand that but I don't often talk about my personal life. With anyone, I mean."

"What are you afraid of?" I asked gently, trying to find the root of his misgivings. "That I would judge you for it? I'm not really in any position to pass judgement, given my own situation."

A smile tugged at his lips and he inclined his head in agreement. "That's true, I suppose."

"And if you're worried I would tell anyone else, I promise you, that's the last thing I would do. I know better than most what it's like to have strangers speculating about your personal business, and I wouldn't wish that on my worst enemy. For all your flaws, Cole, you're hardly my worst enemy."

The fire sparked in his eyes again, taking up my challenge. "You haven't even given me a chance yet. You don't know exactly what kind of enemy I could be."

That was more like it, and I grinned in response. "If you're as good an enemy as you are a lover, then I definitely want to stay on your good side."

He smiled back at me, temporarily diverted, but a moment later, he sighed, his head dropping. "Hardly anyone knows this story, Gemma. I don't want you to think less of me when you hear it."

The idea that he would even think that sent a wave of tenderness rushing through me. Without thinking, I reached out to take his hand, holding it within both of mine.

"Cole, you have no idea how much it means to me that you didn't treat me any differently today than you did yesterday. In the last few months, there's been hardly anyone who did that. I've had people coddle me, patronize me, give me loads of unwanted advice, or just stop talking to me altogether. You acted just the same from one day to the next, and it honestly means the world to me. I promise you that I'll give you the same courtesy."

As he nodded, it felt like I was getting through to him, so I decided to tease him as a final push. He seemed to like my teasing, when the timing was right.

"I mean, unless you took over a small country somewhere. Or turned a bunch of Dalmatians into coats. Or you're responsible for my favourite takeaway restaurant closing down."

"Those are the first things you think of?" Amusement pulled at his lips, just as I hoped. I much preferred that to his uncertainty.

I winked at him, doing my best to ease his discomfort. "Those are just off the top of my head. Unless you really want me to keep guessing, you might as well just tell me."

His hand still rested on mine, and he wrapped his fingers around me, taking control again. It felt comforting and familiar in a way that didn't quite make sense given how short a time I'd known him.

"Actually, in some ways, it's not so different from your story." He looked down at our joined hands as he spoke rather than at my face. "Without the reality TV show part, at least."

I tried to guess what he meant. "You were stuck in a passionless engagement arranged at birth too?"

I got just a flash of his heart-stopping smile. "Okay, maybe not *that* similar, but I was engaged, yes. To the wrong person, just like you were."

That did surprise me. I had no idea he'd been engaged and a dozen questions rushed into my head. Had he actually been in love? How long were they engaged for? What happened? It took a moment to settle on which question to ask first. "When was this?"

"Four years ago. We were together for a year before we got engaged, but the engagement only lasted three weeks."

That certainly contrasted with my own six-year engagement, and I tried to imagine the worst case scenario. Maybe if I suggested something awful, whatever he told me wouldn't sound so bad in comparison. "Did something happen to her? Some kind of accident?"

As I hoped, he quickly shook his head. "No, nothing like that. She's still alive, as far as I know, but I haven't exactly kept tabs on her. I haven't seen her since she left."

So, she left; that answered a few questions, but created many more. "Why did she leave?"

He raised his eyes to meet mine and in their dark depths, I could see both anger and a hint of sadness. "The better question is why she was ever there. I thought we met by chance, that our love story grew naturally, just like any other, but it didn't. She played me from the very beginning."

One word stood out amongst everything he had just said. "You were in love with her?"

His lips curled again, but this time in self-deprecation. "Hard to believe, right? But yes: I was completely, utterly, stupidly in love."

I squeezed his hand a little tighter. "So, what happened?"

"It's a long story, but the short version is that a few months after we met, she convinced me to hire her brother as my personal assistant. That meant he had access to a lot of my personal information."

An uneasy feeling settled in my stomach as I began to see where this might be heading.

"Once we got engaged, I set her up with her own account to handle the wedding plans, setting up our new house, and so on, and I linked the account to one of mine. That's when they worked together to transfer money from my accounts into hers."

He stopped there, as if he'd said enough, but I still wanted to know more. When he didn't continue on his own, I prompted him again. "How much did she take?"

The amount made no real difference, but I thought it might help him to focus on the specifics.

"Nearly ten million dollars."

I hadn't expected it to be quite that much, and I exhaled loudly at the revelation. "Fuck."

Although he smiled again, there was no humour in it. "At first I couldn't understand it. I mean, that amount... it's not nothing, but it's not like it would break me. If she needed the money, why not just ask me for it? Why would she take ten million when, if she married me, she would have access to so much more?"

"Those are good questions." Clearly, they weren't just rhetorical. "What's the answer?"

"It turned out she'd actually been in a relationship with someone else the whole time we were together. Once I set some private investigators on her, it didn't take long for it to come to light. She only ever got involved with me to get to my money. From the very beginning, that had been her plan. She never actually cared for me at all, so once she got what she came for, she ran off with him. They left together and I never saw her again."

As his head dropped again, I couldn't help wrapping my arms around him, trying to pull out some of the hurt that he obviously still felt about it. It might have been years ago, but the wound hadn't fully healed.

Cole didn't return my embrace, but he didn't stop me either. I rested my head on his shoulder as I thought over what he'd said. "So, if you never saw her again, does that mean you never pressed charges?"

He shook his head emphatically. "No, because it would have gone public. The damage to my reputation would have been far worse than the loss of the money. What would it say about me as a businessman if I couldn't even tell when I was being scammed?"

I remembered what he'd told me back at the park the day before, about how he could read people and how accurately he had described Holly to me. It must have been a terrible blow to realize he had been fooled to that extent. He could say that he let it go to protect his reputation as a businessman, but I suspected his personal pride played just as big a role.

He must be hell-bent on ensuring nothing like that ever happened again.

Things were finally starting to make sense to me.

"And that's why you insist on paying the women that you're with now? So no one gets the idea that they're entitled to anything more."

His nod confirmed that I'd understood correctly. "I thought I could tell if someone wanted to use me, but apparently, I have a blind spot I wasn't aware of. It's better this way. Things are clear and simple, everyone knows what they're getting up front, and there's nothing more to it than that."

And he wouldn't get hurt again, although he didn't mention that part. It did make a certain amount of sense, but there seemed to me to be one key flaw in his plan.

"It will be hard to ever fall in love again with all those restrictions."

"I don't intend to." Cole's answer was immediate and firm. "It's not worth it."

I could tell he'd convinced himself of that, and once again, I could see where he was coming from. In his position, I might feel the same.

"My life is full enough," he continued. "I have work, I have family, I have friends, and I have sex. Not necessarily in that order."

Just like that, his smirk returned, and I couldn't help smiling back at him.

"Has that answered your question, Gemma?"

It did, for the time being, but I'd been wondering about something else too, and since he was actually being open with me for once, it seemed like a good time to ask. "Can I ask one more question? On a different topic?"

He raised an eyebrow at me. "Are you changing the terms now?"

"No, this isn't related to our deal. It's just me being nosy."

He gave an exaggerated sigh, but I could tell he was only teasing. "You can always ask, but it doesn't mean I'll answer."

"You might not, but I'm still curious. I know you enjoyed the house tonight, and I think you had fun at the park last night too. So, what, exactly, do you have against Christmas?"

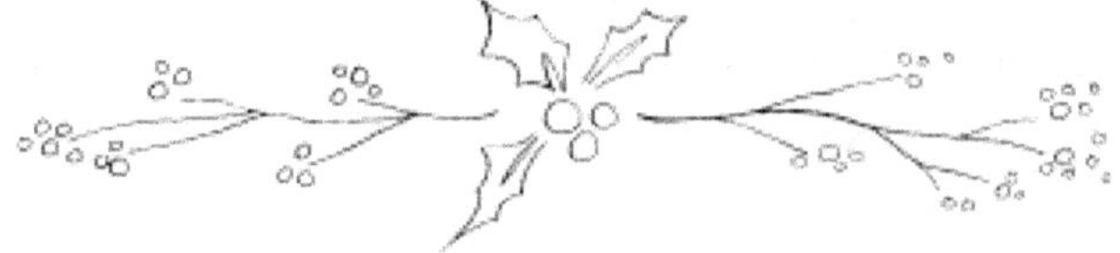

~Cole~

Gemma couldn't have any way of knowing that her question about Christmas was actually very closely related to what we had just been talking about. My dislike of Christmas had everything to do with my failed engagement, and since I had already told her the worst parts, I supposed it wouldn't do any harm to explain the Christmas connection.

Still, I couldn't resist turning the spotlight back on her first. "The real question is: why do you like Christmas so much?"

"I'll answer you if you answer me." Gemma's eyes were as warm and inviting as always, and I could hardly believe how comfortable it felt to talk to her. She made it easy to forget that ten minutes ago, I'd had her tied up and at my mercy, fucking her like there was no tomorrow. Although, when my gaze strayed down to her still-naked body, that was equally hard to forget too.

For the moment, I forced myself to focus back on her face as I answered her question bluntly. "Christmas reminds me of my ex-fiancée. I proposed at the beginning of December and she left me on Christmas Eve."

"On Christmas Eve?" Gemma repeated in horror, as if that detail were somehow worse than the fact that Samantha had robbed me blind.

My chest tightened at the memory. It had been a long time since I'd thought about that night on purpose, let alone told anyone about it. Only a handful of people in the world knew these details, but for some reason, the idea of telling Gemma about it didn't seem unbearable. As she pointed out, I'd already discovered her personal humiliation. She might as well know mine.

"I was really excited about that Christmas," I admitted. "I bought her a new car, one she'd mentioned a few times that she liked, and I planned this whole ridiculous scavenger hunt for her to find it. I even stayed up late, after she'd gone to sleep, to plant all the clues. I left the first one next to her toothbrush in our bathroom. She wasn't a morning person, so it didn't worry me that she might see it before I got up. Usually, I woke up hours before her."

The memory was still so fresh in my mind if I let myself remember: the soft moonlight through the window as I crept into bed beside Samantha, the light floral scent of her perfume as I kissed her goodnight. The last time I saw her.

"But when I woke up on Christmas morning, the bed was empty. I went to the bathroom to look for her, but she had gone and so had the clue. I guess she wasn't in so much of a hurry that she didn't have time to find the car and take it with her, along with all her other presents that were under the tree."

Gemma gasped, her face scrunched up in horrified disbelief. "She didn't even say anything? She just left?"

I simply nodded. There was nothing more to add.

"How long did it take you to figure out what happened?"

"Too long." I tried to laugh, but even I could hear how hollow it sounded. "At first, I thought someone had taken her and I nearly lost my mind. I tried phoning her but there was no answer. I called her brother, but of course, he didn't pick up either. My next call was going to be the police, but something made me call Jackson first. When I told him about the car and the presents being gone, and how there was no sign of anyone breaking in, he suggested I check my bank account before I involved the police. He saw the truth before I did."

"Oh Cole. That's awful." Gemma looked almost more upset about it than I felt, but I supposed I'd had longer to get used to the idea. "It's hard to believe that anyone could be that cruel."

"Ten million dollars can do that to you, I guess." I shrugged, trying not to show that it still affected me at all. "I have to bear at least part of the blame. I should have known something was off. She shouldn't have been able to blindside me so completely."

Gemma's head shook vigorously, her red hair swishing back and forth over her shoulders. "No way. Don't do that. It's not your fault. You put your trust in someone who abused it, and that is on her, completely. You can't blame yourself, Cole."

I disagreed. "I can, but don't worry: I still blame her more. In any case, she showed me that trust is overrated, and so is Christmas." With that summary, I cleared my throat, ready to change the subject. "Now, it's your turn. Why are you so obsessed with this holiday?"

I could tell that Gemma didn't completely support my conclusion, but the Christmas question made her smile softly anyway.

"It's always been my favourite time of year. When I was young, my brother and I would always spend the holiday with my grandparents, my mum's parents. My dad's family was aristocratic, of course, but not my mum's. She came from a tiny town in the Orkney islands, in the north of Scotland. Every year, we'd go up to Mainland just before Christmas, and for the only time all year, we got to be 'normal'. Up there, we weren't the Earl's kids. We were just Gemma and Tom."

I nodded in understanding. From my own childhood, I knew how important those moments were when no one cared about your status.

"The local families let us take part in all their activities, but never gave us any kind of special treatment," she continued. "I suppose it wasn't really anything special, but it seemed like something magical to me. And now, whenever I do something Christmasy, I remember what it felt like when nobody had any expectations of me just because of my name."

My mind returned to the memory that had come back to me earlier that evening of baking gingerbread at my grandparents' house, and surprisingly, I gave in to the urge to share it with her. "Actually, my childhood Christmases were very similar. We went to stay with my grandparents on their farm, far away from the city and all the hotels where the staff treated me like a little prince. My grandparents and I would bake things and go sledding and go for hay rides, and it felt special precisely because it was so normal."

Gemma smiled wider, her eyes taking on that special twinkle they got when she had something up her sleeve. "You know what I think, Cole?"

Her enthusiasm was so contagious, I couldn't help smiling back. "I think you're trouble, but no, I don't know what you're thinking."

She narrowed her eyes at me playfully. "I think you could be persuaded to like Christmas again. You had one bad Christmas... one *very* bad one, I'll grant you, but still only one. That doesn't mean it should ruin the day for the rest of your life. I'm going to make it my mission to save Christmas for you."

The ridiculousness of her 'mission' coupled with the complete earnestness in her voice made me snigger. It sounded impossible, but I had to admit she had me curious. "How do you plan to do that?"

"You said you'll let me fill your schedule, yes?"

I nodded in agreement.

"Well, I have so many things planned, that sometime over the next two weeks, I am going to find the activity that will make you fall in love with Christmas all over again." She looked completely delighted with herself, as if it would be as simple as that.

"You sound fairly certain that you'll succeed." I was far less convinced.

"I am," she replied with a grin. "In fact, why don't we make a wager on it?"

Now, she had my full attention. I could think of a few prizes I wouldn't mind claiming from her. "What kind of wager?"

She tapped her finger against her lips, a habit of hers when she thought about something carefully, I'd noticed. I found it rather endearing. "I bet you that before you leave for New York, I can convince you to wear a Santa hat with me. In public."

I actually laughed out loud. "I have no problem taking that bet. It's not happening. You are doomed to fail."

"We'll see." A sly smile graced her face. "And if I win, I get to ask one favour of you. No restrictions."

That definitely sounded like something worth playing for. "Only if the prize is the same for me if I win. *When* I win."

I offered her my hand and Gemma shook it firmly, pure determination in her eyes.

"You're on, Mr Stamer."

~Gemma~

Cole's eyes darkened once again as I called him 'Mr Stamer', but when he glanced over at the clock on the wall, he groaned. "It's late. We should get you home for tonight. While you're there, you can pack up everything you need for the next ten days and leave it at the front desk in the morning. I'll have it all brought up here for you."

He certainly didn't waste any time implementing his plans. "You're sure you want me around all the time? I understand that you have work commitments while you're here."

"As do you," he pointed out. "We'll ensure that none of our extra-curricular activities interfere with business for either of us. We're perfectly capable of keeping work and play separate."

I had to admit that Cole did a better job of compartmentalizing things than anyone I had ever met before. If anyone could make this deal of ours work, he could.

The only clothing I had with me that night was the red dress Cole had bought for me, so I slipped it back on with Cole's eyes following each movement. He walked back out to the living room of the suite with me, not bothering to put any clothing on himself, and kissed me goodbye at the door.

"I'll see you tomorrow, Gemma." The words were deep and full of promise, and I held onto them tightly as I walked back through the lobby and out into the street.

The next hours passed in a blur. Cole had called a car for me and added my name to his account so I could arrange for one to bring me back in the morning with all the luggage I needed. How exactly did one go about packing for a ten-day stay with a man who was practically a stranger? With work carrying on as usual, I needed my business clothes, but I also needed some more formal wear for some of the events I had planned, and casual things for the others. In the end, it felt like I packed half my wardrobe.

I sent a text to Holly, asking her to come into work early the next morning so I could fill her in. She knew that Cole had taken me out that evening and that there were almost certainly going to be photos of us in the papers in the morning, but I still hadn't explained to her about our deal, and now that we'd agreed to extend it until the end of the following week, I needed to tell her.

By the time I finally crawled into bed, I fell straight to sleep, where my dreams were filled with ribbons of silk, digging into my skin in delicious restraint.

When the car arrived to pick me up at six thirty the next morning, I took a last, quick look around my flat, trying to ensure I hadn't forgotten anything important. I could always come back and pick up anything I needed, and yet, I didn't want to waste a single minute of time that I could be with Cole instead. Our time together would fly by, so I planned to enjoy it while it lasted.

Once I had settled in the back of the car, I pulled up another search on my name to see the photos of me and Cole from the night before. There were a lot to choose from, but instead of the dread I usually felt at seeing my name in print, looking at these photos actually made me feel almost proud. I looked damn good, actually, and Cole did too. Together, we made a pretty attractive fake couple.

Feeling a bit more confident, I skimmed a couple of the articles. They mentioned my history with Edwin and Annabel, of course, but only after spending the first few paragraphs focused on Cole. According to one paper, the previous night had been the first time in several years that he had been seen taking a woman on a date that wasn't to a public event. That fit in completely with what he had told me; he probably hired women to go to events with him, like he had at the Mayfair Mews, but he wouldn't ever just go on a date for fun. Our dinner the night before must have been as unusual for him as it had been for me.

The car stopped outside the entrance to the Lytton and a bellhop hurried out to help me with my bags. When I explained to him that they were to be delivered to Cole's suite, he assured me they were already expecting me. I certainly couldn't complain that Cole didn't follow through on his promises.

With that all sorted, I made my way the few blocks over to our office, stopping to grab some porridge from Pret along the way. Holly already had the tea made, waiting for me in my office when I arrived.

"I saw the photos," she practically squealed as soon as I took my coat off and sat down. "You looked amazing. Edwin is going to be eating his heart out."

Whether Edwin would care or not, I couldn't say, but I knew who would. "I don't think this is the kind of publicity Annabel had in mind when she posted about us in the first place. She wasn't even mentioned until the fifth paragraph."

Holly grinned, rubbing her hands together like a film villain. "It serves her right. She was ready to drag you through the mud again just to keep herself in the news, and instead, they're talking about how you've captured the heart of Cole Stamer, 'untouchable American billionaire'. She must be having a fit."

"I've hardly captured his heart," I corrected her. "That's not what's going on."

She'd obviously been waiting for that opening, since she leaned forward across the table with an eager look on her face. "So, what *is* going on with you two?"

I told her the whole story. I told her what happened on Monday night, where we had gone the night before, and what the plan was for the next ten days. I didn't go into any specifics about exactly what we got up to in his room; that was definitely more than I felt comfortable sharing, especially since I still didn't fully understand my own actions yet, or my reactions to the things Cole had done. But I told her everything else: about our initial agreement, about the Christmas activities, and about me moving into his suite for the next ten days.

When I'd finished speaking, she leaned back in her chair and took a long sip of her tea. "Wow. And you're good with all this, right? It's what you want?"

"Fantastic sex and someone to do Christmas things with me?" I clarified. "I don't know. It's a real hardship, but I'll try to manage."

She rolled her eyes at my sarcasm and we both laughed. "Well, if you're happy, then I'm so happy for you, Gem. Enjoy the hell out of it, and if it pisses Annabel off in the process, even better."

She held up her tea cup as if making a toast, and I obligingly clinked mine against hers.

"Enough about me, though," I said as I finally dug into my porridge. Since I'd done most of the talking so far, I hadn't had a chance to eat yet. "Have you heard anything from Jackson? What are the odds that we'll both have a handsome American man in our beds before they go back?"

"Oh, I'm more than open to it," Holly assured me. "But despite his flirting, I think he's actually a bit of a romantic. I don't know if he's looking for something casual."

"Well, I've got a couple of other events that the two of you could join me and Cole for," I suggested. "If you want to spend more time with Jackson, that is. Including my father's Christmas party."

I hadn't specifically told Cole about that one yet. Every year, my father hosted an extravagant Christmas party at his London mansion for the upper crust of London society. Full-on black tie, ballgowns, dancing, the works, it would be taking place next Thursday evening, the night before Cole and Jackson were leaving to go back to New York.

"I thought you weren't going to the Earl's party this year," Holly reminded me, her eyes wide with surprise.

"I wasn't planning to, especially since Edwin and Annabel will be there, but I haven't officially declined yet either. I was going to make an excuse at the last minute, but now, if Cole's willing to come..."

Holly finished my sentence with glee. "It might be a chance to rub Cole in Annabel's face. In that case, I am definitely in. I want a front row seat for that."

We laughed and talked a while longer until the rest of the team started arriving at the office, at which point we had to get started on work ourselves. As I settled down at my desk to start the day properly, my eyes drifted over to the calendar on the wall. That night, there would be a carol concert at St James's Piccadilly, the church closest to our office. Representatives from many of the businesses in the neighbourhood would be there, and I always attended on behalf of Anchor.

With a smile, I pulled out my phone and sent Cole a quick text to let him know what our plans were, and to tease him in anticipation of the night ahead. As I got back to work, the smile remained at the thought of what his reaction might be when he read my message.

I'm taking you to church tonight. You can see how you like me on my knees. G

Chapter Ten

Role Play

~Cole~

Normally, I wouldn't check my phone during business meetings, but I couldn't help taking a look when Gemma's name popped up, and once I'd read her message, I had a hard time thinking of anything else. My imagination ran wild for the rest of the meeting as images flashed across my mind: Gemma on her knees, her hands tied behind her back. Being punished for something? There were so many delicious possibilities.

By the time the meeting ended, I'd decided what I wanted to do and I quickly found a store online that could get me the items I would need before the end of the day. Normally, my personal assistant would help with purchases, and she'd been the one who found dress options for Gemma the day before and made all the arrangements to have everything delivered to her. I only picked out the final dress from the options she provided me.

However, when it came to my sexual business, I always kept that separate. When I wanted an escort, I arranged it myself, and the things I wanted Gemma to wear that evening definitely fell into a different category from the dress my assistant had helped me with yesterday. Some things were better kept private.

My meetings were off-site in the morning, but in the afternoon, Jackson and I set up in my suite to go over the latest reports from our European hotels. The London hotel project had been placed on hold temporarily until Gemma and Holly signed the agreement, but I didn't really have any doubt that they would. In fact, I suspected that they were already working on some preliminary design ideas for us and I couldn't wait to see what they came up with.

The items I'd ordered for Gemma were delivered just before five and I stashed them in the closet next to her luggage, which I'd already had unpacked for her by the hotel staff. With everything put away, I hadn't been able to resist looking through the various items of clothing she had packed and imagining what she would look like in them. I may have lingered a little longer than necessary over some of the lingerie before shaking my head at myself. This woman had taken over my thoughts in a completely unexpected way.

Gemma herself arrived shortly before six. I had sent her a message to let her know I'd be working and that she could pick up a keycard at the reception desk, so she let herself into the suite when she arrived and gave Jackson and me a cheery wave. Comfortable and confident, she made it seem like joining me after a day's work was something she'd done a million times before.

"Good evening, gentleman," she greeted us as she removed her coat and scarf. "How's the hotel mogul business today?"

Jackson immediately got to his feet, walking over to give her a kiss on the cheek in welcome. "You're a sight for sore eyes, Gemma. Can you please tell Cole that the working day ended an hour ago?"

"It's only one o'clock in New York," I reminded him, still staring at the numbers in the report I'd been reviewing for nearly an hour, trying to understand what I was missing. Our Milan hotel had fewer repeat customers than any of our other Italian locations and I couldn't see an obvious explanation.

Gemma answered Jackson rather than me. "I don't need him until seven, so if he wants to work until then, I can't stop him."

Jackson sighed dramatically. "In that case, will you at least have something to eat with me so I don't have to dine alone again?"

"You ate by yourself one night," I pointed out, my eyes still on the computer screen. We'd eaten together every night since we arrived except for the previous night when I went out with Gemma.

"Are you actually listening to our conversation and reading at the same time?" Gemma asked curiously, coming to sit next to me on the couch. "I'm impressed. I always need complete silence to concentrate."

"I've always been able to multitask." I didn't mean it as a boast, just a statement of fact. My brain had always been good at keeping things separate. "Jackson is right about one thing, though: we should eat. Order whatever you like from room service. I'll have the steak sandwich."

After Gemma and Jackson conferred together over the menu and placed the order, she leaned over my shoulder, looking at the report I still had in front of me. "Where is that hotel?"

"Milan. It opened two years ago but it's not performing as well as we'd hoped. I'm trying to figure out why."

She leaned in a bit closer to the screen, focusing on one of the photos in the report. "Are those LED lights in the guest rooms?"

For the first time since she'd entered, I turned to look at her fully, watching as her finger tapped against her lips. "The design firm recommended them because they're less expensive to run, I believe."

She nodded thoughtfully. "They are, but they tend to have more blue in them, which makes it harder for people to feel sleepy. Personally, I think they're fine for the common areas of a hotel, but I wouldn't use them in the bedrooms."

I glanced over at Jackson to see if he'd come across this idea before, and he shrugged back at me. "The report does mention that some of the guests complained of unsatisfactory sleep, but there didn't seem to be a common reason why."

Gemma nodded again. "That makes sense. It's a subconscious thing. You wouldn't really know why you weren't tired, only that you weren't. It might be worth replacing the lights and seeing if that helps."

Her intelligence impressed me nearly as much as her creativity, and I snapped the lid of the laptop closed to give her my full attention. "Where were you an hour ago when I started looking at this?"

Gemma laughed, her green eyes sparkling warmly. "Do I get a consulting fee if I'm right?"

The food arrived and the three of us ate together, talking about work and London and the day's news. The conversation flowed easily with no tension or awkward silences. Very rarely did I find a woman who didn't let sex filter into other aspects of a relationship, aside from the women I paid, and I could hardly believe my luck that Gemma seemed to have no problem with it. She acted like a friend or a business acquaintance, which was just what I wanted anytime that we weren't in the bedroom.

Just before seven, Jackson bade us goodnight, and Gemma turned to me. "I need to get changed for tonight, but it won't take me long. Did my suitcases arrive?"

I pointed her to the closet where everything had been unpacked and left her to get changed, since I had a feeling if I stayed to watch her, we wouldn't be ready to leave when she wanted to. Fifteen minutes later, she emerged in a pretty, understated black dress with an emerald necklace and earrings that brought out her eyes. In her hands, she held a deep green tie from my closet.

"I hope you don't mind, but I thought this would look great on you tonight." She held it out to me almost hopefully.

I couldn't remember the last time someone had picked out clothes for me to wear, but it didn't bother me that she had. In fact, I kind of liked the idea of us matching. It would act as a visual stamp, a signal to the other men we might encounter to let them know she belonged to me, at least for the night. Without hesitation, I removed the tie I had on and put the green one on instead.

The walk from the hotel to the church didn't take very long. Two photographers waited outside the hotel to take pictures of us again, but clearly, the interest had already started to wane after the stories in that day's papers, just as I thought it would.

Candlelight filled the church interior along with the scent of spices or incense as we entered, and Gemma greeted many of the people inside as we made our way to a pew. Everyone seemed to know her and treat her with respect, I was glad to see. She introduced me by name without specifying any kind of relationship between us, but the smiles on many people's faces told me that our appearance in the morning's papers hadn't gone unnoticed.

The charming and peaceful carol service lasted just over an hour, and though I didn't dislike it, when Gemma turned to me at the end to ask if it had won me over for Christmas, I had to burst her bubble. "I'm going to need more persuading than a few pretty songs, I'm afraid."

Gemma took the news with a shrug. "I would have been surprised, but I thought I'd ask. It's only the first night, anyway; I haven't really started trying yet."

After a few more minutes of socializing on the way out of the church, we were finally on our way back to the hotel, and despite the cool night air, my body flooded with heat at the thought of what awaited us there. The night was still young and neither of us had anywhere else to go. I couldn't wait to get started.

"I think you gave me some false advertising about tonight, Gemma," I told her once we reached the suite, both of us removing our coats and shoes at the door.

"Oh?" she asked innocently. "What do you mean?"

"You promised me I'd see you on your knees," I reminded her, letting my voice turn a bit harder. "But there was no kneeling involved. You lied."

I actually saw the shiver run through her, making it clear just how much she was looking forward to our evening, even if she didn't know exactly what I had planned.

"I didn't intentionally lie, Mr Stamer. I thought we would have to kneel."

I had to bite my lip to stop from groaning. People called me Mr Stamer all day long, but somehow, from her lips, it sounded like the sexiest thing I'd ever heard.

"Were you always this badly behaved, Gemma? Even when you were in school?"

The question took her by surprise, her lips parting in uncertainty, and I pressed ahead to let her know exactly what I had in mind.

"I bet you were. I bet you drove the boys crazy in your school uniform: the short skirt, the see-through white top, your hair in pigtails." Fuck, just talking about it made me hard. "I want to see it for myself. There's a bag in the closet. I want you to go get dressed and show me just how naughty you can be."

~Gemma~

My heart raced as I hurried to the bedroom to follow Cole's instructions. I hadn't noticed anything in the closet earlier, but I'd only been focused on getting my dress for this evening. When I looked for it now, I quickly found the bag laid out on top of my empty suitcases, and when I opened it up and pulled out the contents, my heart started beating even faster.

Cole's 'naughty schoolgirl' comments were obviously not a spur-of-the-moment thing. He'd been thinking about this, had put some effort into it, and I couldn't wait to see exactly what he had in mind once I looked the part.

As quickly as I could, I removed my elegant dress and jewellery and put on the clothing he'd provided for me instead. Inside the bag, I found a white cropped shirt that stopped just beneath my breasts, and a red and black tie to go with it. A red, white and black tartan skirt, ridiculously short, along with knee-high white socks and black Mary Jane shoes completed the 'uniform', and there were also two hair ties, which I used to pull my red hair into bunches as he'd suggested.

I didn't bother putting any underwear on. He hadn't provided any, and there didn't seem any point.

When I had it all on, I took a moment to examine myself critically in the mirror. My hard nipples were clearly visible beneath the white shirt, and if I bent over even a little, my bare ass would be on display too. It looked so ridiculously over-the-top that I loved it, and I knew Cole would too. Just the thought of his reaction sent a flush of anticipation through me.

I'd never done any kind of role play before. The idea of doing anything like that with Edwin was laughable, but Cole seemed to know exactly what he was doing, and I couldn't wait to try it with him. My whole body tingled with excitement as I opened the bedroom door and headed back out into the living room of the suite.

While I'd been gone, Cole had removed his suit jacket and his socks, but otherwise, he remained fully dressed. He sat on the couch with a drink in his hand, which froze mid-air, halfway to his mouth, when I appeared. His eyes combed over me slowly, taking in every detail, leaving all my nerve endings on fire in their wake.

"That is even fucking better than I imagined." His voice sounded thick and his eyelids looked heavy with lust, and pride raced through me at the effect I had on him.

What exactly did he want to do next? I wasn't sure so I decided to ask. "If I'm the naughty schoolgirl, who does that make you?"

His eyes came back up to meet mine, full of heat. "Who do you want me to be, Gemma? This is your fantasy too."

I hadn't expected to be able to choose, and I swallowed hard as the possibilities ran through my head. He could be the star athlete who I seduced in the locker room. He could be my teacher who wanted to give me some extra 'work' for extra credit. He could be the headteacher whose office I got sent to for misbehaving. Or he could be...

My thighs clenched together as the last thought hit me, and I knew exactly what I wanted, if I was being completely honest with myself. Would he judge me for it if I told him? Was it too kinky?

"Tell me." He'd clearly seen my reaction, and the hard and commanding edge to his voice left no room for disagreement. I had no choice but to obey. "Who am I?"

I swallowed again to try to get some moisture back in my mouth, which had gone completely dry. "You're my stepfather. I've just been in trouble at school and they sent me home."

Cole raised an eyebrow at me, letting me know he hadn't expected that, but his mouth turned up into a smile as he thought it over. "Okay. Go back in the room and come out again in a minute."

Though my heart hammered in my chest, I did as he said, trying to commit to the scene just as much as he obviously intended to. When I reentered the living room, Cole still sat on the couch, but he had his laptop open on his lap, staring at the screen. For a moment, I wondered if I had missed something, if he had received a phone call for work and actually needed to do something else, but as soon as he looked up at me with that cold heat in his eyes, I realized it must be part of the act.

"What are you doing home, Gemma? Shouldn't you be at school?"

The words sounded natural from his mouth, like he had rehearsed them for days rather than coming up with it off the top of his head, and I tried to throw myself into my role with the same abandon.

"The teacher's a fucking wanker," I complained, noting how Cole couldn't help smiling at the colourful term. "He kicked me out of class but I didn't even do anything."

"If you used that kind of language in your class, I'd say you got off light." Cole's voice sounded disapproving and cold, just as I wanted it to. "Someone needs to teach you some manners."

I laughed sarcastically. "Like you don't ever swear."

"I'm an adult, Gemma. You're just a child."

A child, huh? How old was I supposed to be? I pouted at him, sticking my chest out in defiance. "Eighteen isn't a child, Daddy."

I didn't know where the 'Daddy' came from. I hadn't planned to say it, but I had to call him something, and Cole's eyes darkened even further when I did. Obviously, he didn't mind.

"It's still young enough for you to get a spanking when you deserve it, Gemma."

As he got to his feet, another thrill of anticipation shot through me at the idea of Cole spanking me. Really? Did I actually want that? I hadn't known that I did, but I was so wet now, it was practically dripping down my legs.

"You can't touch me," I argued, crossing my arms beneath my breasts, pushing them out even further. "Mum won't allow it."

"Your mother's not here." Cole took a step towards me, his eyes fixed on mine. "And you've been teasing me long enough."

He reached out and grabbed my arm, pulling me over to the chair.

"Bend over."

The hard edge to his voice sent shivers of pleasure through me, and I changed tactics, pretending to be scared instead. "No, please, Daddy. I'll be good. I promise."

"You will be," he agreed. "Once you've learned your lesson."

As he pushed me down over the arm of the chair, the angle exposed my bare ass to the air, and a groan echoed from his throat as he realized I had no underwear on. I couldn't help smiling, even as my arms trembled with a heady mix of fear and anticipation.

"Is this how you go to school? Teasing everyone? Showing all the boys this gorgeous ass of yours?"

He rubbed it with the palm of his hand, and it was my turn to groan. My whole body throbbed, aching for his touch so close to where his hand was.

"No, Daddy," I whimpered. "I don't show it to anyone."

His hand came down hard on me, making me yelp in surprise. It stung, but only for a moment, quickly replaced by a rush of pleasure and the strong, gnawing need within me. "Don't lie to me, Gemma. Who else has seen it? Who else has touched you?"

"No one," I repeated, and he smacked me again, the sound echoing through the room.

"You expect me to believe that? That this needy little pussy of yours hasn't been used?"

Fuck. I loved it when he talked dirty to me like that. I was so turned on I could hardly think straight.

"It hasn't, Daddy," I managed to pant. "It's waiting for you."

Cole groaned again, the only sign that this turned him on just as much as it did for me. "You want me to use your pussy, Gemma? What do you want me to put in it?"

Anything. I was almost past caring, I just needed some relief. "Your cock, Daddy, please," I begged.

The next thing I knew, Cole pulled his trousers down and I could feel his hard cock rubbing against my ass. "This is what you want? You want me to fuck you over the chair, just like this?"

God, yes. I pushed back against him, desperate for him. "Please, Daddy. Please fuck me."

As he thrust into me, roughly and desperately, my body turned to liquid. His hands tight on my hips, he took me harder than he ever had, as if he really had been lusting after me for years, and it didn't take long at all before stars appeared behind my eyelids.

"Oh, God, yes!"

"Fuck, Gemma, fucking hell." As I came, clamping down on him, Cole quickly followed me, muttering half-formed obscenities as he pumped deep inside me.

It took a minute for my legs to stop shaking, the force of my orgasm sapping all my energy. Cole pulled out of me just as I got my balance, and I turned around to face him, resting against the arm of the chair that he'd just had me bent over. I couldn't have been more satisfied with how that went, and based on his reaction, I expected him to look the same. Instead, he looked at me with something close to guilt on his face.

"Cole? What's wrong?"

"I'm so sorry, Gemma." He shook his head in disbelief. "I can't believe I did that."

He had me completely perplexed. "Did what?" He certainly hadn't done anything I didn't want him to do.

He looked down at his cock before his eyes came back to me, confusion written all over his face. "I didn't use a condom. I just... I forgot."

~Cole~

I really couldn't believe it. I had been intending to steer our little role play in the direction of my fantasies this morning, to get her down on her knees, sucking me off just like I'd imagined, so I hadn't bothered to bring any condoms out into the living room with me.

But then, the whole thing took a different turn, and I had been so caught up in the moment, so completely lost in the scenario we created, that I completely forgot my real world obligations.

That was not something I did. Ever. I thought that men who claimed to have 'forgotten' were liars or idiots, and I didn't consider myself either of those things. I never thought it would happen to me and I didn't understand how it had.

I expected Gemma to be furious, as she had every right to be.

She looked back at me with wide eyes, her gaze dipping briefly to glance at my clearly unsheathed dick before looking back up at my face. I could almost see the calculations taking place in her head, but then, to my astonishment, she gave me a shrug and smiled.

"It's not a big deal, Cole. It's fine."

Immediately, I shook my head in disagreement. "It's not fine. I shouldn't have done it, and definitely not without asking you."

Once again, she didn't look anywhere near as concerned as I thought she should be. "You're always careful with the women you hire, right?"

Of course. That was why I couldn't believe I had done this. I had never even been *close* to forgetting before. "I am, but that's not the point."

"It is to me." Seeing my confusion, she reached out and took my hand. "You're clean, and so am I. It's okay. I trust you, Cole."

She trusted me? What the hell was I supposed to say to that?

When I said nothing, she gave me a sheepish, almost shy grin. "I got a little carried away too. Sorry if the 'Daddy' thing was a bit too much."

Blood rushed back down to my drained dick at the reminder of what we had just done. Before my mistake, it had been incredibly hot. "I didn't mind. I had no idea that would do it for me, but apparently, from you, it does."

I couldn't imagine many things that wouldn't sound sexy coming out of her mouth. Her little act had turned me on so much that, clearly, I hadn't been thinking straight.

Gemma pulled her skirt down, though it still didn't do much to cover her. "So, do you want me to stay in this, or should I put something else on?"

She really wanted to keep going? I still couldn't quite believe that she was taking this so well, but if she wanted to continue like nothing had happened, I certainly wouldn't argue. Refocusing my thoughts, I put the issue out of my mind and answered her question.

"Definitely stay in that." My eyes narrowed as I looked her up and down. She really did look like a wet dream come to life with her innocent-looking pigtails, her see-through top and that fucking short skirt that didn't leave much to the imagination at all. "We're going to change the game though."

Compliant as always, she nodded, waiting for my instruction. I still planned to have her on her knees before we were through, but I needed a little more time to recover so I'd have to improvise in the meantime.

Before she suggested the stepfather scenario, I assumed we would do a teacher/student scene, and I still liked the idea. After tucking my dick back into my pants and pulling up the zipper, I took a couple of steps away from her, getting into character before turning back with an impersonal, commanding tone. "Take a seat, Gemma. You're late for class."

Without hesitation, she scurried over to the couch and sat down while I looked around as if I had an entire room of students to address.

"Now, as I was saying before Gemma so rudely interrupted us, our topic today is self-stimulation. Female self-stimulation, in particular."

Though Gemma's lips twitched, she did her best to keep a neutral expression.

"I can assure you all that there is nothing sexier than a woman who knows how to get herself off." Still addressing the 'class', I walked over to one of the chairs in the living room and stood behind it. "Of course, the best way for you all to learn about this will be through a little demonstration. Gemma, since you obviously like being the centre of attention, why don't you come up here and walk us through it."

She crossed her legs and pouted at me. "What if I don't want to?"

My lips curled in amusement. That bratty persona would play in perfectly to the next thing I had planned, so I happily rolled with it. "I don't think you want me to send another note home to your stepfather, do you? I've heard he can be rather strict."

She tried her best not to show her amusement, but her eyes sparkled anyway. "No, sir."

With a sigh, she stood up, tugging her skirt down, and walked over to flop down into the seat in front of me. Circling her, I adjusted her in the seat until she was perfectly displayed. Her legs, I lifted up over the arms of the chair, spread wide apart, and I tugged her hips down so they rested near the edge of the chair. I pulled her shirt up to show off her breasts and, grasping one of them in my hand, I gave it a rough squeeze as Gemma gasped in surprise.

"Just making sure you're ready. Now, I'll take a seat and you can lead the way."

With that, I walked over to the couch and sat down in the spot she had just vacated with a perfect, unobstructed view of her beautiful body.

Her eyes still on me, she reached down, almost hesitantly, to brush her fingers across her taut, exposed nipple.

"Explain to the class what you're doing, Gemma," I ordered. "Tell us how you turn yourself on."

That seemed to embolden her and give her a clearer idea of what I wanted. She started to pinch her nipple more forcefully as she wet one of her fingers in her mouth and used it to rub the other nipple, narrating her actions the whole time. Her eyes never left me even though my gaze was focused on following her hands, particularly as they drifted lower, moving toward her swollen clit. By the time she started pumping her fingers into herself, her hips writhing on the chair, I had to unzip my pants again. My palm ran slowly and firmly down my dick as her breathing grew more shallow, her eyes a little more unfocused.

"Tell us what you think about, Gemma," I instructed. "When your fingers are inside yourself, what are you imagining?"

Her eyes went straight to my dick. "I'm imagining it's you, sir. That my fingers are your cock, fucking me hard."

"Dirty girl," I admonished her, my throat tight around the words. "Just for that, I want you to show everyone how you come. Let them all see you fall apart, but not until I tell you."

She whimpered, that fucking perfect sound of hers, as her legs began to tremble.

"You can wait, gorgeous. Just a little longer."

Her hips shuddered as she tried to hold back her release.

"Five. Four." I started counting down slowly as she bit her lip, trying so hard to get the timing right. "Three. Two..."

I held the space between the last two words for longer than necessary and she cried out in frustration. "Cole, I can't. I need..."

"One."

The orgasm shot through her, her whole body convulsing and lifting off the chair before collapsing back again as little aftershocks ran through her, tiny jolts of pleasure.

She looked completely satisfied. And completely fucking perfect.

With her chest heaving, her eyes closed and her limbs hanging limply over the side of the chair, she had to be the most beautiful thing I had ever seen.

~Gemma~

It felt like I was floating, suspended weightless in the air as the pleasure of my orgasm flooded my body and slowly ebbed away. Gradually, the room around me began to take shape again, including Cole, his eyes still fixed on me intently, his hand still moving slowly across his hard-on.

How on earth did he have such power over me? How could he control me to such an extent that I could come on his command? I couldn't help remembering how frustrated Edwin used to get trying to get me to climax, and all Cole had to do was tell me to and I did.

And he made it all feel so safe and so natural. If anyone else had suggested the things we had done together, or even knew that I had thought about doing them, I would have been humiliated. Cole, however, made me feel that there was nothing wrong with it at all, that I could be as filthy as I wanted, more than I'd ever known I wanted to be, and he would find it perfectly normal.

And no matter what we did within these walls, as soon as it was over, he would go right back to treating me just as he always had.

With my arms trembling beneath my weight, I managed to shift my body back in the chair, placing my feet back on the ground. From the state of his cock, I knew Cold hadn't finished with me yet; he was simply waiting for me to be ready to move on, and I honestly couldn't wait to see what he planned to do to me next.

"I'm disappointed, Gemma." Cole's cold tone was at odds with the heat in his eyes, and I understood straight away he was still in his teacher mode. "I told you to wait."

My eyes widened, trying to figure out what he meant. "But I did, I waited until you said one."

"Yes, but you were meant to wait until I said 'come'. I think I might have to fail you."

His eyes twinkled just enough to let me know he wasn't serious. For whatever he wanted to do next, he needed an excuse to tell me I was wrong. Should I argue with him? Or maybe try something else?

Settling on a course of action, I did my best to look apologetic. "I'm sorry, sir. Please don't fail me. Maybe there's something else I could do to earn some extra credit?"

His lips twitched, telling me that he was perfectly satisfied with that response. "Maybe there is. Let's see, shall we?"

In a flash, he stood up, his trousers still open, allowing his erect cock to jut out in front of him. I couldn't help watching it as he walked over to me, which only made him smile more.

"What do you think, Gemma? You think you can do a better job making me come than you did with yourself? Using only that smart little mouth of yours?"

"I know I can, sir." Looking up at him, I licked my lips in anticipation, and his nostrils flared, his gaze growing even more heated.

Reaching down, he yanked the tie off my neck. It burned my skin, the movement was so fast, but I was far less concerned about that than with what he planned to do next. Grabbing my arm firmly, he pulled me up from the chair, onto my feet, and spun me around. His hands went around both my wrists, pulling them behind my back, and the fabric of the tie rubbed against my skin as he bound my hands together. It felt rougher than his fancy silk ties the night before, not as soft on my skin, but I didn't mind.

"There. Now, you won't be tempted to cheat."

With his hands on my shoulders, he pushed me down onto my knees and stepped back around in front of me, his hard, thick cock right at my eye level. My mouth watered at the sight of it, which had never happened with Edwin either.

"Tell me how much you want it," he ordered, grabbing the base of his shaft and smacking it against my cheek. "Beg me for it."

I looked up at him from beneath my eyelashes, trying to put on my best innocent face. "Please, sir. Let me taste you."

He slapped his cock against my cheek again. "That doesn't sound very desperate. Maybe one of the other girls wants it more."

Swallowing down any remaining inhibition, I tried again. I didn't have any experience with the kind of dirty talk that seemed to come so easily to him, but I would do my best.

"Please," I repeated, my voice shaking with need. "I want to taste your cock. It looks so hard and so big. I need it, sir. I need you to fuck my mouth. I want to feel you in my throat, to feel you come down my throat. I need..."

Apparently, that was enough. With a groan, Cole brought his cock to my lips, cutting off my words. I opened my mouth wide and he grabbed hold of my hair, holding both pigtails by the base of them, holding my head steady as he began to thrust into me.

This was unlike any blowjob I'd ever given before. Then, I had always been in control, setting the pace and using my hands, but now, my hands were tied and Cole held my head tight. As his cock filled my waiting mouth, I realized this was no blowjob. He was fucking my mouth, just like I'd asked him to. I could do nothing but keep my mouth open and try to breathe. Tears began to form in my eyes as he pushed in deeper, hitting the back of my throat with each thrust, but I didn't want him to stop. Instead, I looked up at him, trying to keep eye contact as he stared down at me, his eyes glazed as he watched his cock disappearing into my mouth, over and over again.

"Fuck, Gemma," he grunted, obviously getting close to his climax as he thrust even faster. "I love fucking your sweet mouth, seeing those perfect little lips around my dick."

I moaned in response, the sound muffled around his cock, and that seemed to push him over the edge. His eyes closed as he groaned and hot liquid spurted into my throat. I swallowed as much as I could but some managed to spill out of my mouth, dribbling down my chin.

When he finally pulled out, I gasped for breath, coughing, and instantly, Cole was on his knees in front of me. "You okay?"

His dark eyes were full of concern, all the hardness gone from them, and when I nodded, not quite trusting myself to speak yet, his face relaxed into a smile. With his thumb, he swiped the cum off my chin and put his thumb in my mouth. I licked it clean and gave it an extra suck, hard, hollowing out my cheeks.

Cole groaned once more. "You're so fucking sexy, you know that?"

I couldn't say I did. No one had ever said that to me before. In fact, in the past year, people had gone out of their way to tell me the opposite. Based on our time together, I had hoped that Cole thought so, but actually hearing the words from him felt pretty good.

"You're not so bad yourself," I replied, making him smile.

Rising to his feet again, Cole pulled me up and then moved behind me to untie my wrists. After a minute of pulling and tugging which only seemed to make it tighter, he swore loudly. "Shit. I can't undo this knot. Hang on, Gemma, let me find something to cut it with."

He returned with a small knife from the kitchen area of the suite, but it quickly became apparent it wouldn't be sharp enough to cut through the fabric.

"Fuck," he swore again, tossing the knife aside. "I'm going to have to call down to the desk for something. Are you okay for a few more minutes?"

I couldn't help laughing. "The all-powerful Cole Stamer is stymied by a cheap polyester tie?"

His eyes narrowed as he pretended not to be amused by my teasing, even though I knew he was. "It's *because* it's cheap. That's the problem. I'm used to much better quality."

He picked up the phone and placed a call to the front desk, asking for someone to bring some scissors, and he led me into the bedroom to keep me out of sight for when they arrived.

"I'm sorry," he apologized, his hand cupping my face gently, and I could tell that he really did feel bad.

By the time the scissors arrived and Cole managed to cut through the fabric, my wrists had turned a deep red colour and Cole's brow furrowed in worry as he looked at them.

"I didn't mean to hurt you, Gemma." His eyes were filled with regret as he looked between my wrists and my face.

"I know," I assured him. "Don't worry. They're a little sore, but it didn't cut off the circulation or anything. I'll be fine."

He shook his head, though whether it was at what I said or the thoughts in his head, I couldn't be sure. "I don't know why I..." He trailed off before shaking his head again. "You make me lose control, Gemma, but it's no excuse."

I suspected he wasn't just talking about my wrists anymore; he also meant earlier, when he forgot the condom.

He'd looked so guilty about that when it happened that I didn't tell him that it actually worried me a little too. Normally, I took my pills regularly, but with everything going on in the last week since I'd met him, I couldn't be entirely certain that I'd remembered to take them every day. I would need to check in the morning and maybe get a morning-after pill, just to be sure.

In any case, I could deal with that on my own. I didn't want him to worry about it or feel worse than he already did, and I certainly didn't want him to stop doing the kinds of things he was doing to me.

The idea that I made Cole lose control seemed almost unbelievable to me. As far as I was concerned, I had never known anyone so in control at all times.

"It's fine, Cole," I told him once again, gently, dipping my head to meet his eyes. "Tonight was... unexpected, but amazing. I loved it. All of it."

"I did too," he agreed, looking down at my wrists again. "Let me take care of this."

In a minute, he returned with lotion, rubbing it gently into the reddened skin. I winced as he pressed a little too hard, and I noticed that he grimaced in response. It seemed obvious to me that he really did care about not hurting me.

When he'd finished tending to my wrists, he ran me a bath, insisting that I take it even though I told him once again that I was perfectly fine. As I sank down into the warm, bubbly water, he brought in a towel and my pajamas, fussing over me like an overprotective mother hen. Finally, I kicked him out to go do some work so that I could relax.

Leaning back in the bath, I tried to make sense of the mystery of Cole Stamer. So domineering one moment, then sweet and concerned the next, he could switch from businessman to friend to lover in the blink of an eye, and he seemed to take a certain amount of pride in doing so. He relied on that self-control to keep his life in order, and to keep his heart safely locked away.

So, if I made him lose control, what did that mean for him? What did it mean for us?

Chapter Eleven

SHOPPING

~Cole~

By the time Gemma got out of the bath, her wrists looked a little better, but I still cursed myself for not being more careful. Perhaps if we were going to keep engaging in this sort of thing, I should invest in some proper restraints, something designed for it. Something that I would not eventually have to cut her out of.

As she went into the bedroom to get ready for bed, I took a quick look at the same online store where I had bought the costume she'd worn tonight. There were a lot of bondage options, more than I'd been anticipating, and after a few minutes of looking, I decided that Gemma and I should probably look at them together. She might have some ideas on what she would like to try, but I suspected that conversation might get a little... intense. Enjoyably so, but intense nonetheless, and it was late. We would have time to look at it the next day, so I put the laptop away and joined Gemma in the bedroom instead.

The towel she wore when she came out of the bathroom was still loosely draped around her body as she applied lotion to her legs. As I watched her hands moving across her smooth skin, I couldn't help feeling the stirrings of arousal again. "Do you need some help with that?"

She raised an eyebrow at me. "I think I better say no. It's already pretty late, and I know there's no such thing as a quickie with you."

I couldn't help smiling. She wasn't wrong; I'd just closed my laptop for the same reason. "I'm a man of many talents, Gemma, but rushing my pleasure isn't one of them."

"Another time, then." She winked at me as she snapped the lotion bottle shut. Discarding the towel, she slipped a plain black slip nightgown over her head and crawled under the covers.

Though the action in itself was incredibly commonplace, my heart beat slightly faster as I watched her. No woman had stayed overnight in my bed for a very long time; not since that Christmas Eve with Samantha, in fact. All my sexual partners since then had been paid by the hour, and paying someone to sleep made no financial sense.

But with Gemma, I'd asked for all of her time, and obviously, that meant I would have to let her sleep sometimes. In a way, it wasn't any different from eating with her, just another thing we needed to do as part of our day.

"What are we doing tomorrow?" I asked as I climbed into bed next to her.

"You've got a business meeting tomorrow," she replied, burrowing down into her pillow in a rather endearing way. "Your calendar was already full. It's the one day I couldn't squeeze anything in."

It took me a moment to remember what that appointment would be. With everything that had taken place with Gemma, the days had all begun to run together in my mind. Finally, it came back to me. "That's right, I'm meeting with an old college friend of mine. His family's also in the hospitality business. It's just dinner and drinks, nothing formal. You could come along if you like."

I didn't really have any idea why I extended the invitation, as if I couldn't go one evening without seeing her.

Though Gemma smiled up at me, she also turned me down. "I'm sure you'll have more fun without me there. Besides, I could use a late night in the office. I've been a little distracted at work this week for some reason."

The coy smile she gave me was so irresistible that I couldn't help bending down and giving her a quick kiss on the upturned corners of her mouth.

"As long as you're working on my hotel, you can work as long as you like. Goodnight, Gemma."

"Goodnight, Cole."

After I turned off the light and laid back on the pillows, Gemma's breathing quickly evened out, which didn't surprise me. I must have worn her out. Turning towards her, I could just make out her face in the darkness. Gently, so I didn't wake her, I reached out and brushed her hair back over her shoulder. She really was exquisite. Laying there like that, without the sparkle in her eyes, she looked almost vulnerable too. I wanted more than ever to protect her, to keep her safe from everyone who dared to judge her or belittle her. That was the last thought I remembered before I fell asleep.

The next day passed quickly enough. Getting ready with Gemma in the morning felt a bit strange, getting dressed next to each other and chatting about our days, but we kept things light and casual as always. There was one brief moment, as she got ready to leave, when I hesitated, unsure if I should kiss her goodbye or not. I decided not to, but after she'd gone, I almost wished I had.

Once the work day began, the meetings backed into each other, one after another, until the time came for Jackson and I to meet my friend, Wilson, for dinner. Despite being British, he had attended Yale with me, and Jackson got to know him fairly well too. We always tried to get together whenever I visited London or he spent time in New York.

"Cole!" Wilson greeted me enthusiastically as we were shown to the table at the private club that he belonged to. Staid and a little stuffy, the venue perfectly embodied the type of atmosphere I *didn't* want at my hotels. "Good to see you. And Jackson, glad you could join us."

Once we'd all shaken hands and sat back down, Wilson raised an eyebrow at me over his drink glass.

"You've made quite the stir since you've been in town."

I could play dumb and pretend he meant my hotel, but I knew what he was actually talking about: the photos with Gemma, of course.

That gave me an opening to ask him something I'd been wondering anyway. "Do you know Gemma? Do your families run in the same circles at all?"

Wilson shook his head. "No, my family's much too nouveau-riche to fit in with Totnes' set. I've met the son, Thomas, once or twice, but only for business. Never socially."

Gemma had mentioned her brother once to me, very briefly, when she told me about her childhood Christmases, but I knew nothing about him. "What kind of business did you do with him?"

"Leaseholds," he explained. "The Redvers family owns huge chunks of land in central London, which some of my buildings are built on."

It sounded like there must be quite a lot of work involved with that, and I wondered why Gemma had decided to work at Anchor Design instead of getting involved in her family's business. It could just be that there hadn't been an opportunity for her to use her passion and skills within that organization, but that didn't explain why she also worked under a different name. I'd never really given it much thought before.

Actually, when I thought about it, there were quite a few things I didn't know about her, which seemed strange somehow, given how intimately acquainted we were in other areas. I hadn't told her about my family either, though. It simply hadn't come up.

"I hoped you might bring her with you tonight," Wilson continued. "Thought I could see for myself what all the fuss is about."

What 'fuss' was he referring to? Did he mean the pictures of me and Gemma or the stupidity with that reality show?

My silent question was quickly answered as he leaned forward with a conspiratorial tone. "Hard to believe someone that attractive could be so useless in bed, but I guess it doesn't make much of a difference as long as you're getting off. That's why there's a market for sex dolls, after all."

Jackson shifted nervously next to me, as if he anticipated an argument, but that had never been my style. I simply met Wilson's gaze coldly. "I wouldn't know. I don't put any stock in what the tabloids have to say about anyone."

Wilson laughed, unfazed by my reaction. "Oh, of course not, but we all heard it right from the guy's mouth. Her former fiancé, that is. You would have missed it all since you weren't here at the time, but did you know for a while there, after the show first aired, people were using her name as an insult?" He laughed again, as if any of what he'd said was remotely funny. "If someone failed to react to something, you'd say they were being a Gemma. There were some pretty funny memes. I'll have to send you some of them."

He completely failed to notice that I never cracked a smile, and Jackson quickly intervened and steered the conversation onto safer topics.

By the time the dinner ended, I'd reached two decisions. First, Wilson's number would be deleted from my contact list immediately, and second, Gemma and I were definitely going shopping together for some of the new accessories I'd been exploring the night before.

Not online shopping, though.

If everyone thought they knew what Gemma was like in private, maybe the time had come to show them another side of her. I wouldn't waste my time defending her to one ignorant man, but if we made a big enough splash, the whole country might notice. Maybe we needed to let them know exactly how sexy she could be.

~Gemma~

I left Cole's suite on Thursday morning with the full intention of heading straight to the pharmacy and picking up a morning-after pill, just in case. When I checked my birth control that morning, I found that there were indeed three more pills in the packet than there should have been, and I couldn't be sure exactly which three days I had missed. Though it would probably be fine, better to be safe than sorry.

However, as soon as I stepped out of the lift in the hotel lobby, my phone rang with a call from the lawyer's office, wanting to review our contract with Stamer Hotels, and the only time they had available that day was in ten minutes, or mid-afternoon when we were already scheduled to meet with another client whose project was nearing completion. I didn't want to have to reschedule the other meeting if I could help it, so I agreed to meet the lawyers immediately. I could always run out to the pharmacy afterwards.

By the time the meeting with the lawyers finished, I was already running late for the day. I hurried straight to the office and spent the next several hours playing catch-up, even asking my assistant, Denise, to grab lunch for me so I wouldn't have to waste any time going out myself. I did briefly toy with the idea of asking her to run to the pharmacy for me at the same time, but I didn't want to make her uncomfortable or open myself up to too many questions. She didn't know anything about Cole, and it wasn't in her job description.

In the afternoon, Holly and I met with a few different clients, and before I knew it, people had started packing up for the day. I grabbed my coat, determined to take a quick break before coming back to continue the extra work that I'd wanted to do that evening, but I only made it as far as my office door before Holly appeared in front of me.

"Emergency, Gem."

"Get in line. I need to go out for just a few minutes. Can it wait until I'm back?"

She bit her lip in uncertainty. "That depends. Morelli's on the phone for you."

"You mean his office?"

Holly shook her head. "No. Signor Morelli himself."

Damn it. I really couldn't keep him waiting. With a sigh, I put my coat away and sank back into my office chair to pick up the phone.

As I expected, he had called to check why he hadn't heard back from us about his latest project. We would have to tell him that we weren't available since we'd be busy working for Cole, but I couldn't share that until I had delivered the signed contract to Cole himself. For the time being, I had to try to put him off without sounding evasive.

When I finally got off the phone with him, Holly had brought in some takeaway for us for dinner and we reviewed the initial sketches that we'd made for Cole and Jackson for their London hotel. We were hoping to meet with them the next day to review both the contract and our initial ideas.

Eventually, Holly stretched her arms over her head and yawned. "Well, it's time for me to make a move. Not all of us are staying a few blocks from the office, you know."

As I glanced up at the clock, my stomach sank. It was already after nine o'clock. I quickly tried to calculate in my head at roughly what time the night before Cole and I would have been playing our game. It probably would have been right around this time, and I knew that the morning-after pill worked best in the first 24 hours after sex. Maybe I could still make that window if I left immediately.

I wished Holly a hurried goodbye and raced to the nearest pharmacy, cursing my luck when I saw its darkened windows. It had closed hours ago. Pulling out my phone, I found the nearest 24-hour one, which was a cab ride away. When I finally got there, the girl at the counter handed over the box with a sympathetic smile.

"How effective is this?" I had never used one before. With Edwin, I had always been on top of my birth control pills, so I had never needed to.

"95% within the first 24 hours," she told me in a reassuring tone.

I swallowed, resisting the urge to pull my phone out to check the time. I must have missed the 24 hours by now. "And after that?"

"Oh." She suddenly looked a little less certain, which didn't help matters at all. "Around 85% in the first 48 hours, and around 60% before 72 hours."

85% was still pretty good; not as good as 95%, but still pretty good. I thanked her and bought myself a bottle of water to take the pill right there in the store, before anything else could distract me.

By the time I got back to the Lytton, it had just passed ten and Cole had already returned, which surprised me. I had expected him to be out later with his friend.

He sat on the couch in the living room with his laptop, but he looked up and gave me his usual sexy smirk as I came in. "So, is my hotel ready yet?"

I didn't want to tell him that we'd decided to sign the contract since the decision didn't belong solely to me. He could wait and find that out in the office with Holly, so I simply smiled back. "Not quite. I noticed you had some free time in your calendar for tomorrow afternoon, so I've booked you and Jackson to come see us to see some sketches. I hope that's okay."

Cole's smile widened in genuine pleasure. "I'm looking forward to it."

With the late hour and a busy day ahead of us, I didn't know if Cole would have anything planned for us in the bedroom tonight, but when I made my way there, heading to the vanity table to take off my jewellery, he followed me.

"How are your wrists today?"

With how crazy my day had been, I had actually forgotten all about them, but I glanced down at them when he asked the question. They were still a little discoloured, but I had worn long sleeves and I didn't think anyone had noticed. Still, I couldn't help teasing him a little. "Have you been worried about me all day?"

"I don't know if worried is the right word." His voice rumbled through me as he stepped closer. "But you've been on my mind, Gemma."

How did he manage to make that sound so inviting? Still facing the vanity mirror, I glanced at him in it. "What have you been thinking?"

His eyes bore into mine through the mirror glass. "About how I'd like to take a turn at rubbing your legs like you did yesterday after your bath."

If he wanted to give me a message, I certainly wouldn't complain. Placing the last of my jewellery down, I turned around to face him. "Where do you want me?"

The corner of his mouth curled up. "Such a dangerous question, but on the bed is fine for now. Take all your clothes off and lie face down."

I obeyed immediately, stripping my work clothes off and lying on my stomach. Cole adjusted the pillow beneath my head, making sure I was comfortable before he reached over to the bedside table to pick up a bottle of massage oil that I hadn't noticed before.

"Have you got the local sex shop on speed dial?" I asked curiously.

He laughed, the sound deep and deliciously dark. "Something like that. Now, be quiet. No more talking. Concentrate on how it feels."

I shut my mouth and watched as Cole removed all of his clothes. His body somehow only got more attractive to me the more I saw it, and the sight of him pouring the oil onto his hands and rubbing them together to warm it up already had my body aching in anticipation. Finally, he climbed on top of me, straddling my thighs, and I could feel his cock, already half-erect, pressed up against them. Leaning forward, he started with my shoulders, and I immediately moaned as his strong, firm fingers kneaded into my muscles.

He instantly stopped. "I said: quiet. Do I need to gag you?"

Though I wouldn't necessarily object, I shook my head and his hands started moving again. Suppressing my sounds of pleasure proved diffi-cult, but I did my best as his hands worked their way down my back. When they reached my ass, he kneaded the cheeks firmly for a while before climbing off me and turning around to reach my feet, his cock feeling even firmer as he settled onto my lower back. I bit my lip to hold in my groan as he rubbed first one foot and then the other, then worked his way up my legs, getting closer and closer to my centre that already throbbed for him.

When he got off me again, just for a moment, I could hear him open a condom packet. Apparently, he didn't plan to forget again. Every second without his touch felt eternal, but finally, he was back on me, his hands between my thighs, spreading them open just enough to let his thick, hard cock slide in between them and deep inside me.

As he filled me perfectly, I couldn't hold the moan in, but luckily, Cole didn't seem to mind. He grabbed my hair at the roots, tugging it back to turn my face into the pillow.

"You can scream now, Gemma. Scream as much as you want, into the pillow."

Gripping my shoulders tightly, he began to thrust into me, rough and fast. Completely pinned beneath him, unable to move anything but my feet and my hands, which clawed uselessly at the sheets, there was nothing I could do to contribute, nothing I could do but lie there and let him use my body for his own pleasure while he gave me mine.

And I absolutely loved it.

As his pace became more frantic, my cries grew louder. The angle couldn't be more perfect. With each thrust, he hit both my g-spot and my clit as he bottomed out within me.

"Fuck, Cole" I groaned into the pillow, the words muffled beneath me. "That's so... good... fuck, yes!"

I came with a blinding, nearly painful intensity, and through the fog of my orgasm, I could vaguely hear him swearing somewhere above me. His movements slowed as I felt his cock pumping within me, mimicking the aftershocks that still reverberated through my body.

All too soon, he stood up and left the room, returning with a warm, wet towel which he used to wipe the oil from my back and between my legs. Satisfied with his work, he brought over my pajamas and helped me sit up and put them on. I still felt so dazed by the intensity of my orgasm that I just let him do it, barely able to move my limbs. He tucked me into bed and gave me a gentle kiss on the lips before turning out the light and leaving the room again.

The last thing I remembered before drifting off to sleep was thinking, sleepily, that with the tenderness he showed me, he would actually be a really sweet father.

~Cole~

"You're freaking me out, Cole."

Jackson stood beside me as we waited for the elevator down to the lobby, looking at me with a mix of curiosity and confusion.

"I haven't said anything," I pointed out. We'd been working separately all day, seeing each other for the first time as we met to head over to the Anchor offices to take a look at the initial ideas Gemma and Holly were working on for our hotel.

"I know, but you're..." He gestured toward me with his hand and a look of disbelief on his face.

The elevator door opened and we both got in as I tried to figure out what he meant. "I'm what?"

"You're *smiling*."

When I glanced over to the mirrored elevator wall, I was surprised to see he was right. I hadn't even realized it, so I quickly pulled the corners of my mouth back down.

Jackson laughed. "I didn't mean you should stop. It just surprised me, that's all."

I tried to find a reasonable excuse for my uncharacteristic good mood. "I'm thinking about the hotel. I'm excited to get moving on it so we can stop wasting our time."

"Uh huh." He sounded unconvinced. "And it's got nothing to do with the redhead who's designing it?"

His words brought memories of Gemma to my mind in an instant: her body beneath mine the night before, her muscles giving way to my oiled hands, her thighs tight around my dick, and the amazing orgasm I'd had, followed by the peaceful feeling of sleeping beside her in the bed afterwards. Then, there was the way she suggested a shirt and tie combination for me this morning that I'd never put together before, or how we laughed together over our morning coffee. Before I knew it, my lips had started curling upwards again.

"That's what I thought." Jackson's grin made me pull my lips tighter together, flattening them once more.

I hated nothing more than when he got a chance to gloat. "Let's just go."

It didn't take long to walk over to the Anchor office, and I found myself looking up at the Christmas lights along Jermyn Street, the wreaths hung on the lampposts, and for the first time in years, I didn't feel like I wanted to tear them all down. I simply wondered idly if Gemma liked them. It seemed like the kind of thing she'd like.

It had only been four days since the first time we'd visited the Anchor office, which was nearly impossible to believe. So much had changed since then, and now, hopefully, we were about to make our business partnership official. The office bustled with energy as we walked in, and the receptionist had clearly been waiting for us. After taking our coats, she ushered us into Gemma's office where Gemma and Holly were waiting.

A rare moment of uncertainty gripped me as I tried to decide how to greet Gemma. Everyone in the room knew we were sleeping together, but we were still there to discuss business. Luckily, Jackson took the lead, giving both Holly and Gemma a kiss on the cheek, so I followed suit. Still, I couldn't resist letting my hand trail down Gemma's back and across her perfect ass as I pulled away.

When we were all seated around the table, Gemma opened a file folder on the table in front of her and removed a document, sliding it across the table towards us. "Here is the signed contract, gentlemen. We are delighted to accept your offer to work with Stamer Hotels."

She and Holly both beamed at us, and my smile in return was intentional and sincere, unlike my subconscious one earlier. Jackson told them how excited we were to work with them, and we both meant it. The document in front of me didn't only signify a positive development for my hotels; it also meant that Gemma would be in my life for the next three years, one way or another, and the thought pleased me immensely.

Next, she reached down to the floor and picked up another hard-covered folder. "Now, let's take a look at some initial ideas we've had for your hotel."

For the next hour, we reviewed their initial sketches and ideas, and they exceeded even my highest expectations for what we might see at this stage. I didn't love all of the ideas, but there was plenty to work with, and it certainly had the individual style that I had been looking for. Nothing about it could be called computerized or soulless.

A knock at the door startled all of us, and a young woman stuck her head in. "Gemma, you asked me to let you know when it was five o'clock?"

She smiled at the woman at the door. "Thanks, Denise. Have a good weekend."

"You too." She disappeared again, closing the door behind her.

Gemma turned to the rest of us, still wearing her smile. "I knew we'd get too caught up here if I didn't put a time limit on it. What do you all say to a quick drink to celebrate?"

Surprisingly, I felt an irrational annoyance at that suggestion, and I could only guess it stemmed from not wanting to share Gemma's time outside of the office. I was getting used to having her to myself. However, Jackson and Holly quickly agreed, so I had no reason to argue.

Gemma led us to the pub that was practically next door to the office and we all toasted our new partnership. I noticed that Gemma didn't have a beer like the rest of us, opting for a soft drink instead.

When I questioned her about it, she leaned in close to me. "I think keeping my wits about me when you're around is in my best interest." Her eyes sparkled with promise.

Once the drinks were finished, Jackson and Holly suggested dinner, but to my relief, Gemma declined. "Cole and I have tickets to the theatre tonight, so we're just going to grab something quick, but I'll text you later, Hols, about Sunday."

We said goodbye in front of the pub and Gemma and I began walking in the direction of the theatre. However, I had another destination in mind. "I'd like to make a stop before we eat, if you don't mind."

Gemma's eyes registered her surprise, but she quickly agreed. "Sure. Where to?"

"You'll see."

I'd studied the map earlier to be sure I knew where to find it, and as we approached the neon lights of the store, Gemma's pace slowed. "You want to go in there?" she asked, sounding uncertain. "What if someone sees us?"

I simply smiled. "I'm counting on it."

The store was simply called The Sex Shop. That was one of my favourite things about the Brits: they always got right to the point. Before she could ask any more questions, I went up and knocked on the door, which was quickly opened for us, and Gemma hurried inside. She still didn't look completely convinced as I led her first over to the wall full of handcuffs and other restraints.

"I don't want to hurt you again like the other night," I explained. "We should find something fit for purpose. What do you like the look of?"

Gemma glanced around the mostly empty store. Only two other people were in there with us, by design. "Couldn't we have just bought stuff online?"

"We could have, but then you couldn't try them on first." I pulled a pair of fluffy pink wrist cuffs off the wall and held them out to her. "Shall we?"

Her eyes searched mine, and for the first time since she spotted the store, she smiled. "You're doing this on purpose."

"Yes."

"There are photographers?"

"One, over there." I had hired him myself to take and 'leak' the photos. Besides him, the only person in the store was the owner. I'd rented the whole store for the evening so no one else would get in the way.

"Why?" Her question had no accusation in it; she simply wanted to understand, and I did my best to offer an explanation.

"The world got to hear one person's experience with you, something that should have stayed private. But since it didn't, I don't see how it hurts to show them there's a bit more to you than what they'd heard."

I held out the cuffs again in invitation.

"You don't think this is a little too far in the opposite direction?" Though she still resisted, her eyes were sparkling again.

"I already told you, Gemma: nothing with you is ever too much."

I looked down at the cuffs once more, and that time, she offered her wrists without hesitation.

I snapped them closed around her, tightening them snugly. "How does that feel?"

"Softer than your ties. Maybe too soft." She looked back over at the wall, really taking a look at it for the first time. "How does that one work?"

She pointed at a black leather contraption with three loops, so I removed the pink cuffs from her wrists and put them back on the wall before picking up the one she'd pointed to instead, looking it over to figure out how it worked.

"It's a neck collar, attached to some cuffs. Do you want to try it?"

She swallowed, no doubt thinking about the fact that photos of her wearing it could easily end up in tomorrow's papers, but a moment later, she looked up at me with determination in her eyes. "Okay."

Satisfaction filled my chest as I slid the collar around her neck, adjusting the tightness before turning her around, pulling her arms behind her back to attach the wrist cuffs. The soft click of the camera could be heard in the silence of the store but we pretended not to hear it, and once she was secure, I took a step back.

"I think we're getting that one whether you like it or not." My voice had grown thicker, matching the situation in my pants. She looked incredible tied up like that.

Gemma laughed, turning her head to try to see me. "Lucky for both of us, then, that I do like it."

We spent the next half hour and a couple of thousand pounds buying up everything she put her hands on, even if she said she was only curious. Realistically, I knew we'd never have time to use everything we bought before I left London the next week, but I wanted to have plenty of options depending on where our mood took us. After arranging for it all to be sent to the hotel, we stepped out into the streets again, resuming our walk towards the theatre.

I didn't have any clue what theatre we were going to or what show we were seeing. I only hoped it would be short so we could get back to the hotel room as soon as possible. I couldn't wait to decide what we were going to try first.

~Gemma~

After a quick takeaway shawarma from a hole-in-the-wall place on Oxford Street, Cole and I settled into our box at the Palladium. That night, I had brought him to a pantomime version of Cinderella. Attending a panto was a classic British Christmas tradition but something not easily explained to someone who had never been.

So, when I asked Cole innocently if he had ever been to a panto before and he said no, I had to hide my grin. Between the audience participation and the random pop songs and the B-list British actors taking part, he had no idea what he was getting into.

Sure enough, once the show began, it didn't take him long to realize this was not a typical night at the theatre. He jumped when the crowd heartily booed the entrance of the villain, and by the time the first, "Oh yes it is!" was called out, he looked thoroughly bewildered.

When the lights came up for the interval, I couldn't hold back my laughter. "Your facial expressions are more entertaining than anything that's happening on stage."

He narrowed his eyes at me in that stern way I loved. "You might have warned me. What the hell is this? And what does it have to do with Christmas?"

That only made me laugh louder. "Nobody knows, but you have to go to at least one every Christmas. It's a requirement of being British."

He turned his chair to face mine. Our box had four individual chairs which could be moved around to find the best view of the stage, but that night, we were the only people there. "How much longer does it go on for?"

"It's probably a little more than half finished. The second act is usually shorter."

He leaned forward, a smile playing at his lips. "I'm not sure I can wait that long."

I knew in the back of my head that encouraging him would only lead to trouble, but I couldn't help doing it anyway. "Wait for what?"

As I expected, his eyes darkened. "To have my dick buried in your pussy again."

Fuck. I loved how direct he was, and just like that, my body began to ache for him, my thighs clenching as a thrill of excitement travelled from my stomach downwards.

He glanced around the box at the space behind us. "Although, maybe we don't need to go anywhere. We do have quite a lot of privacy in here."

My heart started beating faster, and so did the throbbing between my legs. What, exactly, was he suggesting? "There's no lock on the door," I pointed out.

"No, but what are the odds someone would come in? Pretty low, I'd bet."

Could he really be serious? I looked out at the other seats in the theatre, trying to judge the angles. "The people sitting up there can see in." I pointed to the balcony across from us. "They can see the whole box."

"Only if they look." He sounded confident and unconcerned. "When the lights go down, they'll be watching the stage."

My teeth chewed at my bottom lip as I tried to decide which feeling was stronger: the desire for him or the fear of getting caught.

"I think it turns you on a little bit, Gemma," Cole whispered in my ear, leaning towards me as his hand brushed across my thighs. "The idea that someone might see us is making you hot."

It really did. As soon as I let myself imagine it, anticipation raced through me. What we'd done under the table at the restaurant had been one thing, but he was talking about actually having sex somewhere where a stray glance might give us away.

Before I had a chance to make up my mind, the lights began to dim for the second act and the actors returned to the stage. After a couple of minutes, Cole stood up from his chair and walked to the back of the box. He pulled his chair and the two extra chairs into a line, creating something of a wall in front of him. It wasn't solid by any means, but it would block at least a bit of anyone's view. Finally, he took his coat from the coat hook and folded it over, placing it on the floor. In no hurry at all, he lay down on the floor, on his back, his head resting on the coat, and he waited.

He had no doubt that I would join him, and damn it, I didn't either.

With my pulse racing, I also rose from my seat and pulled my chair back into the line with the others. Trying not to look too obvious, I walked around behind them and straddled Cole's body with my feet while he smirked up at me from the floor, waiting for me to make my move.

With a deep breath, I dropped to my hands and knees, hovering over top of him. Tentatively, I glanced over at the balcony on the other side of the theatre. The wall of chairs did help, but I could still see several faces, all of them turned towards the stage. If any of them should happen to look over at us...

"There's a condom in the pocket of my pants," Cole whispered, pulling my attention back to him. "Put it on me."

It was an order, one he fully expected me to follow, and I had no will to resist him, not when my body ached for him as badly as it did.

Reaching into his pocket, I fished out the condom and ripped it open. Using my body to shield him as much as possible, I pulled Cole's zip down, waiting for applause from the audience to cover the noise. He lifted his hips to help me get his trousers and underwear down and I rolled the condom onto him. He clearly found this whole situation as arousing as I did, since I didn't need to get him ready at all.

Somewhat awkwardly, I managed to remove my underwear, trying to move as little as possible so as not to draw attention to myself. At least I had decided to wear a skirt that day. The manoeuvre would have been a lot more difficult in trousers.

I still couldn't quite believe we were doing this, but as I straddled him again, lifting his cock up to guide it into place, I knew there was no going back. Slowly, I sank myself down onto him, biting my lip to hold in the moan that always accompanied the first feel of him filling me. I'd never felt anything quite so blissful, both satisfying me and making me crave more all at the same time.

Unlike the first time I rode him on the first night we spent together, Cole touched me the whole time. His hands ran through my hair and down to my chest, playing with my breasts through my clothes before finally working their way down beneath my skirt, finding my clit as I raised and lowered myself onto him, as discreetly as possible. The lights from the stage illuminated his face, the different colours ebbing and flowing along with our movements.

A loud burst of laughter from the audience nearly pulled me out of the moment, but the pressure Cole put on my clit helped to keep me focused. Sensing my distraction, he pulled my head down towards him, bringing his lips to my ear as my hips continued to thrust against him.

"Imagine if we were doing this up on that stage, Gemma," he whispered. "Imagine all those people watching you ride me."

I couldn't help whimpering at the thought, but he had anticipated that and his hand had already covered my mouth, drowning out the noise.

"They'd get their money's worth, wouldn't they, Gorgeous? That perfect ass bouncing on top of me, seeing you take my dick so well. Watching you come all over it."

Fuck. I was already so primed for him, so turned on by the taboo of what we were doing and the feel of his body, that just as he suggested, I came on him now, my muscles clenching him, my arms trembling as they tried to support me. That seemed to be what he was waiting for, since just a few moments later, I felt him coming too, the base of his shaft vibrating against me as he pumped into the condom inside me.

In the glow of our mutual pleasure, I almost forgot where we were, but gradually, it came back to me, and now that I wasn't quite so horny, the idea of being seen seemed a lot less appealing. As quickly and cautiously as I could, I climbed off of him, pulling my underwear back on and my skirt back down, and helped Cole get his trousers back up too. Looking around the box, however, I couldn't see any kind of rubbish bin. What was I supposed to do with the used condom? I couldn't exactly leave it in the box.

Cole simply gave me an amused look as he returned to his seat, as if the problem was entirely mine, and turned his attention back to the stage. Why I should find that so sexy, I had no idea, but I loved how unflappable and unconcerned he could be. It only made the moments when he lost control even hotter.

Quickly, I ducked out of the box and headed down the hall to the toilets. Not only could I throw the condom away, I could clean myself up too, and when I went to wash my hands and looked at myself in the mirror, I couldn't hold back my smile.

The previous Friday, I had my first kiss with Cole beneath the mistletoe. Just one week later, I went to a sex shop with him and fucked him at the theatre where anyone could have seen us.

The following Friday, he would be on his way back to New York, and I couldn't even begin to imagine what we would have done together by then.

Chapter Twelve

New Toys

~**Cole**~

Our tryst during the show managed to satisfy me for a little while, but I was still impatient to get back to the hotel and Gemma seemed to be feeling the same. As the show drew to an end, she leaned over to me and whispered in my ear.

"We can head out now to beat the crowd, if you want."

She didn't have to ask me twice. With her hand held tightly in mine, we caught a cab on Oxford Street to take us back to the hotel. No paparazzi were waiting for us at the hotel, but they weren't needed anyway. We'd already taken the pictures that would be in the next day's papers.

Frustratingly, the lobby was full of people and several of them got on the elevator with us, but when we got to my floor, we were finally alone. Just as I had that first night we met, almost exactly one week ago, I pushed Gemma up against the wall in the hallway, loving the way her body yielded to mine. If it weren't for the security cameras in the hall, I would have been happy to take her right there. As it was, I would settle for a little foreplay.

I had just got her leg wrapped around my waist and my hand high enough up her skirt to feel the heat from between her legs when my phone rang in my pocket. With a groan, I took a step back, reluctantly letting her go. I had a feeling I knew who was calling me, and the name on the screen when I pulled my phone out confirmed my hunch.

"Can you give me just a minute?" My voice made it clear I would prefer not to be interrupted, if I had the choice.

She nodded, giving me a teasing smile. "We should probably move inside your room anyway."

I answered the phone as Gemma began walking down the hall towards the suite, pulling out her own keycard from her purse. "Hi, Isabel. This isn't a great time."

"I don't care. I haven't heard from you in a week!" my sister exclaimed. "Someone told me that you were seen at some kind of Christmas carnival over there in London and I assumed you must have been kidnapped."

"What kind of criminal mastermind do you think kidnapped me to force me to attend Christmas events?" I asked as I followed Gemma into the suite. She raised her eyebrows at me as she removed her coat, clearly intrigued by the one side of the conversation she could hear.

"Well, what other explanation is there?" Isabel asked, trying to keep the laughter out of her reply. "You can't expect me to believe you went willingly."

Since I knew genuine concern lay behind her teasing, I didn't give her a hard time. "I'm fine, Isabel. Everything's fine here, and I'm coming home next week as promised. You can bother me every day from then until New Year's, alright?"

"You sound good, actually," my sister said thoughtfully. "Happier, even."

"We can catch up when I'm back," I promised.

Isabel laughed. "Okay, I'm obviously interrupting something. Good. As long as you're not sitting alone in your room like some comic book villain, I'm happy. Have a good week, Cole."

"You too."

After hanging up, I turned back to Gemma, who had been watching me curiously. "You've got someone checking up on you?"

"My sister. She's two years older than me but likes to pretend it's more like twenty."

Gemma smiled. "That sounds nice. She cares." She sounded almost wistful, or even jealous, but a second later, she winked at me, and all thoughts of Isabel went out the window. "Does she have any idea what a bad influence you are on respectable theatregoers such as myself?"

"Respectable?" I repeated, stalking towards her as I removed my suit jacket. "As far as I'm concerned, you're the one who seduced me in that box tonight."

Her eyes widened in disbelief. "Me? I was just sitting there, minding my own business..."

"Crossing and uncrossing your legs in that little skirt of yours," I finished. "Putting all kinds of thoughts in my head."

My tie came off and I began working on my shirt buttons.

"I really can't take any credit for the thoughts in your head, Cole." Gemma's green eyes sparkled in that fucking irresistible way of hers. "Your imagination is far better than mine."

"And what am I imagining now, do you think?" I pulled my shirt down over my arms, tossing it to the floor with the rest of my clothes, then moved on to my belt.

"Why don't you tell me?" The breathlessness in her voice told me more than her words ever could: she wanted my instructions. She wanted to be told what to do.

"First, I'm picturing you naked."

Gemma made short work of getting out of her clothes, stripping off the last item just as I finished pulling mine off. I took a moment to look her over and appreciate her beautiful body once again, and to appreciate my good fortune in having her there with me for another week still. Although I'd already had her in several different ways, several different times, it still wasn't nearly enough.

"Now, go get the shower started. I'll join you in a minute."

Surprise flashed across her face but she didn't question my command. As she left, I dug around in the bags that had been delivered from the sex shop until I found the suction hand cuffs. I hadn't even known they existed until we saw them in the store earlier that night but I couldn't wait to try them out. Before it could slip my mind again, I also grabbed a condom from the bedroom. With the way Gemma distracted me, it would be all too easy to get carried away.

Steam had already started to fill the bathroom when I entered. The large walk-in shower, easily big enough for the both of us, had a rainfall shower head and a separate handheld one. Gemma had already stepped inside, waiting for me, and the sight of her literally dripping, the droplets of water running down her skin, drawing paths my tongue longed to follow, made me even harder than I had been since pulling the cuffs out of the bag.

Placing the items in my hand down on the shower bench, I pulled Gemma to me, pressing every inch of me against her as we picked up the kiss where we'd left off in the hallway. The taste of her never failed to excite me; something sweet yet spicy, it satisfied me but still left me wanting more.

Her hands wrapped around my waist as her hips moved against me eagerly, trapping my erection between our bodies, but I dropped my hands to her waist to stop her. "Not so fast," I admonished, still nipping at her lips. "I've got other plans for you first."

Grabbing the cuffs from the bench, I quickly attached them to Gemma's wrists and raised her arms up over her head. Once the cuffs were securely suctioned to the wall, I pulled the handheld shower head off down from its cradle.

"Let's see what kinds of settings this has, shall we?"

My body on edge with anticipation, just as hers must be, I cycled through the various options before settling on a gentle, pulsing rhythm to start with. Gemma watched me through half-closed eyelids as I moved the wand over her body, letting her feel it on her neck, on her chest, her stomach and her thighs before finally bringing it to rest against her clit. A moan escaped her lips as her arms tensed, but the cuffs held her firmly in place. I used my free hand to spread her folds open, letting the water hit her more directly, while my mouth went to her breasts, my tongue lapping against her nipple to mimic the pulsing of the water.

"Oh, God, Cole," she breathed as her body wriggled beneath the onslaught of sensations. With a flick of the dial with my thumb, the pressure of the water increased and I sucked her nipple into my mouth harder. Her response came out more forcefully too. "Oh, fuck!"

I didn't let up, both the wand and my tongue continuing to work her over until she came, shuddering against the wall. Another person's orgasm had never brought me so much satisfaction; I loved to see her lose control and the beautiful way her body relaxed as the pleasure overwhelmed her.

Switching the shower head off, I let it fall to the floor and I followed it down, onto my knees. With my hands to guide her, Gemma brought her legs up over my shoulders, leaving her supported only by her arms still cuffed to the wall above her head, and I couldn't help groaning in pleasure as I buried my face between her legs.

As much as I loved the taste of her mouth, her pussy was just as sweet, and I took my time exploring her and working her back to a frenzy after her first orgasm. By their very nature, my paid encounters were less about my partner's pleasure than they were about mine, so I hadn't gone down on a woman in a long time, and that gave it a novelty that only increased my enjoyment of it. My tongue explored every inch and crevice of her, and I loved the way she moved against me and the sounds she made as I circled her clit, teasing her and drawing out her pleasure as long as I could. By the time I finally clamped down on her clit, sucking hard, she had been fully primed for it and she came again, her legs trembling around my neck.

It still staggered me that Edwin called her unresponsive. Maybe she had been so frustrated for so many years that I was reaping the benefits of unlocking her need for submission, claiming all the orgasms that could have been his over the years. Whatever the case may be, I could only count my blessings that I'd found her when I did.

Gently placing her feet back on the ground, I stood back up. "Are your arms okay?" I asked, running my hands down them gently. Gemma nodded, looking up at me with sex-soaked eyes, and I smiled. "Good, because I'm not quite finished with you yet."

My wet fingers slipped against the foil as I tried to open the condom wrapper, and finally, I had to give up and use my teeth. Once I'd rolled it on, I grabbed Gemma's legs again, wrapping them around my waist as I thrust into her hard against the wall.

We both groaned in unison as our bodies fully combined. She felt so fucking perfect wrapped around me that way. I kept my hands beneath her ass, squeezing it as I began to move inside her, first with long, deep strokes and then faster and harder, slamming her into the wall as her arms trembled above her head. Each time I entered her felt like coming home, like this was exactly where I was meant to be.

"Fuck, Gemma," I grunted, barely aware of the water anymore or the steam or anything but the feel of her body against mine and encasing me. "I never want to let you go. I want to keep you chained to my wall, just like this, so I can fuck you whenever I want to."

She whimpered into her climax, and as it had so many times already, that sound pushed me over too. My pace slowed as my dick pumped but I didn't entirely stop, rocking with her a few more times until my heart rate began to return to normal.

As I placed Gemma's feet back on the ground, her arms were still shaking, so I quickly released her from the cuffs and sat down on the bench with her in my lap. She melted against me as I held her, neither of us saying anything for several minutes as we rested in the steamy warmth.

Finally, Gemma raised her head and smiled at me. "I'm going to fall asleep if we stay here much longer."

"Okay. Let's get you ready for bed, then."

Standing her up again, I quickly washed her hair and body before wrapping her up in one of the big, fluffy hotel towels and picking her up in my arms. Still naked and dripping wet myself, I carried her to the bed and gently placed her down, got her pajamas on and helped her into bed.

I couldn't explain why I liked taking care of her that way. I'd never really done it with anyone else before, but for some reason, the more she submitted to me during sex, the more I wanted to look after her afterwards. It wasn't that I didn't think she was capable of taking care of herself. Somehow, it almost felt like a thank you to her for trusting me, for letting me take control for the both of us, and making sure she knew that I took that trust seriously.

As I pulled the covers up and placed a kiss on her forehead, the words I'd said to her in the shower came back to me, like an echo in my mind. I couldn't quite believe I said them, but she didn't seem to have noticed, or she must have just thought they were said in the heat of the moment. Looking at her, though, I suspected part of me really meant it. There was a part of me that didn't want to let her go.

~Gemma~

It took me a moment to remember why my arms were sore when I woke up on Saturday, but as the memories of the night before came back to me, of being suspended, helpless against the shower wall while Cole made me come over and over again, I had to smile. Everything we did together always turned out even better than I could have imagined. With my eyes still closed, I stretched my arms out to ease the stiff muscles.

"Good morning." Cole's deep voice came from further away than I expected, and I opened my eyes to see him standing at the doorway to the bedroom with a tray in his hands and an almost sweet smile on his face. "Breakfast?"

"Only if there's tea too," I mumbled, blinking at him sleepily as I sat up in bed. Did he ever sleep? It felt like I always went to sleep before him and woke up after him.

"Of course." He kept smiling as he brought the tray over to the bed, placing it down next to me. There was indeed a cup of tea, along with a croissant, some fresh fruit and a yogurt pot. "I wasn't sure exactly what you wanted, but we can always order more."

There were perks to living in a hotel, I had to admit. "This looks great," I assured him. "What time is it?"

"Nearly eight o'clock."

He really must have worn me out the night before. I hadn't meant to sleep so late. "Okay, that should give me enough time. The car's coming for us at half nine."

"Car?" he repeated, looking almost disappointed as his smile faded. "Are we going somewhere? I'd been hoping to have more time to play with some of our new toys this morning."

A shiver ran through me at his tone, combined with the memory of some of the things we had picked up in the shop the night before, but I wasn't going to let him distract me. "There will be time for that later, I promise, but first, I want to take you to a house out of town."

Cole sighed, but before I could remind him that he still had to keep up his end of the deal, he acquiesced. "What's special about this house?"

"This is one of my favourite houses in the world," I told him, taking a warm, satisfying sip of my tea. "It's the reason I decided to become an architect."

That got Cole's attention. "Alright, Gemma, I'm intrigued. Where is it? Would I have been to it before?"

"It's possible, but I wouldn't be surprised if you haven't. It's an old stately home outside the city called Wilby Park."

No trace of recognition registered in his eyes. "I don't think I've heard of it. What makes it your favourite?"

"I'll explain when we're there," I promised. "They're open to the public today as part of their annual Christmas opening."

"I should have guessed it was Christmas-related." He sighed again, but I could see the teasing light in his eyes. "Eat up, then. We better get ready."

Two hours later, we were settled in the back seat of the hired car while the driver headed out of London. We talked about different architectural styles and development in London as the car led us through different neighbourhoods, and once the city had fallen away and we were out in the countryside, we talked more about Cole's business and his expansion plans in Europe. So far, Stamer Hotels had mainly focused on city centre locations in Europe, but he was considering opening some countryside resort-style retreats. He had a lot of ideas for the kind of places he wanted to create and I loved listening to the passion that he had for his properties.

By the time we pulled into the grounds of Wilby Park, the time was nearing noon and, as always, the first view of the property across the parkland took my breath away. With its perfect symmetry, the towers, cupolas, and the many, many windows, it almost looked like something from a fairy tale.

"Wow." Cole leaned forward in his seat, his face close to the window. I had rarely seen him so openly interested in anything. "That's impressive. Elizabethan?"

"Yes," I confirmed. "I'm impressed that you knew that."

He turned back to me, smirking in his confident, sexy way. "I'm not just a pretty face, Gemma."

I couldn't help myself; the opening was just too good. "I never said your face was your best feature."

Cole nearly choked on his surprised laughter, making the driver glance back at us with concern. "You're going to pay for that later," he whispered in my ear, his mouth still twitching with amusement.

I certainly hoped so, but for the time being, I tried to direct his attention back to the property. "The house originally dates from the 1570s. It's still privately owned by the same family that built it."

"I'm surprised it's not better known," he mused, looking back out the window. "Americans would eat this up."

I had an explanation for that. "The family likes their privacy. It's only opened for three weeks in the summer and three weeks at Christmas each year so they can claim tax exemptions as a tourist attraction."

The car pulled up along the gravel drive to the front of the house where a good number of other visitors, mostly with grey hair, were milling about. The property wasn't a particularly family-friendly destination, not bothering with the child-oriented activities that a lot of the other big houses brought out at Christmas time.

"We can grab something to eat first if you like." I pointed Cole in the direction of the stables once we were out of the car, and we made our way to the cozy café where we both got a bowl of home-made soup and fresh bread. Refreshed and energized, we bought our tickets and made our way inside the house.

The entrance hall was fairly typical for the period with stone walls and stone floors, decorated with weapons on the walls and a large fireplace, and in a nod to the season, a large Christmas tree had been set up in one corner with home-made ornaments. Cole looked around with interest as I pointed out some of the key architectural elements as well as a few of my favourite decorative flourishes. An older couple also stopped to listen to me for a while, asking their own questions, which amused Cole.

"Do you moonlight as a tour guide here?" he teased me. "If not, maybe you should."

"I used to," I admitted. "On my summer holidays when I was in school."

He raised his eyebrows in surprise. "You weren't kidding that this place is important to you."

"I wasn't lying. I really love it."

"Why? I mean, why this one out of all the houses in the world?"

I simply smiled and took his hand, pulling him through the next door. A large staircase filled the hall in front of us while generations of men looked down on us from gilded frames. I led him over to the first one, the smallest portrait, showing a man in 16th-century dress. "This is the man who built this house. His name is Frederick Redvers."

"Redvers?" Cole peered at the man carefully before his dark eyes moved back to me. "Your family?"

"Yes. They all are." I indicated all the paintings on the walls around us. "This is my family's house. One of them, anyway."

Cole hadn't expected that, and he looked around the room again, as if seeing it for the first time. "And you still have to pay to get in?"

That made me laugh. "We probably didn't have to, but I didn't want anyone to make a fuss about us being here. Most of the staff who work the opening are seasonal, they don't know me."

"So, you grew up here?"

"No, not really. We only spent a few weeks here every year. My father prefers his London house, and my brother and I went to boarding school, but I always loved the time we spent here, and as I said, it inspired me to learn more about architectural design. It's a special place."

"I can see that," Cole agreed. His eyes searched the room again, looking over the portraits as if he might see a resemblance to me in them. "In that case, Gemma, if this is your house, I want the private tour. Not the one you give to everyone."

"There's a lot of good information in that tour," I protested, which only made him laugh.

"I'm sure there is. But I want to see the things no one else gets to see." His voice dipped lower as he brought his mouth closer to my ear. "I want a more intimate perspective. To go deeper."

He was being very subtle by his own standards, but his meaning still came through loud and clear. God, he really was insatiable, and I couldn't stop my mind from wandering to all the hidden nooks and crannies of the house where we might get a bit of privacy.

"I might know the kind of place you're looking for," I admitted. "When we get upstairs. Can you wait until then?"

He smirked at me, his eyes dark with desire. "As long as you make it worth the wait."

~Cole~

Gemma's tour of the house kept me genuinely entertained as she led me from room to room, pointing out little architectural details and anachronisms in the decoration. It really was an interesting building, and the fact that it belonged to Gemma's family only made it more fascinating. My family had money, certainly, but that wealth came from my father and from me, both of us building the Stamer Hotels brand from a couple of hotels to a worldwide chain. It felt completely different to the kind of history that stretched back hundreds of years with old oil portraits of ancestors lining the halls.

As we walked, I tried to picture Gemma as a young girl in these rooms with their museum-quality works of art and furniture. Did she play hide-and-seek in the dozens of grandiose chambers, or come close to knocking the vases off their perches while running races with her friends? Or was she a more quiet kind of child, reading books in the window seats and studying the details of the wood panelling?

She seemed at home here, yet she also seemed equally at home in her offices at Anchor Design, or in her ridiculous Santa dress the night we met. She reminded me of a chameleon, blending in wherever she went. Which version of herself was the truest one? One of those, or perhaps the Gemma that only I got to see, alone in my hotel suite?

As much as I enjoyed the educational diversion, when she finally headed towards the staircase, my excitement only grew. She had suggested that we could be alone when we went upstairs, and I was looking forward to it immensely. I already had a few ideas about what I'd like to do when we got there.

"This bedroom was built for Elizabeth I to stay in if she ever visited Wilby Park," Gemma told me as we walked into a room with more priceless old paintings lining its wood-covered walls, and a large canopy bed in the centre. "However, there's no record that she ever actually came here."

I couldn't resist such an easy setup, or the chance to make her smile. "They did call her the Virgin Queen. I doubt she came many places."

Gemma covered her mouth with her hand to hide her smile, looking around at the other people in the room. They were all engaged in their own conversations; no one had heard us, but she shook her head at me playfully anyway. "Not your most mature humour, but I did give you an opening."

She wanted immature humour? I could do better than that. "Any time you give me an opening, Gemma, I'm going to fill it."

She laughed out loud, and the people closest to us turned to look at her. "You're going to get me in trouble," she whispered, turning away from me in an effort to remain professional.

"I do like putting you in a tight spot," I reminded her, leaning over her shoulder to whisper in her ear.

"Okay, stop now," she pleaded, but I could still hear the smile in her voice. "If you don't behave, I won't take you on the detour I had planned in the next room."

"That's an empty threat, since I know you're looking forward to it as much as I am." My arms went around her waist, and she melted back against me immediately. "You've been thinking about it ever since I first mentioned it."

A soft sigh left her lips. "Do you ever get tired of being right all the time?"

"I'll let you know when it happens. For now…"

"Let's go to the next room," she agreed. When she turned back to me, her eyes were sparkling merrily. "But only because I say it's time."

"Of course," I humoured her. "It's your tour."

She rolled her eyes at me, trying to look annoyed, but the smile on her lips betrayed her. Taking my hand in hers, she led me into the next room, which was actually just a small antechamber between the bedroom we'd just been in and a formal sitting room. On one of the side walls, there was a narrow door, and after looking around to ensure that no one could see us, Gemma opened the door and ushered me through, following close behind.

The door led to a small passageway, only wide enough for one person to pass through at a time. "Go straight ahead," Gemma whispered from behind me. "Third door on the left."

Following her instructions, I opened the third door and found myself faced with a narrow spiral staircase.

"These were the servant's passages." The whispered explanation came from behind me again. "Just step down for a second, and I'll lead the way."

I took a step down as she'd requested so she could squeeze past, and followed behind her as she climbed the stairs to the next floor. A couple of steps above me on the narrow stairs, the sight of her ass at my eye level made me even more impatient. When we reached the next landing, we were met with another narrow passage, and Gemma passed two more doors on the left before stopping.

Placing a finger on her lips to keep me quiet, she very slowly opened the door, peering gingerly around it once the gap was wide enough. With a sigh of relief, she threw it open widely and stepped inside.

I followed her into a much smaller and more modern-looking bedroom than those we had just been visiting. Besides the door we had entered through, the room had two additional doors, one on either side of us as we entered, but both were closed. Gemma moved over to them quickly and locked them both while I closed the door behind me, noticing that it had no lock on it. I supposed her ancestors hadn't considered it necessary to lock the doors to the servants.

"Okay, we shouldn't be disturbed here," Gemma said, speaking at a normal volume again. "This is part of the family's private quarters, and neither my father nor brother are here right now."

"It doesn't concern you at all how easy it was for us to get in here? Anyone on that tour could have done the same thing."

"Anything really worth stealing is in the rooms that are on the tour," she replied with a shrug. "Since the house is opened such a short time each year, my father never felt it necessary to spend a lot of money on security measures."

That seemed short-sighted to me, but there were other things I would rather be focusing on. "So, why did you choose this room to bring us to?"

Gemma grinned and took my hand again, pulling me over to the windows on the far side of the room. The parkland stretched far into the distance, rows of ancient trees opening to fields where deer roamed and, close to the house, formal gardens were laid out. Despite it being early December, plenty of flowers were still in bloom.

"This is my favourite view," she explained, looking out over it with a nostalgic gleam in her eyes. "I always wanted to sleep in this room when we would come to stay here."

I could see why, but I wanted to hear more about it from her. "What did you think about when you stayed here, looking out at the view?"

She seemed a little surprised by the question, but as she thought it over, a soft smile lit up her face. "I used to imagine what it would have been like for the other women of my family who lived here in the past. I would make up stories about their lives, their romances and their adventures. I had a story to go with just about every person you saw on the walls downstairs."

I could definitely work with that. "Did you have a favourite story that you invented?"

As I hoped, Gemma's eyes twinkled mischievously. "I was particularly fond of my backstory for Lady Margaret Redvers. In real life, she eventually married the Duke of Norwich who was nearly forty years older than her, but in my story, she first had a passionate love affair with a tall, handsome stablehand. Sadly, they were parted when she had to be married; star-crossed lovers and so on. Just the kind of thing a teenage girl finds hopelessly romantic."

She couldn't have set me up any better. I already knew Gemma was up for a little role play, and I couldn't think of a better place to do it than where she'd spent her time imagining those kinds of things.

Leaving the window, I moved around the room to see what my options were for props. Gemma watched me for a minute before her curiosity got the better of her. "Are you looking for something in particular?"

"Something thin and hard," I told her, opening the doors to the wardrobe.

"Like the fire poker?" she asked innocently, pointing to the heavy iron instruments by the fireplace.

"No, not quite that hard." As always, I didn't want to actually hurt her. I had been picturing something like a riding crop, but perhaps unsurprisingly, I couldn't see anything that quite fit the bill. It was a shame we didn't have access to some of the things we bought at the shop the night before.

As I cast one last look around the room, I caught a glimpse of myself in the mirror and realized two things: first, I was wearing a belt, which would probably work just fine for what I had in mind, and second, the mirror's position would add an extra dimension to our fun.

"Never mind," I told Gemma, turning back to her with anticipation. "I've got everything I need."

"To do what?" she asked, still not having a clue what was in my head.

"To let Lady Margaret and her stablehand have some fun before the wedding."

Chapter Thirteen

Family History

~Gemma~

My lips parted in surprise at Cole's words and the confident, determined glint in his eyes. I hadn't had any inkling that when he asked me about my teenaged daydreams, he was actually fishing for information he could turn into a role play for us. My eyes immediately drifted to the bed where I had spent many summer nights on my own, imagining the very scenario he had just offered to act out with me. I had pictured myself as the unfortunate Lady Margaret, engaged to a man old enough to be her grandfather, and I had imagined how she would stand at the window, watching the stablehand working with the horses, how their eyes would meet, their attraction undeniable. Looks would turn to touches, and finally, he would take her innocence one night in the stable.

That part of the fantasy would have to stay a fantasy, since we couldn't exactly go out to the stables with all the visitors hanging around, but the second part of my imaginings, when the stablehand found a way to sneak into Lady Margaret's room at night through the servant's passage... that, we could definitely work with.

My pulse raced, my body already feeling nearly weak with desire at the idea of combining several of the things I'd loved doing with Cole over the last few days. First, it had the role play element and second, just like at the restaurant and the theatre, we ran the risk of being caught. Even though we were in private and this was technically my family's house, we definitely weren't supposed to be there in that room. And third, he had just told me he was looking for something hard, something that I could now only suppose he wanted to use as part of our play. As I remembered how he'd spanked me the other night during our game, the memory set off an even stronger throbbing pulse between my legs.

I couldn't have explained to anyone why I wanted him to be rough with me, but by that point with Cole, I was past questioning my desires. My body told me that I wanted it, and I knew without asking that whatever I wanted, he would give to me.

"I wish I had a proper dress," I said, more to myself than to him, but of course, Cole heard it too.

His eyes immediately darkened, the telltale sign that he was aroused too. "You would look incredible in an 18th century ballgown. I'll make a note of it."

I laughed, having no doubt that he actually would go out and buy me one if the fancy struck him. "Well, for now, I guess we'll have to work with what we have."

It didn't really matter what I was wearing, after all. I'd be out of it soon enough anyway.

"Set the scene for me, Gemma," Cole commanded. "What's happening?"

How did I want to approach it? There were so many possibilities, all of them equally appealing, but eventually, I settled on one that I had played out in my head before. It had vanished to the vaults of my memory ages ago, but being back in that room and talking about it with Cole brought it back to the surface.

"I've tried to get out of my engagement, but I can't. I have to leave tomorrow and I'll never see my lover again."

"One last night to remember, then?"

I nodded in confirmation. He was always right on my wavelength. "Exactly."

"Okay. What do I call you?"

In our previous role play, he'd simply called me Gemma, but in keeping with my fantasy, we would be stepping into different roles. "Lady Margaret or 'my lady' when you're being formal. Meg when you're not."

"Meg," he repeated, a smile pulling the corner of his lips. "And do you have a name for me?"

A blush rose in my cheeks as I remembered I had called the stablehand in my fantasies 'Eddie', after an actor who I had a crush on at the time. However, thanks to more recent events, the name Eddie made me think of Edwin, and I had no desire to be thinking about him at all.

"What do you want me to call you?" I asked instead.

He thought about it for a moment. "Maybe something Irish? I think I've seen too many movies with old British estates and Irish staff."

"I think it's okay as long as you don't try the accent," I replied with a laugh. I couldn't imagine anything other than Cole's blunt New York accent coming from his mouth.

"Owen?"

"Owen is Welsh," I corrected him. "Get your accents straight."

He broke into one of his rare, genuinely amused grins, and I couldn't help beaming back at him. It seemed crazy to me how I could be so comfortable with him, joking around and teasing each other, knowing that in a matter of minutes, he would have me naked and be doing unimaginable things to me.

"I like Owen, though," I agreed. "Let's go with that."

The scene set, Cole left the room, stepping back into the narrow passageway that we'd entered from, and as soon as I was alone, the anticipation rushed back in, sweeping through me. Every time I had sex with Cole felt like the first time, full of excitement and uncertainty. I never knew what to expect from him, only that whatever he did, it would be amazing.

Knowing that he would fully commit to the scene, I made my way back to the window, trying to look pensive as I put myself in the shoes of Lady Margaret: promised to a man I didn't love while the one I did care for was here but out of my reach.

The door from the servant's passage opened, and I gasped in pretended surprise, turning towards the sound. Cole stood just inside the door with a dark scowl on his face. If I hadn't known he was acting, I would have almost been frightened. He looked genuinely intimidating.

"Lady Margaret," he greeted me, his voice low and deep, and a shiver ran through me. 'Lady' was actually my proper title, though I never used it, and for some reason, hearing him use the title struck me as incredibly sexy. "I've heard that you're leaving tomorrow. Were you going to go without saying goodbye?"

I did my best to look conflicted. "What's the use, Owen? There's nothing I can do. I have to go, and seeing you only makes it harder. You shouldn't be here."

"That's a lie, my lady." He stalked towards me, his face still dark and brooding. "There is something else you could do: you could run away with me. I've told you before, I can take care of you."

"I can't," I protested. "My father would find us. He'd kill you."

"Not being with you will kill me," he claimed, pulling me tightly into his arms and I couldn't help marvelling at how good Cole was at all of this. He could have been an actor if his career path hadn't already been chosen for him.

"It's impossible, Owen," I cried, probably a little too melodramatically, but Cole's intensity never wavered. "Just let me go."

"Not until I remind you what you'll be missing."

With that, Cole swept me back into a deep kiss, his arms cradling me firmly, the only thing keeping me from falling over entirely. It almost reminded me of being on the ferris wheel with him, kissing him while we moved through the air and losing all sense of space.

The kiss was so hard, so unyielding, that my lips almost felt raw as he pulled away.

"Your duke will never kiss you like that, Meg." His dark eyes were fixed on mine, daring me to contradict him.

"N-no, he won't," I agreed, my voice genuinely breathless, no acting required. "But we can't live on kisses."

"You really won't come with me?" he demanded.

I shook my head apologetically. "I can't."

His jaw clenched in convincing frustration. "Then give me tonight, Meg. Give me a night you'll never forget."

I tried not to look too eager as I nodded, aching for him more than ever. "Yes. We have tonight."

Another bruising kiss followed, his hand holding the back of my head as his tongue explored every inch of my mouth, and when he finally let me come up for air, he took my hand and pulled me roughly to the centre of the room, standing me before the mirror.

"Everything I do to you tonight, Meg, you're going to watch. When you're lying in bed with that old man on top of you, you can close your eyes and remember this."

My thighs clenched as electricity jolted through me. I'd never watched myself while having sex before but I already knew I was going to love it. How did he know I would?

Cole let go of my hand and moved around my back, looking me up and down. As he'd instructed, I kept looking in the mirror, watching his movements and trying to anticipate what he might do next.

"Take off your clothes," he ordered, meeting my eyes in the mirror. "I want to see all of you."

I hurried to obey, but when I looked down to unbutton my shirt, Cole's hand immediately came under my chin, lifting my head back up.

"Watch the mirror," he reminded me. "Never take your eyes off it."

My fingers trembled with excitement as I did as he said, watching myself get undressed. Once I was completely naked, he circled me once more while I followed his movements through the mirror, watching him inspecting me like a prize animal going to the fair.

"You'll be wasted on that duke, Meg." The name surprised me for just a second; I'd been so focused on the way my body was feeling that I had almost forgotten what we were doing. "This glorious ass." His hands reached down and grabbed it firmly, making me gasp in surprise. "These beautiful breasts." Still standing behind me, his hands reached around to cup my breasts, squeezing them gently. "And this tight, wet little pussy."

His left hand stayed on my breast but his right one dipped down between my legs, his finger immediately pushing its way inside me. My breath caught again as I watched him, and I moaned as his thumb began rubbing my clit.

"You're perfect, Gemma," he whispered in my ear, his eyes locked on mine through the mirror. "See how beautiful you are as you come."

Gemma? Did he realize he'd used my real name? I couldn't have asked even if I wanted to. I couldn't speak at all. Even keeping my eyes open was a struggle, but I did, watching as Cole kissed my neck from behind, one hand pinching and playing with my nipple, the other building into a steady rhythm as his fingers pumped into me, his thumb still playing with my clit. Somehow, feeling what he was doing and seeing him do it at the same time made it even more intense, and I approached the peak of my orgasm in hardly any time at all, getting achingly close to that blissful release.

"Keep your eyes open," he reminded me. "Watch yourself fall apart."

His words were all I needed to do just that, and I forced my eyes to stay open even as my vision blurred and blackened at the edges. My legs buckled but Cole's strong arms were there to support me, his mouth curling up into a satisfied, proud smile.

"That's what I get to see each time, Gorgeous," he whispered, still looking at my reflection. "Do you see now why I can't get enough?"

~Cole~

As soon as Gemma's legs were able to support her well enough to walk again, I led her to the bed, letting her sit on the edge while she got her strength back. Watching her watch herself had been just as good as I'd expected. In fact, I'd gotten so caught up in it that I almost forgot about the scene we were playing, but I was ready to return to it as soon as she recovered.

"You can pretend all you want, Meg," I said as I slipped out of my suit jacket. "You can pretend you're a duchess once you're married to him, but I'll always know the truth."

"What truth?" Gemma's eyes followed my hands as I loosened my tie.

"That you're just the same as any whore I can buy in town." I pulled my tie off and set to work on my shirt buttons. "The only difference is that you'll be letting him fuck you for his title instead of his money."

I could see the excitement flare up amongst the glazed submission in Gemma's eyes. It still turned her on to think about being paid for sex, as I thought it would. After all, that was the basis of our entire agreement, even if no actual money changed hands.

"In fact, you're even worse than they are, because I don't have a title or money, and you still want me to fuck you, don't you?"

"Yes." The word came out as almost a whimper. "I want you to."

I pulled my shirt off roughly, my anticipation just as high as hers, and began undoing my belt. "Would you take anyone off the street? Are you that desperate?"

Her eyes widened and I honestly couldn't tell if I'd genuinely surprised her or if she was still playing her role. She was damn good at this.

"You were my first, Owen, you know that. You're the only man who's had me."

"Until tomorrow, when you leave me and marry that bastard. Do you know how that makes me feel, Meg?"

"It's not my fault," she protested. "I'm sorry."

"You will be when I show you just how much it hurts."

Holding the metal buckle of my belt in the palm of my hand, I wrapped it once around my fist, leaving a good length of it free. Gemma's eyes widened once again as she looked at it, and that time, I felt certain she wasn't faking her response. She hadn't expected that, but I saw the gleam of excitement that accompanied her surprise.

I pulled her back to her feet, turning her to face the mirror again. "I'm going to give you something to remember me by, Meg. Pleasure and pain." I leaned in closer, tucking Gemma's hair behind her ear as I whispered to her. "You remember your safeword?"

She nodded at me, her eyes locked on mine in the mirror.

With her agreement secured, I took a step back behind her, surveying her body as I tried to decide where I should strike her. Since I'd never done anything similar before, I would definitely start gently, but I knew she liked it when I spanked her during our previous role play. Not only that, but when we were at the sex shop the night before, she picked out a few different impact play items that caught her eye. She was definitely interested in it, and I would be happy to explore it with her if she wanted to, as long as I didn't cause her any real harm.

"This is for every time that you'll kiss him," I told her, keeping in character.

Using a little less force than I would have with my hand, I brought the belt down across Gemma's ass.

She jumped, but it seemed to be more in surprise than pain. When I rubbed where I had hit her, I couldn't see any redness there.

"Do you want it harder?" I asked in her ear again, letting her know I was asking her and not her character.

"Yes," she whispered back. "A bit harder."

With that in mind, I stepped back again, surveying the beautiful landscape of her skin once more.

"This is for every time that you'll let him touch you."

I struck her across her upper back, a little harder, as she'd requested. It seemed to work better as she gasped, her body instinctively pulling away from the pain but her hips pushing back towards me. A faint red line appeared where the belt had touched, and I rubbed it with my hand to ease the sting.

"This is for him playing with those breasts that belong to me."

The belt hit her on the back of her thighs and her knees buckled, but she kept her balance.

"For his fingers inside you."

A stroke on her lower back.

"And this, Meg, this is for when he fucks you."

I smacked the belt against her ass again: once, twice, and a third time, and red welts appeared almost instantly. The belt dropped from my hand, hitting the floor as I gathered Gemma into an embrace, holding her back against my chest.

I met her eyes in the mirror again, and I could see the tears that gathered in the corners of them. But the way her arms held onto mine, the way she clung onto me, plus the fact that she hadn't used her safeword, all assured me that I hadn't gone too far.

"Shhh," I soothed her, reaching up to brush her hair from her face as a soft whimper broke from her lips. "I know it's not your fault. I know you don't want him. I know you hate it as much as I do. Let me make you forget, just for tonight."

"Please." Gemma's voice sounded almost desperate as I moved her back to the bed, helping her onto it on her hands and knees.

"Don't forget the mirror," I reminded her, and she turned her head so she could see herself, kneeling there beautifully on display for me.

Quickly, I took off my remaining clothes and grabbed the condom from my pocket. I'd started to make it a habit to always carry one or two when I would be with Gemma, since I could never guess when one might be needed and I didn't want to be caught short.

Rolling it onto my ready dick, I positioned myself behind her, resisting the urge to run my hands across the red, raised skin on her ass. Part of me wanted to ease any discomfort she might be feeling, but my rough hands might only make it more sore. In the mirror, she watched me, just as I'd told her to, and when I turned to it, our eyes met through the glass.

"I promise you won't ever forget this." By that point, I didn't know if I was speaking to Meg or Gemma, but it really didn't matter. We both watched the mirror as my dick pushed into her, disappearing into the delicious warmth of her body. *Fuck.* That felt like heaven, and I groaned in pure pleasure while Gemma moaned in response, both of us lost in the dual joys of both watching and participating.

Gripping her hips tightly, I kept my thrusts slow and unhurried, letting her watch as I slid in and out of her, burying myself fully each and every time. I knew from her reaction that the angle was good for her, her breath growing more shallow each time I bottomed out.

"You see how perfectly you take me, Gemma?" I asked, my voice thick with desire. I loved being able to see her face in the mirror, to see her reactions to my words and my actions, seeing what she was seeing. "Your pussy was made for me."

"Cole." My name sounded strangled, almost pleading as it came out of her, and a moment later, she came again, her body trembling in bliss as she dropped to her elbows, her arms giving way from under her.

"That's it, Gorgeous," I encouraged her. "But I'm not done yet. I think you've got one more in you, just for me."

My pace grew faster as our skin slapped together. Loud moans and sighs filled the air of the room where generations of her family had probably fucked before. Neither of us held back, both of us completely lost in the pleasure of the moment. I was so close but I wanted her to come again first, so I returned to my stablehand role once more.

"Lady Margaret," I growled, keeping my eyes locked on hers through the mirror. "My beautiful lady. My perfect fucking whore."

Gemma cried out my name once more, my real name, as her inner walls clenched around me and she collapsed once again.

"Fuck, Gemma," I breathed out as I came too, the release stronger than ever after all that build-up. I honestly couldn't remember it ever feeling that good.

Gemma lay face-down on the bed as I pulled out of her, so I gently lowered her hips down, rolling her onto her side. Removing the condom, I joined her on the bed, curling up behind her as our bodies moulded against each other.

I could have lain there happily for hours, but less than a minute passed before there was a loud knock on one of the doors, making both of us jump. The knock was quickly followed by a loud, angry voice.

"Who's in there?"

~Gemma~

The knock at the door pulled me out of my blissful post-orgasm haze immediately.

"Who's in there?" a voice called, and my stomach twisted. I knew that voice all too well, but what would he be doing there? And how much, exactly, had he just heard? It looked like I would have to explain myself or at least come up with a reasonable excuse for why I was there. I certainly didn't intend to tell him exactly what I had been doing.

"Just a minute," I called out as I sat up on the bed, wincing as the sheets rubbed across the sore spots where Cole had hit me with his belt.

My clothes were still in a pile on the floor where I'd left them, so I raced over and started putting them back on.

"Get dressed," I whispered to Cole, who lazily sat up on the bed, an amused look on his face.

"What's the problem?" he asked. "This is your house, right?"

"It's my father's house," I corrected him, still whispering. "And he doesn't know we're here."

"Is that him at the door?" He still hadn't made any move to cover himself.

"No, thank God. It's his valet."

"His valet?" Cole snickered. "What century are we in?"

"Will you please at least put your trousers on?" I begged. I had pretty much finished getting dressed and he hadn't even started yet.

With a shrug, Cole reached down and pulled his trousers back on. Once he had them zipped up, I went over to the door and opened it just a crack, blocking any view of the room with my body.

"Good afternoon, Roger," I greeted the angry-looking man at the door. "How are you?"

His face froze in surprise as he saw me. "Lady Gemma? What were you..." He trailed off, unwilling to finish that question and unable to meet my eyes. Clearly, he'd heard enough. "I apologize for interrupting. Your father didn't let me know that you would be here today."

"The visit was a spur-of-the-moment one. I'll be leaving shortly."

Roger's brow furrowed into deeper confusion. "Leaving? Without speaking to His Lordship?"

Speaking to him? Did that mean my father was actually there at the house too? I had hoped that Roger was just travelling in advance of him, but apparently not.

"I'm sure he's very busy," I demurred as smoothly as I could. "I just came to see the Christmas opening. I don't need to disturb him."

"On the contrary. I have a feeling he would like to see you and your... friend."

I couldn't stop myself from glancing back into the room to see if he could actually see Cole, but I quickly realized that he couldn't. He only knew I had company because of whatever noises he had just heard. Despite my best efforts to control it, a blush crept up my cheeks as I turned back.

"We actually have another engagement in London this evening, so we really can't stay." That was a lie, but he didn't need to know that. I simply had no desire to see my father.

"It won't take long. I insist, Lady Gemma." Roger's eyes had grown harder, a look that I was all too familiar with from childhood admonishments whenever I did anything wrong. Arguing wouldn't get me anywhere. "Please go to the blue drawing room when you're... presentable. I'll let His Lordship know that you're there."

He turned on his heel before I could argue.

Closing the door behind me, I leaned back against it and looked over at Cole. He had almost finished dressing, just putting his tie on, still as unhurried as always. "So, how would you like to meet my father?"

"It doesn't sound like I have much choice," Cole observed, smirking at me in his casual, confident way. How did he always manage to look so calm and collected? I really needed him to give me lessons. "Should I be worried?"

That was not a simple question to answer. "He probably won't be directly rude. He'll just insult you in that underhanded way that really posh British people do."

"You say that like you're not one of them. You don't consider yourself a 'really posh British person'?" Cole asked, still looking completely unruffled.

I turned the question back on him. "Do *you* consider me a really posh British person?"

He smiled. "Sometimes. And other times..." He reached down and adjusted the belt around his waist. "Not at all."

Heat rushed through me at the simple reminder of what we had just done together. For no earthly reason that I could think of, I liked him hitting me with the belt. *Really* liked it. My orgasms had been even more intense than they usually were with him, and I knew Cole wouldn't ask me to explain, or make me feel strange that I enjoyed it. He simply accepted it and gave me what I needed. What I'd never known I needed.

While he finished straightening himself out, I went to the ensuite bathroom to clean myself up and quickly fix my hair and clothes so that I looked 'presentable', as Roger said. Having done as much as I could, I led Cole out of the bedroom and down the hall to the blue drawing room, the less formal of the two reception rooms in the private part of the house.

The family pictures in that room were much more recent ones than the oil portraits downstairs, and Cole took his time walking around the room, looking at them all curiously.

"Is this you?" he asked, picking up a picture of me and my brother on the lawn outside the house. In it, Tom was about seven, which would make me four.

"Yes. That one too." I pointed at the one next to it which showed the four of us: me and Tom with our parents, photographed in the formal drawing room downstairs.

Cole picked that one up and looked at it more closely. "You look like your mom, or at least how she used to look. Do you still look like her now?"

"She died ten years ago."

Cole looked up at me in surprise, a rare moment where I'd caught him off guard. "I'm sorry, Gemma. I had no idea."

I knew he didn't. He hadn't looked up any information about my family, the same way I hadn't looked up anything about his. I liked that about spending time with him, and I suspected he felt the same. People so often knew things about me that I hadn't told them, and finding someone who only wanted to learn things directly from me felt incredibly refreshing.

Cole had just put the framed photo back down on the table when my father walked in, and out of sheer force of habit, I pulled my shoulders back, straightening my spine, as if preparing myself for inspection.

My father had never been an affectionate man, and things only got worse after my mother died. He viewed my brother and I as chess pieces to direct as he pleased, to serve his larger strategy, rather than as people in our own right. My brother didn't seem to mind, so long as he inherited the title and the houses and the businesses and everything else that went along with being the Earl's heir, but I had let my father down hugely when I went into business for myself. He had ranted and raved about how no woman of my position should take on a 'trade'. He insisted that his name not be associated with it in any way, which was why I had taken my mother's maiden name, Sudlow, as my professional name.

And then, even worse in his eyes, I had completely humiliated him earlier that year when Edwin broke off our engagement. In my father's opinion, the entire thing had been my fault. If I had simply been a more satisfactory partner, it would have never happened. Edwin's father, my dad's closest business partner, hated Edwin's involvement with Annabel, considering her crass and fame-hungry, and he also blamed me for the whole thing. The two of them were completely put out that their long-term plan to marry Edwin and I off to each other hadn't worked out.

My father and I had barely spoken to each other since the whole thing went public, so to say that I was less than enthusiastic to see him would be a bit of an understatement.

"Gemma." My name almost sounded like an insult from his mouth. "I trust you have a reason for showing your face here today."

Showing my face? That was surprisingly direct. As I'd mentioned to Cole, my father was usually much more obliquely insulting than that. He must really be angry.

"Good afternoon, sir," I replied, doing my best to appear unbothered. "I came to show Mr Stamer the property. This is Cole Stamer, a new friend and business associate of mine. Cole, my father, the Earl of Totnes."

Cole obligingly came forward and offered his hand to my father, who looked at it as if it were diseased.

"Forgive me, Mr Stamer. I don't make a habit of shaking hands with men determined to ruin my daughter. Not to mention I don't want to imagine where that hand has been."

Cole recoiled in surprise as his hand fell back to his side. I couldn't imagine anyone had ever spoken to Cole that way before, and I couldn't stop the shame that ran through me, knowing I was to blame for it. I tried to bring my father's attention back to me.

"I assume you know that Mr Stamer and I have been seeing each other." I guessed that must be the explanation for why he was so bent out of shape.

My father's steely glare turned back to me. "Is that what you call it? 'Seeing each other'? When the papers print photos of you flaunting your disgusting fetishes?"

The colour drained from my face as his words sunk in. I had completely forgotten that the photographs from the sex shop would have been released. I hadn't seen what photos had been printed, and I had never even considered that my father might see them. At the time, when Cole suggested letting the photos be taken, it had seemed almost liberating, but now, beneath my father's withering glare, I felt dirty and degraded.

"Did you consider your reputation at all?" my father demanded, full of self-righteousness. "Did you consider mine? This family? Do you ever think of anyone but yourself?"

That was rich, coming from him, but I couldn't deny that I hadn't been thinking of anyone else. I had only been thinking of me and Cole, and that magical way he had of making the rest of the world seem unimportant.

"You're out of line, Lord Redvers." Cole's eyes flashed with anger as he stared down the Earl, his voice firm. "There is nothing 'disgusting' about those photos, and Gemma has done nothing wrong. She's an adult and her actions, right or wrong, don't reflect on you any more than yours do on her."

I wanted to tell Cole not to waste his breath trying to convince my father of that, but part of me couldn't help feeling grateful that he was standing up for me. No one had ever done that for me before.

The vein on my father's forehead began to pulse, a surefire sign that he was nearing the end of whatever patience he had left. "This is none of your business. I don't care how much money you have, Mr Stamer. My daughter is not one of your prostitutes."

My mouth went completely dry as the word echoed into the air around us. My father couldn't know about the way we met, could he? That seemed like far too specific an insult to be something he had come up with out of the blue.

Cole's eyes glinted once more, his hard, dominant side on firm display. "I've known a lot of prostitutes with far more civility than you. I can see now why Gemma doesn't use your name in her business. I wouldn't want to be associated with you either."

Before my father could respond, Cole came to my side.

"I think I've seen more than enough here, Gemma. Are you ready to go?"

Though I could feel my father's furious glare burning into me, I kept my focus on Cole. "Yes. I'm done."

I took his arm and we headed to the door. As we reached it, my father called out behind me: "I'll expect you at my Christmas party next week, Gemma. Alone. This is your last chance. If you can't fix this..."

I didn't wait to hear the rest of his threat. Cole and I were already gone.

Chapter Fourteen

FEATHER LIGHT

~Cole~

We didn't speak until we were back in the car. Gemma held onto my arm the whole way from her father's drawing room, back through the public parts of the house, and out to the waiting car, and I could feel her hand trembling against me. As soon as we had settled in the back seat, I put my arm around her, pulling her close to me without a word.

The Gemma I saw in that room with her father was the first version of her that I didn't find utterly irresistible. The rigidity of her posture, the hesitancy in her eyes, and the timidity in her voice, all of it was so unlike the feisty, fun woman I had come to know, and completely different to the way she behaved with me in private. Although she was submissive in both instances, when she submitted to me, she did so by choice. She chose to give up control. But the way she submitted to her father's harassment made it clear that control was being taken from her rather than given freely, and I hated that anything or anyone ever made her feel that way.

"Does he always speak to you like that?" I asked after several minutes of silence as the car drove out through the estate parklands and back towards the highway.

Gemma raised her head from my shoulder to look me in the eye. The cornered, hunted look I had seen in her eyes before had gone, thankfully, but she still looked subdued. "Not exactly like that, no, but if you're asking if he's always so critical, then I guess the answer would be yes. I can't honestly remember the last thing I did that was good enough for him."

"What about your brother? Is he treated the same way? Does he back you up?"

"He has his own life and his own problems. We don't speak much."

I remembered what she'd said the night before when my sister called, that she found it nice that Isabel cared enough to check up on me, and I remembered the hint of longing in her voice as she'd said it. "Any other family that you're close to?"

Gemma shook her head. "No, not really, but it doesn't bother me, honestly. You don't need to feel sorry for me."

"I'm not," I protested, but as I stopped to think about it, maybe she had a point. Maybe I did feel a little bad for her, but only because she deserved so much better.

As if she could hear my thoughts, Gemma smiled knowingly at me. "Yes, you are, but I'm fine. My life is fine. I've got good friends and I love my work. I don't have to worry about money. It's a lot more than a lot of people have."

True as that may be, it didn't take the place of having her family's support, which she should also be entitled to.

"What was he talking about at the end? He mentioned a party?"

"His annual Christmas party," she confirmed. "It's this Thursday. I was going to take you, but obviously, I won't subject you to it now."

"You're not actually going to go, are you?" I couldn't believe she would even consider it.

She grimaced unhappily. "I'm not sure. It might be worth putting in an appearance, just to appease him."

"You don't owe him anything, Gemma." I'd only met him for a couple of minutes, but I could clearly see that.

"I don't need to decide now. Let's talk about something lighter, like politics or religion."

Since she clearly wanted to change the subject, I gave in, and we chatted easily for the remainder of the ride back to London. When we arrived back at the hotel, it was nearing five o'clock and Gemma suggested that we walk around the city to look at the Christmas lights. Although I would have preferred to go to my room, I couldn't resist the excited twinkle in her eyes, so I followed her as she led me through Mayfair and Soho, through decorated arcades and light-strung small alleys, beneath the showy displays on Regent Street, through the crowds at Carnaby Street and along dozens of side streets, our hands clasped tightly together the whole time.

We stopped for dinner at an outdoor table in a hidden courtyard. The restaurant had space heaters to keep it warm enough for us to eat outside despite the chill in the air. I suggested we order a bottle of wine with dinner, but Gemma told me she'd been craving hot chocolate instead, and as I watched her lick the whipped cream off her lips after each sip, I couldn't really complain.

After finishing our meal and taking the scenic route back to the hotel, we finally arrived back at the suite nearly twelve hours after we'd left that morning. Part of me wondered if Gemma liked torturing me on purpose, making me wait to be with her and building the anticipation with each passing minute, but since I also enjoyed the time we spent together doing other things, I couldn't complain too much about that either.

"Is your back sore at all?" I wished I could have taken care of her after our play that afternoon, but with the valet's interruption, I hadn't had a chance.

"Not too much," she assured me, removing her coat and boots. I loved to watch her undress, even just her outer layers. What lay beneath her clothes was no longer a secret for me, but I still enjoyed watching her reveal it, each and every time. "I felt it a bit when we were sitting on those hard chairs at dinner, but I didn't mind. It kept reminding me of the whole thing."

That answered the question I hadn't asked yet: I wanted to be sure she had enjoyed it, and since she liked being reminded of it, it seemed that she had.

"I want to take a look. Get undressed."

The instant calm that passed over her, the instant response to my command, told me better than her words ever could that she was looking forward to the rest of this night as much as I was. She quickly stripped for me, removing each item confidently until she stood naked in the centre of the room. Circling her, I took a look at the remnants of our earlier activity. A faint red line could still be seen across her lower back, and a couple of bruises on her backside. I pressed against one of them gently and she inhaled sharply but didn't pull away.

"Wait here," I instructed while I went into the room where our purchases from the night before had been moved. After finding everything I wanted, I returned to the living room, finding Gemma exactly where I had left her. "I'm going to try something. This is new to me too, so tell me if you don't like it, okay?"

As she nodded in agreement, her eyes fell to the bag in my hands, trying to see what I had chosen, and I shook my head in disapproval.

"You don't need to see it. In fact, you don't need to see anything."

I pulled out the blindfold first, tying it around her eyes just as I had my tie the other night. With that in place, I moved on to the collar and cuffs that she had tried on in the store, securing the collar around her neck and tying her hands together behind her back. The apparatus looked even better on her now that she was naked.

"How's that?" I asked as I adjusted the collar around the neck. "Can you breathe?"

"It can be tighter."

So, she liked the pressure. I made a mental note of it as I tightened the collar further and stepped back to survey her. "Spread your legs."

Once she'd widened her stance, I adjusted it a little bit wider, and once she was in position, I pulled out an item that we'd chosen from the sensation section of the store: a long, wide peacock feather, soft on the edges, with a hard, stiff spine.

With a light, tickling touch, I ran the soft, feathery edge down her back first. Gemma shivered against it, her hands clenching in the cuffs as I moved around the front of her and circled it gently around her breasts, the circles getting smaller and smaller until it brushed over her nipple which stiffened and peaked beneath its touch. A sigh whispered from her parted lips, the only sound in the air that had grown heavy with our mutual anticipation.

The feather moved down her side, tracing the curve of her waist and her hips, down to her knee and back up her inner thigh. I could see her body tensing as it drew closer to her centre, but before it got there, I pulled back and brought it up to her face instead.

Gemma jumped in surprise at the sudden change, but she smiled as the feather ran across her lips and down her neck. I took it straight down between her breasts that time, not stopping until it rested just above her clit, at which point I pulled it back again.

She groaned in frustration, which only made me smile. I went on that way for quite a while, playing down her back, letting the feather slip between the cleft of her bruised ass and down the back of her legs, leaving a trail of goosebumps in its wake. Over and over again, I came close to where she wanted it most, always pulling back at the last second.

"Please, Cole," she begged after I had lost count of how many times I had teased her. "Please, touch me."

Without warning, I bent down and took one of her nipples in my mouth. As she gasped, I took advantage of her surprise to run the feather through her folds, pressing the hard spine of it against her clit.

A moan of pleasure, of pure satisfaction, came from deep in her throat as the feather brushed back and forth through her wetness. I took her nipple in my teeth, biting down on it gently as my free hand reached up and grabbed her hair, tugging it a little less gently. All the while, the feather continued to play with her clit.

Gemma squirmed against her restraints, her hands tied helplessly behind her back, unable to touch anything and unable to see anything, completely at my mercy. "Come for me now," I ordered, and no sooner had I said it than she did, her whole body shuddering in a total release.

Could she be any more perfect? I really didn't see how.

~Gemma~

As the last waves of my orgasm washed over me, Cole stepped back. In the absence of his touch, I felt even more exposed. I still couldn't see anything and didn't have any idea what he was doing. It made me more aware of every little thing, every whisper of breath, every sound, every touch.

I could hear him moving around: the rustle of clothes and the sound of his zip. He must have been getting undressed, and the idea made me shiver in anticipation. He could make me come in so many different ways, that much was clear, but my favourite was still with his cock deep inside me, when he lost control too.

I didn't know how long I stood there waiting, my sense of time affected by the pleasure still echoing through my body and the lack of visual cues, but eventually, he took my arm and pulled me gently forward before turning me around. In that position, I could feel his legs on either side of mine. "Sit down, Gorgeous." The words came from somewhere behind and below me. "I'm ready for you."

Bending my knees, I lowered myself while his hand guided my hips, until I could feel his hard cock pressing against my entrance. As soon as I was in position, he pulled me down firmly, letting his cock fill me in one swift stroke as I sank onto him.

"Fuck," I breathed, moaning with the pleasure of it. It didn't seem to matter how many times he was inside me; it always felt just as satisfying.

"You're going to ride me now, Gemma," he instructed. "Push yourself up and I'll pull you down."

I wasn't entirely sure what he meant, but I did my best to obey anyway. My arms were still tied together behind my back, so I pushed up with my legs, my core contracting to help me. The clenching in my abdomen seemed to also have an effect lower down too, as Cole groaned from behind me, feeling the tightening around his cock. When I had raised myself up to the tip, I suddenly felt a sharp, downward tug on the restraint connected to my collar. The force quickly pulled me back down, letting him fill me again.

The pressure caused the collar around my neck to tighten, but I didn't mind it. In fact, I kind of liked it. The brief breathlessness only heightened the feeling of fullness from him inside me.

We repeated the action, again and again, me raising myself up slowly, him dragging me firmly back down again.

"Faster," Cole said, the word somewhere between an order and a plea, and I did my best to obey. My thighs were screaming at me, the muscles not used to the motion, but I didn't plan to stop. Each time he released the pressure on my collar, I gasped for air to get me through the next restriction. The pressure built for me with each stroke, just as I knew it must be building for him. I was right on the edge.

As if sensing that I needed it, Cole gave me his permission. "Let go, Gemma. Come, now." Just like that, I did, surrendering to the waves of my pleasure at the same time that I felt him tightening inside me. He swore, followed by a moan of satisfaction. "Fuck, yes."

In my breathlessness and bliss, my body felt completely limp, weightless and floating in the darkness that still surrounded me. Cole pulled me back against him, letting me feel his whole body for the first time since he had put the blindfold on, and he held me there until my legs had stopped shaking.

"What do you need?" he asked, the words whispered against my ear as he began to free me from my restraints. "Do you want a bath? Another massage?"

These acts of caring for me were important to him, I had come to realize, so I agreed to a bath more for his sake than mine. He sat beside me the whole time, his hands trailing across my skin as we talked idly about nothing important. When I finished, he helped me get ready for bed again.

"You haven't looked at your phone all day, have you?" he asked as he tucked me into bed.

"No. Why? Should I?"

"I just wondered if you wanted to see the pictures that were published from last night?"

Once again, he had made me forget all about the real world and the problems I had to face there eventually. I hadn't thought about the photos since we were in the car. "I suppose I should."

He quickly brought them up on his phone and handed the device to me. The first photo showed me in the collar and cuffs that we had just used, which I expected. The second one had the two of us looking over a display of vibrators, and another one showed me holding some kind of edible underwear as Cole and I laughed over something one of us had said. I didn't bother reading the article, and I certainly didn't read the comments. I couldn't care less what people were saying about it.

To me, the most striking thing about all the photos was how happy I looked and how comfortable Cole and I looked together.

I handed the phone back to him. "Thanks."

"Do you regret going through with it?"

He watched me carefully as he asked the question, the answer obviously important to him, so I took a moment to really think about it. The photos were going to cause me some headaches, my father being the biggest one, but Cole had been right in what he had said to my father earlier: we weren't doing anything wrong and there was nothing disgusting about it. I didn't regret a single thing I had done with Cole, so why should I regret the photos either?

"No. I don't regret it."

Cole's face softened into a satisfied smile. "Good. Let's get some sleep."

When he climbed into the bed and nestled up against me, it didn't take long at all before I fell into a deep, restful slumber.

The next day dawned bright and sunny, one of those perfect London winter days with a crisp blue sky and just the right amount of chill in the air. Cole and I showered together in the morning, with a lot of groping, a hand job for him and a finger fuck for me, and when we were dressed, we headed out to meet Holly and Jackson for lunch.

I had booked us into a little restaurant in Covent Garden which had plants hanging from the ceiling, creating the feeling of being beneath a canopy of greenery. Cole and Jackson were both intrigued.

"Is this where you got your inspiration for the Mayfair Mews?" Cole asked, looking up again once we were all seated.

"One of the places, but don't worry, I didn't bring you here just for the scenery. The food is also really good."

We had a lot of fun over lunch, all of us happy and comfortable with each other. Holly hadn't told me yet if anything happened between her and Jackson after we left them at the pub on Friday, but they seemed as flirty with each other as usual. I remembered what she said about Jackson not wanting a casual fling and I tried to make a mental note to remember to ask Cole about it later.

From there, we walked down the Strand until we reached Somerset House, the grand building along the Thames that had once been a stately home but now served primarily as an arts centre. In the winter, it also became the venue for one of the city's most popular ice rinks, which was the reason I had chosen to visit it that day.

Cole had been as relaxed as anyone so far, but as soon as we entered the courtyard, he immediately went tense. I followed his gaze, trying to see what would have caused his reaction, but I could only see the rink and a couple of small market stalls selling food and Christmas crafts.

"Are you okay?" I asked him quietly, holding him back while Holly and Jackson walked on ahead.

"Are we going skating?" he asked in reply, his voice stilted and brittle, nothing like his usual cool confidence.

"Yes," I confirmed. Was that a problem? Maybe he didn't want to look foolish? "Don't worry, I'm not any good at it either."

"It's not that, it's just..."

He trailed off, and my confusion grew deeper. The only time I had ever seen him look so unsure was the night he told me about the woman who had hurt him. "Does it have to do with your ex-fiancée?"

He blinked over at me in surprise. "How did you know that?"

"The only time I've seen you this way was when you told me about her."

"You're too clever," he said, shaking his head. "I definitely need to watch myself around you."

He was avoiding the question, so I simply waited to see if he would say anything else. He looked out over the rink again and his lips tightened.

"I proposed to her while we were skating. In Central Park."

Immediately, I understood. The whole scene must remind him of how much he had cared for her and how much she had fooled him.

"We don't have to skate if you don't want to. There are lots of other Christmas things to do in the city. I have a whole list."

"I'm sure you do." A hint of his smirk reappeared on his face, making me smile. His eyes still hadn't left the rink, watching the people as they made their way around the ice. "You know what? Let's do it. It's just a rink. It's about time I stopped letting the memory have any control over me. We choose what we let control us, right?"

He turned to me with the last question, as if it held some special meaning. Maybe he meant our relationship, or was he talking about my father? I couldn't be sure, but either way, it made me glad to see that he was making an effort to put the past behind him. He had helped me so much to get over what happened with Edwin that if I could repay the favour even a little, I definitely wanted to.

"Right," I agreed firmly, giving him a wink as I linked my arm through his. "Now, let's get some skates and get you tied up."

He smirked back at me with the sly glint in his eyes I loved so much. "I thought that was supposed to be my line."

~Cole~

Gemma hadn't been kidding when she said she wasn't a good skater. Her ankles wobbled dangerously as she stepped onto the ice in her rented skates but she managed to keep herself upright, looking particularly proud of herself that she had. I might be a stuffy New York businessman, particularly while wearing my suit on the ice, but I could skate circles around her.

"Maybe we need to get you one of those penguins that the little kids are using," I suggested, pointing at two young children pushing plastic penguins with handles to keep their balance.

Gemma narrowed her eyes at me in mock offense. "I'll have you know, Mr Stamer, that I can usually get the whole way around the ice and only fall over once or twice along the way."

I laughed and leaned in close to her. "You can hang onto me instead of the penguin then. But don't go calling me Mr Stamer unless you're in the mood for something considerably hotter than ice skating."

She shook her head at me, but I could see the smile on the corner of her lips.

Circling around behind her, I put my hands on her waist. "Let me show you how it's done. Just keep your feet pointed straight ahead."

Gemma shrieked in surprise as I pushed her forward, her hands gripping mine tightly. "Slow down, Cole. It's too fast!"

"Nonsense. I'm right behind you, Gemma. I won't let you fall."

She let out another squeal as one foot swerved to the side, but she got it back under control and I could feel her starting to relax, at least until we approached the end of the rink and she called out again. "We need to turn!"

"Lean back," I instructed. "Lean on me, and I'll get you through it."

She obeyed, her back pressing against my chest, and I leaned into the corner for both of us, easily making the turn.

"You see? Nothing to be afraid of."

We circled the ice four or five times that way, our bodies pressed tightly together, and Gemma got more and more relaxed with each pass. "It feels like flying," she exclaimed as we sped down the inside of the ice, past all the people holding onto the boards at the edges, her red hair flapping in the wind.

I pulled her right to the middle of the ice and spun us around in a circle, and Gemma laughed in delight, her head resting back against my shoulder.

When we'd finally stopped moving, I let her go and moved around to the front of her. She smiled up at me happily, her green eyes sparkling in the sunlight. "That was amazing."

I couldn't help chuckling. "That wasn't even very fast, honestly."

"Let me see how fast you can go," she challenged. "I'll wait here."

I would be happy to show off for her, but as I looked back out at the sea of slow-moving skaters, it didn't seem like a good idea. "I don't think I can go much faster with all these people. I'd run into someone."

Though she pursed her lips in disappointment, she knew I had a point. "Well, then, we'll have to do this another time. We can rent out the whole rink and you can really show me what you've got."

The idea of it made me smile until I remembered that it was Sunday already and I would be going back to New York in five days. We didn't have all that many 'another times' left. The realization left me feeling strangely empty.

"Are you thinking about her?" Gemma asked, taking hold of my hand. "Your ex-fiancée?"

Where on earth had that come from? "No. At least, I wasn't until you brought it up."

Her eyes widened with horror. "Oh my God, I'm sorry, Cole. You just got that look on your face, and I thought..."

"Gemma." I placed a quick, gentle kiss on her lips. "I'm teasing. I'm fine."

I actually was. I hadn't thought of Samantha since we got on the ice, and even now, when I tried to picture that moment when I had proposed, the one that had always been so vivid for me, I couldn't quite capture it. The picture seemed faded somehow. Blurred. When I tried to imagine Samantha's face, Gemma's features came to mind instead.

Jackson and Holly glided up to us, hand in hand. "No making out on the ice," Holly teased. "Either get skating or let's get off and get some mulled wine."

I wasn't ready to let go of this feeling of freedom just yet. "Do you want to go again?" I asked Gemma, and she nodded enthusiastically. With a smile, I circled around behind her again. "How about a race, Jackson?"

He grinned at me, surprised and delighted by the suggestion, before looking over at Holly. "You up for it?"

She laughed at his eagerness. "To be your dead weight? Sure." Soon, we were lined up at one end of the ice, me behind Gemma and Jackson behind Holly as Holly counted us down. "Three, two, one, go!"

Shrieks and laughter filled the air as we both pushed off, racing down the middle of the ice, pushing the women in front of us as the other skaters stopped to watch us. Those at the end of the rink moved out of the way as we approached, and Gemma grabbed the boards at the end about a second before Holly did, claiming victory for us.

"Champions!" she yelled, as applause and laughter broke out among the onlookers, most of them smiling at us, amused by the whole spectacle. I couldn't stop grinning either. God, I couldn't remember the last time I'd done something like that, so completely childish and stupid and just plain fun.

We did a couple of more circles of the ice before getting off, trading our skates for our regular shoes once again. As promised, Holly tracked down the mulled wine which she and Jackson drank while I got a beer and Gemma went for hot chocolate again. Gemma invited Jackson and Holly to join us back at the hotel for an early dinner at the hotel restaurant, and though I would have preferred to go straight up to my suite with her, the night was still young. There would be time for what I wanted to do later.

To my surprise, as we started walking back to the hotel, Holly fell into step beside me while Gemma hung back with Jackson.

"So, Cole." Holly eyed me curiously, and I looked back at her, slightly bemused. In all the time we'd spent together, she and I had never actually spoken directly to each other very much. "Gemma tells me you met the Earl yesterday."

Ah. She wanted to talk about Gemma's father. "I did. I wouldn't exactly call it a pleasure."

She sighed in agreement. "The man is a menace. Gem does her best to pretend it doesn't bother her, but it does. She tried for so many years to get his approval and she even almost ended up marrying that waste-of-space fiancé. Edwin leaving her was the best thing that could have happened to her, even if he was a total ass in the way he did it. They should have broken up years ago."

I didn't disagree with her overall conclusion, but I also didn't understand why she was sharing it with me. "Does Gemma know you feel that way?"

Holly laughed. "I'm not very good at keeping my opinions to myself. Trust me, she knows."

We walked a few steps in silence before Holly looked back over at me, the amusement in her expression gone and her tone completely serious.

"Look, I can't pretend that I understand whatever deal it is that the two of you have worked out. but I do know that I haven't seen her this happy in a very long time. Hell, it might be the happiest I've ever seen her. So, if this really is just for a few more days, you better make damn sure it ends well, or I will haunt your nightmares, Cole Stamer. You got that?"

I couldn't help the smile that crossed my face, which only made Holly scowl.

"I'm serious. You mess with her, you're going to answer to me. Her father might not care enough to give you a talking to, but I do. Don't fuck it up."

"I hear you loud and clear," I assured her. "Nobody's going to get hurt. We're both completely clear on what's happening."

She glared at me a little longer before her eyes softened. "Alright. But just remember, I'm decorating your hotels now, so if you do screw it up, I've got years of potential revenge in store for you."

"Noted."

To my relief, we arrived back at the hotel before she could threaten me further. That had to count as one of the strangest conversations I'd ever had, but it made me glad to know that Gemma had someone watching out for her, someone who would be there even after I was gone, even if the idea of not being there for her myself made me feel more uncomfortable with each passing day.

Chapter Fifteen

ICE COLD

~Gemma~

Although Cole ordered the most expensive wine on the menu for our table at dinner, I had to tell him that I only wanted sparkling water. He didn't seem to be getting suspicious that I kept choosing non-alcoholic drinks, but I didn't feel right about drinking until I knew for sure that I wasn't accidentally pregnant. I also didn't want to tell Cole the reason behind it, since I didn't want him worrying unnecessarily. The odds of me being pregnant were very low, but better safe than sorry, I figured.

When Holly told me that she wanted to talk to Cole on the walk back to the hotel, it surprised me, but I figured he could handle himself. Besides, it gave me a chance to check in with Jackson. I asked him gently probing questions about him and Holly, and he didn't beat around the bush. He told me straight out that he liked her but that he wasn't interested in a short-term relationship and Holly wasn't looking for anything long-term. So, they had agreed between themselves to stay friends, with a lot of flirting thrown in. Neither of them seemed to be upset about it, at least.

He also asked me, equally gently, how I felt about Cole.

"I'm having a great time with him," I answered honestly. "But there's an expiry date on it, so it is what it is. Besides, he lives in New York and I live here. That's not really conducive to a real relationship."

"Cole can pretty much live wherever he wants," Jackson pointed out. "He travels so much anyway and half our work is done virtually. Don't think of that as a deal breaker."

"That doesn't change the fact that he only wants something with strict boundaries," I reminded him. Jackson seemed to know as much about my arrangement with Cole as Holly did.

"And what do you want, Gemma?"

The question was kind and free of any judgement but even so, I couldn't come up with an easy answer. What did I want? I didn't want to feel like I had with Edwin. I liked the way I felt with Cole, but I had agreed to the terms of our deal, and it didn't seem fair of me to try to change them so far into the game.

I stayed quiet for so long that Jackson took it as a sign that I didn't want to answer. "Listen, you don't have to explain it to me, but you should think about it. *Seriously* think about it, and talk to Cole before we leave, because I can tell you that whatever boundaries he thinks he's put on this, they're paper thin. It wouldn't take much to knock them all down."

Before I could ask him to explain exactly what he meant by that, we arrived back at the hotel, and Cole turned back to take my hand as we went inside. Over dinner, the conversation flowed just as easily as it had all day, and once we finished eating, Jackson and Holly took their leave. They were planning on going for a walk along the South Bank to visit the market and see the lights, but they didn't ask us to go with them. They must have known we would rather stay at the hotel instead.

As soon as they were gone, Cole made a stop at the front desk before leading me back to the lift.

"What did you need at the desk?" I asked.

"A few supplies for tonight." His eyes glinted provocatively, suggesting the 'supplies' were of a personal nature.

"You didn't buy enough at the shop the other night?" I teased him.

"I had a new idea today. I can't help it if you keep inspiring me."

Apparently, he had no intention of telling me what he had in mind, and I didn't really want him to. I was more than happy to put myself in his hands and let him do what he wanted.

When we got to the suite, Cole pulled me into his arms almost immediately, kissing me softly. His hands ran through my hair as I slid my own hands beneath his suit jacket, feeling his firm chest through his shirt. "Undress me," he whispered against my lips.

That was new. He'd always taken his own clothes off, never really letting me have free rein to touch him as I wanted, and he never got naked first. Eagerly, I took him up on the offer before he changed his mind.

Since my hands were already beneath his jacket, I used them to slide the jacket up over his shoulders, down one arm and then the other. He tossed it away onto the floor as soon as he was free of it. Our lips never parted the whole time.

Moving on to his shirt, I unbuttoned it one button at a time, tugging the tucked bottom up from his trousers. When the buttons were all open, I finally broke our kiss, but only so I could move my lips to his chest instead, kissing and licking my way across it as I opened his shirt wider. My tongue flicked over his nipple before moving lower, tracing the hard edges of his abs and licking between each line that defined them.

Cole groaned as I got lower still, finding the trail of hair leading down into his trousers. The bulge in his trousers grew more prominent with each passing minute, so I quickly finished taking his shirt off and dropped to my knees in front of him. My fingers trembled as I undid his belt, remembering again what he'd done to me with it the day before. He made no move to stop me as I pulled it from the loops and put it aside, moving on to the button and zip of his trousers.

Gently, I pulled his trousers and underwear down, pulling it over his erection which sprung out hard and ready. Although I hadn't completely finished undressing him, I couldn't resist the chance to take his cock into my mouth. He had never let me explore him that way before, and

I wanted to take full advantage of it. He groaned again as I swirled my tongue around his head and his hands threaded through my hair, but not in a controlling way. For a change, he let me take the lead.

I took my time, running my tongue over every inch of him, taking his balls into my mouth as my hands stroked his shaft. Whenever I glanced up at him, he was watching me, his eyes dark with lust, and the look on his face only made me want to please him more. When I'd teased him long enough, I took him fully into my mouth, relaxing my throat to take him as deep as I could.

"Fuck, Gemma," he moaned. His hands tightened in my hair as I moved faster, taking him in as far as I could each time. With one hand at the base of his shaft and the other playing with his balls, I could feel them tighten just before he came. I swallowed it all down before releasing him from my mouth and placing a kiss on the head of his cock as he drew in a ragged breath above me.

No sooner had I finished than someone knocked on the door, startling me until I remembered Cole having placed an order at the desk downstairs. "Perfect timing," he said, smirking down at me. "You want to get that?"

He quickly pulled his trousers the rest of the way off and went to sit on the couch, where his nakedness wouldn't be immediately obvious. Wiping my face to make sure no evidence remained of what I'd just been doing, I opened the door to find a bellboy with a room service cart containing a bottle of champagne on ice and two glasses, and the happiness I'd just been feeling dimmed slightly. How could I explain to Cole that I didn't want any champagne without revealing why?

Teasing seemed like a good place to start. "Are you trying to get me drunk?" I asked after the bellboy had pushed the cart into the room and left. "You know you don't need to in order to have your way with me, right?"

"It's not for drinking; or at least, not in the way you're thinking." He stood up from the couch, his muscled, naked body looking somehow even more enticing because I remained fully dressed. "Bring it into the bedroom and strip," he instructed.

Obviously, he had taken control again, and that was fine with me. I did as he said, bringing the cart with me into the bedroom before removing all my clothes, waiting for him to tell me what to do next. While I undressed, Cole pulled out a set of handcuffs from our purchases from the sex shop, and he led me over to the bed and had me lay down on my back, putting the cuffs on and securing them with a metal chain to the lamp on the wall so my arms were up over my head, leaving my body completely exposed to him.

From my restrained position, I watched as he went over to the cart, but instead of grabbing the champagne as I expected, he pulled out one of the ice cubes from the bucket instead.

"I had an idea seeing you out on the ice this afternoon." He walked back over to me with the ice cube between his fingers and a dangerous smirk on his face. "I couldn't help picturing you laid out on it, completely naked."

If I hadn't already been turned on, that would have done it. Excitement raced through my veins as I tried to guess what he might intend to do next.

"I wondered what it would do to your body," he continued, his eyes moving across my naked form. "I tried to picture how you would react to the cold. Let's find out, shall we?"

Having given me fair warning, he placed the ice cube onto my stomach and I shivered immediately, partly from the cold and partly from the anticipation of what was to come. With one finger, Cole began moving the cube slowly across my skin. First, he circled my navel, letting the melted water drip into my belly button. Next, he moved it up, rubbing it against the underside of my breasts, first one and then the other. Goosebumps erupted across my body and my nipples stiffened, partly from the sensation and partly from the intensity of his gaze.

"Interesting," Cole teased, his eyes fixed on my breasts. Controlled by his finger, the cube circled my left breast before running over the nipple, the ice shockingly cold on the sensitive peak, and I couldn't keep from gasping in both surprise and pleasure. Pulling his finger back but leaving the ice cube in place, he leaned down and took both the ice and my nipple into his mouth. The heat from his tongue contrasted with the cold of the ice, making me writhe and wiggle beneath his touch and the contradictory sensations.

When the ice had fully melted in his mouth, he stood up and returned to the cart. I expected he would get another cube, but instead, he opened the champagne, pouring a small amount into one of the glasses and bringing it back with him to the bed.

"Now let's see what the effect is if, instead of just cold, we add a little fizz."

Taking a small sip of the champagne into his mouth, he bent down and took my other nipple into his mouth. I gasped again as the bubbles sparkled against my skin, aided by Cole's clever tongue. I'd never felt anything like it, but I loved it, moaning as drops of champagne escaped from his lips, trailing down my body.

Swallowing what was left, Cole sat back up, looking down at me with a challenge in his eyes. "Now that you've felt both, which do you think will feel better on your clit?"

Oh, fuck. Just the thought of either one sent a shudder through my whole body while Cole raised his eyebrows, waiting for me to reply.

"Maybe... maybe the champagne?" I managed to stutter.

He nodded. "Good choice. If we do the ice first, it might numb you too much."

First? Did that mean he would do both eventually?

"Spread your legs, Gemma."

I did as he requested, and, taking another mouthful of champagne, Cole positioned himself between my thighs.

The explosion of bubbles against my clit, building on the arousal that had been rising in me ever since we got back to the suite, nearly made me come immediately. "Oh, God, Cole," I moaned as his tongue brushed over my skin, making everything more intense. The swirling of the bubbles and his tongue on my swollen clit was too much. "Please, I need to come."

I could feel his chuckle more than I could hear it. "Go ahead, Gorgeous."

His mouth clamped down on me and I saw stars, surrendering to the blissful release that cascaded over me. As pleasure echoed through me, I couldn't help wondering how I went so many years thinking it would be okay to marry someone who never made me feel that way?

And that wasn't even the end of it. Before I had recovered, Cole was back on his feet again, grabbing another ice cube from the bucket. After his earlier comment, I knew what he was going to do with it, but it didn't make the sensation any less intense when he pressed the cold block against my already-overstimulated clit.

Pleasure and pain combined, melding together beautifully as I whimpered against it, and the ice began to move lower, brushing against my folds and probing at my entrance. Was he really going to...?

My back arched off the bed as he pushed the ice cube inside me, my hands pulling at my restraints. *Oh, my God.* I could feel it moving deeper and also feel it melting, the water dribbling out of me as my internal heat, the heat of my arousal, warmed and thawed it. Cole licked away every drop that came back out.

"Was that alright?" he asked, and I simply nodded, unable to speak. His smirk sent another jolt of pleasure through me. I loved when he was satisfied. "Good. There's just one more thing I want to try."

One more time, he stood up, grabbing a condom from the bedside table and rolling it onto his cock, which was hard and ready again. Using yet another ice cube, he ran it up and down the condom, cooling the whole thing, hissing against the cold and making me even more curious about what it would feel like inside. Without any further warning, he popped the ice cube in his mouth and quickly mounted me, pushing deep inside before the effect was lost.

The cold didn't compare to the cube itself, but I definitely felt the coolness along his whole length as he filled me up, my pussy contracting around him in response. Cole groaned at the sensation, and he leaned down and kissed me, letting the ice cube fall into my mouth as his tongue chased it.

It only took a few thrusts of his hard length before it heated up again, but I didn't mind. I loved having him inside me no matter the temperature, and when I came again, he was right behind me, calling out my name as he followed me over the top.

In the wake of our orgasms, we were both silent for a long moment, only the sound of our heavy breathing filling the air, until we both heard Cole's phone ringing in the other room.

I let out a huffed laugh. "That's not your sister again, is it?"

He smiled, giving me a kiss. "It shouldn't be, but I should see who it is. Not many people have my personal number. Are you okay here for just a second?"

He asked because I was still tied to the wall, but I assured him I'd be okay. He pulled out of me and rolled the condom off, tossing it in the rubbish bin as he went back into the living room to find his phone. I couldn't hear the entire conversation, but I heard Cole's tone quickly shift into his take-charge, professional side.

When he came back into the room, his expression had turned somber. "I'm sorry, Gemma. There's been an incident at one of my hotels and I need to go to handle the PR. In person."

"Right now?" I asked in surprise.

"I'm afraid so. As soon as possible. The plane will be waiting for me at Heathrow." His distracted frown melted into a small smile as his eyes moved over me. "I'll untie you first, though."

He quickly did just that, removing my hands from the cuffs and giving me another kiss.

"I really am sorry. Trust me when I say that I would much rather stay here."

"I believe you," I assured him. I could see that he didn't want to go, and I didn't want him to go either, but he did have a life outside of this room. We both did. "How long will you be gone?"

"A day or two is my guess, but I'll let you know as soon as I know more. You can stay here if you like. You've already got the key. Anything else you need, just call the desk and ask for it."

I thanked him for the offer and helped him quickly put a few of his suits into his suitcase while he got dressed. With one more kiss, he headed out the door, and the room fell silent again, but unlike in the aftermath of our intimacy, the quiet felt oppressive and a little bit lonely.

I had spent most of the last year on my own, I reminded myself. I was more than used to it, so why did the idea of a day or two without Cole suddenly seem unbearable?

~**Cole**~

The flight to Tokyo felt endless. On the way, I spent a couple of hours on the phone with the local hotel manager and our corporate PR team to get the full story: apparently, two senior members of staff at the hotel had been running an elaborate scam to steal credit card and other personal and financial information from our guests. The police had conducted an early morning raid to arrest them, dragging them out of the hotel in handcuffs, and the story was all over the local news.

The hotel manager had done his best to reassure people that these kinds of activities were in no way normal or indicative of all Stamer hotels, but the board felt my physical presence would help to reinforce that message. Normally, I would have completely agreed; my name was on each and every property and I took everything we did personally.

However, leaving Gemma behind in the hotel in London, knowing that it would mean losing a couple of days from the few days we had left together, I couldn't help wishing that someone else could handle it instead.

From the plane, I also spoke to Jackson to let him know he'd have to handle our London meetings on his own for at least Monday and probably Tuesday as well. Without knowing how long I'd have to stay in Japan, and taking into account the flights and the time difference, I couldn't predict when I would be back and ready to work again.

Finally, I sent Gemma a text before trying to get some sleep. My fingers hovered over the keys for several seconds as I tried to figure out what I wanted to say. I could tell her that I missed her, or that I wished she was with me. Both things were true, but they were also trite and sentimental, and not part of our arrangement. In the end, I settled for something suggestive and flirty instead.

Just hit a bit of turbulence. It would be a lot more fun if it happened when I was inside you. C

It must have been after midnight in the UK by then, but the reply came almost immediately.

Invite me along next time then. ;) G

The message made me smile, but it also made me think: *could* I have invited her? Would she have come with me if I asked her to? She had work commitments, but maybe she could be flexible. I hadn't even considered it, and now I could only kick myself that I'd be going to sleep alone in the queen-sized bed on my private plane when even a chance existed that Gemma could have been beside me.

After a restless few hours of sleep, we finally touched down in Tokyo on Monday evening local time. The hotel manager was waiting for me, looking exhausted after a full day of dealing with the fallout from the arrests. We spoke for an hour where he filled me in on everything that had happened, including the fact that we were going to hold a joint press conference in the morning with the police.

When I had all the details I needed, I told him to go get some rest and he had one of the assistant managers come to show me to my room. Although night had fallen in Tokyo, I was still on UK time and not tired at all. The assistant manager must have sensed that because as he turned to go, he asked if he could get anything for me. Food, drink, entertainment? Female companionship?

Any other time, I might have taken him up on that. In fact, I very well might have in the past. The way he looked at me suggested that he knew that final offer would appeal to me.

"That's not necessary. I'm..." I trailed off as I realized what I had been about to say: the words on the tip of my tongue were 'I'm seeing someone'.

That was ridiculous. Gemma and I weren't in any kind of relationship. We had never even specified that we would be exclusive for the length of our deal. If I wanted to have a woman come to my room, there was absolutely no reason that I couldn't. And yet, I didn't want to. The thought of it completely turned me off.

"I'm tired," I lied instead. "Thank you for your help."

I closed the door behind him when he left and looked around at the empty suite, at something of a loss about what to do with myself. The clock on the TV told me it was almost midnight, and a quick calculation in my head worked out that it must be about three o'clock in the afternoon in London. Gemma would still be at work, which meant I shouldn't disturb her, but I would have liked to hear her voice anyway.

Shaking my head at myself, I went into the bathroom and took a shower instead. As soon as the water hit my body, my mind returned to the last shower I'd had on Sunday morning with Gemma. The memories were only good ones: the feel of her hands on me, the feel of my hand in her, and the wonderfully sexy sounds she made as I touched her.

Soon, I was touching myself, imagining it was her instead: her hands, her mouth, her wet, warm pussy. *Fuck.* I groaned as I came, half in pleasure and half in frustration. How could it even be possible that I wanted her more at that point than I had when we first met? My last solo session in the shower had been the night she'd left me alone in my suite when I'd confused her for a prostitute, and it almost made me laugh when I thought about it.

How had I ever thought there was anything artificial about the way she reacted to me? How had I ever thought that magical sparkle in her eyes could be bought? That anyone could ever put a price on her?

Stepping out of the shower, I dried myself off, grabbed my phone and composed a text.

Arrived in Tokyo. Need to make some appearances tomorrow but should be able to leave straight afterwards. Hopefully, I'll be back by Tuesday pm, but I'll let you know for sure when I'm leaving.

After hesitating a moment, I added one last line.

Thinking of you. C

As soon as I hit send, I wanted to take it back. Would she find it too much? Was I being clingy? Maybe I could play it off that I had been thinking of what I could do to her, rather than just of her in general.

Before I could stress too much, the dots popped up on my phone, letting me know Gemma was typing, almost as if she had been waiting for me to get in touch. That idea pleased me more than it should have.

Jackson sent me the link to the story this morning. I'm sorry you have to deal with this. Hope it goes well. I'll be working late tonight, but missing you. G

Those simple words filled my chest with a lightness, a feeling of buoyancy, that almost made me feel I could fly. What the hell was going on? The fact that just a few words from her could so completely alter my mood scared me, and yet, I had to admit that I didn't completely dislike it either.

As the realization slowly hit me, I sank down onto the couch to try to get my bearings. Examining all the evidence, I couldn't deny it any longer: Gemma made me feel things. Things I hadn't felt in a long time and things I hadn't even thought I wanted to feel again. But now that I did, I didn't want to stop feeling them. I felt nervous and unsure and, yes, a little scared, but the point was that I *felt.* For the first time in years, I felt alive again.

Being with her made me happier. I cared about her happiness in return, and the thought of not seeing her again after Friday, or of only seeing her in a business capacity, made it feel like one of my limbs was about to be severed, like part of me would be missing without her there.

Even with that realization, I didn't know if she felt the same way at all. Were those feelings completely one-sided, the way it had been with Samantha? Gemma had been happy to take my deal, not asking anything more of me than what I offered her. Did that mean she wasn't interested in anything else? She'd just come out of such a long-term relationship that she might not be looking for anything serious.

Was it too late for me to renegotiate our terms?

Whatever the truth might be, I wouldn't be able to figure it out over text. I would have to talk to her when I got back and try to find a way of asking her if she had any interest in turning the relationship between us into something real. I couldn't even begin to imagine how I was going to do that, but first, I had to figure out how to reply to her text. One place I could always feel in control with her was the bedroom, so I steered the conversation to the one thing I knew she did expect from me.

Can you do something for me tonight?

Her reply came in a second. *Of course. What is it?*

I couldn't help smiling as I typed. *Lie naked in the middle of the bed, spread your legs wide, and make yourself come while thinking of me. Take a picture of your face immediately afterwards and send it to me.*

Her reply wasn't quite so immediate that time. I could almost see the way she would have bit her lip when she read it, the way her breathing would have sped up just a little.

When her reply came, it was succinct and to the point.

Yes, Mr Stamer.

I groaned again into the stillness of the empty room. I had to put a stop to that train of thought before I ended up having to get back in the shower.

Goodnight, Gemma. See you soon.

Goodnight, Cole. xx

Walking into the bedroom, I placed my phone on the bedside table. I wanted that picture to be the first thing I saw when I woke up. That way, I could almost pretend she was right here with me, and with that in mind, I climbed into bed, counting the hours until I could be with her again.

~Gemma~

By the time I left the office on Monday evening, the church bells had already rung for nine o' clock. I still had work to catch up on, which kept me busy, but the main reason I stayed so long was that the idea of going back to Cole's room without him there didn't appeal to me very much at all. Seeing his clothes in the closet or his things in the bathroom only made me more aware of the fact that he had gone and that we were missing out on time we were supposed to have together.

I had been planning for us to visit another museum that evening, one that showed the evolution of Christmas celebrations and decorations in England over the last few centuries. I had also been hoping to convince Cole to wear a Santa hat with me while we went, so I could win the bet we made the previous week. With all the excitement of the sex shop and the drama of running into my father at Wilby Park over the weekend, I had nearly forgotten about the bet, and I suspected Cole had too. I was still determined to win it, though, and my chances to do so were getting fewer.

On my way out the door of the office, I glanced at the calendar on the wall, and as I saw in black-and-white just how quickly Friday would arrive and how few days I had left with Cole, an uncomfortable, gnawing feeling settled in my stomach. As I locked the office door behind me and made my way back through the nighttime streets to the Lytton, beneath all the coloured Christmas lights, I remembered what Jackson said to me the day before: I needed to really think about what I wanted and talk to Cole about it. It felt like he was suggesting that Cole would be open to something more than what we had originally agreed on.

But was that just Jackson being his usual optimistic, cheery self? Cole himself hadn't done anything to suggest to me that he considered it an option. The closest he had come was the text he sent earlier that day to say he was thinking of me. It really surprised me, but I appreciated it too. It made me feel warm and safe and protected, despite him being a continent away from me. Somehow, just knowing that I was on his mind made a world of difference.

Back at the hotel, I let myself into the empty hotel suite, and everywhere I looked, I could imagine Cole there. Sitting on the couch working on his laptop when he pretended to be my stepfather. Naked and dripping wet in the shower when he had me cuffed to the wall. Holding an ice cube between his fingers in the bedroom as he walked over to me, my body restrained and at his mercy.

Just thinking about it started to turn me on, and I hadn't forgotten what Cole had asked me to do for him. Feeling the same tingles of anticipation I felt whenever he was involved, I headed for the bedroom, quickly stripped down and took my place in the centre of the bed, just as he'd instructed, keeping my phone nearby.

My mind wandered back over all the different encounters we'd had and all the different things we'd done together as my hands explored my body. I imagined he could see me, that he was somehow watching me at that very moment, and a shiver of excitement ran through me. In my mind, the fingers playing with my clit and pressing into me weren't mine at all. They were Cole's fingers, or his tongue. I could almost feel the scratch of his stubble against my thighs and hear the low rumble of his laugh.

Getting close to my peak, I imagined him telling me to come, ordering me to, and that was enough to make it actually happen as pleasure and release flooded over me. As quickly as possible, I grabbed the phone and snapped a photo of myself from the neck up.

When I had fully recovered, I took a closer look at the picture. My eyes were half-closed, my lips parted and my cheeks flushed, and I had a feeling he'd be pleased with it. He would certainly be able to tell I hadn't faked it.

It would be early Tuesday morning in Tokyo by that time, and I couldn't be sure what time Cole would be up or when his press conference started, but I sent the photo to him anyway with a quick message.

I imagined you were here, but it doesn't compare to the real thing. G

I left the phone on the bed as I threw on my pajamas and went through my nightly routine in the bathroom. By the time I got back to the bedroom, Cole had already replied.

I agree. The picture is beautiful but the real thing is so much better. Press conference starts in an hour. Will update you when I can. C

The fact that he took the time to write to me even when he obviously had a lot going on filled me with warmth. It must mean he considered me important enough to devote his time to. If our relationship still hung entirely on our deal, he wouldn't need to keep in touch with me while he was away. That must mean he felt something more too, didn't it?

I sent him another short goodnight text and went straight to bed. The faster I fell asleep, the quicker morning would come, and hopefully, the next day would bring Cole's return with it.

When I woke in the morning, I grabbed my phone off the bedside table eagerly, hoping for the message that would tell me that Cole was on his way, but instead my spirits sank as I read his latest text.

New complications. Some of the affected parties are suing the company, need to meet with lawyers and do a further public appearance. Hope to fly out this evening but will confirm to you when I can. I'm sorry I'll miss the gardens tonight. C

Despite the bad news, the ending of his text made me smile. The whole time we'd been in our arrangement, he'd never paid attention to the things I put in his calendar. He appeared to be content to just go along with me to whatever I had planned without question, but he had obviously looked to see what I had planned that night, which was the lights at Kew Gardens. I took that to mean he really did feel bad about missing it, or that maybe he just missed me too.

Teasing him felt like the best response, and hopefully it would give him something to smile about during what sounded like a stressful day for him.

Sorry to hear that. Guess I will find myself another handsome American billionaire to go with me tonight. ;) G

Cole's reply was nearly instantaneous.

You're still mine until Friday.

That response left me more confused than ever. On the one hand, his quick reply and the fact that he called me 'his' made me think that he didn't like the idea of me being with someone else. However, he also mentioned our Friday deadline again, which suggested he still intended to end things on Friday as planned.

What was I supposed to make of that?

Since I still wanted to go to Kew Gardens that evening, I invited Holly and Jackson to go with me. We had a good time, but it definitely felt like something was missing. Some*one* was missing. Everything felt a little less vibrant, a little less special without Cole there to share it with. More than once, I caught myself about to turn to him to tell him something that had crossed my mind, only to remember that he wasn't there.

Finally, as I got back to the hotel on Tuesday evening, the text that I'd been waiting for came in.

On the plane now. Should arrive in London around 10 am Wednesday. Will probably try to get some sleep when I arrive, but will be available when you're off work. Can't wait to see you. C

The whole text made me happy, but the last sentence really elevated my mood. He couldn't wait to see me, and I couldn't wait to see him either. Those two days without him had made things a lot clearer to me: I didn't want whatever was happening between us to end. I didn't know how it would work in the long term, but I would be willing to put in the effort to find out.

I just had to figure out how to tell him that, and hope that he felt the same way too.

Chapter Sixteen

TOGETHER AGAIN

~Cole~

Though I would have liked to sleep on the plane on the way back to London, I still had a lot of work to do, speaking with our PR team as well as our lawyers both in Japan and in New York. I managed to grab a couple of hours of sleep, but not enough to be as alert as I needed to be for my scheduled meetings when I arrived back in the UK. Since being rested up for my evening with Gemma sounded more enticing, I let Jackson know he'd have to do without me for one more day.

By the time I arrived back at the hotel, it was close to noon on Wednesday, and Gemma was still at work. Even without her there, I could smell her perfume lingering. Seeing her makeup bag in the bathroom and her clothes hanging beside mine in the closet made the place feel more like home than my actual home in New York had felt like in a long time.

After setting my alarm for four o'clock so that I'd be up and ready for her when she got back from the office, I got in bed and tried once again to rest. Sleep only came fitfully, though. I was wound up too tightly, excited to see Gemma again but nervous about talking to her about everything I'd been thinking about over the last few days.

When three o'clock hit, I decided there was no point in staying in bed any longer and turned my alarm off. After showering and getting dressed in a fresh suit, I headed out into the busy streets. The sheer number of people took me by surprise until I remembered it was mid-December and most people were probably out Christmas shopping. As I passed the store windows full of elaborate displays, I found myself wondering what kind of present Gemma would like. What would make her eyes sparkle as she opened it up on Christmas morning? How excited would she be on the actual day when she planned a whole month's worth of activities leading up to it?

The smile on my face caught my eye in the reflection of one of the store windows, and I shook my head at my own foolishness. My imagination was running away with me when I didn't even know if she wanted any kind of relationship with me after the end of the week. I had no reason to think we would spend Christmas together.

Eventually, my steps led me to the Anchor office, arriving there at quarter to five. Would Gemma think it was charming if I showed up a little early, or desperate? My indecision frustrated me. Second-guessing myself had never been my style. I never had with Samantha, but that was before I knew what it felt like to make a complete fool of myself over someone who didn't actually care for me at all. That didn't seem to be the situation with Gemma, but then, I hadn't thought it was happening with Samantha either. How could I trust my judgement?

Either way, standing outside the office door like an idiot wasn't much better, so I went inside. The receptionist recognized me and gave me a warm, but slightly confused smile. "Good afternoon, Mr Stamer. You don't have an appointment today, do you?"

"No, I'm just here to see Ms Sudlow when she's finished for the day." Gemma's office door was closed, giving me no indication of how soon that might be.

The receptionist said she'd let Gemma know and invited me to take a seat, but before either of us could move, Gemma's door opened and she stepped out, already wearing her coat and hat. She didn't see me there, walking over to her assistant's desk across from her office instead.

"Denise, I'm heading out a few minutes early. If anyone needs me, let them know I'll get back to them in the morning."

As she turned to go, I stepped out into her path. "Are you in a hurry? I was hoping to steal you away."

Gemma's eyes widened in surprise as she took me in, and her face lit up with a genuine smile that warmed me through and through. "Cole! I didn't know you were coming here. Should I have?"

She went to pull out her phone to look for a missed message, but I put my hand on hers to stop her. "No, I just decided to come. I hope that's okay."

"Of course." She looked around at her staff who were trying a little too hard to look like they weren't paying attention to us. "Let's head out then, shall we?"

I let her lead the way and once we were out in the courtyard, away from the curious eyes inside, she turned back and gave me a hug.

"It's really good to see you, Cole. I missed you."

My cheek pressed tighter against hers as I smiled. "I missed you too."

I hadn't completely thought things through, I realized. If I had just waited for her at the hotel, we would have been in private. Instead, we were out in public, when what I really wanted was to feel her naked body against mine. I was an idiot.

"It actually works out well that you came." Gemma pulled away and took hold of my hand as we started to walk back out to the street. "We were going to be quite rushed for dinner, so this gives us a little more time."

"There's no chance of skipping tonight's entertainment?" I really just wanted to get her alone, to get her moaning beneath me for a while, and then to talk.

"I'm afraid not," she replied, giving me a wink that told me she knew exactly why I asked. "This is the one thing the whole month that I really can't miss."

That was frustrating. I had looked at my calendar today to see where we were going, and it only said 'gingerbread'. Since I didn't know what that meant, I had hoped it might be negotiable. "What are we doing?"

"It's a gingerbread house contest," she explained, her eyes twinkling with excitement. "Children from disadvantaged schools across the city get teamed up with professional architects to help them put together a gingerbread house. All the pieces are already prepared from designs I sent over earlier, and we have three hours to decorate it and put it together. It's a lot of fun, and the schools of the winning teams get some really good prizes. I've been working on this year's design since March, and I've got a good feeling that my team is going to win."

I hadn't been expecting anything like that, but I could see just how excited she was about it, and her enthusiasm was infectious. "What's my job, then?"

"We'll see when we get there," she teased. "I'm going to let the kids put you to work."

Gemma explained more about the contest to me as we stopped for a quick bite to eat, and afterwards, we took a taxi to the Dorchester Hotel. The event would be taking place in their ballroom, but when we arrived, we were ushered into a smaller meeting room where the children assigned to Gemma's team were gathering with their parents.

"Are you okay with kids?" Gemma whispered to me as we waited for the last team members to arrive. "Or are you afraid of them, like clowns?"

My eyes narrowed in mock indignation at her teasing. "I told you, I'm not afraid of clowns, I just don't see the point of them. Children have a purpose, so they're fine."

Gemma almost snorted with laughter. "You 'see the point' of children, do you? How benevolent of you."

I had to fight to keep the smile off my face, not wanting to let her know just how much I enjoyed her teasing. "I thought it was quite magnanimous."

"But do you like kids?" she followed up, looking at me with genuine curiosity.

Though she couldn't have known it, the question brought a lump to my throat. I hadn't told Gemma that part of the story with Samantha. I hadn't mentioned how I proposed to Samantha in part because she told me she was pregnant, and I hadn't told her how excited I'd been at the prospect of being a father and having a baby with the woman I loved.

I had to assume now that it had just been another lie, another thing Samantha told me just to hook me in deeper. Surely, if she had actually been pregnant with my child, she would have tried to get more money out of me somehow. Since she hadn't, it must have meant she'd never been pregnant at all.

In any case, I didn't want to bring all of that up right at that moment. I didn't want to think about Samantha at all, so I decided to give Gemma a pithy answer that I hoped would change the subject. "Children are fine as long as they're someone else's."

A flash of something that almost looked like disappointment crossed her face, but before I could find out what it meant, a man with a clipboard came over to us. "Ms Sudlow, all the members of your team are here now."

I stood back as Gemma gathered the kids around her. There were eight of them ranging in age from about eight to fourteen, and she showed them some pictures of the house they were going to make and gave them a pep talk that had them all laughing and ready to go. Soon, the time came for us all to head into the ballroom and find our table.

Gemma and I were the last to go, and she reached into her bag and pulled out two Santa hats. "What do you say, Cole?" she asked, slipping one of them onto her head and offering me the other. "It's for the kids."

My eyes moved from the Santa hat to Gemma's inviting smile. I had nearly forgotten about our bet, but after everything that had happened between us, the idea of being able to ask a favour of her, with no restrictions at all, appealed to me even more than it had when we made the bet. As tempted as I might have been to give in to her, I wanted to win even more.

"You haven't convinced me quite yet, I'm afraid."

A look of such genuine disappointment crossed her face that I almost changed my mind right then and there out of guilt. But a moment later, she put the hat away and gave me a challenging grin. "Alright. I'll just have to come up with something even better tomorrow, then. For now, let's go out there and win this thing."

~Gemma~

By the end of the night, Cole's expensive suit had been covered in bits of icing and candy. The children designated him the official 'gingerbread holder', meaning he had to hold the pieces of the house together until they dried while the kids decorated the house around him.

He took it all in stride, gamely letting them climb over and under him to get to where they needed to go, and only slightly wincing every time a stray bit of decoration landed on his custom shirt or jacket.

Despite what he'd said, I could see he was actually really good with kids, especially the younger ones. Although his response when I asked him if he liked kids disappointed me, I tried not to read too much into it. After all, most men didn't sit around dreaming about having babies. He probably wouldn't know for sure how he felt until he had one of his own, and I still couldn't help feeling that he would make a great dad based on the way he stood up for me and protected me even in the short time we'd been together.

In the end, I reminded myself that I probably wasn't pregnant anyway, so getting worked up about his glib response wouldn't do anyone any good. I had enough real things to worry about without inventing new problems for myself.

Like how to talk to Cole about our relationship and what I wanted it to be, for example. Or what I was going to do about my father's party the following evening.

I hadn't told Cole yet that my father's valet messaged me earlier in the day to remind me that my father expected me at the party, and that I was not to bring a guest. Holly could still come, as she'd been issued a separate invite, and apparently she could still bring a guest, but I couldn't. It seemed that my father wanted me to show up looking single and repentant, though repentant for what, exactly, I couldn't be sure. For having the bad form to be left by my fiancé? Or for actually admitting that I was a woman who liked sex?

Whatever the case may be, I still thought it would probably be in my best interest to go, to make an appearance to satisfy my father, and hopefully, I wouldn't see him again for another six months or more afterwards.

When the buzzer sounded to signal the end of the competition, we all stepped back from our masterpiece. The house I designed was a fanciful version of Wilby Park, with the same basic structure as the actual house but with decoration drawn purely from the imaginations of the children on my team. They'd done a brilliant job.

After a tense round of judging, we were awarded second place out of the twenty teams there. I was a little disappointed, as I really thought we had a chance of winning, but the kids' school still got some great prizes and the kids themselves were happy enough.

Cole was much more upset on my behalf. "The other team cheated," he complained as we got into the taxi to head back to the Lytton. "They propped up the rear wall because it couldn't support the weight of the roof on its own. Yours was free-standing and perfectly proportioned."

"It's okay," I assured him, amused by how invested he'd become. "We'll always know in our hearts that ours was the best."

He recognized the teasing in my voice, and his eyes darkened. "Just because I know you're the best doesn't mean the world shouldn't recognize it too."

A shiver ran through me, as it often did when he adopted that tone of voice. Why did it feel like we weren't only talking about the house anymore?

By the time we arrived back at Cole's suite, it had already passed ten o'clock. As much as I wanted to spend some time being naked with him, I also wanted to talk to him that night and I wasn't sure we had time to do both. As I tried to figure out how to tell him that I only wanted to talk, he shocked me by saying the exact same thing.

"Gemma, I've been thinking about having you in that bed ever since I left, but if it's okay with you, I'd like to talk to you about something first."

"Sure. What is it?"

He invited me to take a seat on the couch in the living room and sat down beside me, sitting at an angle so he could look at me directly, our bodies not quite touching.

"I'm really not good at this kind of thing," he started, his hand gripping the back of his neck in an almost nervous gesture, and a surge of affection rushed through me, seeing him so unsure of himself. "Negotiating and making deals, that's where I'm comfortable. But being away from you for the past few days made me realize that this thing between us, it's more to me than just a deal. I hoped... well, I hoped maybe it was for you too."

Could he literally read my mind? It felt that way. How did he know what I was going to say? "Cole, I wanted to tell you exactly the same thing. I just didn't know how."

Something sparked deep in his eyes, something that almost looked like hope. I hadn't ever seen that expression on his face before. "You mean that?"

"Of course." I reached over to take his hand in mine, the warmth of it making me feel safe and grounded. "Our time together has been incredible. You're incredible. I feel like a different person when I'm with you, in the best possible way. And I like that person. I like being her."

"I like her too." His eyes gleamed with that promise of passion that I always found irresistible, but also with a hint of tenderness that was new. "I don't know exactly what I'm suggesting, Gemma. I don't have a plan, and I have to admit that kind of terrifies me. All I know is that I don't want Friday to be the end of us. I want you in my life for a lot longer than that."

"I want that too."

Words didn't seem enough to show him how much, so I pulled his face down to mine and kissed him. He kissed me back eagerly but gently too. For the first time, it felt like we weren't kissing just as a way of moving on to something else. The kiss was the endpoint. It was the only thing that mattered.

I couldn't guess how long we stayed there, simply kissing and holding each other, but eventually, Cole pulled back, giving me a sweet smile. "I had all kinds of plans for tonight, but I have to admit I'm completely exhausted."

I knew what he meant. I felt elated that we were on the same page, that he wanted us to be together too, but it also felt like we had run a marathon to get to that point. On top of that, he'd been travelling and dealing with time zones and all the other stress of the last few days. He must be absolutely knackered.

"Let's get some sleep," I suggested. "We'll have plenty of time tomorrow to carry out your plans after my father's party."

The smile on Cole's face faltered. "We're going to that party?"

"I am," I clarified. "Just for a little while, and then I'll come straight back here to you."

His smile fell away completely, replaced by a scowl. "You're not going there alone. Either I come with you or you don't go. Those are the options."

"It's not a big deal," I tried to assure him. "There will be so many people there, I probably won't even speak to my father. I just need to be seen, to keep up appearances."

"Gemma, this isn't negotiable. I will keep you tied to that bed all night if I have to, but you are not going alone."

"Is that supposed to be a threat?" I teased him, trying to distract him from the issue at hand. "You know I have no problem with you tying me up."

I could see his desire warring with his protectiveness as he looked back at me. "Well, we can always do both. I'll go with you to the party, so you can be seen, and then we can come back here and tie you up in as many ways as possible."

He obviously didn't intend to give in, so I decided to press my advantage. "You can come with me on one condition."

He raised an eyebrow at me. "And what's that?"

"You have to wear a Santa hat with me as we walk in."

His eyes narrowed and for a moment, I thought I had actually angered him. But a few seconds later, his face broke into a smile, that genuine, boyish smile of his that was so rare and all the more precious for its rareness. "Very well, Gemma. You've outplayed me. I'll wear your damn hat."

"It won't be the last time I outsmart you," I teased, giving him a seductive wink.

His smile only got wider. "God, I hope not."

~Cole~

Waking up the next morning with Gemma beside me in the bed, I could hardly believe that the previous night really happened. Our talk might have been brief, but it was still everything I could have hoped for. She felt the same way I did. She wanted to be with me. It seemed almost too good to be true.

I hadn't been so happy in a long time. Probably not since Samantha had agreed to marry me, which had also felt too good to be true, and look how that turned out.

My good mood began to fade, but I tried to push my doubts aside. I didn't have any reason to be suspicious of Gemma's motives. She wasn't Samantha, and it wouldn't be fair to her to make that comparison.

Gemma began to stir, so I leaned down to give her a soft kiss. "Good morning."

Her smile felt like the sunshine through the clouds, flooding my whole body with warmth. "Good morning. What time is it?"

"Only just after six. I need to get up though, I've got a lot of work to catch up on from the last few days. I can order some breakfast for us if you want?"

We ate together and she got ready for her day while Jackson joined me in the living room to review the meetings we had coming up. He had pushed back a couple of things from earlier in the week that needed my personal attention, so our day would be completely full. I wouldn't have a spare minute until the time came to get ready for the party that evening.

Jackson surprised me by telling me he would be going to the party too. Apparently, Holly had invited him as her guest, and I was glad to hear it. The more people that had Gemma's back, the better. We could make sure no one got a chance to bother her and that the night went as smoothly as possible.

Gemma came over to give me a kiss before leaving for the day. It wasn't the first time she'd done so, but that morning, it felt different. More meaningful, somehow. More of a promise than a goodbye.

Jackson couldn't hide his grin after she'd gone. "Okay, you've both got that sappy in-love look, so I'm guessing you had 'the talk'?"

I knew what was coming, so I encouraged him to get it over with. "Go ahead and say it: you were right. I like her and apparently I'm lucky enough that she likes me too."

"That's a good start." To his credit, he didn't look smug about it. He just looked genuinely happy for me. "But what happens next?"

"We haven't figured it all out yet," I admitted. "I still have to go back to New York tomorrow. My sister's having her big Christmas get-together this weekend, and she'd kill me if I missed it. But after that, we'll see. We'll figure something out."

Jackson nodded. "Good. I'm so glad, Cole. Gemma is great, and I think she's perfect for you."

I was really starting to think so too.

The day flew by and before I knew it, I was back in the suite, getting changed for the evening. I hadn't brought any formal wear with me for the trip since I'd only been planning on focusing on business, but this party was a black-tie affair. I asked my assistant to find me something appropriate, and earlier that day, someone delivered a formal suit with tails and a waistcoat. The style didn't match my usual look at all, but she assured me that men in London were wearing them.

I'd almost finished getting ready when Gemma rushed in. "I'm so sorry, I got caught up in a meeting, but I just need a few minutes..." She trailed off as she caught sight of me, and a wide smile lit up her face. "Well, don't you look like the proper British gentleman?"

I put on my best fake British accent to answer her. "That's what I was going for, love."

Gemma laughed loudly, her eyes sparkling in amusement. "Okay, don't ever do that again." She came over to me, still chuckling, and gave me a sweet kiss. "But you do look wonderful."

"I can't wait to see what you're wearing." I wished we had more time before the party to get her out of her work clothes before she had to put something else on.

"I was tempted to wear my Santa dress from the night we met," she teased as she walked into the bedroom. I followed her to the door, watching as she walked over to the closet and opened it up.

"I wouldn't have any problem with that. You looked amazing in it."

"Well, hopefully you'll like this one just as much." She turned to see me standing there, and made a shooing motion with her hands. "You have to wait until I'm ready though. Out."

Normally, I gave the orders, but I let her have her way, returning to the living room to wait for her to make her appearance. When she did, I could hardly believe my eyes.

The dress matched the colour of her skin almost exactly, overlaid with a light gauzy material covered in fake diamonds and sequins, in swirling patterns. It made it look like she hardly wore anything at all, although in reality she was completely covered. As she moved, the sequins caught the light, making it look like she glowed from within, like her own special light shone out of her.

I couldn't take my eyes off her.

When I finally raised my gaze back to her face, she gave me a nervous smile. "What do you think? My father's probably going to hate it."

"That makes it even better, then. You don't need to worry about what anyone else thinks. You've got eyes, Gemma. Look in that mirror. You're exquisite."

The nervousness in her smile lessened. "Thank you, Cole. I'm glad you're coming tonight."

"I am too."

We made our way downstairs to where Holly and Jackson were already waiting so we could all take a car over together. The ride didn't take very long, and soon, we pulled up in front of a large, elegant townhouse behind a cast-iron fence. The house wasn't as old as the one in the country that Gemma had taken me to, but it had clearly still been there for at least a couple of centuries.

Once the gate had been opened for us, the car drove us right up to the front door. Two men in tails and top hats stood on either side of the double doors, which were open wide, and another man came over to open the car door for us.

I got out first, offering my arm to Gemma, and Jackson and Holly followed behind us. Just inside, an elegant woman in heels checked the guest list on an iPad. Gemma gave her name and Holly's, and the woman frowned as she scrolled through her list.

"I have Ms Chapman and guest here, but Lady Gemma, it doesn't say that you're bringing a guest."

"There must be some mistake," Gemma told her, her voice clear and strong and confident. "This is my father's party. Surely, I can bring anyone I like."

I squeezed her arm, proud of her for not backing down, and the woman blushed. "I'm sure you're right. Please, enjoy your evening."

Gemma led us to the small room being used as a coat check, and we shed our outer garments. Before Gemma handed over her coat, however, she pulled out two Santa hats from an inside pocket.

"Time to put your money where your mouth is, Cole," she challenged, offering one to me.

I didn't say anything as I took it from her and placed it on my head while she tucked hers over her beautiful red hair.

Meanwhile, Jackson stared at me in utter shock. "I need a picture," he cried out, reaching for his coat again. "This is the end of the world. I have to document it."

Gemma laughed and grabbed his arm before he could retrieve his phone. "Come on, let's go inside."

The sounds of people chatting and music playing got louder as we walked down the hall towards a beautiful, large ballroom. A small orchestra played jazz-infused versions of Christmas songs while trays of food and champagne were circulated among the very well-dressed guests. I had been to a lot of parties in my life, and even I had to admit to being impressed. The Earl had clearly spared no expense.

"How long are we staying?" I asked Gemma under my breath. I had more than one reason for asking: I didn't want to give her father or anyone else a chance to bother her, and I also wanted to get her back to the suite for our last night before I flew out the next day. However long it would be until I saw her again would be too long.

"Just long enough for people to know we're here," she assured me, leading us into the room. "No more than an hour, tops."

The next half hour was filled with the usual inane small talk that typically made up those kinds of events. I found Gemma's father in the crowd shortly after we arrived, so I'd been doing my best to keep us away from him. He wouldn't be pleased that I came, but I doubted he would make a scene in public at his own party. Even so, it seemed prudent to avoid him anyway.

Holly and Jackson had gone to the dance floor while Gemma finished making polite conversation with another older couple. Just as I was about to ask her if she wanted to dance, someone else appeared in front of us; someone that I recognized.

"Gemma and Cole." A smile graced Annabel's face, but her eyes gleamed with something far less appealing. Gemma stiffened next to me and I put my arm around her waist to try to reassure her. "I was hoping to run into you here."

"This is my father's party," Gemma pointed out. "It's not a stretch that I would be here, but we don't have anything to talk about, Annabel."

"Oh, of course we do." Annabel's laugh was as fake as her hair colour. "I'd heard that you might not make it, or at least that Cole might not. I'm glad that wasn't true. It would have spoiled the surprise."

Obviously, she knew that Gemma had been told not to bring me. How would she know that? My guess was that it came through Edwin's father.

"What surprise?" Gemma asked through gritted teeth.

Annabel tutted at her. "I'm afraid it's not for you. It's for Cole." She turned to me with a look of gleeful anticipation. "Someone special who flew in to see you."

Someone to see *me*? What the hell was she talking about?

Before I could ask, she turned around and pulled the woman behind her over into my line of view, and my stomach dropped to the floor.

"Hello, Cole," Samantha said.

Chapter Seventeen

GHOST OF CHRISTMAS PAST

~Gemma~

I had no idea who the woman with Annabel was. Elegantly dressed and beautiful, with long, dark hair, her bright blue eyes were fixed on Cole as she spoke to him.

Clearly, *he* knew who she was. His face turned deathly pale as he caught sight of her and he took a step back, almost losing his balance, as if someone had shoved him. I quickly put my arm around him to steady him.

"What are you doing here?" he asked, his voice betraying his surprise. It almost shook, not sounding anything like his usual confident self.

Whatever effect she had on Cole, it looked like the woman felt almost equally anxious to be seeing him. She glanced over at Annabel, who wore a smug smile, obviously enjoying the drama she had caused. "Annabel invited me," the woman replied, which even I could tell wasn't much of an answer. He wanted to know *why* she'd been invited.

Cole's gaze moved between Annabel and the mystery woman, his eyes narrowing as he tried to make sense of it. "How do you two know each other? Is there some secret club you both belong to? A place where pathetic, manipulative women get together for fun?"

Annabel's smile widened, making me even more confused. Why did she look so pleased? There had to be something else at play, and as my eyes darted around, trying to figure it out, I noticed the phone in her hand.

"Annabel's recording this," I whispered in Cole's ear, turning my head so that my lips couldn't be seen. "She wants you to lose your temper."

I didn't know what she planned to do with the recording, but I could only guess it involved buying herself another thirty seconds of fame somehow. Cole's grip on my waist tightened in acknowledgement, letting me know he saw it too. "We've got nothing to say to either of you," he told the two women. "Gemma, I'm ready to leave if you are."

"Cole, wait." The woman I didn't know spoke up again. "I need to talk to you. That's why I came. I knew you wouldn't agree to see me otherwise."

"You're right about that, at least," he agreed. "And I won't talk to you now either."

He turned to go, but she stepped forward, taking hold of his other arm, the one that wasn't around me, and whispered something in his ear. Any colour that had come back to his face immediately drained again as he heard whatever she had to say.

"You're lying," he said, but I could tell he wasn't sure of that. His voice sounded weaker than ever.

"I'm not," she argued. "I can prove it. Please, just give me a couple of minutes."

The muscles in his face twitched as his jaw clenched. Whatever she'd said had really shaken him. I hadn't seen anything affect him that way other than when he told me about his ex-fiancée, and my eyes widened as I made the connection. It couldn't be, could it? Why would she be here? How would Annabel know anything about her?

Those were the same questions Cole just had, I remembered, so maybe it really was her. It would explain a lot.

Cole turned to me, his eyes unsure and conflicted. "I need to talk to her. I won't be long."

Since he was obviously struggling, I didn't object. "Do you want me to come?" I offered instead.

He shook his head. "No, it's alright. I'll explain it to you later. Maybe Holly can keep you company?" He looked towards the dance floor, trying to seek her out.

"I don't need a bodyguard," I assured him. "Go ahead. I'll wait for you here."

He nodded, clearly distracted as he and the other woman headed for the door, looking for a place to talk. I watched them go until I couldn't see them anymore, lost in the sea of people.

"It's such a shame when an ex shows up and stirs up old feelings, isn't it?" Annabel's nasal voice grated in my ear.

That confirmed my suspicions about the woman's identity, but I still didn't know what Annabel had to do with any of it. When I turned back to face her, she still held the phone in her hand, waiting for my response, but I had no intention of giving her anything else to work with.

Before she saw it coming, I grabbed the phone out of her hand, threw it down on the floor and stomped on it with the heel of my high-heeled shoes.

"What the... you can't do that!" she shrieked, her face twisted in disbelief and outrage.

"You're not in any position to tell me what I can or can't do," I pointed out, stepping closer to her. "I'm not your puppet, Annabel. You don't have any power over me. You wanted Edwin? You got him. There's nothing else for you here, so move on and leave me the hell alone."

I hadn't realized how loudly I spoke, but between the volume of my voice and the smashing of her phone, we seemed to have attracted a small crowd. Annabel noticed it too and I could almost see the wheels in her brain turning, trying to figure out how to use it to her advantage.

"You're the one who hasn't moved on yet, Gemma. It's really sad, bringing your fake boyfriend here to try to make Eddie jealous. Especially after you posed for all those staged photos at the sex shop? Everyone knows you'd never do anything like that for real. It's so obvious. You just want Eddie back."

She didn't actually believe the words coming out of her mouth, did she? Was she just trying to paint herself as the victim, to get sympathy through some bizarre fantasy she'd invented?

"That is the last thing I want," I told her, keeping my voice calm but still firm. "Why would I want a man who never satisfied me? I guess it's lucky for him that you're so much easier to please."

Her mouth fell open in shock, and a thrill of satisfaction ran through me. Cole had been telling me so all along, and I finally saw just how true it was: my lack of response to Edwin had never been my fault, and blaming myself for it was ridiculous.

Even though he wasn't beside me right at that moment, I could hear Cole's voice in my head and feel his support, urging me to stand my ground and not give Annabel an inch.

"Bel?" Edwin rushed to Annabel's side, apparently having caught wind of the confrontation between us. He gave me an apprehensive look as he took her hand. "What's going on?"

I answered for her. "We were just clearing the air. Annabel seemed to think that I wanted to win you back, but nothing could be further from the truth. I'm actually really happy that you two got together. It seems like you deserve each other."

Edwin's face went nearly as pale as Cole's had earlier. His eyes darted around the group of people who were watching us, hanging on every word. "Gemma, there's no need to make a scene."

I couldn't help it: I laughed in his face. "Is that what I'm doing? And what do you call what you and Posh Barbie here pulled on that ridiculous TV show?"

Cole's nickname for Annabel slipped out without me even thinking about it, and I could see several of the people around us snickering at it while Annabel's face turned a very interesting shade of red.

"That wasn't the best way for us to have handled things," Edwin admitted, which was the closest thing to an apology I'd ever got from him.

"I'm over it," I assured him. "And I'm definitely over you. Merry Christmas, both of you."

Before either of them had a chance to respond, I turned and walked away without a backward glance.

Holly and Jackson were immediately at my side. They must have heard at least part of the exchange because Holly was grinning ear-to-ear. "I can't believe you finally told him off! That was brilliant, Gem. Highlight of my year."

I smiled back at her, but as the adrenaline left my body, my hands began to shake. I wanted to leave before my father found me or anything else unexpected happened. "Let's find Cole and get the hell out of here."

~Cole~

Samantha followed me down the hall, both of us looking for somewhere private where we could talk while the words she had whispered in my ear continued to ring in my head. I didn't want to believe they were true, but I had to admit they could be. Would she really risk coming to the party and showing her face to me again if they weren't?

Either way, I didn't want Gemma exposed to whatever new scheme Samantha had up her sleeve. Gemma had enough on her own plate without dumping my baggage onto it. By agreeing to speak to Samantha in private, I hoped I could cut through all the garbage, find out exactly what she wanted and get back to Gemma as quickly as possible.

Finally, we reached an open door leading into a small sitting room that appeared to be empty, the lights off. We both stepped inside and I flipped the switch to illuminate the room. As soon as I'd closed the door behind us, I turned around and got straight to the point. "What the hell do you want from me, Samantha?"

She took a step back, clearly not accustomed to my anger. I never raised my voice to her when we were together, but any tender feelings I'd once had towards her were long gone.

"I told you," she repeated, blinking at me in the way she always had, which I'd always taken for innocence. When she did it then, it just seemed ridiculously fake. "We need to talk about your daughter."

"I don't have a daughter." My voice was low and filled with warning. The days when she could manipulate me were over. Nothing she said would be taken at face value.

"I told you I was pregnant before you proposed," she reminded me.

She actually had the gall to stand in front of me and talk about our engagement? Was she really that shameless?

"You also said you loved me," I pointed out. "You said a lot of things that weren't true. Why should I believe this is any different?"

She opened her mouth to reply, but I cut her off, changing my mind.

"Actually, the first question I want answered is: what are you doing here? At this party? How do you know Annabel?"

"I've been trying to get in touch with you, but none of your friends will talk to me."

If that was true, I owed a debt of gratitude to any of the friends that Samantha might have approached.

"I found Annabel on Instagram, posting about how she was spending time with you. I sent her a message and she said she could arrange for us to meet."

Annabel claimed to be spending time with me? That was quite a stretch. I couldn't see what she had to gain from helping Annabel, other than getting more attention for herself, or maybe just causing trouble for Gemma. Maybe that was all she wanted.

"And this sudden interest in finding me? What brought that on?"

"Our child," she stated once again. "As I already said. You have a daughter, Cole."

She planned to stick to that story, apparently. "If that were true, it's not something that happened recently. Why would you just be telling me now?"

She pursed her lips, clearly not getting the reaction from me that she wanted. As I tried to figure out what reaction she expected, it suddenly became clear to me.

"You want money."

Of course she did. It always came down to that.

Samantha winced, but she didn't deny it. "It's not for me. It's for your daughter."

"And what happened to the ten million you took from me?" My anger began to fade as I grasped the game, and my usual calm control returned to me.

"Cole, I never meant to..."

I didn't know where she was going with that, and I didn't care. "Don't insult my intelligence. We both know what you meant to do."

I didn't want to hear anything else, and certainly not any excuses she might have come up with to try to explain what she'd done. If she had come to me two weeks earlier, it might have sent me into a tailspin, making me question everything and doubt myself. But that evening, having spent the last two weeks with Gemma, I could see Samantha for exactly what she was.

Finally, it had become crystal clear to me: the Samantha I thought I loved never existed. I had always been so careful with her, eager to please her, because part of me always felt like she might slip away. With Gemma, I felt none of that. Gemma gave herself to me completely; not just her body, but her spirit and her wit and her laughter and her support. She withheld nothing. What we had together, that was real, the most real thing I'd ever experienced.

No matter what the truth turned out to be, whether I had a child or not, I wouldn't let Samantha control me or affect my relationship with Gemma. She didn't have any power over me anymore.

"Is there really a child?"

A hint of a smile appeared on her face. She thought she had me, but she had no idea what I was really thinking. "Yes. Of course there is."

"In that case, call my office in New York and they'll arrange for you to take her to a doctor of my choosing for a paternity test. But I won't just give you money, Samantha. If I really do have a daughter, I want to be part of her life. My lawyers can discuss custody arrangements after the tests are completed."

Her eyes widened in disbelief, making it clear she hadn't been expecting that. "You can't be serious. You don't want..."

"Don't tell me what I want." I cut her off once again. "You have no idea. And don't think you can hide from me either. If you don't call my office, I will track you down. I let you go before, I didn't bother trying to find you, but that time you only hurt me. I won't let you use my daughter too, if she truly exists."

"You can't take her from me." For the first time, I really believed she might actually be telling me the truth. The fear in her eyes looked real, but we couldn't go back now. She'd put the idea out there, and I would see it through.

"That's not what I said, but if what you're saying is true, then that's exactly what you did. You took her from me, and I won't let you keep doing it. You chose to come here tonight, to try to squeeze me for just a little more, but I'm not the same man who fell for your lies. I've changed, and it's time you did too. Now, if you'll excuse me, I need to get back to my date and the woman that I actually care about."

Leaving her speechless in my wake, I left the room. As soon as I turned back towards the ballroom, Gemma appeared at the other end of the hall, flanked by Holly and Jackson.

Just the sight of her lifted my spirits, but she had said she'd wait for me in the ballroom. Had something happened? I walked towards her, wanting to make sure she was okay, but all I could see in her face was concern for me as she came up and took hold of my hands.

"Are you alright?" she asked first.

I could feel her support enveloping me like a warm, gentle breeze. "Yes. I need to tell you about it, but I'll do it back at the hotel. Are you ready to go?"

She gave my hands a firm squeeze. "Definitely."

After retrieving our coats from the coat check, we were almost at the door when a voice called out from behind us. "Gemma."

I recognized her father's voice immediately. Gemma told Holly and Jackson to go ahead, and she and I turned together to face the Earl. He glared at both of us as he moved closer, his voice lowered.

"I warned you to come alone tonight. Not only did you disobey me, but now I've just been told that you caused a scene with Edwin and Annabel?"

She had? I looked down at her in surprise, and when our eyes met, I could have sworn she was trying not to smile. What a shame I'd missed it.

"You're the one who should be embarrassed," she said to her father, taking me by surprise once again. "Why would you invite them to your party in the first place after what they did to me? If that's who you'd prefer to spend your time with, then it's fine with me. I won't come back."

Pride coursed through me, hearing her stand up for herself that way. It also clearly shocked her father, taking the wind right out of his sails. Whatever threat he'd been planning to give her, she'd obviously just outmaneuvered it. He sputtered for a moment before settling on a new line of attack.

"Whether you're in this house or not, you're still a representative of this family. And I won't have you out there doing God knows what..."

That was more than enough. I knew that Gemma was capable of standing up to him herself, but she shouldn't always have to. I wanted her to know that I would always have her back too.

I took a step towards the Earl, forcing him to step back. "If you truly believe that Gemma represents you, then you should consider yourself damn lucky. And if you can't see the brilliant, successful, charming woman in front of you for what she is, then it's your loss." I turned to Gemma. "Shall we?"

She smiled up at me. "Absolutely. I'm finished here."

Without a word of goodbye, we left the party for good.

~Gemma~

I felt almost giddy in the taxi on the way back to the hotel. I couldn't believe that I had just spoken to my father that way, or that I had shut down Annabel and Edwin either. It felt like it had happened to someone else, like I had been watching someone else's life rather than my own. It almost didn't seem real, except for the firm grip of Cole's arm around me as we sat in the car, reminding me that no matter how unlikely it seemed, this was reality.

When we arrived back at the Lytton, Holly and Jackson headed for the hotel bar to grab another drink and talk a bit more. That evening marked their last night together too since Jackson would be leaving the next day, along with Cole. I didn't know yet when Cole would be back, but I knew he would; Jackson returning was less certain. He and Holly might not see each other again, and I felt bad that nothing was going to come of their obvious attraction. But that was their choice, I supposed, just like I had made the choice to jump in feet-first to whatever the future held for me and Cole.

At that moment, all I wanted to do was make the most of our night, the last one we'd have together for a while. However, I knew something had happened at the party, something that woman had said to him that he'd promised he would tell me about, so I asked him about it as soon as we were in the door, before we moved on to anything else.

"Annabel said the woman at the party was your ex. Was she your fiancée?"

He exhaled deeply as he removed his coat and his suit jacket, making himself more comfortable. "That's right. That was Samantha."

Although I had guessed it, a sudden fury raged through my veins on his behalf. How dare that woman turn up after what she'd done to him? And what did Annabel have to do with it? "I can't believe Annabel invited her. It's one thing for her to stick her nose in my business, but she had no right..."

Cole cut me off with a smile, placing a gentle finger to my lips. "I think we're in agreement about how terrible Annabel is. We don't need to waste any time on her, but I do have to tell you what Samantha said. Let's sit down. Do you want something to drink?"

I still didn't want any alcohol, so I asked for water instead. At least with Cole leaving the next day, I wouldn't have to keep making up excuses to avoid drinking with him. In another week or two, I should be able to take a pregnancy test and put my mind to rest about the whole thing.

When we both had our drinks, he sat down opposite me. I couldn't quite read the look on his face as he took a deep breath. "Before I tell you what she said, I just want to make it clear that it doesn't change anything between you and me."

That didn't necessarily make me feel any better. What could she have said that would necessitate that kind of warning? "I'm assuming she didn't apologize," I guessed, trying to make him smile.

It worked. His lips curved upward, just slightly. "Hardly. She wanted money."

My mouth fell open in disbelief. He couldn't be serious. "What happened to the money she already took from you?"

Cole laughed darkly. "I asked that exact question, but she didn't give me an answer." His face turned serious once more, and he leaned closer to me, looking me straight in the eye. "The reason she thought I might give her money now was to support her daughter. A daughter that she claims is mine."

My mouth opened again, but no sound came out. I hadn't been expecting that at all, and I could only assume that Cole hadn't either. His face held no clues as to how he felt about it. He only looked concerned about me and my reaction. He'd just said it didn't change anything between us, but maybe he thought it would for me?

"Is it true?" I managed to ask, realizing he had used the word 'claims'.

"I don't know, but it could be. At the time she left me, she had told me she was pregnant. I thought afterwards that she'd been lying, but perhaps she wasn't. It's possible."

"Either way, it's awful," I couldn't help pointing out. "Either she lied to you in the first place and is lying again now, or she's telling the truth and she kept your own child from you all this time."

Cole's look of concern softened into a gentle smile. "Yes. She's awful. You'll get no argument from me on that."

That was some good news, at least. It didn't seem like seeing her again had rekindled any old feelings on his side, as Annabel suggested it might. But how was the news affecting him? I remembered what he'd said just the night before when I asked him about whether he liked kids. What did he think now that he might suddenly have one that he never knew about?

"How are you feeling about it?" I asked, trying to keep the question as open-ended as possible.

He leaned back and rubbed his hand over his face. "Honestly, I don't know. When we were together and she told me about the pregnancy, I was excited about it. And if there really is a little girl, and she's mine, then I want to know her. I want to be there for her, and it bothers me how much I would have missed already. It would kill me that she was out there all this time and I didn't know it. But I'm trying not to get angry or hopeful or anything, really, because I still don't even know if it's true. Does that make sense?"

"Of course it does," I assured him. It made perfect sense to me, and it made me glad to know that he would want to be a part of his daughter's life, if he really had one. "For what it's worth, I think you're taking it very well."

"I guess so. I don't know if there's a standard way to deal with something like this." He grew quiet for a second, his dark eyes examining my face closely. "You're taking it well too. Does it bother you that I might suddenly have a kid I didn't know anything about?"

Was that what he'd been worried about? I couldn't see that he'd done anything wrong at all. "Cole, you never lied to me about anything. You were honest with me about your past, and that's all I could ask for. You couldn't tell me about something you didn't know yourself. No one can prepare for every possibility, no matter how many rules you try to put in place."

I gave him a playful nudge, and he narrowed his eyes at me in that way of his that told me he was actually amused.

"I told you that I want to be with you," I continued. "And that includes dealing with new things that come up. Life's going to keep throwing things at us, at both of us. After the year I've had, I know better than anyone that you can never tell what's coming around the corner. Having your support these past two weeks has been amazing, and I will support you too, for as long as you want me to."

Genuine relief flashed in his dark eyes. "Gemma, that sounds, as you would say, 'bloody brilliant'." He put on his fake British accent again for the last two words, making me laugh. He smiled back at me, his eyes warm with humour. "I'm so glad it doesn't bother you, but to be honest, I somehow knew it wouldn't. I knew I didn't need to be afraid to tell you, and the fact that I can tell you things, even hard things, means a lot to me."

He took my hand in his, rubbing his thumb across the top of it, his touch firm but soft at the same time.

"I guess this is as good a time as any to talk about what happens next."

I assumed he meant what happened next with us, and I was very curious to hear what he would suggest. He had mentioned the night before that he didn't have a plan, so had he come up with one in the meantime?

"I have to fly back to New York tomorrow, as I always planned," he began. "There are several things coming up that I can't miss. But once the end of the year is out of the way, I want to see you as much as possible. So, I want to know: how flexible is your work? Do you need to live here in London?"

I honestly hadn't anticipated that he would want me to move, but on the other hand, it shouldn't have surprised me either. Cole never did anything by half-measures.

I'd also never really thought about living somewhere else, but I couldn't think of any particularly good reason not to. What did I have to keep me in London? My job, of course, but now that we had the contract with Cole, most of my time would be spent designing for him anyway, and I could do that anywhere. I had Holly too, but I knew she would kill me if I turned down a chance to move forward with Cole because of her. She would probably stick me in a packing crate and ship me off to him herself.

Clearly, I had no family worth sticking around for. So, what was there to stop me?

"I don't need to live here," I heard myself saying. "I would need to visit occasionally to spend time at the office, but it doesn't need to be full-time."

Cole smiled widely, that genuine, almost boyish grin of his that I absolutely loved. "And how would you like to live in New York?"

"You want me to move in with you?" I wanted to be sure I understood the question correctly and hadn't read too much into it.

"I do," he confirmed immediately. "As soon as possible."

"It will take me a little while to make the arrangements," I said, trying to temper his enthusiasm just enough that he wasn't disappointed that I couldn't go with him the next day. "But I'd love to, Cole."

He leaned forward, took my face in his hands and placed a gentle kiss on my forehead. "You don't know how happy that makes me, Gemma."

"I think I do, if it's anywhere near as happy as it makes me."

He kissed my cheek, then down to my neck, and I started to melt against him. He'd never been gentle or tender like this. As much as I loved his rough side, the unusualness of this softer treatment made it even more special.

"Wait, there's one more thing we need to talk about," I told him before I completely lost my train of thought.

"What's that?" he murmured, his lips still nuzzled against my neck.

"The bet. You wore the hat tonight with me, so now you owe me a favour."

He laughed, his lips vibrating against my skin. "Alright. What do you want from me, Gemma?"

I pulled back so I could see his face. This had been the thing I wanted to ask him ever since he first told me the story of what had happened with Samantha, and I really hoped he would agree. "I know you have to leave tomorrow, but will you come back and spend Christmas Eve here with me?"

Chapter Eighteen

Christmas Future

~Cole~

I wasn't completely sure I'd heard Gemma correctly. "You can ask me for any favour in the world, and you're asking me to spend Christmas Eve with you?"

I couldn't even begin to imagine what Samantha would have asked for if I told her I would give her any favour she wanted. With Gemma, it had never even crossed my mind to be concerned about what she might ask for, and she just proved exactly why I didn't have to be.

"I know it's a difficult memory for you," she said, her eyes bright as they looked into mine. "So I want to give you a new memory to take its place. We can go to the carol service at Westminster Abbey, then go home and watch Love Actually and all the good British Christmas films. In the morning, you can open the present I got you."

"You already got me a present?" Nobody shopped for me for fun. In fact, everyone constantly told me I was impossible to buy for. And though it had crossed my mind to get *her* something, I hadn't actually bought anything yet.

"Yes, but don't get your hopes up," she warned me with a teasing smile. "It didn't cost me anything."

That intrigued me even more. What would she have got me for free? Had she made something? What hidden talents did she have that I had yet to discover? I couldn't wait to find out.

My last few Christmases had been less than memorable. If I didn't make plans to work, my sister insisted that I stay with her and her family, and as much as I liked my sister's family, I preferred to spend the day working. There was nothing like watching a happy family on Christmas morning to make me even more aware of what I had lost.

Gemma offered me an entirely different kind of Christmas, and as long as I spent it with her, I knew it would be one I would never forget. "I might have to move some things around, but I'm sure it can be done. After all, you won the bet, fair and square. So, yes. I'll be back here on the 24th."

Her face lit up in delight, and I couldn't wait any longer. I pulled her to me in a deep kiss before standing up, lifting her off the couch with me and heading for the bedroom.

I honestly hadn't even really known that I would ask her to move in with me until the words were coming out of my mouth, but I didn't regret it, not for a second. Picturing her in my apartment and imagining coming home to her there at the end of the day was the best thing I could imagine.

For three years, I had believed that I didn't want to fall in love again, that what I felt with Samantha wasn't worth the pain I felt after she left. My mistake had been believing that what I felt with her was actually love. In two weeks, Gemma had shown me a deeper connection than I'd ever had with Samantha, and it seemed to be getting stronger every day.

As I'd already told Gemma shortly after we met, when I found something I really wanted, I went for it, all in.

Placing her on her feet, I helped her out of her dress, my lips only leaving hers to pull the dress up over her head. Once I had her naked,

I laid her down on the bed, and as I quickly removed all my clothes, a new thought crossed my mind. Telling her to stay put, I headed back to the living room. It took me a few seconds to find it, but eventually I returned to the bedroom with the Santa hat I'd worn at the party placed back on my head.

"You like the hat now, don't you?" Gemma teased, watching me with equal parts humour and lust. "Are you going to be my personal sexy Santa?"

"Exactly," I confirmed, and her eyes widened in surprise. She hadn't been expecting that, so I explained my logic to her. "If I had won the bet, I was going to ask you to dress back up in that Santa dress of yours so I could fuck you while you were still wearing it, just like I'd planned to do the night we met."

Just the thought of it made her shiver. I loved her fertile imagination and how she reacted to my words..

"But since you won, it's only fair that you get to have Santa at your service instead."

With that, I pulled the hat down so the fur trim sat just above my eyes, and I started kissing my way down her body. As I'd hoped, the fur trim of the hat tickled Gemma's skin, adding an extra layer of sensation to the work my lips and tongue were doing. As I got lower, she began squirming even more.

Spreading her legs wide, I pulled the hat down even further, right over my nose. I couldn't see, but that didn't matter. What mattered was that as I tasted Gemma, as my tongue played in her tight, wet pussy, the fur from the hat brushed against her clit. The way her thighs tightened around me and the soft moans I could hear coming from her confirmed just how effective it was.

"Cole." My name from her lips sounded somewhere between a plea and a curse as I teased her, switching between slow and fast movements, bringing her close but not letting her go all the way.

Knowing she was close, I decided to try something I'd been curious about ever since she had come on my command the night we did our student role play out in the living room. I pulled entirely back from her so no part of me touched her and pulled the hat back up so I could see again. Entirely removed from her, I gave the order.

"Come for me, Gemma."

Just as I'd hoped, her hips pressed down into the bed as her back arched off of it, her body writhing in ecstasy as her climax finally hit. Being able to bring her that kind of pleasure with just my words gave me a feeling of power unlike anything I'd ever experienced. It was an incredible turn-on.

Grabbing a condom from the bedside table, I rolled it on and entered her before she had even finished pulsing. I could still feel the last few aftershocks as I pushed into her, feeling her contract around my dick, drawing a groan of pure satisfaction from my throat.

Once we were joined together, I didn't want to rush. Christmas Eve was ten days away, meaning I would have to be without her for nine nights, so I wanted to make that night last as long as possible.

She seemed to feel just the same, not urging me to go faster or to do anything other than what I was doing, kissing her lips while moving slowly within her, drawing out each stroke as long as I could. I had no concept of time, no idea how long we stayed that way, but finally, my need grew too great and my pace increased, thrusting harder and faster into her until she came again, bringing me right along with her.

We fell asleep still naked and tangled in each other's arms, and the morning came far too quickly.

Almost before I knew it, Jackson and I were on the plane heading back to New York. Gemma had left the hotel before me in the morning, needing to go to work. We didn't bother with a long, drawn-out goodbye, knowing our separation would only be temporary. After she'd gone, I made arrangements for her things to be returned to her flat that evening. It seemed strange to realize that in all the time we had spent together in the city where she lived, I had never seen her flat, but I would see it on Christmas Eve, when I came back to see her.

Jackson seemed subdued on the flight, unusually for him. When I asked him about it, he simply said that he was disappointed that he and Holly weren't on the same page when it came to relationships. I hadn't realized he'd been so interested, but then I supposed I had been pretty preoccupied with my own relationship. I tried to make up for it by talking it all out with him since we had the time then.

He said that Holly was exactly the kind of woman he would be interested in, but she had no interest in a long-term relationship, while he was ready to commit to someone. She'd suggested they get involved but keep things casual, but he didn't want to get too attached. In the end, they hadn't done anything more than kiss a few times. I felt bad for him, but sympathizing was really all I could do.

When we landed, my regular driver met me at JFK to take me directly to Isabel's house. My sister was expecting me for our usual pre-Christmas extended family gathering, taking place on Saturday. I would stay with her the whole weekend.

After I got in the door and went through the usual round of greetings, I sat down with my sister in her kitchen as her children, my niece and nephew, ran circles around us and from room to room. A bittersweet melancholy filled me as I watched them. My nephew was nearly three years old, only a little older than my daughter would be, if she even existed. I'd watched him change so much, and it hurt me to think that I might have missed all those same moments with my own child.

"So, who is she?" Isabel asked, drawing me out of those thoughts and dropping me into thoughts of Gemma instead.

"What makes you think there's a she?" I countered, taking a sip from the scotch she'd offered me. We always played this game: she did her best to get information out of me, and I made her work for it.

She smirked at me. "I'm not blind, little brother. Even if I hadn't seen the photos, I would be able to tell just by that smile on your face."

It surprised me that she would have seen the photos. "I didn't know you subscribed to the British tabloids," I said, still avoiding her question.

"I don't," she replied just as drily. "But when your brother is photographed looking at dildos, the pictures find you."

I couldn't help laughing at that, and Isabel grinned.

"God, it's good to see you laugh again, Cole. I love this woman already. Now, drop the act and tell me everything."

~Gemma~

Returning home to my flat for the first time in ten days felt very strange. I felt Cole's absence keenly, but I was also equally aware of him despite him not being there. He texted me regularly and phoned me from time to time, keeping me up to date on what he was doing and asking what he could do to help me get ready to move.

Once Holly got over her shock about me moving to New York, she was completely delighted for me, even though she swore she would miss me terribly. I would miss her too, more than I could even say. She had been my rock for the last year, the one who kept me sane when everything else fell apart, but we both agreed that between video chats and cheap flights, plus the fact that we'd still be working together even if not in the same office, it would almost be like nothing had changed at all.

I made arrangements to have things from both my office and my home shipped to Cole's apartment in New York in early January. He told me he could have one of the rooms in the apartment made into an office for me, or that I could have an office at the Stamer Hotels headquarters where he worked. Or both. It seemed like nothing would be too much trouble. I wasn't used to that kind of generosity from anyone, but I knew that from him, it came without any kind of strings attached. He wouldn't do it if he didn't truly want to.

A few days before Christmas Eve, I was still deep in work at the end of the day as everyone else packed up to go home. There weren't many people in the office to begin with since we'd given most of the staff the week before and the week after Christmas off, in celebration of our new contract with Stamer Hotels and in recognition of the hard work that they'd be expected to put in on that contract in the new year. I'd hired a temporary receptionist for the week so our regular one could have the time off, and she buzzed me to let me know a man was there to see me, someone who didn't have an appointment.

My heart leapt in hope. Could it be Cole? It would be just like him to surprise me, to show up without telling me he was coming. I told her to send him in and quickly checked myself in the mirror, trying to see myself as he would see me, making sure nothing was too out of place.

However, when the door opened, my heart sank right back down again. It wasn't Cole at all.

The anti-Cole stood there instead.

"Edwin?" I asked, hardly able to believe my eyes. "What are you doing here?"

He lingered in the doorway nervously. "I'm sorry to bother you at work, but I didn't think you'd see me at home. Do you have a few minutes? I'd like to talk to you."

Now he wanted to talk? After leaving me with no explanation, abandoning me to the fallout he knew was coming, and months of complete silence ever since?

Part of me was tempted to send him away, but I hesitated as I remembered how Cole dealt with *his* ex at the party. He told me just a couple of days earlier that speaking to her helped to make it clearer to him just how much of their relationship had been built on illusions and who he wanted her to be. Perhaps speaking to Edwin would help me find a similar sort of closure, especially since I would be leaving the country in a matter of days. There was a good chance I would never see him again once I did.

Steeling myself, I invited him in. "I don't have a lot of time, but I can give you a few minutes. Take a seat."

He exhaled, as if he'd been holding his breath, making it clear he hadn't been sure whether or not I would agree.

Normally, I met with clients at the table in my office, but I wanted to maintain more distance between us than that, so I sat back down at my desk while Edwin sat across from me, his fingers twisting together restlessly.

"I don't really know how to say this," he started, not looking me quite in the eye. "But I wanted to tell you that I'm sorry. For all of it."

Well, that was something, at least. Not much, but something.

"I felt terrible when the show came out and I saw the way people were treating you. I should have said something then, I know that, but I was embarrassed. And you didn't do anything about it. You never responded to anything, or tried to contact me, and I guess I just convinced myself that you really didn't care. I figured I'd meant so little to you that it didn't even bother you."

Had he really thought that? Or had he convinced himself he did to ease his guilt?

"When we ran into you in Hyde Park a few weeks ago, and you were so calm, I took that as proof that I'd been right the whole time. You'd clearly moved on. I saw all the pictures of you and that American bloke in the papers, and I was happy for you, Gemma, really. I'm glad you found someone who makes you happy."

Despite my misgivings, I could feel the sincerity of his words. He really did mean that, in the same way that I could have been happy for him and Annabel if the circumstances were different.

"But then I saw you at your father's party," he continued. "The way you spoke to me and to Bel was the first time I had any idea that the whole thing had affected you in any way. It made me feel awful that perhaps it had been bothering you the whole time when I didn't think it had. So, although I know it's too little, too late, I still just wanted to let you know that I am sorry."

I knew Edwin well enough to know that losing my temper wouldn't get me anywhere with him, so I kept my tone calm. Faced with confrontation, he would just close himself off completely. "Of course it affected me, Edwin. We might not have been madly in love but I did care for you, and I thought you cared for me too."

His face twisted into a grimace. "I did care for you, Gemma. I do. But when I met Bel, it was so different. It was wild and exciting, and I let myself get caught up in it, and I made choices that I shouldn't have made. The situation wasn't fair to you, and I see that now. I don't expect you to forgive me, but I thought you should know that if I could change things, I would. I would do it very differently."

His eyes finally met mine directly, and I could see how difficult he found it to say those words. We had never talked about our feelings that way, but I appreciated him making the effort.

"I also want to apologize for Bel inviting that woman to the party. I didn't know anything about it beforehand, I swear. She only told me afterwards."

Perhaps I could satisfy my curiosity on that one point, at least. "Why did she invite her? What did she hope to achieve?"

He grimaced again. "It all comes back to the show, I'm afraid. Bel was... disappointed, I guess, when you didn't respond publicly to the whole scandal when the show first aired. I think she wanted it to turn into a big rivalry between the two of you, a storyline that would keep her in the spotlight for a while, but obviously that never happened because you didn't engage. So, when she found out you were seeing someone new, she tried to find a way to get herself involved in that too."

Complete consternation and disbelief filled me as I listened to him. How could he explain her actions like that, as if there was nothing wrong with them? "You see how messed up that is, don't you?"

He simply shrugged. "I don't agree with everything she does, but I love her. I can't help it. She's it for me."

That was the first thing he'd said that I could relate to. Now that I had Cole in my life, I finally understood why people did crazy things for love. It didn't make it right, but at least I could begin to understand.

"Anyway, that's all I wanted to say, really." He gave me a tentative smile. "And I thought today would be the best day to do it."

My eyes immediately went to the calendar on the wall, and I almost laughed. Of course. We were supposed to be getting married that very day.

I had completely forgotten.

I'd been so wrapped up in thoughts of Cole and the upcoming move and our Christmas together, it hadn't even crossed my mind.

"Well, thank you for coming by," I told him. "Have a good Christmas."

He nodded. "You too. Goodbye, Gemma."

I could hear the finality in that goodbye, and I echoed it with my own. "Goodbye, Edwin."

As he walked out of my office, a smile spread across my face. Cole had been right. Talking to Edwin only reinforced what I already knew: he'd never been the one for me. Maybe in some alternate reality, Gemma and Edwin were getting married that day, but I was glad I didn't live in that reality. At that moment, I was exactly where I wanted to be.

~Cole~

When I arrived at work on December 23rd, there was an extra spring in my step. My plane was scheduled to leave New York late that evening, arriving in London mid-morning on the 24th. Gemma said she would work until noon, so I hoped to meet her at her office, take her out for a nice lunch, then head back to her flat for some time alone, preferably with both of us naked for a good part of it, before we went back out for the midnight service at Westminster Abbey.

However, my best-laid plans were upended when my assistant called me at noon. "Mr Stamer, you said to let you know when Samantha Weston called? She's on line three now."

That strange feeling that had been surfacing every time I thought of my potential daughter came up again, a mixture of excitement and dread. I hated the uncertainty of it, so I could only hope that Samantha was calling to settle things one way or the other.

"Thanks Hayley, I'll take it myself." She put the call through to me and I answered in a professional monotone. "Samantha, it's Cole."

She sounded surprised that I had answered, no doubt expecting to speak to one of my staff instead. "Oh. Hi. I was just calling like you said, about the paternity test."

That seemed to settle one thing: there must actually be a child if she would go this far with it. It also confirmed she must be desperate for the money too. All that remained was to determine if the child was mine.

"When can you come into the city?" I had no idea where she lived, but I would arrange for them to fly in if necessary.

"Actually, we're here now. Me and Madison."

Madison. My chest tightened at the sound of the name. Samantha and I had talked about using it for our baby if we had a girl. It had actually been my suggestion, and I couldn't believe she'd gone ahead and used it. She truly had no shame, but I tried to focus on the other part of what she'd said, that they were there in the city.

"Are you free today? Can you go to the clinic now?"

"Yes, we're free for a while. We're going to see Santa at Macy's later this afternoon, but we have a few hours before then."

Once again, my heart constricted at the thought of my little girl, if she really was mine, visiting Santa without me.

"I'll put you back through to Hayley and she'll arrange a car for you. I'll meet you at the clinic."

I wanted to watch the whole process: the blood draws and the analysis. I wanted to be completely certain that there could be no mistake, no chance that anything had gone wrong or been tampered with.

After transferring her back, I sent a quick text to Gemma to let her know what was happening and that I'd be out of the office for a while. She came back quickly with a message of support.

It will be good to know for sure. Call me if you need to talk, doesn't matter how late. G

Shoving my phone back in my suit pocket, I grabbed my coat and headed downstairs. The private medical clinic was only a couple of blocks away and, thanks to Hayley, they were already expecting me when I got there.

"How long will it take to get the results?" I asked the doctor who ran me through the whole process.

"It's usually about 12 hours for the computer to complete the analysis," he explained. "We can prioritize it for you so we'll have the results first thing tomorrow morning."

He drew my blood and showed me how the sample was processed. With that finished, I went back to the waiting room to wait for Samantha to arrive.

Only a few minutes later, she walked in carrying a little girl, bundled up in a winter coat and hat. The doctor took us all directly into the examining room where Samantha removed all the girl's outer layers, revealing a beautiful, miniature version of herself. She had the same dark hair and the same oval-shaped face as her mother; only her eyes were different. Instead of Samantha's blue eyes, the girl's were dark. Like mine? Maybe. It was impossible to say.

Even so, I couldn't take my eyes off her.

Samantha noticed me staring so she walked over to me as the nurses played with the girl, distracting her with bubbles and toys while they drew blood from her hand. "She has a lot of you in her," Samantha said, trying to sound casual, as if she weren't trying to sway my opinion.

"What happened to the guy you were with?" I asked, refusing to engage on the topic of Madison until we had the results for certain. "Where is he?"

A storm flashed in her eyes, bitter and deep. "He left and took the rest of the money with him."

I let out a small huff of disbelief. That explained why she needed more money, and why she had decided to come back to me for it. I couldn't help thinking it served her right, but the girl didn't deserve it.

"He was always a little resentful that Maddie wasn't his daughter," Samantha continued, clearly looking for sympathy.

Once again, I didn't respond to that, but my heart hurt even more for the little girl in front of me. Had the other man taken that resentment out on her? Not given her the love that she should have had? I didn't even want to think about it.

When the blood had been taken, I followed the techs back to the lab to watch them input that sample for processing too. The doctor assured me that once that had been done, the results couldn't be manipulated. We just had to wait for the computer to run the tests, but whatever news he had for me the next day would be the truth.

Samantha was still in the waiting room when I returned, wrapping Madison back up in her winter clothes. She called over one of the nurses to play with Madison again while she walked over to me. "You know, Cole, you could come with us to Macy's if you want to."

Was she serious? Every time I thought we'd reached the limit of her shamelessness, she found a new level. I would have to shut down any of those kinds of ideas before she got carried away. "Samantha, I'm only being civil to you because I don't want to upset your daughter, who may or may not be mine. But we are not doing anything together, and we are definitely not playing happy family. If that's what you're hoping for, you can forget it right now."

She pursed her lips, not pleased with my response. "Well, what about tomorrow? You'll have the results then. Will you come and see your daughter on Christmas Eve?"

Though my anger flared, I was still very aware of the little girl in the room with us. I couldn't let it out while she could hear. "What about the last two Christmas Eves? I missed those too, but only because I didn't know she existed."

"She doesn't remember," Samantha insisted. "But she will now. If you do something special for her, it will help her get to know you."

As I looked at Samantha, I could only wonder how I had ever fallen for someone so manipulative. However, a small part of me still hated the idea of abandoning my daughter on Christmas Eve, even though no sane person could claim it was my fault.

I quickly did the calculations in my head, working out the flight times and the time difference. "Bring her back here at eight o'clock tomorrow morning. We can get the results together and I'll give her a present. That's all. I already have plans for Christmas this year. If the results show she's mine, then we'll work out custody first thing in the new year."

"And support payments," she added.

Of course she would be most concerned about that. "Naturally," I agreed through gritted teeth.

As they left the room, Samantha bent down and whispered something to Madison, who turned back and gave me a shy little wave goodbye. It was the first time she'd looked directly at me, and my chest tightened yet again, hope and doubt filling me in equal measure. Part of me wanted her to be mine. It would mean at least something good would have come out of the whole sorry mess with Samantha. The other part of me wanted the result to be negative, since a positive result meant that Samantha would be part of my life going forward, no matter what.

I really didn't know what to feel.

The only thing I did know was that I needed to update Gemma, so as I walked back to the office, I sent her a quick text.

I'm so sorry, but I'll be arriving a little later than planned tomorrow. I'll still be in time for church and to spend Christmas with you. I can't wait to see you. C

~Gemma~

Cole's text the night before disappointed me, but when I spoke to him and he told me what was going on, I completely understood.

Samantha was trying to manipulate him, obviously, but he knew it as well as I did. He wouldn't fall for it, but neither would he punish the little girl for her mother's behaviour, and I respected him all the more for that.

In the end, he would still be coming, which was all that mattered to me. I couldn't wait to see him again, so as I left my flat for work on the morning of the 24th, my spirits were high.

Since I no longer had lunch plans, I stayed at the office a bit later than I'd originally planned, well after everyone else had left. It gave me time to put the finishing touches on my present for Cole and to add a few bits to it that I thought he would appreciate.

Cole sent a text around two o'clock saying that he was on the plane, just waiting to take off. He said he knew the results of the paternity test but he wanted to tell me in person. I didn't press him on it. There must be a reason he wanted to wait, so I just replied and said I couldn't wait to see him. That much was definitely true.

When the time came for me to pack up and go home for the last time that year, I walked over to the calendar on the wall and pulled it down, scanning over all the handwritten events. The 1st of December had been our staff party, the night that Cole and I had met. The party at the Mayfair Mews followed, where we saw each other again, and so did the Winter Wonderland at Hyde Park, the first night we had sex. Just over a week later was the gingerbread house contest, the night that we had admitted to each other how we felt. Reading over each entry brought up so many memories and I decided I would keep the calendar, or at least this page of it. I wanted to remember this time always.

Just before I tucked it away, my eyes landed on the night I had taken Cole to the carol service. That was the night we'd done the schoolgirl role play back at his hotel, the night he'd forgotten the condom. Nearly three weeks had passed since then, and I hadn't had a period since. With all the excitement of the upcoming move, I had forgotten all about it.

It didn't necessarily mean anything, I told myself. My birth control pills had been slightly mixed up at the time, so my whole schedule was off. Even so, it had been long enough that I should be able to do a test and find out for sure. So, once I had packed up and got ready to go, I made a quick stop at the pharmacy to pick up a pregnancy test before making my way home to my flat.

After putting everything away and tidying up the flat a bit in preparation for Cole's arrival, I finally went into the bathroom and followed all the instructions. My stomach fluttered strangely as I waited for the results, filled with a feeling I couldn't quite pin down.

I had bought one that gave the results clearly, in plain English, not wanting to worry about lines or plus signs or anything else. When the time was up and I turned the test over, the result was there, clear as day.

Pregnant.

I was actually pregnant.

The fluttering feeling in my stomach grew stronger, and I finally recognized it as excitement. I was actually excited. I hadn't planned for it, but now that it was happening, I didn't regret it either. The thought of having a child with Cole made me truly happy. He would be a wonderful father. I could see how much he already cared about Samantha's daughter, not even knowing for sure if the girl was his or not.

But how would he feel about my unexpected pregnancy? He had always been so careful about using a condom, except for that one time, not to mention that he had literally found out that same day whether or not he already had a child with another woman. The timing was hardly ideal.

Our whole relationship was so new. Yes, he had asked me to move in with him, but that didn't necessarily mean he wanted to start a family and commit to me in such a permanent way. Still, whatever his reaction might be, I knew I had no choice. I had to tell him immediately, as soon as he arrived. After what he'd been through with Samantha, I didn't want to keep it from him for even a second. I wanted us to be completely on the same page.

As night drew in, I got dressed for the church service, checking my phone every few minutes. Cole's flight should have been landing any minute, and at just after ten, the message came through.

Had to circle for a while, but we're on the ground now. Probably easiest to meet you at the church. Let me know where to find you. C

Just knowing he was back in the country made my heart soar, and I quickly sent back a reply.

We have tickets to get in so I'll wait for you outside, by the ticket office. Call me if you can't see me. Counting the minutes now. G

I waited another half hour before leaving for the Abbey. The night was cloudless and cold, a few stars twinkling above the London lights, and I pulled my scarf a little tighter and cinched my coat tighter too. As it tensed against my stomach, it reminded me of the little life already growing there. By the following Christmas, I would have a baby. Cole's baby. Just the thought of it helped to keep me warm and put a smile on my face. I really hoped he would feel the same way about it that I did.

Minutes ticked by while I waited outside the church, and as Big Ben chimed 11:30, I sent another text to Cole, asking if he knew how much longer he'd be. He quickly replied that it should only be a couple of minutes, and finally, as the clock drew close to 11:45, a town car pulled up outside the church, and he appeared.

Maybe I should have played it cool and waited for him to come over to me, but I couldn't help myself. I ran to him, throwing myself into his arms as soon as his feet were on the ground.

"Gemma." His deep voice in my ear sounded like heaven as his arms enveloped me. "I've missed you so much."

"I missed you too," I assured him, my words muffled against my scarf.

"Last call for ticket holders," a member of staff at the Abbey called out, reminding us both where we were and why.

I pulled back from him and took his hand, but Cole looked at the church and back at me, a rare look of apology on his face. "I know you've been looking forward to this, but would it be okay if we just go somewhere and talk instead?"

That actually sounded perfect to me. The idea of sitting next to him for an hour in the church without being able to tell him my news or to hear his was almost unbearable.

I quickly walked over to the staff member looking for any last ticket holders and handed him the tickets in my hand. "I can't use these after all. If there's anyone who wants them, please, pass them on."

He thanked me, and I returned to Cole, taking his hand and leading him over to the river. Neither of us spoke along the way. The things we had to say were too big to blurt out until we were settled somewhere, somewhere where we could see each other's faces and talk properly.

The lights of the London Eye and Westminster Bridge reflected in the dark waters of the Thames as we walked along the Embankment. There, in the waning moments of Christmas Eve, we found a bench, a quiet place to see the river and also see each other. Keeping my hand tucked firmly in his, Cole sat down next to me and turned to me, his dark eyes full of an emotion I couldn't quite name.

"First things first, I wanted to say thank you, Gemma, for being so understanding about me arriving late. I know we didn't plan on this."

Why was he wasting time on an apology? "Cole!" I admonished him. "Just tell me the results already."

He smiled, a look of true affection on his face but still with a hint of that unnamed something in his eyes. "Madison is not my daughter."

"Not?" I repeated in genuine surprise. I didn't realize until he said it how much I had convinced myself that she must be. I had been fully prepared for it to be true.

He shook his head. "No, she's not. It came as a surprise for me too. I believe that Samantha truly thought she must be. She was shocked when we got the results, and I don't think she faked her response. She must have honestly thought all this time that I was Madison's father, but the doctors assure me that I'm not."

"So, she was actually sleeping with the man she left you for while you were still together?" I asked, wanting to make sure I understood what had happened. Cole said Samantha had told him about her pregnancy before he proposed.

Cole nodded. "Apparently. And I guess he thought the whole time that he wasn't the father, because Samantha had convinced herself I was. And he left her partly because of that, when Madison had actually been his daughter all along."

"That poor little girl," I couldn't help saying.

Cole's brow furrowed in a look of pain. "I know. I hope you don't mind, but I decided on the flight over here that I'm going to give Samantha some money anyway, just to keep her on her feet. I'll also set up a small trust fund for Madison, in an account that Samantha won't be able to touch. Even though she's not mine, for a little while I thought she might be. She's completely innocent and I don't want her to suffer just because her mother can't be a decent human being."

"That's very generous of you," I told him sincerely. I had no idea why he cared if I would mind or not. The money belonged to him, and I was much more worried about how he felt about everything. "Are you disappointed?"

He smiled almost wistfully. "A little. It's a strange thing to suddenly be told you have a child and then just as suddenly be told you don't. But it is what it is and at least now I know. Besides, I still have a lot of other wonderful things in my life to keep me occupied."

He raised his hand to my cheek, stroking it gently.

"So, you're not opposed to the idea of being a father?" I clarified, trying to steer the conversation towards my own news.

"I'm not opposed to it. I would like to be, eventually. Hopefully, I can do it properly next time, from the beginning."

He couldn't have given me a better opening than that. Taking a deep breath, I gave Cole's hand a tight squeeze. "What if the beginning came sooner than you expected?"

His eyebrows drew together as he looked at me, trying to figure out what I meant.

"I just found out this afternoon," I told him, giving him a small, hopeful smile. "Cole, I'm pregnant."

Chapter Nineteen

CHRISTMAS PRESENTS

~Cole~

Gemma's words seemed to linger in the air between us for a moment until a new sound rang out: Big Ben just behind us, marking the hour.

Gemma looked over her shoulder at the clock tower before turning back to me with a bright smile. "It's midnight! That means it's Christmas Day now. Happy Christmas, Cole."

"Merry Chris... " I started to respond automatically before catching myself, still trying to wrap my head around the first thing she'd said. "Wait, hold on. Back up a second. You're pregnant?"

She nodded, still smiling, her green eyes sparkling under the street-lights as she looked up at me. "Like I said, I just found out this afternoon."

Could she really be serious? It didn't seem like a joke, but how would that even happen? I mean, I knew how it happened, but I only forgot to use a condom that one time. What were the odds? I woke up that morning thinking I might have a daughter, found out I didn't, and now, it seemed like I was going to be a father after all, but to a new baby. My equilibrium had been completely thrown off and I almost wondered if I could be dreaming, it felt that surreal.

"Cole? Are you alright?" Gemma's eyebrows drew together curiously as she tried to read my expression, making me wonder how long I'd been sitting there speechless.

More to the point: *was* I alright? Obviously, neither of us had planned or intended a pregnancy at that point, but as I let myself really take it in, a new feeling took root inside me, one I hadn't felt in a long time. The best way I could describe it would be... joy.

The incredible woman in front of me, the one I'd already decided I wanted to be with, the one who made me happier than anyone ever had, was going to have my baby. And she had to ask me if I was okay with it?

"Gemma, that's amazing." I took her face in my hands, wanting to be sure she saw the truth behind my words in my eyes. "I never expected it right now, but as long as you're happy with it, then I'm absolutely delighted."

"Really?" The most beautiful, hopeful smile lit up her face beneath the city lights.

"Really," I assured her. "But how do you feel?"

"I was surprised," she admitted. "But I'm actually really happy about it, especially if you are too."

"I am. I really am."

My lips pressed down on hers, not caring that we were in public, not caring how many people might see us there. I wanted her to feel my certainty. Her news had to be the best Christmas present I could have imagined, and I groaned internally as I realized the only thing that would have made the moment better would have been if I could give her my present. Unfortunately, I'd sent it to her apartment along with the rest of my things.

I'd have to wait and give it to her in the morning, but I could live with that. We had enough to celebrate already.

"Do you want to go back to my flat?" Gemma asked against my lips.

"God, yes," I muttered, making us both laugh.

We caught a taxi and before long, we were letting ourselves into Gemma's home after picking up my bags from the driver outside. She paused for a moment in the doorway after unlocking the door, making me nearly run into her.

"Not so fast," she teased me. "You know the rules."

Her eyes moved upwards and I followed her gaze to the mistletoe hanging over the door. In my mind, I was immediately taken back to that first night with her, the night we met, when she kissed me under the mistletoe. The night everything started.

I didn't need any further invitation. In less than a second, I had her in my arms, kissing her deeply as we stumbled further into her flat.

"Do you want a tour?" she asked, laughing as she wriggled from my grasp.

"Later. For now, just show me the bedroom."

With a grin, Gemma took my hand and led me down the hall to the master bedroom. There would be time later for me to take a look around, learning what I could about her from the decoration, but for now, I couldn't take my eyes off her. I needed to be inside her again. Everything else could wait.

She bit her lip as she sauntered to the middle of the room. "If you don't mind, I actually have something in mind for tonight."

That immediately piqued my interest. Up until then, I had always been the one with the plan. "I suppose it is Christmas, your favourite day. We can do things your way, just for tonight."

She grinned even wider. "That's what I hoped you'd say. And since we're doing it my way, the first thing I want you to do is strip."

My eyebrows raised in surprise as she gave me an order. It made for a complete reversal of our usual dynamic, but since it was Christmas, I supposed I could give her the reins for one night. She took a step back and watched me as I removed my clothes. I had worn a suit that day for flying on the company plane, but for the rest of my time in London, I had actually brought sweaters and jeans. It would be the first time she would see me wearing something other than a suit or nothing at all.

The latter was my current situation as I stood before her, naked, my dick already hard with anticipation. Longing filled Gemma's eyes as she looked me over, a longing I would bet was reflected in my own gaze, but when I stepped towards her, she held out a hand to stop me.

"Just wait," she teased as she went over to her closet and pulled out a set of individual cuffs that we had bought at the sex shop, turning back to me with a mischievous smile.

"Gemma." My voice rumbled with a low warning. What exactly did she have in mind?

"Trust me," she requested, and how could I say no to that? Of course I trusted her.

So, with just a little trepidation, I followed her instructions to lie down on the bed, where she attached each of the cuffs to my wrists and tied them to her headboard. With my arms immobile, she pulled out a blindfold and held it up to me.

"This one is your choice: if you can promise to keep your eyes closed until I'm ready, I'll leave it off, but if you're going to peek, then it's going on."

"I promise I won't peek." Being cuffed to the bed felt strange enough; being blindfolded might be a step too far, but I kept my word and closed my eyes, waiting for her to tell me to open them. Fabric rustled as Gemma moved around the room, but from the sounds alone, I couldn't guess what she was doing.

At last, she was ready. "Okay, you can look now."

As soon as I opened my eyes, my dick immediately jumped, the rush of blood to it nearly making me weak. She was wearing the damn Santa dress, the one she had worn the night we met. Her red hair flowed down over her shoulders and her green eyes sparkled at me, gleefully taking in my body's reaction to her.

"Fuck, Gemma," I grunted, pulling at my restraints. I wanted so badly to touch her, and she must have known I would. She cuffed me for that exact reason. When did she get so sadistic?

"Tell me, Cole," she said, crawling up onto the bed on her hands and knees, moving slowly towards me. The view down her dress was even better than I remembered it and almost more than I could take, and I groaned in both frustration and desire. "Have you been a good boy this year?"

I narrowed my eyes at her teasing tone. "You know damn well I haven't."

Her laugh seemed to float with happiness. "Well, lucky for you, Santa's feeling generous tonight."

She dropped her head, licking her way up my inner thigh and onto my dick, her tongue flicking back and forth up the shaft, making it jump again towards her. It felt so good that I wanted to close my eyes and enjoy it, but I also didn't want to miss a second of seeing her in that dress, her mouth on me. Taking hold of my dick at the base, she stood it up, licking her way up it again and taking the head in her mouth.

"Fuck, yes," I groaned. I had been dreaming of being inside her again for the last ten days, and it didn't matter which way she wanted to do it. Her mouth felt like heaven.

She teased me a while longer, licking my shaft and my balls and sucking on me gently before taking me in her mouth deeply; once, twice and a third time. I couldn't keep from thrusting my hips upwards, trying to feel as much of her as possible. My arousal couldn't get much higher, but to my frustration, she pulled back completely.

Her eyes continued to twinkle merrily despite the state she'd left me in. "As much fun as that is, I haven't been able to stop thinking about how you said you wanted to fuck me in this dress."

I groaned again, pulling at the cuffs once more. "Yes, I did, Gemma, but in none of those fantasies was I tied to this fucking bed."

Her light laughter filled the room. "Don't worry. I promise it'll be worth your while."

She crawled further up the bed, bending down to give me a hard, demanding kiss as she straddled me, and even as we kissed, she reached down to lift my hard dick once again. The words were on the tip of my tongue to stop her and remind her to get a condom when I remembered that we didn't need one. She was already pregnant; what else could happen? *Fuck.* That just made me look forward to being inside her even more.

As she slid down onto me, not wearing anything beneath her dress, I couldn't help thinking that I was the luckiest man alive. She felt absolutely amazing, her warm, wet pussy enveloping me, taking in all of me until she was grinding against me.

"Cole," she murmured, her own eyes closed as she adjusted to me. "I've missed you."

A deep laugh rumbled in my throat. "I missed you too, Gorgeous."

When she started riding me, the fur trim of her skirt brushed against my stomach as she leaned down over me. There was nothing for me to do but lie there and take it, to revel in the sights and sounds of her and the unbelievable feel of her against my bare dick as she brought me higher and higher, to ever greater planes of pleasure, until finally, she clamped down on me in the throes of her own orgasm, pushing me over the edge too as I pumped into her, deep inside her, with nothing between us.

It felt like nothing would ever come between us again. This was exactly where we were meant to be.

As we both caught our breath, she leaned down over me one more time, giving me a soft kiss on the lips. "Happy Christmas, Cole."

"Merry Christmas, Gemma," I whispered back.

When she asked me to spend Christmas with her, she said her goal was to give me a new memory to replace the one of Samantha disappearing during the night, and in that, she had most definitely succeeded. Whenever I thought of Christmas Eve from then on, for the rest of my life, the night we'd just shared would always come to mind first.

~Gemma~

For the first time since I'd known him, I woke up before Cole in the morning. He lay facing me, his mouth slightly open and his eyelashes resting on his cheeks. I could barely resist the temptation to take advantage of the rare opportunity to touch his face and trace all his handsome features with my fingertips, but I didn't want to wake him after his flight and all the emotional upheaval of the previous day. Instead, I simply lay there studying him until his eyelids fluttered open.

"Good morning," he mumbled as he caught sight of me, a half smile on his lips. "What time is it?"

"It's Christmas," I reminded him. "Time doesn't matter."

He chuckled sleepily. "What's the plan for today, then?"

"It's up to you. I've got some food for breakfast and to make a somewhat traditional Christmas lunch. We can eat when we're hungry and maybe go out for a walk later. I've still got your present too, don't forget."

Putting his hand on the back of my head, he pulled my mouth to his, giving me a gentle, warm kiss. "You've already given me everything I could want, Gemma."

His other hand trailed down my body, coming to rest on my stomach, and my heart skipped a beat. I couldn't be happier that he had embraced the fact that we were having a baby, and the idea that my child would have such a caring, supportive father, so unlike my own father, filled me with joy.

When he told me the night before that Madison wasn't his daughter, I saw the disappointment in his eyes, but that morning, it all seemed to have gone, replaced with his enthusiasm and excitement over our own future.

"So, what do you want to do first?" I asked him when he finally let me breathe again. "Presents or breakfast?"

"Presents, definitely," he replied, giving me a sexy smirk that made me wonder exactly what kind of present he had got me. "Do we need to put clothes on?"

The question made me laugh. "My present to you doesn't require any clothes, but I don't know what you have in mind."

He laughed too. "No, mine is clothing-optional as well. I just wondered if you were going to insist on pictures or anything like that."

That made a lot more sense. "Not this year, but next year might be a different story since it will be our baby's first Christmas."

Cole's eyes lit up at that thought and he rolled me over onto my back so he could bend down and kiss my stomach. The sweet gesture nearly brought tears to my eyes.

"Let's get presents out of the way before you get carried away," I teased him, and he looked back up at me, his dark eyes shining.

"You said time doesn't matter today," he reminded me.

"It doesn't, but I really want to give you your present already."

With another laugh, Cole admitted defeat and rolled away from me, standing up to grab his suitcase from the floor where he'd dropped it the night before. I had already hidden his gift under the bed the day before, so I only had to reach down to retrieve it from its hiding spot. The package was cylindrical and wrapped in mistletoe-covered paper, and he eyed it curiously as he sat back down on the bed, holding a cube-shaped box in his hands for me.

"Who's going first?" I asked him. As curious as I was about what he'd got for me, my excitement to see his reaction to my gift was stronger.

It came as a relief, then, when he told me he wanted to open mine first. After placing his box down on the bed, he reached for the present in my hands, and his eyebrows raised in surprise as he took it from me. "Oh, it's light. Not wine, then."

"You thought I was going to give you wine that I didn't pay for?"

He laughed again, his rare boyish enthusiasm on full display. He had hardly stopped smiling since the moment he woke up. It was so unlike him, but wonderful at the same time. "I really don't know what to expect with you, Gemma, and I wouldn't have it any other way."

Tearing the paper off, he pulled out the cardboard tube that was inside, and shot me another questioning look. "Just open it," I encouraged him. The anticipation was killing me.

Curiously, he flipped the lid off the top and reached inside, his fingers sliding the rolled up paper out of the container. As he slowly unrolled it, my heart raced even faster. I really hoped he would like it. There were so many things I could have bought him, but he had more money than anyone I had ever met. Anything that he wanted, he could buy for himself, so I had decided to make him something instead, something completely personal for him.

The gift was an architectural drawing of a London street, but not any street that actually existed. Instead, it represented a map of our relationship, showing, from left to right, all the places that Cole and I had visited together on our two-week 'deal'. First, the Lytton hotel where we'd met at the Christmas party. Next to it stood the Mayfair Mews hotel, where we had run into each other again at the opening. Each location had a special meaning for us and a special memory. The Anchor office was there, the Winter Wonderland in Hyde Park, Dennis Severs' House, St James's Piccadilly church, and the Palladium theatre where we saw the panto. Then there was Wilby Park, my family's house in the country, transplanted into London for the sake of the drawing, followed by the Dorchester hotel where the gingerbread house contest took place, and finally, my father's London home where we had attended the party.

Cole's eyes travelled from place to place, taking in every detail, for what felt like hours even though it couldn't have been more than a few minutes. He didn't say a word, and I waited as patiently as I could, even though I grew more desperate to know what he was thinking with each passing second.

When he finally looked back up at me, I was shocked to see there were tears in his eyes. "Gemma, this is incredible. No one has ever given me such a thoughtful gift."

My teeth caught against my bottom lip, overwhelmed by his reaction. "You really like it?"

"I love it," he stated firmly. "And I love you."

He hadn't said those words before. He'd asked me to move in with him, he'd been happy I was having his baby, but he had never outright said he loved me.

"I love you too, Cole."

I didn't have to think about it for a second. As soon as the words were out, I tried to kiss him, but he turned away, moving his arms away from me, still holding onto the drawing as if it were some priceless treasure.

"Hold on. Let me put this away safely." Chuckling, he rolled it back up and returned it to his tube. "We can frame it and put it up in the apartment in New York," he promised. "I want to see it every day."

As pleased as I was that he really did like it, I still wanted to kiss him. As he placed the tube down on the bed, I tried once again to pull him to me, but still, he resisted.

"Wait, you still need to open your present. Then, I promise, we can spend the rest of the day doing whatever you want."

I groaned at the delay, but as he picked up the box and handed it to me, my curiosity took over. The box wasn't wrapped, so I lifted the lid to reveal... another box. I raised my eyebrows at him but he just smiled, waiting for me to continue. When I pulled out the second box and opened it, I found another, smaller box inside.

"Is the actual present the size of a pea?" I couldn't help asking.

"Keep going," was all he said, his eyes shining as they watched me.

On it went. Finally, the sixth box looked different, not a gift box like the others but a small, velvet jewellery box, and I looked up at him in surprise. I hadn't expected anything significant, especially since I had already told him I hadn't spent any money on his gift.

"Open it," he pleaded, his own patience clearly nearing its end.

With my fingers slightly trembling, I flipped open the lid to reveal a beautiful ring, unlike any I'd ever seen. A sparkling solitaire diamond was nestled beneath a cluster of tiny emeralds, with even tinier pearls. The pattern of the gemstones almost looked like...

"Mistletoe?"

I raised my eyes to Cole's as I asked the question, and he smiled back at me, that genuine, boyish smile of his that I loved so much. "Exactly. The diamond is us," he explained, placing his finger on it, pointing at the large stone before running his finger over the other gems. "Under the mistletoe."

I could hardly believe it. The ring was stunningly beautiful, and so incredibly thoughtful. He must have had it specially designed, and the fact that he would go to so much trouble meant more to me than any dollar amount ever could. I absolutely loved it.

"It's not just a ring though," he said, his voice getting softer. "There's a question that comes with it."

My heart raced again as I looked back into his dark eyes once more, trying not to get ahead of myself.

"Gemma, you know I've spent the last few years living by the rules I set for myself, but now, I'd like to set some different rules. Just one rule, really. One that says that you're with me, and I'm with you, forever."

Forever? The tears that had previously been in his eyes seemed to have transferred to mine as the meaning behind his words sunk in. It didn't seem like I'd got the wrong idea at all.

"So, what do you think?" he asked me with an almost tentative smile. "Will you marry me, Gemma? Do we have a deal?"

Both of us had been in that moment before, with other people, but I knew my previous proposal hadn't felt anything like this, and judging from Cole's expression, it felt new to him too. And just like him, I didn't have a doubt in my mind. "It's a deal."

With the biggest smile I had ever seen on his face, Cole took the ring from the box and slid it on my finger, and then there was nothing on earth that could have stopped us from making the most of our nakedness and the fact that we had nowhere else to be.

It might have been a mistake that brought us together that night under the mistletoe, but I knew in my heart it was the best mistake we could have ever made.

~~THE END~~

IF YOU ENJOYED THIS...

Holly and Jackson's story continues in the next book in the series, *Candy Cane Challenge.*

Turn the page for a preview from the first chapter!

CANDY CANE CHALLENGE

~Jackson~

People always say that love finds you when you're not looking for it. That couldn't be more true of my best friend, Cole, I had to admit, as I watched him tying the bow tie of his tuxedo. He met Gemma, the woman he was about to marry, when he least expected it, and they both did their best to deny the depth of their feelings for each other as long as possible. It had been incredibly frustrating to watch from the outside, but incredibly satisfying in the end when they finally admitted what I had known right from the beginning: they were absolutely made for each other.

Maybe there was a lesson in there for me, a reason why I hadn't had any luck finding the right woman yet. Maybe I tried too hard, but to stop looking would be easier said than done. I wanted to find my partner, the love of my life, and I didn't hide it. One-night stands and casual flings were not for me. When I went in, I went all in, and I wanted to find the woman who felt the same way about me. It didn't seem like too much to ask for.

"Does this look alright?" Cole asked me, giving himself a critical look in the mirror.

I couldn't help laughing. He never cared what anyone thought of anything he did, except when it came to Gemma. He wanted the day to be absolutely perfect for her, still not seeming to understand that all she really wanted was him.

"You know she'd be happy no matter how you looked, right? She probably wouldn't mind if you turned up naked."

"Don't tempt me," Cole muttered, straightening his tie again even though it had been perfectly straight to begin with. "Then we'd really give people something to talk about."

Despite Cole's efforts to keep the wedding relatively quiet, word had somehow leaked out and the paparazzi had gathered outside to take pictures of all the guests as they arrived. After all, it wasn't every day one of the richest men in the country got married, and to the daughter of a British earl, no less. That would be enough on its own, even before throwing in Gemma's previous engagement and the British media interest in it.

It frustrated Cole anyway. He preferred to have more control.

"People are happy for you," I pointed out. No one could say anything negative about two people so obviously in love with each other. "Let them take a picture or two. Don't let it ruin your day."

He sighed, closing his eyes briefly. "I've told you that I hate it when you're right, haven't I?"

"A few times," I replied drily, giving him a smug smile. "Now, what do you need me to do? We've still got about twenty minutes before the ceremony. Any last-minute best man duties?"

"I'm fine, but could you go make sure Gemma's got everything she needs? She left her phone back at the apartment so I can't call her."

I would bet anything that Gemma's maid of honour had everything under control, but I also knew that Cole would feel better if I went to take a look, so I didn't argue. Stepping out into the hall, I made my way down the corridor and across the church foyer to the room set aside for the bridal party to get ready.

My knock on the door was followed by a call of "just a minute" in a crisp, British accent. A moment later, the door opened just a crack, revealing a face I hadn't seen in almost a year.

"Well, well, well. Someone cleans up very nicely. I'm impressed, Jackson," she teased, opening the door wider as she looked me up and down. Holly Chapman was Gemma's best friend and colleague, as well as her maid of honour. She'd flown over from London for the wedding, but had only arrived late the day before so we hadn't had a chance to catch up yet. I was laying eyes on her for the first time since the previous December.

"No one will be looking at me when you look like that," I replied, returning the compliment sincerely. "You're a vision, Holly. It's wonderful to see you."

One year on, Holly was just as beautiful as I remembered. Her blond hair had been swept up into an elegant twist, her cheeks and lips perfectly pink to match the pale pink dress that hugged her curves in all the right places. Her skin was somehow still tanned and glowing in the middle of winter, and her blue eyes stood out against her slightly bronzed face, drawing me in just as quickly as they always had.

Holly and I had spent a fair bit of time together in London on the same business trip where Cole met Gemma. I had been attracted to her right from the start and she assured me the attraction was mutual, but to my disappointment, she wasn't interested in a relationship, especially not with an American only in town for a couple of weeks.

She suggested that we simply enjoy each other's company instead, including in bed, but that had never been my style. I declined her offer to get more physical and we spent time together seeing the city and getting to know one another, as well as spending time with Cole and Gemma. I loved every minute we spent together, and since returning home, she had crossed my mind far more often than I would ever admit. Even so, I had never reached out to her and she hadn't contacted me either. There didn't seem to be any point. I had plenty of friends I could call up when I needed a pleasant conversation. What I had wanted from her was something more, something that wouldn't happen if she didn't want it too.

"So, what brings you over to our side of the church?" Holly asked with a laugh. "Shouldn't you be keeping the groom from getting cold feet?"

"That's the least of my worries," I scoffed light-heartedly. "When Cole decides he's doing something, he doesn't look back. Nothing is stopping this wedding from taking place today."

That answer seemed to satisfy Holly as she gave me an approving nod. She wanted Gemma to be happy, and we both knew how happy Gemma and Cole made each other, so we had nothing to worry about on that end.

"What can I do for you, then?" she asked, reminding me that I still hadn't got to the point about what had brought me to her door.

"Cole just sent me to make sure everything's under control. Is there anything you need?"

"I think we're okay," she said before turning back into the room. "Gem? Jackson wants to know if you need anything?"

Gemma came around the corner of the door with a smile on her face, and the sight of her in her wedding dress nearly knocked me over. I put my hand to my heart, taking a staggered step back. Both women laughed at my dramatics, but I was only half-faking. She looked truly stunning.

Since Gemma moved to New York to live with Cole at the beginning of that year, she had become one of my best friends. The three of us often hung out together, and during the later stages of her pregnancy, whenever Cole had to travel for business, I stayed behind to take her to her doctor's appointments or get her whatever she needed.

Sometimes, it felt like I lived vicariously through their relationship, but seeing just how devoted they were to each other gave me hope. True love really did exist, and eventually, I would find it for myself. But not right at that second. Not until after I watched my best friend marry the love of his life.

"Cole's not going to know what hit him," I told Gemma sincerely, taking another moment to admire the sheer perfection of her dress and the way the whiteness of it brought out her flaming red hair and sparkling green eyes. No one would ever guess by looking at her in that dress that she gave birth less than three months ago to the most adorable little boy I had ever seen.

Cole was a damn lucky man.

"Alright, well, you better stop distracting us and let us get back to work," Holly instructed, shooing me back out into the hall. "We only have about ten minutes left. I guess I'll see you at the altar, Jackson."

She gave me a wink, and I grinned back, even though her words gave my heart a little twinge at just how close to my own secret desires they hit. "See you at the altar, Holly."

~Holly~

As soon as I closed the door behind Jackson, I let out a long breath, letting the tension in my shoulders release. Ever since Gemma asked me to be her maid of honour, I had been simultaneously dreading and anticipating that exact moment, the moment I came face-to-face with Jackson again.

I'd lost count of how many times over the last year he'd crossed my mind, usually late at night when I went home to my flat all alone. Lying in the dark, I remembered his warm smile, the way the corners of his eyes crinkled and his adorable dimples came out when he laughed, which happened often, and the way his lips felt when they brushed against mine the last time I saw him, the night we said goodbye.

Over and over again, I questioned whether I had been wrong to push him away as I had. He seemed so sincere when he said he felt a connection between us, that he wanted something deeper than just a casual fling, and I could still see the look of sadness in his deep blue eyes when I said I wasn't interested.

However, I'd heard promises that sounded sincere before. They always sounded sincere in the beginning, but sooner or later, it would all fall apart. I had been through that pain too many times and I had learned my lesson. I wouldn't get my hopes up again.

Undying love was all well and good for someone like Gemma, and I couldn't be happier that she'd found it, even if I still found her whole relationship with Cole a little mystifying. But I also knew that kind of happy-ever-after wasn't in the cards for me, at least not with a guy like Jackson, so I cut it off before it even had a chance to start. I had to protect my heart.

"Alright, Hols?" Gemma asked me with a look of concern on her face. She'd always been far too tuned in to my mood. Even though we hadn't spent much time together in person since she moved to New York, she still knew me better than anyone.

"Of course," I lied, putting on my best cheeky smile. My sad love life had no place in her wedding day. "Just trying to decide how it's even possible that that man is better looking than he was a year ago."

Gemma's worry dissolved and she laughed, convinced by my joking that I only had Jackson's appearance on my mind. And I wasn't lying about that part: since I saw him last, Jackson had cut his hair shorter and grown a short beard and it really suited him. Combined with the tux he wore for his role as best man, it made him look almost impossibly suave. My only concern was that the beard made it harder to see his sexy dimples when he smiled, and that was a real shame. I had been hoping to get a few more memories of those to keep me company when I went home to London in a few weeks' time.

At that moment, though, all I needed to focus on was ensuring everything was perfect for my best friend's big day. I double-checked Gemma's dress, hair and make-up, but I didn't need to do a thing; there couldn't be a more beautiful bride. Just a few minutes later, one of the ushers knocked on the door to let us know that they were ready for us.

"This is it!" I exclaimed, giving her one last squeeze. "Last chance to bail and head back to London with me."

Gemma laughed without a hint of hesitation. "I think it's a bit too late for that. Besides, my two favourite men in the world are out there waiting for me."

For a second, I thought she was talking about Jackson, until I realized that of course she meant Cole and their son, Noah. I really needed to stop thinking about Jackson.

Gemma and I headed to the back of the church to wait for our cue. She only had me as a bridesmaid since they were keeping the wedding fairly low-key, or at least as low-key as possible for two people of their status. Gemma had chosen the beautiful and historic Trinity Church in lower Manhattan for their ceremony because, of all the churches they'd visited in New York, it felt most like the churches we'd grown up attending at home in England.

The opening strains of their beautiful wedding song began to play over the church's audio system and I gave Gemma a big smile. "Ready?"

"Ready," she agreed, her eyes shining with excitement.

Turning around, I took a deep breath as I stepped into the church, all eyes in the room on me. Gemma and I had talked about walking in together since she didn't have anyone to give her away. Neither her father nor her brother were attending the wedding, and neither of them deserved to be a part of her day anyway. She hadn't heard a word from either of them since she left the UK.

So, she had considered the two of us walking in side-by-side, but in the end, I insisted on coming in separately. This was her day; all the attention should be on her when she walked in.

Wearing a sincere, happy smile, I walked slowly down the aisle, past all the beautiful fresh white and red flowers decorating the end of each pew. Of course Gemma had gone with red and white Christmas colours for her theme, but she let me choose a pink dress since pink went far better with my colouring than red did. As a combination of red and white, it worked.

The lyrics of the wedding song filled the air of the beautiful stone church as I walked, reminding me once again just how perfect Gemma and Cole were for each other. They had chosen the song In Whatever Time We Have, and the words highlighted that although life could be navigated alone, it would be better to have your partner at your side. Who would want to be alone?

Tears unexpectedly pricked at my eyes as the words hit home. That was exactly what I had decided for myself: I *did* want to be alone. From my point of view, it seemed preferable to the alternative of getting my heart broken over and over again. Reminding myself firmly that this day was *not* about me, I quickly blinked the tears away and turned up the brightness of my smile instead.

As I approached the altar, my gaze landed on Cole standing there, looking as serious and brooding as always. Gemma assured me he was capable of laughter, and I figured she must be telling me the truth, but I hadn't seen any proof of that. I wasn't looking for him anyway; the person I really sought was the man next to him, the one standing there watching me with an appreciative smile on his face, as if I were the only woman in the room.

What would it be like to be the one walking down the aisle with Jackson waiting for me at the end? For just a second, I let myself dream before filing the memory away as just another one in the list of my beautiful but impossible dreams.

When I reached the front, I took my place on the opposite side of the altar from Jackson and Cole, leaving a space for the person everyone was waiting for. The whole congregation got to their feet and a hushed gasp spread through the crowd as Gemma appeared. I could hardly blame them. She looked absolutely stunning. Though everyone in the whole building gaped at her, she only had eyes for one man, the one next to me who stared right back at her, his mouth hanging open in awe.

I caught Jackson's eye and he nodded his head towards Cole and raised his eyebrows, making me giggle. He saw the same thing I did: Cole was completely smitten.

The ceremony sped by, each part of it beautiful and emotional. Gemma and Cole wrote their own vows and there wasn't a dry eye in the place as they described what they meant to each other. I had come prepared with a few tissues tucked into my cleavage, so I pulled one out as discreetly as I could to dab at my eyes. As I tucked it away again, I felt someone's eyes on me, and glanced over to see Jackson watching me, his own eyes looking a little watery. We shared a quick smile before I looked away again.

Noah slept almost all the way through the ceremony, but then, with perfect timing, when the minister asked if there were any objections, his loud wail filled the church, making everyone laugh. Cole's sister, Isabel, who'd been watching him, quickly excused herself, taking him to the back of the church to calm him while the minister carried on with the ceremony.

Almost before I knew it, they were pronounced man and wife and with one hand on her waist and the other around her neck, Cole gave Gemma a passionate, dominating kiss that nearly took *my* breath away even though I only watched it happen.

They walked together back down the aisle to the cheers and applause of everyone gathered, and Jackson walked over to me and offered his arm with a warm smile.

"Looks like it's our turn now. Shall we?"

~Jackson~

I could hardly believe they'd actually done it. Not that I ever had any doubt that Gemma and Cole were meant to be together, but with everything they'd both been through with their past engagements, to see them officially married and looking so happy together as they shared their first dance at the wedding reception seemed almost like a miracle.

We were in the Rainbow Room on the 65th floor of Rockefeller Centre, and Cole had rented the whole place out for the night. No cameras were allowed besides the official photographers; everyone had to surrender their phones at the door. The New York skyline twinkled in the distance, the Empire State Building lit up in red and white as if it were part of their wedding decorations. Maybe it was, who could say? I wouldn't put it past Cole to have arranged for those colours to be shown tonight. There didn't seem to be anything he couldn't do if he really wanted to.

My eyes drifted around the room before landing on Holly standing across from me on the other side of the small dance floor that had been created, watching the happy couple with a soft smile on her face. Seeing that smile pulled me back to the first night we met, just over a year earlier.

Cole and I ran into Gemma in the hallway outside a Christmas party, and she looked just as gorgeous then as she did at her wedding, even if her dress was completely different. I told Cole that night that Gemma was my dream girl, but that didn't stop him from going up to his hotel room with her that night. It had happened before that Cole caught the interest of a girl I would have killed for a chance with, but I never held it against him. He didn't do it on purpose. People were just drawn to him, they always had been. Hell, even I was. Something about being around him made anyone in his presence feel special. It felt invigorating in a completely indefinable way.

But the following night, we went out to an industry event and ran into Gemma again, and that was when I met Holly.

Although I said just the night before that Gemma was my ideal woman, I had to make an immediate mental retraction of that statement when I laid eyes on Holly. With her sleek blonde hair and bright blue eyes, and the way her elegant dress wrapped around her body, showing off every perfect curve, she looked like something straight out of a dream. I greeted her warmly and she returned my smile with one of her own that nearly made me weak in the knees.

Something special lingered in her smile and the way her eyes twinkled, looking somehow fearless and vulnerable at the same time. I could see in that look the promise of all I'd ever wanted.

If only she'd felt the same.

As she caught me staring at her across the wedding dance floor, she flashed me that same smile, a hint of a challenge in her eyes as she gestured towards the dance floor with her head. With the first dance wrapping up, we were expected to join in as best man and maid of honour, and we walked across the open space of the dance floor towards each other like two magnets being drawn together until we met in the middle.

"May I have this dance?" I asked formally, bowing to her in a way that I knew would make her laugh.

Sure enough, her beautiful blue eyes shone as she grinned. "Do you know how to dance? Maybe we should have practiced this ahead of time."

"I'm available for practice whenever you like," I teased her back, holding out my hand, and she stepped into my arms like we'd done the move a million times before.

"So, they really did it," Holly said as her hand slid over the top of my shoulder, close to my neck, sending a tingle of excitement through my body. "After being engaged to Edwin for six years, I never would have guessed that Gemma would be married to someone else a year after breaking up with him."

"Sometimes, you just know when a thing is right," I pointed out. "It's got nothing to do with time."

A hint of sadness flashed in Holly's eyes as she looked away from me. "Or sometimes, things that seem right fade over time."

That was the biggest glimpse she'd ever given me into the world inside her head, but before I could ask her to explain what she meant, she turned back to me with her smile back on, as if that little moment had never happened at all.

"So I'm here for three weeks now, until New Year's." I knew that already; Gemma had mentioned it to me several times. "I know Gem's got some plans for me, but she's hardly a native New Yorker. What are the can't-miss things I need to see while I'm here?"

Taking the bait, I began to tell her about some of my favourite places, the list growing bigger as I kept thinking of more things she should see.

"I think I'm going to need you to write that all down." She laughed as I twirled her across the floor.

"I'd be happy to show you around," I offered, completely unplanned. "I've taken most of the rest of the month off. Since Cole's out of the office, there won't be any major deals going on, so my work can all wait too. I might have to stop in every now and then, but most of my time is free."

Holly looked up at me in surprise, her face tantalizingly close to mine as we moved to the music. "You don't have any plans? What about your family? Aren't you going to spend the holidays with them?"

The details of my family life were hardly the kind of light-hearted talk suitable for a wedding dance, so I kept my answer vague. "I mostly planned to relax. I've got a few days booked in to babysit Noah, but otherwise, I'm pretty flexible. If you're interested, I'm at your service."

She raised an eyebrow at me, a smile playing on her lips as her gaze dropped down my body and back up again. "Exactly what kind of services are you offering?"

I knew she meant it as a joke. Flirty and upbeat had always been our dynamic, but after everything I'd been thinking about all day and watching my best friend get his happy-ever-after, I couldn't bring myself to smile back. The implication was perfectly clear: Holly only wanted me in the way she always had, and nothing more. I hadn't really expected her position to have changed, or at least I had told myself that I hadn't expected it, but it stung anyway to hear her say it.

Luckily, the music drew to an end just then, so I gave her a quick kiss on the cheek to avoid answering. "Thanks for the dance, Holly." Without giving her a chance to reply, I turned around and headed for the outdoor terrace, needing to get some air.

After a few minutes of pushing through the crowd, I finally made it out into the night air and breathed deeply as I tried to push down the lump in my throat. Why was I so disappointed? She'd made it clear enough the year before that she only saw me as a good time. Why should I have hoped for anything else?

"Hey, are you okay?" Holly's British accent cut through my self-pity, forcing me back to the present. She stood just behind me as I turned around, a worried look on her face. "Did I say something wrong?"

"Of course not," I lied. "It was just getting a little stuffy in there."

"You're not a very good liar." She saw through me immediately, but her expression was soft and kind. "You don't have to tell me if you don't want to, but can I at least make it up to you?"

She held out her hand with a peace offering: one of the candy cane favours Gemma had ordered to complement the red and white colour scheme. They were raspberry vodka flavoured rather than peppermint and dangerously good. Gemma and I had tasted a few a couple of nights earlier and managed to get ourselves a little tipsy, though she had a better excuse than I did since she hadn't been drinking for the last year because of her pregnancy.

"Thanks." I took the candy from her and opened it while she unwrapped one of her own. Turning back to the view of the skyline, I put the end of the candy cane in my mouth and Holly did the same with hers, coming to stand beside me.

"You grew up here in Manhattan, right?" she asked as we looked out over the city lights together.

"Right," I confirmed. We had talked about that briefly the year before. "Up in Washington Heights. Born and bred."

"Have you ever wanted to live anywhere else?"

I looked over at her, trying to gauge if her question held a deeper meaning, but her eyes remained focused on the skyscrapers as she twirled the candy cane absent-mindedly in her mouth.

"I can't really imagine calling anywhere else home, at least not permanently. This city has an energy all its own. It's like it won't let you just sit back and wait for life, you need to go out and find it. I've travelled a lot through my work and I've never found anywhere like it."

I sucked a second longer on my candy cane before biting off the end of it, and Holly turned to me with a grin. "That was hardly more than a minute! I thought you'd last longer."

I had no idea what she was talking about. "Last longer at what?"

"Your candy cane," she explained, still smiling as she gestured to the piece that was left in my hand. "At school, we used to try to suck the whole candy cane without taking a bite, and it's a lot harder than you think. It's so tempting to snap it off. You need to have a lot of self-control."

"I have plenty of self-control," I teased her right back. "You just didn't tell me what we were doing. I bet I could hold out longer than you if you'd told me the game."

Something flashed in her eyes, looking almost like desire mixed with hesitation. "I'm not so sure about that, Jackson. I bet I could get you to give in first if I really tried."

She stepped closer to me and her hand brushed against the front of my pants, subtly but obviously not accidentally. Combined with what she'd said on the dance floor, her meaning couldn't be clearer: she still wanted to get into bed with me, but she had no idea how much self-control I really had.

The time had come for me to be clear about that too. I took hold of her hand and kissed the back of it before looking her straight in the eye. "Holly, nothing has changed for me. I still think you're beautiful and fun and smart and all-around amazing, and I would love to give whatever this is between us a proper shot. But I'm not going to sleep with you unless we're in some kind of committed relationship."

Her lips pursed, showing her disappointment. "I really don't understand," she said, the frustration clear in her voice as well. "You just said you find me attractive, and I've made it pretty clear that I feel the same. Why can't we just have some fun and then see where it goes?"

"Because that's not the kind of guy I am, Holly. I told you that last year."

"You did, but it still doesn't make sense to me." Her brow furrowed as she tried to understand. "You're not the guy who does a one-night stand, fine. What kind of guy are you, then, Jackson Hanmer?"

There was a challenge in the question and I took a deep breath before deciding to tell her the truth, a truth I'd hardly told anyone before.

"I'm a virgin."

MORE FROM THE AUTHOR

<u>Historical Romance – 18+</u>

Lady in Waiting Series
Lady in Waiting
King in Training
Princess in Hiding

<u>Contemporary Romance – 18+</u>

Standalones
Charity Case
A Set of Three
Hired Lover
A Work of Art

Christmas in the City Series
Mistletoe Mistake
Candy Cane Challenge
Tinsel Temptation
Gingerbread Gamble

Contemporary Romance – New Adult/Clean

It Figures duet
It Figures
Figuring It Out

Paranormal Romance – 18+

Cold Lake Pack Series
The Curse and the Prophecy
The Spell and the Legacy
The Dream and the Destiny

Mismatched Mates Series
Mismatched Mates
Misguided Motives
Mistaken Meanings

Serena's Story
The Alpha's Second Chance
The Returned Mate
The Vampire's Consort

Sacrifice Series
Blood Donor
Life Giver

Paranormal Romance – New Adult/Clean

The Alpha's Prey

KEEP IN TOUCH

My Patreon account has daily updates from my works-in-progress, bonus chapters and more – join me there to comment and read along as my next books are being written:
www.patreon.com/melodytyden

You can find and follow me on Facebook at:

facebook.com/melodytyden

Join the Facebook group Melody's Romance Corner for fun games, interaction with the author and exclusive news and excerpts.

You can also sign up to my newsletter at www.melodytyden.com for all the latest news.

www.ingramcontent.com/pod-product-compliance
Lightning Source LLC
Chambersburg PA
CBHW051005180726
48291CB00006B/1985